...ed to be abl...

...wer, she put 'writer'. Then it asked what Carol did for relaxation, and she put down the truth—'writing'. The third question asked for her hobbies. Well, not wanting to look obsessed, she crossed her fingers and answered 'swimming'—but, given that the chlorine in the pool does terrible things to her highlights, I'm sure you can guess the real answer!

Cathy Williams can remember reading Mills & Boon books as a teenager, and now that she's writing them she remains an avid fan. For her, there is nothing like creating romantic stories and engaging plots, and each and every book is a new adventure. Cathy lives in London. Her three daughters—Charlotte, Olivia and Emma—have always been, and continue to be, the greatest inspirations in her life.

FORBIDDEN TO THE POWERFUL GREEK

CAROL MARINELLI

CONSEQUENCES OF THEIR WEDDING CHARADE

CATHY WILLIAMS

MILLS & BOON

First Published in Great Britain 2022
by Mills & Boon, an imprint of HarperCollins*Publishers* Ltd,
1 London Bridge Street, London, SE1 9GF

www.harpercollins.co.uk

HarperCollins*Publishers*
1st Floor, Watermarque Building,
Ringsend Road, Dublin 4, Ireland

Forbidden to the Powerful Greek © 2022 Carol Marinelli

Consequences of Their Wedding Charade © 2022 Cathy Williams

ISBN: 978-0-263-30069-7

02/22

MIX
Paper from
responsible sources
FSC® C007454

This book is produced from independently certified FSC™ paper
to ensure responsible forest management.
For more information visit www.harpercollins.co.uk/green.

Printed and Bound in Spain using 100% Renewable Electricity
at CPI Black Print, Barcelona

FORBIDDEN TO THE POWERFUL GREEK

CAROL MARINELLI

MILLS & BOON

PROLOGUE

'WHAT HAVE THEY done to you now?'

Almost thirty years ago, six-year-old Galen Pallas had heard the weariness in his *yaya*'s tone as he'd stepped in their home high on the hilly Greek island of Anapliró.

Galen's shorn black hair had been full of mud, his clothes torn and his face bruised, so there had been no denying that there had once again been trouble...

And, again, it had seemed it was all his faut.

'Galen!' Yaya had been cross when she'd found out the reason the boys had again ganged up on him—and she'd blamed Galen. 'You don't tell your teacher that she's got bigger after the summer.'

'She said it to me, though...' Galen had frowned. It was the first thing everyone said when they saw him!

Yaya had turned from the stove and held her hands apart. 'I meant you don't comment on someone's size...' Yaya had looked skywards for guidance and muttered some prayers. 'I am too old for this...'

'I didn't say it to them, though,' he'd pointed out, 'just the teacher.'

'They are boys being boys and you provoke them. Trust me on this,' Yaya had insisted. 'Sometimes it is better to say nothing, or even to lie. Your first thought, your first response, is not always the appropriate one. Galen, you offend people...'

With the table laid Yaya had brought over dinner, and though Galen had closed his eyes as they'd said prayers, his mind had been somewhere else, and as she'd started to serve he'd told Yaya the truth. 'I would never kick someone, or spit on them, or call them names, no matter how much they offended me.'

And they offended him daily! Calling him a *rompot*, or robot, for his undemonstrative ways. Laughing because he lived in the hills with his *trelós yaya* as they all called her. Yes, she was eccentric, and she wept in church, and at times openly on the street.

Galen knew she was almost demented with grief at the loss of her family. His *papu* had died before Galen had been born, and when he had been two Galen had been in an accident that had claimed his parents.

Yaya had been left to raise him and, as he was frequently told, it was not an easy task.

'Galen, you are different...'

He watched how Yaya's glass of water trembled as she brought it to her mouth, and he hated the trouble he caused her. 'You need to think before you speak *every* time. You want to fit in, don't you?'

As a child, and later as a teenager, Galen simply hadn't.

Oh, but as a man...

His brilliant brain had soon been so in demand that the world had rather quickly decided it might be wiser, as well as extremely profitable, if it chose to fit in with him.

CHAPTER ONE

'GALEN.' HIS PA placed a large take-out coffee on his desk, though it went unacknowledged for he was deep in his work. 'Sorry to interrupt, but Costa keeps calling—says you were supposed to be meeting him and Leo for dinner at V's?'

The restaurant was opposite Galen's head office in Kolonaki Square, a very upmarket neighbourhood in Athens. Both he and Costa had bought, and now worked from, the once dilapidated building. Their businesses were separate entities, though—Costa was into property, and Galen's passion was technology. And right now, he was exceptionally busy.

'No,' Galen said. 'I've told him I can't make it.'

'Sure.'

'Kristina!' Galen called her back. 'The care home called this morning with the treatment regime?'

'Yes,' she nodded. 'It's on the report.'

'I just saw.' Galen took a breath. Had she told him about Yaya he would have gone over today. Then again, he had insisted on not being disturbed and the care home did call a *lot*. 'Let me know if it's regarding treatment.'

'Noted.'

He heard the slightly tired edge to her tone, reminding him that she was heavily pregnant. 'Go home?' he suggested.

'I don't need favours.'

'It's not a favour. We've got a busy weekend coming up and I want you fully on board.'

Galen was by most accounts brilliant...mathematically, technically, fiscally... As for his looks...he was way more than the requisite tall dark and handsome, with intense hazel eyes and an incredible body. His thick black hair, when he had time, was superbly cut. Even by Athens' high standards, he dressed impeccably.

Not that he cared for fashion. His mind was filled with more important things.

Numbers. Food. Sex. Or numbers. Sex. Food.

Most of the time it was just numbers.

Charts.

Code.

Programming…

Galen didn't notice the lights going off outside his glass office—he had blacked out the glass. Nor them coming back on as the cleaning team arrived—they knew not to come into his office when he was deep in work.

There were many satellites that orbited Galen's world—legal, admin, social media, maintenance… The list went on, but Galen loathed all the distractions they created so, in as far as it was possible, they orbited his world offsite.

Onsite, though, aside from the developers, quants, programmers and such, was a small vital army who, apart from one very lazy exception, worked away all the days and nights so that Galen and the team could immerse themselves in tech.

And, yes, while Galen's brilliance might pay an awful lot of wages, at the core they were a very loyal and exceptionally devoted team to their aloof, at times arrogant and rather remote boss.

A short rap on his door had him frowning, but he remained immersed in work until he heard his name. 'Galen.'

'What?' Galen sighed when he saw that it was Costa. 'I already said I can't get there…' Though come to think of it he was a little hungry. 'Maybe a quick dinner.'

'Galen, it's almost midnight.'

'Oh!' He had long since lost track of time.

V's generally did not do take-out, but there were always exceptions, and Costa handed over a container. 'Here.'

'Thanks.'

The chef would probably weep as his carefully prepared lamb tenderloins drizzled in his signature sauce, with delectable baby potatoes and a delicate side salad, were all scooped onto a piece of pitta and rolled up as Costa asked, 'How's it all going?'

'Do you want the long or the short answer?' Galen asked, because he was more than aware now of how people's eyes tended to glaze over when he spoke of his work.

'I won't understand either of them,' Costa admitted. 'The drift...'

'Well, the first of the ICOs went well.'

'You've already lost me.' Costa grinned.

'Initial coin offerings. Although there is still...'

Galen saw that Costa had tuned out, so he took a large bite of his wrap, but then frowned as Costa produced from a bag a bottle of champagne and two glasses.

'What's this?' Galen checked, hastily swallowing as Costa popped the cork. 'Are you going to tell me you love me, Costa?' he joked. 'Because if you are, then it really has to wait. I need a clear head to work...'

'Galen, I've got news,' Costa said, handing him a glass and then sitting down.

'Okay...'

'*Good* news,' Costa said—and, yes, he was telling him how to react, Galen realised. 'Mary and I are getting married.'

'Mary?' Galen frowned. Frankly, he couldn't quite keep up with Costa's love life, but Mary was the most recent one. 'You're serious?' Galen checked. 'But you only recently met...'

He was more than a touch bemused. It had nothing to do with his own views on relationships and marriage, more that Costa really wasn't the settling down type. Still, even though Galen was actually itching to get back to work, it was indeed good news and so, remembering his manners, he halted his own impatience and raised his glass. '*Yamas...*'

'*Yamas.*' Costa shared in the toast and then put down his glass. 'Galen,' Costa said. 'I'd like you to be my *koumbaros.*'

'Me?' Costa was asking him to be his best man. 'Doesn't that involve speeches and...?'

'Yes.' Costa nodded. 'Speeches and dancing and being Mr Sociable and everything you hate...' Costa smiled. 'Look, we go back for ever. Long before...' He gestured to the *very* sumptuous surroundings. 'Of course it has to be you.'

'Well...' Galen blinked. 'Thank you.' He was both stunned

and flattered, yet a little uncertain as to whether this was…well…
A set-up. This was Costa after all! 'So…' Galen checked the
little he knew about the sudden bride-to-be. 'Mary's English?'

'Yes.'

'Will you get married there?'

'It's still a bit up in the air…' Costa was toying with the champagne cork. 'I'm hoping the service will take place at my hotel
in London.' Costa was very guarded to most, yet now he shared
a confidence with Galen. 'Mary's father is in prison there; I'm
trying to get his leave approved and surprise her.'

'I do have a good lawyer in the UK…' Galen offered.

'I've already pinched him,' Costa freely admitted. 'Anyway,
the plan is to marry there, spend whatever time we can with her
father, then fly back to Anapliró for a church blessing and reception.'

Galen felt his guts tighten a touch even at the mention of the
island. He had left as a teenager and had, of course, gone back
to visit Yaya. But she was now in a nursing home here, close by,
and had been for years.

Galen felt neither the need nor the desire to return to Anapliró.

In fact, he hated the place.

Still—his analytical mind ticked over—he had to deal with
the family home there, which was no doubt going to ruin. It was
one of those jobs he'd been putting off, but this wedding might
be a good time to put things in motion.

'A big Anapliró celebration, then.' Galen commented, trying to keep his mind on the conversation and wedding plans and
all the things that just did not interest him. But when it came to
friends, he had trained himself to listen.

'No,' Costa corrected. 'Without Mary's father that's not fair,
so I'm keeping the reception to twelve and that includes us…'
He gestured to Galen.

'And the bride,' Galen added.

'Indeed, and then there's Leo and Deacon, Yolanda of
course…' She was Costa's mother. 'Your plus one.'

'I shan't be bringing anyone,' Galen said—not that Costa
was listening.

He could not believe he was sitting here discussing Costa's wedding. The two men were both seriously single. Well, in different ways. Costa dated and borrowed Galen's PA to make bookings and to send flowers when it all invariably went wrong. As for Galen... Well, suffice it to say there were no flowers required when it was simply sex. And while that might appear cold, both Galen and his partners would contest that assumption—not that they cared what others thought.

In fact, his phone was buzzing now.

'I thought your calls were being diverted to Kristina.' Costa frowned. 'I've been trying to get you all night...'

Galen offered no explanation as he read the message and saw that it was one of his partners.

Catch up?

Galen fired a rapid response.

Can't now.

He added a sad face to his message.

And received a sad face in response.

His sex life really was as delightfully uncomplicated as that.

Right now, though, he dragged his focus onto Costa, who seemed to have everything planned.

'I'm going to offend a lot of people by keeping the reception small,' Costa admitted. 'But there will be a big party on the beach afterwards for everyone on the island—'

'*Pias to avgo kai kourefto.*' Galen shrugged. It literally meant grab an egg and shave it, but it referred more to the *Catch-22* situation Costa was in. 'It's not your job to please everyone. And anyway, that's an impossible ask on Anapliró.'

'Yes, well, I need to keep the locals happy, given that I didn't sever all ties like you.' Indeed, Costa had both masterminded and financed the development of a lavish retreat there. Once the impoverished poor relation of the islands, Anapliró was now an exclusive destination for the extremely well heeled. 'You still haven't seen the retreat.'

'I know,' Galen said. Costa had long since been pushing for him to fly over, yet Galen, thankfully, had always managed to be too busy. Yes, a trip to Anapliró was long overdue, and of course he would not miss Costa's wedding just because he loathed the place. 'When are you looking at?' Galen asked. 'I will ensure everything is cleared in my schedule...'

'Galen,' Costa said, and he tapped the champagne cork on the desk a few times, 'the wedding is on Saturday.'

'Excuse me?' Galen had long ago been taught not to not say the first thing that came to mind and rapidly deployed his filter rather than shaking his head and stating the truth—*that's impossible!*

'Yes.' Costa nodded. 'We fly to London tomorrow, the wedding is the following morning, and we go back to Anapliró that afternoon.' Costa took a breath. 'I know it's short notice...'

Short notice?

There was absolutely no way Galen could be there. He had to make a major announcement regarding a partnership on Saturday. And there were vital system updates to be checked and run. Every hour between now and then was accounted for.

Even sex was being forfeited!

While Galen didn't expect Costa's nuptials to be arranged around his schedule, in the same vein Costa was more than aware of the importance of the coming days for him.

'Galen,' Costa said into the ensuing silence, 'as God-awful as the timing is for you, believe me when I say there is a reason the wedding is so soon and it's *not* the one you are thinking—Mary isn't pregnant.'

'Why would I be thinking that?'

Costa laughed, but then he took a drink. Putting down the glass, he let out a sigh. 'There's stuff going on...'

Hearing the sudden gravity in Costa's voice, Galen frowned.

'Heavy stuff. But I honestly can't discuss it...'

'That's fine.' Galen was the least nosey person. Drama and gossip irritated him, and certainly he would never delve.

'I'm really asking you to be there.'

For many reasons Galen couldn't be, and yet…

Galen and Costa went way back.

Leo Arati too.

While they might all be successful now, in their own rights, it hadn't always been so. They shared a past only those who came from Anapliró could understand.

Conform or suffer—that had been the unvoiced motto of Anapliró.

All three, in their various ways, had refused the former and endured the latter. If you weren't one of the bullies or one of the popular crowd…if you were in any way different…then your life was made hell.

Costa's father had left when Yolanda had fallen ill, and his parents' had been the island's first divorce.

Leo had suffered dreadfully—ostensibly for being tiny, but really for his effeminate ways.

And Galen, well…

They were unlikely friends, perhaps, but friends all the same, and that mattered.

'You know I'll be there…' Galen said, and there was another clink of glasses—and a smile—as his brain asked, *What the hell?* 'I'll message Kristina now…sort out…' He halted. Usually he would fire his PA messages at all hours, and yet, despite appearances, he *was* mindful that her due date was nearing.

'It's all done.' Costa waved him away. 'Flights and everything. London's booked and you've got the Temple Suite on Anapliró—it's amazing…the best on the retreat.'

'Shouldn't that go to the bride and groom?' Galen frowned.

'My villa's actually better.' He grinned and topped up Galen's glass.

'Of course it is.'

'I've put Leo and Deacon down for the bridal suite.'

'I'm sure that will be appreciated.'

'Hey, why not stay on for a few days…?'

'I shan't be joining you on your honeymoon, Costa.'

'I wasn't inviting you to, but it's been years since you've been back and—'

'There's nothing there for me now, and no reason to return,' Galen abruptly cut in. 'Your wedding is the exception.'

A very inconvenient exception at that!

The moment Costa left Galen began firing urgent messages to Joe and his development team, telling them to get here *now*. And, despite the late hour, he sent a quick one to Kristina, asking her to pack, and also to send his usual brief to both the London hotel and the retreat, so they were prepared to his specifications.

And also, in regard to Anapliró…

Ensure a good Internet connection!

Costa had said the retreat was amazing and that it had every luxury, but Galen had grown up there after all. It had been beyond poor then.

Merda! His announcement on Saturday wasn't just big—it had been timed for maximum impact.

Everything had been factored in…

Except for a damned wedding!

CHAPTER TWO

ROULA DRAKOS WAS rather certain she had the best office in the world.

Well, not her *actual* office. But often in her working day she paused to admire the endless theatre of the sky merging into the Aegean Sea. In the five years she had worked there the beauty and grandeur of the retreat still held her enthralled...

Still, there was no time to pause today.

She clipped at pace towards Reception and breezed into her *actual* office. Sitting down at her desk for the first time since she had arrived at work, Roula Drakos, Guest Services Manager, retrieved her to-do list from her rather untidy desk. She pushed a stray red curl out of her eyes and, snapping off a piece of her favourite dark chocolate, scrolled through the guest requests to ensure all had been met and found she was smiling at the sight of an old friend's name.

Galen Pallas plus one

Familiar faces were not particularly frequent amongst the guests here as Anapliró had once been very poor. Though locals often returned to the island, very few could afford to stay at the retreat.

Leo Arati was a renowned fashion designer, and he was here regularly, but Galen...

No.

She knew that he was friends with the owner, Costa, but Roula hadn't seen her old friend for...she thought back...nineteen years.

Well, they hadn't been friends, exactly. Galen had been several years older. But he had always been so kind to her.

She'd been Roula Kyrios then.

It really had been a lifetime ago.

'Roula.' The receptionist's rather loud rap on her door had her looking up. 'They're just leaving Thira.'

'Thanks.' Roula nodded. 'Is everything okay out there?'

'Mia's getting a little…' Stephanie made a wavering gesture with her hand that indicated the retreat's head chef was having her customary pre-function meltdown.

'So what's new?' Roula gave a nonchalant shrug and as always appeared unfazed. For the past thirty-six hours—since the news as to the identity of the bride and more pertinently the groom had been revealed—Roula had being doing her best to calm the staff, reminding them that although the groom was their boss, ultimately it was just another high-end wedding. Anapliró was now a very coveted destination and the retreat had seen many weddings, from royalty, to billionaire tycoons, to seriously wealthy celebrities.

'Let me finish this update and then I'll come by the kitchen.'

'Thanks.'

Roula wouldn't usually be flying quite so solo today. However, Yolanda, the retreat's manager, was also the groom's mother, and Beatrice, the wedding co-ordinator, was overseeing the London event.

Roula wore many hats.

Professional Roula was unflappable, breezy and efficient, and her focus was always on the guests. That was why in the five years since her husband's death she had moved through the ranks and was now Guest Services Manager.

She was gunning for Head of Guest Services—a role that Yolanda had pointed out did not exist.

Yet!

Her professional persona was by far the most comfortable fit—here she was completely in control. Her thick curly red hair was clipped back, and she wore subtle make-up and a neutral shade on her nails as was the policy. Her uniform consisted of a stone-coloured linen suit and a pale top, which she wore with heels or ballet pumps as required. She was poised and groomed right down to the requisite pearls in her ears and she wore her name badge with pride.

Her legs were toned and smooth, her figure for the most part trim, and yet beneath the coiffed appearance she was somewhat neglected. Roula could barely stand to be naked and always showered hurriedly, quickly taking care of the essentials. Even alone in the bathroom she put her underwear on beneath a towel, pulling on vast knickers and ensuring her large breasts were flattened by two sports bras before she emerged.

Nobody really knew Roula...

Updating the data to reflect that all suites were up to standard, she caught sight of her wedding ring—of course it was not a requirement of the retreat that she wore it...more a silent policy here on Anapliró. There was no question that she remove it. Eyebrows had already been raised when, a year after Dimitrios's death, Roula had stopped wearing black.

Seeing that the plaster on her thumb was fraying, she took a fresh one from the drawer to replace it. Roula had thought she'd kicked her nail-biting habit, but since her twenty-ninth birthday celebration it had resurfaced—though at least it was confined to one thumb nowadays.

'Roula!'

She looked up at the anxious calling of her name as Mia flew through the door.

'It's a disaster.'

'Mia.' They had been best friends growing up—although, to Mia's chagrin, they weren't as close now. Still, with her professional hat on, Roula poured Mia a glass of water then waved her to a seat. 'Sit down.'

'I haven't got time to sit down.'

'I'm sure your staff have it all under control...'

'How can a wedding with less than thirty-six hours' notice ever be under control?'

'Believe me...' Roula rolled her eyes. 'I get it. Come on, you can take two minutes.'

'This is our *boss*. It's the most important meal of my career...'

Roula halted her. 'It's Costa. We were at school with him. He likes burgers...' Roula reminded her. 'He orders souvlaki at midnight—not from your kitchen, but from the stalls down at the tourist beach.'

'Yes…' Mia had finally sat down and was taking deeper breaths now. 'But his guests are all high-end and…'

'Leo?' Roula rolled her eyes. 'Come, now. Yes, he's famous now, but we have lunch with him on Santorini and the two of you go clubbing. He's a friend, and anyway I've made sure he has his favourite tipple. Who else are you worried about?'

'Galen Pallas and his guest.' Mia gulped.

'You honestly think that Galen is going to cause problems?'

'He's mega important now!'

'Please…' Roula shrugged. 'Galen invented that digital game my nieces play on.'

'He does way more than that…he's some tech guru…' Mia's gestured helplessly. 'He's seriously powerful and…'

'Come off it,' Roula dismissed. 'I remember Galen when he thought jam was a treat. He's the least of your worries. Mia, you have cooked for royalty, you have cooked for celebrities, you have more awards and stars than the website can keep up with and you can *absolutely* do a perfect wedding lunch for twelve.'

Mia finally took a deep breath.

'Twelve,' Roula reiterated.

'So, why didn't Costa want me to cater for the beach party?' the easily offended Mia asked. 'Does he not think I'm up to it?'

'It's a barbecue on the beach. The whole island is invited and they want you there for the party as a guest,' Roula said. 'You just have to hand over your kitchen to the Santorini chefs and have some fun. Just focus on the lunch, and some meze for the private guests after the beach party…'

'Yes.' Mia was breathing again. 'God, how do you hold it to-gether, Roula? You're always so in control.'

'It's my job to be,' Roula said, and she had found out she was very good at it. 'You've got this.'

'I do.' Mia nodded, but instead of heading back to her be-loved kitchen she sat still, and her eyes narrowed a touch. 'You knew it was Costa's wedding before the rest of us, didn't you?'

'I knew a little earlier,' Roula admitted, 'but I was told in confidence.'

'And you didn't think to share it with me?' Mia challenged. 'We're supposed to be best friends.'

'Let's not bring personal issues to work.'

'But you're the same out there.' Mia pointed beyond the retreat and her eyes were both hurt and angry. 'You never tell me anything any more. We shared everything growing up. God, Roula, your wedding was my first big event…'

'I know.'

'It's been five years since Dimitrios died!' Mia had stood up now, and was almost shouting. 'I've tried to be patient, but you keep shutting me out—'

'Mia,' Roula broke in. 'Not now.'

But there was no stopping Mia. 'Look, I'm not saying I understand what you're going through, but Dimitrios was my cousin and I loved him too. You used to talk to me, Roula…we used to share everything.'

No, not everything—and certainly not where her late husband was concerned.

Nobody knew Roula.

For, despite her bright smile at work and her suitable widow persona in the village, at her very core Roula felt as if she had been annihilated. And her withdrawal from friendships, her slow self-annihilation, had taken place long before Dimitrios had died.

Roula had wanted to finish her studies, maybe study in Athens if she got the grades… But she had come home from school one day and been told she was to marry the popular and charismatic Dimitrios Drakos, who had his own fishing boat, and that his parents would gift them a cottage on the foreshore.

When Roula had cried her mother had come to speak with her. Pappa was ill—dying, in fact, she had told her. His dearest wish was to walk his daughter down the aisle. He had chosen wisely and wanted to be sure Roula was taken care of when he was gone.

She had been so naïve, so innocent, she hadn't even known the questions to ask.

Once a week to keep him happy.

That had been the full sum of her sex education.

So Roula had lain there on their wedding night as Dimitrios snored. She'd listened to the waves, but they had not soothed her, for she'd felt shocked, sore and ill. Not even the sound of birds greeting the dawn had brought comfort.

The only consolation Roula had had was that it was done for another week... But then Dimitrios had stirred, rolled over, lifted her nightdress and done it again before he headed off night-fishing.

And again on his return.

Again and again and again...

No, Mia didn't need to know that about her cousin.

'Mia, I really don't think this is the time or place to be discussing our private lives...'

'There's *never* a good time with you, Roula,' Mia retorted, and went to flounce off. But she saved her parting shot for the office door. 'Since Dimitrios died it's as if I don't know you any more.'

Breathe out, Roula, she told herself. *And in.*

Roula buried her head in her hands and told herself that she would get through this and that she had survived much worse. Calming, she picked up the little glass frame on her desk and read the passage she loved so much. For despite everything, even if she'd questioned it and challenged it at times, Roula had clung on to her faith.

And I will restore to you the years that the locusts have taken.
Joel 2:25

And God had. Now she had peace in her life, and a career that she loved. And yet as she dragged in air Roula could almost feel the life she had rebuilt being snatched away...

For there was *another* secret.

One that would, by Roula's own doing, soon be getting out.

Her world was about to crumble, and here on the island only the bride and groom knew.

The bride wore...

Well, although she was dying to know, Roula hadn't had a chance to see yet. The bridal party had been whisked from the church straight to the private function. Roula had been busy with the beach party preparations as the meal was served.

Now, though, she might finally get a glimpse.

Roula stood out of sight in the archway of the minor function room, waiting to liaise with Beatrice. It was minor only in size, and perfect for intimate parties. It had been built around the remains of an ancient pillar and archway. She and Mia had used to play hide and seek on this very spot. The room was mainly windows, allowing nature to star and taking advantage of near-panoramic sea views. Right now, they were tinted a little, to avoid the afternoon glare of the sun, but tonight—weather allowing—the room would be bathed in stars.

'Fifteen minutes or so,' a waiter whispered. 'The *koumbaros* is just wrapping up.'

And then Roula heard a voice.

It wasn't necessarily a familiar voice, for it was very low, deep and measured, yet even if she couldn't see him, she knew unmistakably it was Galen.

'Well, I did warn Costa that I am the least suitable person for this role.'

Roula found that she wanted to move, to step out of the archway and glimpse her old friend.

Of course she couldn't step out, but she listened intently as he spoke.

'I am not good at jokes, nor am I sentimental, and neither do I share anecdotes...'

'The very reasons I didn't choose Leo,' Costa quipped, and the small gathering laughed.

Yes, Roula could well imagine Leo had plenty of colourful stories—it would seem Galen was indeed a wise choice.

'Mary…'

Roula heard Galen addressing the bride now, and lightly jesting with her.

'If you are feeling exasperated, please know that you are not alone. If you need someone to speak with, I'll completely understand. In truth, I have considered ending my friendship with Costa many times. A kitchen fire might not sound like a good reason,' Galen said. 'However, I was overseas and hadn't even spent a night in my new apartment. Nor was I aware it was being used for a New Year's Eve party…'

Roula smiled at the disgruntled edge to Galen's voice.

'Worse, though, was his attempt to paint over the fire damage. When you are back from your honeymoon I invite you to see what I mean.'

His serious tone had everyone really laughing, and Roula smiled again, because this intimate crowd would know that Galen was serious indeed—that brilliant mind let nothing go. He was affronted, only nicely so.

'Still,' Galen continued, 'each time I consider calling it a day I am forced to reflect—and, really, a more loyal, annoying, generous, exasperating…'

She didn't get to hear the rest as Beatrice had made her way over. 'Yolanda's starting to struggle. She's asked if you can make up a bed…'

'Sure.' Roula nodded, for she needed no further explanation. Yolanda had MS, and the sudden wedding would be taking its toll, though she would never let it show. It would be wise that she rest during the lull in proceedings before the beach party.

Roula left then, and by the time Yolanda arrived there was a bed in the area between the offices—a space big enough to accommodate both the bed and her electric wheelchair.

'Rest…' Roula said as she quietly shut the door to the offices, and then winced as the receptionist called to her.

'The Bridal Suite wants absinthe!'

'Shh…' Roula hushed her, because Stephanie could be rather loud. 'They have it.' Roula knew that because she had placed it there herself. 'You do mean the Bridal Suite—*not* the bridal party?'

'Leo Arati.'

'I'll call him,' Roula said, and promptly did so from her office, pulling his details up on the computer.

'Roula!' Leo greeted her warmly. 'You remembered!'

Sure enough, he had just found it. She snapped off more chocolate, for there had been no time for lunch or a break.

'What's absinthe?' Stephanie asked as she took another incoming call from a guest.

'Nobody can remember!' Roula laughed at her own joke, but then stopped smiling as the one problem she hadn't anticipated arrived.

'Temple Suite.' Stephanie replaced the phone and rolled her eyes. '*Not* happy!'

'Did he say why?'

'Not to lowly me—he wants management *now*! I said the guest services manager would be over shortly...'

That didn't sound like the Galen she had known. Still, because it was her job to anticipate, Roula hazarded a guess as to what might be upsetting a tech wizard. She took a black bag from her drawer, then made her way over. And, yes, she was curious, as with bittersweet chocolate still melting on her tongue her mind wandered back to long-ago bittersweet days...

Oh, how she'd hated school when she'd first started.

Hated it!

The noise, the teasing about her red hair, the games she hadn't been invited to join... It had been too big, too scary, and Roula had started to wet her knickers.

Mortifying.

It had first happened in assembly, in front of the entire school.

Then again in her class.

Her peers had laughed and squealed, and she'd been scolded by her teacher and sent to change. A tall lady had wrapped her wet knickers into a paper parcel and told her off again.

'*Roula Kyrios, this has to stop!*'

She had wanted it to stop.

Roula had been placing the parcel in the bag on her peg, embarrassed to go back inside the classroom, when tears had threatened.

The other children would tease her more for that, Roula had known. She'd taken a breath and bunched her fists, and had been looking to the sky, fighting not to cry, when she'd heard his voice.

'*It will all be okay.*'

She'd jumped, because she had thought she was in the corridor alone, but it seemed Galen Pallas had been sent out of class.

'*I don't want to go back in,*' *she'd admitted.*

'*I know.*' *He'd nodded.* '*But you are brave.*'

'*I'm not.*'

'*Well, I think you are.*'

And because the cleverest boy in the school had considered her brave, it had kind of made her so. At least enough to head back into class. Enough that a couple of years later, when he had again been beaten up and his lunch tossed away, Roula had left her little group and gone over to him, offered to share her lunch.

'*No!*' *Galen had said sharply, without looking up. He'd been sitting on the grass, his knees pulled up, his head down as he'd plucked at the grass. But then he had added,* '*Thank you, though.*'

'*Please,*' *Roula had said.* '*I hate fig jam.*' *She hadn't—it had been her complete favourite.*

'*Go and join your friends or they'll tease you for speaking to me.*'

'*I don't care if they tease me. I'm sorry for what Nemo did to you.*'

Galen had looked up. His eye had been swollen, his lip bloodied, and she had known that was why he'd been looking down when she had first spoken to him.

'*It's not just your brother.*'

'No...'

After that, every now and then, they would share her lunch.

By then Roula had always asked her mother for fig jam on her bread. Galen would help her with her maths problems and let her practise her English, which Roula was good at, though she'd struggled in art and maths.

Of course he'd got older, and so too had she. Roula had become popular, and best friends for ever with Mia, and had started to skip and hopscotch her way confidently through playtimes.

And then it had seemed as if she'd looked around one day to find that Galen was gone. He hadn't even said goodbye....

And now he was back.

Roula put her smile firmly in place and then knocked on the door.

She was met with familiar hazel eyes—but that was the only thing familiar.

Galen had not just grown from the lanky awkward youth she had last seen, he was very tall and although slim, somehow broad. His hair had always been clipped, but now it was worn longer and thicker, glossy and raven-black. Gone were the scruffy homemade clothes, and he was polished and elegant in his wedding suit.

Her breath hitched—for of course he would look different all these years on. But this new Galen, the thirty-something one, had hit her with an impact she had neither expected nor anticipated.

He was beautiful—and Roula had never contemplated male beauty before.

Ever.

Not even once.

He was standing there, phone in hand, dressed in a dark suit with a sprig of flowers in the lapel, a white shirt and silver tie. And, most noticeably, he was no longer awkward.

The awkward one was Roula, but she refused to acknowledge it, even to herself!

'Sir, I'm...'

'The guest services manager...' Galen finished for her as he looked at her badge.

He was doing his level best to hold on to his patience, but name badges irritated Galen. Always had. Especially when the person wearing one introduced herself with the title on the badge… Especially when he'd already been told that the guest services manager would be with him shortly…

He took a breath, aware that he was not, despite smiling since the crack of dawn, having the best day. But then he really saw the name, and he looked up and met dark brown eyes and— Who could forget that hair?

'Roula?'

'Yes,' she said. 'The guest ser…'

'Roula Kyrios?'

'Well, it's Drakos now.'

'*Really?*' Okay, not the best first response. Congratulations might have been better. But Galen didn't correct himself.

Married? Well, of course she would be, living here. And Dimitrios… He cast his mind back. Well, Galen hadn't moved in his circles, but he remembered him as good-looking and popular. As for Roula—well, she was seriously beau—

Galen abruptly halted his own thought process with a glance at her wedding ring.

'How can I help?' she asked.

Oh, yes, the Internet… Except this was *Roula*!

'So you're the guest serv…?' God, he was going to say those dreaded words again. He stopped himself. 'Still living here?'

'I am.' She smiled patiently. 'I was told that you wanted to speak to management.'

'Yes—I'm having trouble getting online. I can't even make a call.'

'There's no signal here. No internet either…'

'Excuse me?' He flashed her an incredulous smile.

'It's a health retreat. People come her for a digital detox—well, for many different types of detox, actually, but—'

'No, no,' Galen cut in. 'I'm not here to detox. I'm here for a wedding. A wedding I only found out about on Thursday night.'

'Yes.' Roula nodded. 'I thought it might prove an issue, and that is why I brought over the satellite phone…'

She held out a black bag and he took it and peered at the brick inside.

Good grief!

He took a very deep breath before attempting to explain the priority this was. 'There is an announcement soon to be made and I need to be online for it. I have one hour before I have to head out to the beach and plaster this grin on again…'

'I'm aware of the schedule, sir.'

He tried another angle. 'I bet Costa's villa has Internet access. I can guarantee it…'

'You would have to discuss that with him. There are guest-to-guest calls, of course…'

'Good,' he clipped, and went to stalk off. 'I'll do that now!'

'Yes,' Roula said. 'Why don't you call the groom and his new bride and ask to drop in on them? I'm sure Costa would be delighted to help you resolve this urgent matter.'

That stopped him, but not for long as he pondered how long a post-wedding bonk might take. 'How long do you think they'll…?'

Roula halted his inappropriate question with the tiniest raise of her brows—it was a tactic she occasionally used with difficult guests and, sadly, Galen was fast becoming one.

'Roula,' he said very patiently, 'I *know* that the Internet can be turned on.'

'It can't.'

She shook her head and he watched as a long titian curl sprung forward and freed itself from its confines, like some old-fashioned jack-in-the-box. *Surprise!* And, like those old-fashioned boxes, the spring did not straighten out, and nor did it jump back. It draped, amber, gold and spent, across her cheek. Galen wanted to reach for her hair…he would like to pop that curl back, to tuck it in, and then for it to surprise him all over again.

'Pardon?' Galen said, because while watching her hair he had lost track of her words.

'I said, even if you were the King of England, I could not give you a signal or Internet access. What I *can* do is give you the use of my office once the bridal party has moved down to the beach.'

'How about now?'

'I'm sorry.' She shook her head, loose curl and all. 'I'm sure you understand that the smooth running of the wedding has to remain my priority.'

He stood silent.

'Is there anything else I can help you with?' she asked.

'Actually, yes. Didn't you get the brief from my PA?'

'The brief?' she frowned. 'Regarding...?'

'Bed linen.' Galen said. 'I prefer plain.'

Roula looked past the columns to the sleeping chambers. The Temple Suite was beyond anything she had ever seen, and the very best of the luxurious retreat. It had its own vast internal pool, and beneath an incredible dome was a bed so high it looked like an altar—and it was dressed in the bespoke Temple Suite bedding: a pale velvet with a *very* subtle hand-embroidered star constellation.

And he was complaining!

'I don't believe I did get that.' Roula gave a tight smile, trying to be diplomatic because she didn't want his PA to be in trouble, but, no, of *course* she hadn't got a brief! 'I believe Costa arranged all the bookings.'

'But I specifically messaged Kristina...'

'I apologise for the oversight.'

Oh, Galen, Roula thought, her smile fading as she let herself out. *How you've changed.*

CHAPTER THREE

IT WAS A minor glitch.

So very minor in the scheme of things.

Mia was hyperventilating as the chefs from Santorini commandeered her kitchen. Yolanda had been difficult to wake up, and so tired she'd actually needed a little help from Roula into her chair. And Leo Arati had had to be gently prompted, several times, and told that it was time to head to the beach for the party.

There were just a million balls, but Roula was actually very used to juggling them at work.

She stood, her work smile on, as the party took off. All were invited. The chefs, waiters and security guards were all externally hired, and rarely the retreat was running on a skeleton staff for a few hours.

Beatrice and Roula were the skeletons!

'Aunty Roula!' Dimitrios's twin nieces came running towards her, all dark curls and huge brown eyes, the sweetest girls on earth.

'There's going to be dress-up soon!' the leader of the two declared.

'But you're already dressed up!' Roula teased, for she knew what they meant. Soon the music would start, and there was a dressing up area and a photo booth for all the children, and *of course* the twins knew it. 'You both look beautiful.'

'But they're starting to give numbers out...'

'Are they?'

'We're going to be last.'

Roula smiled and then put her hand in her pocket and took out two numbered tokens. 'Shh...'

'Will we be first?'

'No,' Roula said, 'that would not be fair.' She gave them a tiny wink. 'But you will be third and fourth!'

They were the sweetest, cheekiest pair, and she waved to their father as the little ones scampered off. Stephanos, Dimitrios's brother-in-law, waved back, and then helped the baby he was carrying wave too.

Roula smiled, but then blew out a breath. Her confrontation with Mia had shaken her, perhaps? Or was it her knowledge of the news to come? Would she see still be able to see the twins? Roula had held them the day they were born…

It fully dawned on her then that her time here might be ending. That her family, her home, her career were silently coming undone—the truth, when revealed, would *not* be setting her free.

Galen wasn't faring so well either.

In dutiful *koumbara* mode he worked the beach. He loathed mingling and small talk at the best of times, but he kept his smile on and made dreaded chit-chat. Yet his eyes kept drifting.

There was no doubt the retreat was marvellous, but it was the village in the distance he scanned. There was the church where he had stood silently as his *yaya* had openly wept each week. He looked upwards at the lush hilly terrain, at the winding road that hugged steep slopes and had claimed his parents and almost him.

'You must see a lot of changes…?' someone said.

'No,' Galen responded, and saw the startlement of the small group nearby. 'Well, of course the retreat is incredible. I meant the village looks the same…'

'But it's completely different,' one of the man insisted. 'Designer shops now, cafés and restaurants, a medical centre…'

'Of course,' Galen agreed, choosing not to explain that he had meant the skyline, and the roads carved into his brain so clearly he could almost see the school bus heaving it slow way up the hill.

'Some familiar faces…?'

'Yes,' Galen said. 'Your father was the postmaster…'

'Still is.' The man nodded. 'Well, he retires soon. Hey, Pa…' He called the elderly man over. 'Remember Galen?'

Again his gaze drifted, though now it swept the beach. On the edge of the activities stood Roula, talking and laughing with two little girls who were identical twins.

'Who else have you caught up with?' the postmaster asked.

Galen had the memory of an elephant—except when it came to irrelevant names.

'Yolanda, of course…' Galen said. 'And Mia…' He had never really liked Mia, but today he was *koumbara*, Galen reminded himself. 'The wedding lunch was excellent...' Galen smiled politely, even though he felt the gnaw of indigestion.

'Poor Roula...' One of the women followed his gaze. 'We were just saying how hard today must be for her...' She sighed dramatically. '*She* was promised to Costa...'

Galen almost laughed in her face—and not pleasantly. Roula would have barely been at school when that ridiculous promise had been made. But the money-hungry Kyrios family had changed their mind when Yolanda had fallen ill and her husband had left her. Bastards.

Still, it was not Galen who disputed the observation.

'No...' the old postmaster corrected. 'I told you—Roula misses Dimitrios.' He must have seen Galen's frown. 'You didn't know?'

It was then that he found out that Roula had been widowed.

'So sad...they were so happy. You know...' the postmaster leant in a little closer to Galen '...five years on and she still sleeps on the couch.' He tapped his nose. 'I deliver parcels. She tries not to let me see in...'

'Excuse me, please.' Galen pushed out his plastic smile. God, but he loathed this place and the gossipmongers—like hyenas with a carcass. And he fed himself into another group, but the conversation was much the same.

The bride was too thin...a little too clingy.

Oh, she'd done *very* well for herself.

And Roula was one of the topics too.

Her career was all she had.

Such a shame they'd never had babies.

Galen hated this place.

There were, though, some friendly faces.

'God!' Leo gave a dramatic sigh when they caught up with each other. 'Kill me now.'

'Good to be back?' Galen grinned.

'I absolutely adore coming to the retreat,' Leo admitted, 'but there you're rather shielded from the locals and my ghastly family. How are you faring, Galen?'

'It's a good wedding,' Galen said, because he just didn't bitch—even with friends. And, of course, some people were lovely. But it was the maliciousness behind certain smiles that rankled. The opinions so readily voiced.

He glanced over towards Roula and found that he was frowning.

He watched her look up to the sky and saw her shoulders lift, and he remembered that day—gosh, years ago…decades, perhaps—when she'd stood at her peg and wept. He saw her hands clench and he was certain now that she was about to break down…

Not here, Roula, he silently urged.

There were already enough poisoned arrows flying around. He could just imagine how the locals would feast on it if she cried. And even before that thought had been processed Galen left his friend and walked towards her.

'You said you could get me a connection.'

'Sorry?'

Roula was startled. Her eyes were brimming, and Galen knew he had been right. She was on the very edge of tears and needed to get the hell away from here.

Now.

'I need to get online,' he snapped. 'So either you get me to an internet connection now, or you find someone who can…'

'Of course.' She gestured towards the main offices. 'This way, please.'

They came into an empty reception area and she took him behind the desk, then gestured to her own office. Galen pretended not to notice her glassy brown eyes and the pink tip of her nose.

'Please,' Roula said. 'Help yourself.'

'Thank you.'

Galen took a seat and looked not at the computer but at the endless items that crowded her desk. The chocolate he understood, but there were photos, quotes, flowers, rosary beads… There was even a little dragonfly stuck to her computer screen. Galen was untidy himself, though his desk was cluttered with coffee cups and food, not endless pictures of grinning twins staring back at him. How the hell did she work in this riot?

'Galen?' Roula knocked, but stood outside the door. Unlike the postmaster, she made no attempt to peer in. 'I apologise—you will need my password.'

'It's fine. I'm already in.'

'But I didn't give it to you…'

'Easy guess,' Galen said. 'You really need something more secure.'

He grimaced when he saw the dip in charts his absence had caused, but then flicked off the page, and called the care home to find out how the new treatment regime that had been arranged before he'd flown off was faring. Yaya was on her second unit of blood, he was told, but had twice removed the IV.

'She has one-on-one care, though?' Galen checked, because it had been agreed she would while she was receiving treatment.

'Of course—but she is quick.'

'Very quick for ninety,' Galen said. 'One-on-one care,' he reminded them, and then dropped the phone.

Despite the rather rich lunch, he ate some of Roula's chocolate. He was annoyed with the carers and glad for a brief respite in a long, long day, with the private after-party still to come.

Roula also wished the day was over.

She looked at the sky as the blazing sun dipped down and could already feel the throb of music from the beach. Thankfully she had composed herself by the time Galen reappeared, and she looked up and smiled.

'Did you see the announcement?' Roula asked as she stood up.

'Sorry?'

'The one you needed the Internet for?'

'Oh, that.' He gave those hazel eyes a little roll. 'I was supposed to be making the announcement. Well, my foundation. But…'

Roula gulped. 'Did it cause problems? The delay…?'

'The price has crashed, but that happens a lot in crypto… It will recover.' He considered for a moment. 'Well, maybe.'

Oh, no! She should have woken Yolanda earlier, got this man to a connection… 'I'm so sorry.'

'Roula, don't worry about it.'

He gave her a smile then, and possibly it was the scent from the candles—only they weren't lit yet—but she breathed in something beautiful, something soothing, just a moment of calm…

And Roula felt something she had not felt for so long now. Normal.

CHAPTER FOUR

THE BEACH PARTY was over.

Finally!

Roula's heels were about to come off for the final time as she updated the overnight team. 'The beach is almost cleared,' Roula said. 'The private party will go for ages, but I'm out of here.'

'Not yet, you're not.' Stephanie halted her. 'Costa's just asked if you could bring some more cake. Mia is just slicing it.'

'Can't someone else do that?' Roula groaned. She was honestly exhausted—but then she stirred herself. Mia had already been invited for a drink, Beatrice too. It was just Costa being polite with the senior staff. 'Of course I'll go.'

'Here.' Mia handed her the tray she had prepared but did not meet Roula's eyes.

'Thank you,' Roula said. 'I've heard from the guests that lunch was amazing...seriously so.'

Mia said nothing in return.

Roula carried the tray in—of course with a smile. It really was a small gathering. Yolanda had retired and it was just the happy couple, along with Galen, Leo and Deacon, and a few people who were, she guessed, Athens friends.

'Roula!' Costa looked up. 'You're off duty now.'

'Soon.' She kept her *no problem* smile on.

'I meant join us,' Costa said. 'Please. Relax.'

'Thank you, though not for long—'

'Roula,' Costa interrupted. 'You're staying.'

'Old friends,' Leo chimed in. 'Gosh, how long since we've all been together?'

'Leo, I see you all the time.' Roula smiled.

'I meant us four.'

Roula didn't answer.

They were soon back to whatever they'd been discussing before Roula had arrived.

'She was awful to Mary,' Costa said, and then politely brought

Roula up to speed. 'We're discussing Galen's PA. I had to bribe her with a babymoon just to get her to pick up Mary from the airport. You could not meet a colder woman.'

But Galen shrugged. 'Kristina is not employed to pick up your girlfriends from the airport, Costa…'

'Fair enough,' Costa conceded. 'Though she's not exactly looking out for you either.'

'Rubbish,' Leo interjected. 'She's devoted.'

'No, I work in the same building,' Costa insisted, 'Kristina wouldn't notice if he was dead at his desk…'

It was light-hearted banter, really, and Roula actually slipped off her shoes as she sipped her champagne.

'I'm serious,' Costa continued. 'Once Kristina left him in the office on a Friday, after he'd already been there all day. She came back on Monday and didn't even look in on him…'

'I'm not an infant,' Galen said. 'I had said I was not to be disturbed. I wanted to focus.'

'He collapsed when he came out,' Costa informed the people at the table, and they all laughed. 'Dehydrated. All that brain and he forgot about H2O.'

'I got a hell of a lot done though…' Galen shrugged and took a drink of his iced tea.

'I know Kristina's married and everything…' Leo pressed on. 'Due to have a baby soon?'

'Correct,' Galen nodded. 'She's in her third trimester.'

Roula felt a little uncomfortable now—just as she had when they were at school and the boys would tease Galen and he'd never realise until too late that they were…

'It's the million-dollar question, really.' Leo sighed dramatically. 'Come on, Galen, we're just dying to know. Were you two ever, or are you still—?'

'Leo,' Galen cut in, and his voice was calm but there was the sharp edge of warning. 'I would never discuss one of my staff's personal life—not with them, and most certainly not with you.'

'Ooh!' Leo beamed as he was duly told off. 'Well, you can't blame me for trying to find out.' Unfazed, he turned his gossipy smile to Roula. 'How was your day, dear Roula?'

'Busy!'

'Do the locals all still think you're upset over him?' Leo asked, and gestured with his head towards Costa, who laughed.

'Some do.' Roula nodded. 'You know what they can be like here.'

Leo sighed. 'This place! Can't they accept you might just be grieving your husband?'

Galen noted Roula's brief grim smile and then he looked away.

Five years since her husband had died and yet it was spoken about as if it was a recent event.

Still, time did not move on readily here—and neither did widows… Galen knew very well the rules of this place. Just as his *yaya* had, Roula would attend church for all souls on a Saturday, as well as go on Sunday, and then there'd be his annual memorial…

Where, he wondered, did beautiful widows go for relief? And Roula was undeniably beautiful…

It didn't enter his head that she might not have such requirements, because he so often did. It was necessary. Like food, like water…

Admittedly, he forgot to eat or drink on occasion, as had been outlined tonight by his friends. But after famine came feast…

He considered her options and found there were not many—for there was no chance of her taking a discreet lover in Anapliró that Galen could see.

So where do you go, Roula?

Did she take the ferry to Santorini and meet a lover? Galen was quietly turned on at that thought of her leaving it all behind for a steamy afternoon. Or maybe an occasional stolen sultry Santorini night, before returning to Anapliró as if butter wouldn't melt…

He liked that thought.

Galen remained seated when the others decided to go around popping balloons—there had apparently been a specification from Costa that there were many.

Roula, it would seem, was not a popping balloons type of person either, for now it was just the two of them at the lavish table, and Roula was fiddling with a plaster on her thumb.

'Did you enjoy the day?' Roula asked politely. 'The beach party…?' Her voice trailed off as clearly she recalled the internet issues he'd raised. She moved to safer ground. 'Everyone said the meal was beautiful.'

'It was a bit too rich for me,' Galen said.

He was just being honest—his guts had been burning since lunch and usually he had the constitution of an ox. Galen watched her lips, parted ready to jump in and defend her friend Mia, but then she pushed out her work smile.

'The guest is always right, Roula.' He was gently provoking her, and with specific intent. 'Isn't that so?'

'Of course,' Roula responded politely.

Galen waited silently for the real Roula to be revealed—for the fiery person he'd known to fire back a tart retort. Yet it never came.

'How is Kupia Florakis?' she asked, about his *yaya*. 'She's in Athens, yes?'

'Doing well for ninety.' He nodded. 'She misses here.'

'Will you go up to the house?' Roula asked. 'Perhaps take something back for her?'

'It was all very last minute. I was only told about the wedding on Thursday night.'

'We didn't find out much before that,' Roula admitted, glancing up as a couple who were topping up their drinks in between balloon-popping chimed into their conversation.

'Nor us—we were taking bets about your plus one, Galen.'

'Not a chance,' Galen said.

'Told you!' The woman smiled at her partner. 'I said he'd be here on his own.'

'Have you just broken up with someone?' Roula asked.

'No.' He shook his head. 'Nothing to break.'

'Oh, sorry. I thought when they said they were taking bets…'

'They were being facetious.'

'About you being single?'

'I don't date,' Galen said. 'Believe me, the thought of a long weekend entertaining someone…' He shook his head. 'No.'

'"Entertaining"?' Roula checked.

'Breakfast, flying together, driving to the airport, getting ready…' He must have seen her frown. 'I don't do well with relationships.'

'Well, I'm sure you'll…'

Roula looked, and then looked again. Because even if she was dead inside—well, there was no denying Galen was stunning.

'I'm sure the right person is out there.'

'Roula,' he said, and looked directly at her. 'I think we may have crossed wires—I actively *choose* not be in a relationship.'

'Oh…' Roula said, relieved they had found a common thread. 'Like me.'

For the first time that evening their eyes met.

Galen didn't flirt—there was no need when he were as beautiful as he was—but, more than that, romance was not an arena he played in. His refusal to acknowledge her entrance to the party had been…well, deliberate. For he was skilled at a certain game. He was also discerning and discreet.

And he chose his moment now, when the rest were distracted, and offered invitation with his eyes.

If Roula was interested he was about to find out, for she now glanced towards him and met his gaze.

Her eyes were brown—that he already knew—and yet for the first time Galen ventured into their burnt umber.

Where do you go, Roula? he asked silently, and when she did not look away his hazel gaze delved a little further. *Do you want to go there with me?*

Roula found herself caught in his line of vision and for a brief moment had the sensation of being pulled by a gentle undertow—floating mindlessly, willingly, as the noise of the revellers around them seemed to dim.

It was the oddest sensation—to be locked in another's eyes—

but perhaps only because she'd never been asked if she'd like to indulge before, had only ever been taken, Roula misread the question.

Was he still cross about earlier? she wondered. Because she felt a little… She wasn't sure what. Anxious, perhaps…scrutinised, maybe?

Roula flicked her gaze away.

'Hey, Galen…' someone called.

A little bewildered, Roula stood. 'Excuse me.'

'You're going?' he checked, and she saw that he wore just a smudge of a frown.

'Not yet.'

Roula was warm, and also a little flustered as she briefly escaped to the bathroom. She did what she had to and then, washing her hands, decided to top up her lipstick.

It was a party after all.

Yet even as she added a slick of coral she was still replaying that moment with Galen and trying to interpret it into a language she knew. Perhaps he didn't appreciate staff mingling with the guests? Or was he still irritated that she hadn't been able to get him online…

Her thoughts stopped as the door opened. 'Mary!' She turned as the bride came in. 'You look completely beautiful.' Roula was actually in awe of the fact that a bride could still look so gorgeous after midnight. The formal dress had been replaced by the slip version which she had worn earlier on the beach, and her blonde hair tumbled. 'Stunning.'

'Just happy.' Mary smiled. 'I never dreamt we'd be having the actual wedding service in London…' Her eyes brimmed with tears. 'Did you know?'

'There were *many* back-up plans,' Roula told her. 'I am so glad it all came together.'

'I just wasn't expecting my dad to be there. Yolanda too, and Galen…' She gave a low, devilish laugh. 'Mind you, apparently Costa thought he'd lost him at one point…'

'Lost him?'

'He was catching up with a *friend*, apparently.' Mary gave an exaggerated roll of her eyes. 'As you do at six a.m. on the morning of a wedding.'

'I'm not with you…'

'Galen was with one his catch-up girls.' Mary laughed again. 'It would seem that he has a very devoted fan base in every port!'

Roula's laugh came a little too late. She was so out of step with everything. She'd been thinking Galen was single, or even celibate, perhaps, when actually… Gosh! She replayed their conversation and realised it would seem that when it came to relationships, Galen cherry-picked the parts he wanted…

And they were the very parts Roula most certainly didn't!

'How are you doing?' Mary asked.

Roula dragged her mind back to more familiar terrain. 'Oh, it's been busy, but…'

'How are you holding up?'

Costa had no doubt asked Mary to corner her like this, to find out how she was faring. Roula had immediately known the reason for the rapid wedding—and, no, it wasn't as half the island was suggesting. Costa just wanted the woman he loved by his side and out of danger.

And, as Roula had recently found out, her older brother Nemo might be very dangerous indeed…

'Have you heard anything?' Mary asked anxiously.

'No.' Roula shook her head and then reminded Mary of what they'd been told. 'The police said not to discuss it.'

'Even so…'

'Mary.' Roula was practical. 'This is your wedding! Focus on enjoying it!' She refused to let anything spoil Mary's day. 'Get out there and have fun. Guest Service Manager's orders.'

'You're off duty,' Mary pointed out.

'Then *I* want to have some fun,' Roula lied, because in truth she just wanted to head for home.

Nobody knew Roula.

They returned to the table. Roula's smile was back in place, and she even took her jacket off and placed it over the chair, to denote that she was reluctantly—not that she showed it—staying.

She refilled her glass, but with water this time, and took

a grateful refreshing drink. Galen was still there and, given Mary's recent revelation about him, she was embarrassed at her earlier reply.

Gosh, had Galen been flirting with her or coming on to her? Had he thought she was doing it back at him?

Yikes.

'Galen?' she said, and when he glanced over, she corrected her earlier response to his single status. '*Not* like me!'

To his credit, Galen gave her a very nice smile. 'Pity.'

Roula almost laughed. Gosh, he'd certainly been barking up the wrong tree with her. And now, very politely, he'd stopped barking.

Not that he had been really, but… Well, there were no more undercurrents, no stolen looks—just the last moments of a gorgeous wedding.

And of course Roula had work the next day…

'I'm going to head off,' she whispered to Leo.

'Don't you dare,' Leo said as she attempted to depart discreetly. 'Stay and hear my speech at least…'

'Leo, no.' Galen was assertive, but he combined it with humour as he stood and averted disaster—because Leo was less than discreet. 'You are *not* stealing my thunder—I give the best man speeches.'

To everyone's relief he took to the microphone and his speech was very concise.

'Mary and Costa: *ee ora ee kale!*' Galen offered his best wishes for perhaps the twentieth time that day. 'The time is good,' he said, and then he added, 'Now we dance.'

Oh, they danced!

Well, not Galen. He remained seated and Roula wondered if she could slip away. Mary and Costa were draped around each other as Leo, deprived of the microphone, played DJ, and the others joined them.

'Come on, you two!' they urged, begging them to join in, and he looked over to Roula.

'We're killjoys,' Roula said.

'I always am.' Galen nodded. 'I hate dancing—I find it pointless.'

Roula found that she was smiling, and they shared an eye-roll as they were summoned again.

'Shall we?' he offered.

Whatever the silent conversation they'd briefly engaged in had meant had long since been dropped, and for old times' sake she smiled. 'One dance,' Roula said, 'then I'm really going to go...'

He held one of her hands up, as if they were in a half-formal dance, and felt her fingers cold beneath his. The other was light on her bare upper arm.

It was a polite dance.

Galen *was* polite.

Always.

At least out of the bedroom...

But he only played with the very willing, and Roula had made it clear that she wasn't, so he'd ended the game back at the table.

His grip did not tighten, and nor did he touch her hair, which was uncoiling down her back. It was a dance with a long-ago friend.

Pointless.

Two people standing fully dressed and moving, but going nowhere.

And this was a particularly wooden dance—or rather one with a porcelain figurine. For she was rigid in his arms and held herself back from him.

'I ate the chocolate on your desk,' Galen said.

'I know you did.' Roula nodded. 'How did you know my password?'

'I'm good at retaining numbers. Your date of birth,' Galen said. 'And your little dog Benji...'

She gave a soft laugh. 'I still miss him.'

Perhaps dancing wasn't quite so pointless.

Her hair smelt like sunshine, and her once cold hand had warmed to match the temperature of his, and the almost imperceptible beginnings of a thaw was taking place in his arms. Not much…just the dusting of her curls on his chin as she moved a little more freely…yet it felt so rewarding.

They were polar opposites.

Roula was a nice Anapliró girl, and that generally meant commitment before bed—or at the very least dinners and conversation and all the things he just did not do. Though he would like to stroke the skin on her arms beneath his fingers. Just to feel the shiver that was, he was almost sure, there between them.

Not acknowledged.

Not quite…

Roula felt his shift in awareness and could not quantify it, for they were dancing the same dance and he held her the same way. Yet his scent made her want to breathe deeper. And from nothing of note she felt a band of constriction from the two bras which she always wore to flatten her generous breasts.

It was just a moment during a dance, but what had felt simply natural suddenly flustered her as the moment—whatever it was—dispersed.

'Are you okay?' Galen asked.

Roula frowned, for it was as if he had felt her sudden tension. 'Of course.'

Yet she wasn't. It really was time to go home. But she was saved from making an excuse to leave, because the music suddenly died and they both looked over at the sound of a crash.

Leo had faded rather abruptly!

It was quite fun, watching Deacon carry him out, and then Mary and Costa were cheered and clapped off to bed, and like soapy bubbles the little crowd started to disperse.

'It was nice to see you again,' Roula said.

'And you,' Galen agreed. 'Roula, I heard about…' He faltered. 'Well, I'm sorry—'

'Please…' she rapidly cut in, and then corrected herself. 'You weren't to know.'

'How many years *has* it been?' Galen asked, and he was not discussing her late husband. 'I mean since we saw each other?'

'I'm not sure,' Roula said, but there was a slight edge to her voice as she spoke. 'You're the one who's good with numbers.'

He found himself staring into unblinking umber eyes and saw that there was turmoil there. Despite popular opinion on the island, Galen was not a robot—or *rompot* as he'd been called in Greek.

'Are you...?' He didn't know how to ask if she missed her husband. 'Weddings must be hard.'

'There's one every week here.'

'I meant—'

'Please don't try to guess about me, Galen. It's the national sport here.'

Galen looked at her then, at that gorgeous hair in the moonlight, stripped of colour, and her face so pale. It felt surreal to be here. To stand in a place so familiar, with someone he'd once known and yet no longer recognised.

He thought of her near tears on the beach—not that she was aware he knew she'd almost cried. But she was hurting today. Galen was sure.

And so he broke the heavy silence.

'Anonymous conversation helps sometimes, I believe...' he said.

'You're not anonymous, Galen.'

'Sort of...' he said.

'No, thank you,' Roula said, and then rather tartly added, 'To both offers.'

Galen knew exactly to what she was referring—for, yes, there had been two offers made tonight.

Roula pushed out her best guest services manager smile. 'I hope the remainder of your stay is a pleasant one.'

'Roula...?'

'Goodnight, Galen.'

Roula slipped away into the dark of the night. She could hear the roar of the sea and feel the whip of wind on her cheeks, and she was hurting and confused and so cross, so furious, that she felt like screaming.

Instead she walked faster, almost at a run.

Mia had upset her, Roula told herself as she marched along dark familiar streets. And Mia was wrong. They had grown apart long before Dimitrios's death.

She had tried to broach her issues once, at a girls' lunch. Ella, his sister, had been pregnant with the twins, and had told them that Stephanos wanted to get the snip, so they could 'do it' worry-free.

They had all laughed.

Her face burning, Roula had broached the subject, desperate for some advice. 'Dimitrios wants it all the time...'

'Newlyweds!' Ella had smiled. 'We never came up for air. But wait till you have kids...'

'Young love...' Mia had sighed. 'I'm jealous—the only thing keeping me up at night is meal prep!'

Roula had come away even more confused, and had never so much as hinted at her private hell again.

Never.

Even when it had got worse.

The lunches with friends had stopped. The sex and violence had not. There had been no babies, and that was all her fault, and each month his rage had increased.

Her retreat had started.

'I might apply for work as a chambermaid,' she had said one day as she'd put down his dinner, nervous to admit to him that she had already put in her application.

'Why would you work for Costa Leventis?' Dimitrios had stood up from the table. 'You wish you'd married him, don't you?'

'Of course not. Dimitrios, please...'

'Why would you want to work for him when I'm working night after night to provide for you?'

To say they'd 'made love' would not be the term she would have used even in her most naïve times.

To say they'd 'had sex' did not suffice either...

Roula was crying as she let herself into her little fisherman's cottage, the flashes of memory too much. All she had held in during this long, dreadful day burst like a dam as she went through the door—only to be greeted by her wedding photo.

'Damn you!' she said, and took off her wedding ring and placed it on the mantelpiece, then turned down the photo as she always did when she was home alone.

Roula headed into the bedroom to retrieve her bed linen from the wardrobe. Usually she did not so much as glance at the marital bed as she passed it, but tonight—or rather early this morning—she glared at it.

The coastguard had come to her door in the middle of the night to say Dimitrios's boat had been spotted ablaze, and as his family had arrived she had dashed to the bedroom to get dressed.

Dressed in whatever one wore wear when one's husband was missing at sea.

Get dressed, Roula, she'd told herself.

She had walked into the bedroom and closed the door. The sound of a helicopter had been loud overhead and the wail of the sirens urgent as she'd glanced at the bed.

A couple of her long red hairs had lain on the pillow. She usually picked them off and then turned the pillow over. But that morning her hand had reached out and then pulled back...

She'd heard the wailing and sobbing starting up outside as she'd stood there and stared at her marital bed.

Please God, she had silently begged, may I never have to set foot in that bed again.

And to this very day Roula slept on the couch.

CHAPTER FIVE

GALEN HEADED BACK to the Temple Suite, peeled off his suit and took a long drink of water.

It was icy cold and pure, and so instantly refreshing that he conceded there was one thing about Anapliró he missed.

Galen refilled the glass, took the sprig of flowers from his lapel and placed them into the water.

Duty had been fulfilled.

It was done.

Well, not quite.

He stripped off and got into the pool and lay on his back, liking the weightlessness, choosing not to reflect on the day.

It had been a disaster workwise.

Galen hauled himself out of the pool and lay on the now plain linen and looked up at the dome. He'd forgotten just how beautiful the stars were here. How, as a child, he would creep out at night just to stare up at the Milky Way and try to spot the stars he had read about.

Yaya had said he wandered.

No.

Sometimes…

But usually it was to sit or to lie and stare up, as he did now.

Galen found Scorpio easily and thought that the stars above did not itch like the ones that had been on the bedlinen…they were soothing…

Roula must have thought him a right bastard, Galen thought. A demanding guest. Perhaps he was? But the guest services manager did not need to know of his issues with fabric, or the chaos missing his announcement had caused. Perhaps it was a good thing he couldn't get online now and see the charts!

Rarely, he wished for a moment to explain himself. He had long ago given up on doing that, but he would have liked to explain things better to Roula.

Galen took a breath, and to distract himself fixed his gaze

on the star Antares. But there was no escape there, for with its reddish glow he thought of her hair uncoiling.

Roula Kyrios… With her fiery red hair she had once been so strong with her opinions, and with a laugh so infectious that he could recall it now.

Ha-ha, breath, ha-ha-ha, breath, ha-ha-ha-ha…

She hadn't laughed that way tonight.

Maybe your laugh changed after childhood? he considered.

Possibly.

Or perhaps it faded away when your husband died?

Where do you go to, Roula?

Galen decided he would not be going there!

Instead, he hauled himself from the bed. Hopefully Kristina had managed to brief his maid properly and his running gear would be there.

It was, so he dressed and put on his small running pack. Under a pre-dawn sky he took the familiar road up the hill towards his old home, but that was not his destination. It took ten, maybe fifteen minutes to get into rhythm, and then he made his way up the steep incline.

The last of the stars were fading in the sky when he first saw the *kandylakia* for his parents. The roadside shrines were dotted amongst all these hilly roads. Each different, some were like little houses, but his parents' shrine was a tiny replica of the village church where they had married and were now buried together. It was set high on a stone, near where the accident had occurred.

It was not the gradient Galen was tackling that had his throat hitching as he jerked in air—more that he could see a candle was lit inside it.

The locals had always taken care of these roadside memorials, but he had thought that by now… Or rather he had tried *not* to think about it standing neglected, like the house…

It had not been neglected.

He opened up the little door and took out a few fading flowers. He put in the ones he had worn yesterday. There was a box of matches inside, and fresh candles.

He had always turned his head away as they'd passed it on

the school bus. Today, he saw its beauty. And he wished he had faith, but he stuck to logic.

He looked around, examined the tree, and could barely locate the scar on it. His parents had died here, and the trajectory of his whole life had changed right at this spot.

It offended Galen's consciousness that he couldn't remember a thing about it. Nor could he remember the months in hospital afterwards.

And so, instead of standing there and trying to remember what he could not, Galen ran down towards the *theatron*, where he and Costa had used to train.

As Galen took the steps again, he recalled being small and running up and down, over and over. Preparing to face a day of being shoved. And then getting taller and wider and still running, because he'd thought his brain might explode if he stayed there much longer.

Yet one night here and he was already considering staying on for another…sorting out the house…just getting it done…

For things had been left undone.

Galen's run finished rather abruptly, and as he dragged in air he took a seat reluctantly. The silence was actually beautiful here on Anapliró. There was a haze of sea mist over the Aegean, softly fading into a clear blue sky, and it was a colour he could not describe. There was no hum of traffic, no lights or anything. It was like a power-cut, when all appliances stopped, and you realised the world you sat in was not so silent after all.

Maybe he did need that digital detox, Galen thought wryly, because his mind was actually feeling a new version of clear.

'Galen!'

He looked up when he heard his name being called, and then frowned when he saw that it was Costa. 'What the hell?' Galen asked. 'Haven't you got better things to do the morning after you marry?'

'I do—but I need to speak with you, and of course there was no chance to do so yesterday. I guessed I might find you here.'

They both sat on a damp, dewy step and Costa handed

Galen some water. 'Are you and Mary the fastest break up ever?' he asked.

'No…' Costa was turning his own water bottle over and over in his hand, as he had the champagne cork. 'But I need to ask you to do something.'

'What? More speeches!'

'Kristina is taking six weeks off, yes?'

'What's that got to do with you?'

'I'm going to ask you to employ someone. You're going to say no, but I—'

'I'll save you the trouble,' Galen cut in. 'The answer is no. Stay out of my work!'

'Galen, I told you there was stuff going on.'

Galen turned at the gravity in Costa's tone.

'This is a serious matter…'

And Galen knew that it must be if the groom was here at seven in the morning the day after his wedding.

'Please just listen?'

Galen gave a reluctant nod.

'This can go no further—ever.'

'You know it won't.'

'You know that Roula and I were briefly promised to each other—'

'Oh, please,' Galen cut in. 'You were kids. Anyway, she married Golden Boy…'

'I know that, and so does Roula, but her brother Nemo—he's my head of security…'

'Another reason never to employ family or friends,' Galen said, because Nemo was a brute and had made his life hell.

'You're right,' Costa agreed. 'Because when I brought Mary here for the first time he tried to set her up as a thief. I now believe he wanted to break us up…'

Galen frowned at Costa's ominous tone.

'I tried to speak to Roula about it—she's been odd for weeks…'

'And?' Galen snapped, impatient for information now.

'On her birthday she found a gas cylinder hidden in her brother's garage. She recognised it from Dimitrios's boat.'

'She's sure?'

'Sure enough that she went to the police. They're taking it very seriously. It would seem there have been several suspicious transactions made by Nemo.'

'You're saying that Nemo killed Roula's husband to clear the way for her to marry you?'

'He hasn't been charged,' Costa said, and then added, 'Yet. But there's a lot of resentment there. Now that I'm rich, Roula's family are bitter that they pulled out of the arrangement.'

'She's not a piece of real estate.'

'Tell that to Nemo.'

Galen closed his eyes. *This place!*

'The Drakos family are going to kick off, and her family too, when they find out that she was the one who informed on her brother—'

'I get it,' Galen cut in. No wonder Roula had been upset yesterday.

'If you offered Roula a temporary—'

'No.' Galen shut down Costa's solution straight away, for he did not bring his personal life to work in any way shape or form. 'Arrangements have already been put in place. But I've got the guest apartment. Tell her she's welcome to use that.'

'Roula can't know I've discussed this with you!' Exasperated, Costa waved a hand. 'Believe me, I have tried to help, but she says she has it all under control. Mary approached her last night, but she was quickly shut down...'

'Then maybe she *does* have it under control.'

'Galen,' Costa said. 'Roula was going to walk into the police station without a lawyer.'

Galen swore.

'Roula will only take the job if she thinks it's a genuine one.'

'Then I'll find her something...'

'Something!' Costa gave an incredulous laugh. 'Galen, she's very career-minded. Believe me, she's not going to leave here for some admin role in one of your offsite offices, but a temporary PA position for Galen Pallas would look good on her CV…'

'I don't like this, Costa.'

On so many levels Galen did not like it—he did not want his worlds colliding, and he chose his staff carefully. He loathed emotion and drama—the very things this island thrived on.

There was another issue too, but he pushed that out of his mind for now. Instead, he thought of a day long ago, when a little girl had walked away from her friends, from her own brother and the children who had beaten him, and bravely insisted on being his friend.

'Six weeks.' He nodded tersely and dug deep to retrieve his business self. 'I'm not running a drop-in centre, and whatever you think of my current PA it's a damn hard job. I don't do hand-holding.'

'Just put it to her. She might say no.' Costa stood while Galen still sat. 'But if she does take the job you might want to book her in with Leo and sort out her wardrobe.'

'Why?'

'Trust me on that.'

Galen could not give a damn what Roula wore. Well, so long as there were no patterns… They irritated his brain. Just that.

But she'd been in neutral colours yesterday, apart from the blaze of red hair, and he was hardly going to ask her to dye that.

Maybe she'd ditch the name badge.

First, though, he had to speak with her.

'You're wanted,' Stephanie told Roula loudly, the second she arrived. 'There's an issue in The Temple Suite.'

'He's probably having Internet withdrawals.' Roula rolled her eyes. 'Don't worry, I'm headed there now.'

'Pretty flowers!'

'Yes.' Roula hadn't slept either. She had been into the hills and picked a gorgeous spray from the bougainvillea that draped his *yaya*'s home and had wrapped the end in wet cotton wool and some plastic. 'They're from his *yaya*'s,' Roula said. 'Hopefully it will appease him…'

Roula did not feel appeased in the least when the door to the Temple Suite opened to the sight of Galen wearing a bemused frown and not much else. She tried to ignore the fact that he was dripping wet and there was only a towel around his loins—after all, she'd seen many guests wearing less.

'Good morning!' She gave a cheery smile. 'I have moved things around so you can have the office if you choose...' He was the boss's most important guest after all. 'And I have brought the satellite phone...'

'That was quick!' Galen commented. He had clearly just got out of the shower and made the call before getting dressed. 'What are these...?' He looked at the flowers she held.

'For your *yaya*.' Roula said. 'From her home.'

'I don't think so...'

'She'll love them,' Roula insisted, holding them out at arm's length and trying not to look at him. 'It would be really nice for her.'

Reluctantly he took them. 'Please, come in.'

'As I said, I have arranged for the office—'

'Roula,' Galen cut in. 'I want to talk with you without others around. Actually...'

He stopped. She thought he must have seen her scalding cheeks.

'If you can excuse me a moment? I'll go and get dressed and maybe then we can speak.'

She turned and stood in the bright morning sun, as if it might bleach the image of his bronzed wet skin from her eyes, and the memory of the dark hairs on his chest and the glimpse of flat stomach...

She'd walked in on guests wearing practically nothing. Actually nothing at times!

Roula had seen a *lot*, working here!

But, while it might bewilder her a little, unsettle her at times, reassure her at others, this felt different.

For there had been beads of water on Galen's shoulders and arms, and as he'd taken the flowers she'd seen the darkness of his underarm hair, and she'd tried not to look at his chest, and even that had caused a certain sense of disquiet in the most unfamiliar of ways.

'Sorry about that.'

She turned at his voice.

'I honestly wasn't expecting you to get here so soon.'

He was dressed in dark linen trousers and a thin top that was a little damp, for perhaps he hadn't dried all those beads of water before pulling it on...

She fixed her smile as she spoke. 'Well, apart from the happy couple, you are currently our top guest. And you're upset...'

'No. That was just to get you here,' Galen said. 'Please, come in. Tell them my complaint was a major one! Maybe say that the flowers did the trick,' he suggested as she came in. 'Please, take a seat.'

'Thank you.' She perched on the edge of an extravagant chair. 'How has your stay been...?' Roula started, but Galen shook his head.

'Roula, my PA is soon taking six weeks' maternity leave.'

'Only six weeks?'

'I noticed how well you dealt with the wedding yesterday, especially given the short notice. I need someone like that.' Galen shrugged. 'I just thought I'd run it by you.'

'You're offering me the role of your PA?' Roula frowned.

'Yes—well, it's a short-term position, and I have to warn it's a very demanding role.'

'I don't mind demanding, but...' She swallowed. 'I'm very happy here, Galen...' Her voice trailed off as she thought of the weeks ahead and wondered if that happiness would still apply. 'My home...'

'I have a furnished apartment,' Galen said. 'I keep it for temporary staff.'

'Oh?'

'Your computer skills...?'

'Are good.' She'd been on a refresher course last month. 'Well, my passwords clearly don't suffice...' She stopped the mild joke because his expression was very serious.

'Our cyber security is way beyond what is to be expected here, but you'd be versed in that only after contracts are signed.'

'I see.'

He addressed another issue. 'Roula,' Galen said, 'if we reminisced a little too much last night...'

Her eyes flew to his. 'Did we?'

'I don't think so, but...'

Ah, the eye-meeting.

'I want to make it clear that was me on a rare day off and visiting home.'

'Of course.'

'What I am saying is that I am completely different at work. For one thing, I don't engage in small talk.'

'Small talk?'

He hesitated. 'This...'

Roula's eyes widened and she was about to say that *'this'* was just conversation. Still, their fig jam days had been long ago—he was a very different person from the one she had known then.

'Should you take this role you will have some access to my private life—mainly my grandmother and liaising with the nursing home. We are doing our best to keep her peaceful...'

'Peaceful?' Roula smiled at the irony. 'That's not the Kupia Florakis I remember—she was always very vocal.'

'Roula.' Galen spoke rather sharply. 'Perhaps I should make things a little clearer.' He looked right at her. 'An old friend might suggest I take her flowers from her home—my PA most certainly would not.'

'I see.'

'Do you?' Galen checked. 'Because for this to work that needs to be understood.'

'Galen, if you don't think I'm suitable, then why are you even offering it to me?'

'I do think you're suitable.'

Galen knew that it was then that he outright lied, for never in a million years would he hire a woman whose scent reached him from across the room, as it was doing so now, who tripped wires and crossed firm boundaries with every throaty word those full lips delivered.

Damn you, Costa!

'I am just stating how it is, and then it is for you to decide.'

Say no, he pleaded silently. Because the mystery of her dark brown eyes was too distracting for his workspace.

Say no, he pleaded silently. *Because right now I want to take you to that bed and lay you down and taste you.*

'I'm flattered…' Roula said. 'But I have commitments here. And also…'

He watched as those lips parted and she drew a breath to continue, but then those gorgeous lips closed. Worryingly for Galen, he found he *wanted* to be privy to her thoughts.

She gave him a very efficient smile. 'You understand that I need time to consider this?'

'Of course.' He moved to hand her a business card, but then seemed to change his mind and took up a pen. 'Usually all calls go through my PA,' he said, 'but this is my personal number.'

'I see.'

'If you…'

How did he say that if she needed a friend, if she was ever in Athens, or here on Anapliró, and it was all too much then she should call him? How did he resume their friendship when she might soon be working for him?

More pertinently, how did they both ignore this attraction?

And it was mutual. Galen could feel it, breathe it, almost touch it.

Yet he could not *see* it.

Her skin was pale, her eyes cool when they met his, and there was no visible sign of the vibe that thrummed in the air between them…

Galen was aware that he was not brilliant at reading people. Yet, he'd known Roula once…

Not now.

How he hated this ruse already.

'Whatever happens, you have my number.' Galen concluded

the conversation and hoped that if she needed to some day then she might read between the lines.

There was little time to think about it as most of the prominent guests were helicoptered off the island and the retreat was being prepared for the next.

Late that evening—way past her rostered time—Roula checked that all was in order for the upcoming bookings. But she scrolled down and saw that, indeed, Galen's PA was due to come to Anapliró for her babymoon in two weeks' time.

And then she looked up Galen on the Internet. Gosh, she known about the platform game, but she'd had no idea how prominent he was in the tech world.

And what the hell was DeFi and Blockchain?

Working for Galen Pallas, even temporarily, really was a career opportunity. And of course the upcoming drama with Nemo made it doubly tempting…

But there was another issue to consider. One that Roula had never dealt with in any way shape or form before, because it was startling to acknowledge that she was attracted to him.

Roula hadn't just shut down that side of herself—it had never even existed. Possibly there had been a shy curiosity about her body once, but it had died on her wedding night.

And then she laughed out loud.

Gosh, she'd barely coped with a dance! Roula knew she would run a mile from a kiss… A relationship with a man was an impossible dream at best, and from all she had learned—had been told by him, in fact—Galen was not interested in that.

And Roula was not interested in sex.

So she had a slight crush on him? Her very first.

Then again, she had seen Galen at his impressive, sociable best, groomed for a wedding.

He had told her himself he was different at work.

More, Galen made her feel…not nervous, not scared…but, just as he always had, he made her feel brave.

Roula took from her bag her rarely used phone and dialled

the number he had given. Her heart was pounding when she got an automated response.

'Galen…' Roula took a breath. 'I don't think I thanked you properly for the opportunity.' She hesitated. Then, 'Yes,' she said. 'I would like to accept…'

Her time had run out, for the phone clicked off.

She'd done it.

Roula stepped out into Reception a little stunned at her own boldness. Surely she should have discussed things first with Yolanda? Or her mother? Or…?

Her eyes were drawn to the occasional table and a beautiful arrangement of bougainvillea there. A frequent sight, perhaps, but she would know those blooms anywhere, for Roula had cut them herself.

'Where are these from?' she asked the cleaner, who was vacuuming.

'One of the guests left them.' She turned off the vacuum cleaner. 'I hope that's okay? It just seemed a shame to waste them.'

'Of course,' Roula agreed. 'Did the guest forget them?' she asked, while knowing it was a pointless question, for the butler would have done a sweep of the rooms. Not so much as a phone lead would be left behind by a Temple Suite guest.

'No, they were in the trash,' the cleaner said, and went back to vacuuming.

Oh, Galen…

CHAPTER SIX

FOR ALL HE KNEW, the two weeks building up to her leaving were passing slowly and for Roula. But for Galen life was on fast forward, and there was a lot to get through.

A lot!

Galen took the elevator up to his suite of offices, but frowned when he saw Kristina there, immersed in work. 'Shouldn't you be at the airport to meet Roula?'

Kristina barely looked up as she responded to his query. 'I've organised a driver.'

'Good,' Galen said, glad that it was all taken care of. Except… 'Cancel him and call my driver. I'll greet her myself.'

He was in his office when Kristina came in, and she looked startled when she saw him swigging from a bottle.

'Antacid,' Galen said, licking his chalky lips.

'Again? Do you want me to schedule an appointment…?' Kristina stopped when he shot her a look, and got to the reason why she had followed him in. 'Galen? If you want me to collect the new temp personally just say. I'm pregnant, not ill.'

'I know.' He nodded. 'But I've told the team I'm taking today off. I'll be too busy on Monday to take Roula over to the care home…'

'I can take her over this afternoon.'

'It's no problem.'

'You're sure?' Kristina checked. 'Please don't go soft on me now, Galen.'

'I'm not.'

Galen wasn't altering his stance for Kristina, and nor would she want him to. She had insisted on working right up to the end, and no doubt had gone for her usual dawn run on the hilly Athens streets…

It wouldn't enter Kristina's head that this was…

What?

Something in Anapliró's unwritten code that you would be

met at the airport? A certain rule that you greeted an old friend personally when she arrived?

Galen had long stopped following the lines in that rule book.

'Do want me to schedule Hector for next week?' Kristina asked.

'No. Tell him the wedding has derailed things...' Galen paused. 'Actually, maybe suggest dinner tonight.'

'But he's in Rome for the convention.'

'I know he is.' Galen smiled. 'At least he can't say I didn't try!'

Arrivals was busy. So busy that as his eyes skimmed the latest batch of passengers dragging their luggage Galen failed to spot Roula.

'Galen!'

He almost looked through her. In the space of two weeks, in his mind he had turned Roula into the goddess Aphrodite, with lush curves and tumbling red curls. So Galen blinked as a woman in a maroon and royal blue zig-zag skirt and a white top dotted with little circles walked towards him. Her hair was tightly scraped into a high knot and the fringe pinned tightly, as if in an attempt to squeeze every drop of colour out of it.

Galen realised then the reasoning behind Costa's warning about her clothes. For out of her smart official uniform Roula dressed... Well, even the residents in Yaya's nursing home were more up to date!

'Galen,' she said again, and gave a little wave.

Her shoes were brown, sturdy and laced, and as for her mismatched bright fabric luggage and the orange cool bag she carried... It was a drama on his eyes.

'Roula!' He righted himself. 'Welcome.'

She gave him a tense smile. 'I wasn't expecting you to meet me.'

Clearly not, Galen was about to say, but thankfully stopped himself, for her attire was completely none of his business. 'Well, there's a lot to get through. I thought we could speak in the car and stop by the care home on the way.'

As they made their way towards the waiting vehicle those zig-zags on her skirt were dancing before his eyes like a pre-migraine aura. He was irritated too by those little circles on her top, for the seams did not align. Galen could not abide patterns—even the hint of a check on a suit would have him wanting to strip it off. And of course Leo took care of all that, ensuring all his attire was plain...

'Kristina will take you to the apartment and brief you a little later.'

'She must be exhausted,' Roula said, 'working so long into her pregnancy. I have never heard of someone taking just six weeks off to have a baby—'

'Roula,' he cut in. 'I don't think it is appropriate to discuss Kristina's decision-making regarding her maternal leave.'

Plus, it made him sound like the worst boss in the world.

She felt awkward, seated in the car beside him—so awkward that she did not even take in the view.

For two weeks she had told herself that the little spark that he'd ignited would fade.

It had not.

And then she had hoped it would puff itself out on meeting him again, for surely if he was not dressed in wedding day best...?

Oh, no, it hadn't.

He wore a dark suit and a white shirt and a gunmetal tie, and his jaw was unshaven. And he was even more beautiful than she had remembered, or dared now acknowledge.

'How was your trip?' he enquired politely, in a voice rich and deep with the vibration of a purr.

'Long.'

'Long?' Galen checked. He had thought, given the circumstances, that Costa would have arranged a comfortable passage. 'Didn't you take the chopper to Thira?'

'The helicopter is for guests, Galen.'

'Of course.' He took a breath. Now that he thought about it, Costa would not be wanting to raise any flags with the locals. 'Look, if you want to go to the apartment first, freshen up, have a break...'

Change out of that skirt!

'No.' She shook her head. 'We agreed I'd start at two. I came ready to hit the ground running.'

Or to go hiking! Very deliberately, he did not look at her shoes.

'How was it?' Galen asked her. 'Your leaving?'

'It was...' Roula even opened her mouth to tell him about her hellish two weeks, yet quickly pulled back. 'Fine.'

However, it seemed Galen really wanted to hear how she was. 'Roula, you're not working for me yet.'

'No, and before we commence work I thought I could give you this.' She pointed to the little cool bag she'd been carrying. 'It's just some cheese from home, *chlorotiri*, and some *melitza-nosalata* that I made last night—for your grandmother...'

'You didn't have to do that.'

'I would *always* do that.' Roula smiled. 'You can take the girl out of Anapliró, but you can never...' Then she felt a little embarrassed by his discomfort over her small gift. 'If that is overstepping the mark...?'

'It's not that. We're trying to keep her calm...' Galen explained. 'Peaceful. Any talk of Anapliró only confuses her.'

'So you don't mention it?'

He looked at her then, their first real eye contact since meeting, and she saw there was a warning in his eyes. 'I do all I can to avoid upsetting her,' he clipped.

'Of course.'

'I should also warn you that she gets confused at times. It varies. She can be very lucid, but there are times she thinks I'm my father. At other times I am ten, or...' He ran a finger around his shirt collar. 'She can be a little personal.'

'It's fine.'

'I apologise in advance.'

They drove on in silence. Roula twisted a strand of hair that had escaped rather than bite her nails. They passed the very police station where she had given the statement that would condemn her brother.

'We're here,' Galen said.

There were no care homes on Anapliró, but even so, this was not how Roula had envisaged one. Really, it was more like stepping into a five-star hotel from a glossy magazine. There were glamorous elders chatting in a lounge to one side, as if taking high tea, and there was even someone playing the piano.

'Galen!' A very sprightly man held up his stick.

'Sir!' Galen nodded.

The staff were all immaculate, though they appeared a little surprised to see him.

'Galen! We weren't expecting you today.'

'This is Roula,' Galen introduced her. 'From Monday you will be liaising with her.'

'Of course. It's nice to meet you.'

'Likewise.' Roula smiled, and listened as they brought Galen up to date.

'Kupia Florakis is still refusing to dress and is really quite distressed. We are about to give her something a little stronger than her usual medication. Would you like me to take you through?'

'I know the way.'

He was coming across as abrupt—but then, Roula recalled, that was Galen. He dealt in facts and of course he didn't need an escort.

'How often do you manage to visit?' she asked, assuming from the staff's evident surprise that his appearances here were rare.

She had assumed wrong, Roula quickly realised.

'I try to take coffee with her most days during the week, though I don't generally come on a Friday. I prefer to work uninterrupted over the weekend.'

Roula was shocked when she saw Kupia Florakis dressed in her nightwear and standing rubbing the window, as if to clear it, as two staff tried to tempt her to a chair.

Gosh, she was so tiny. Or was it that Galen was so tall as he walked over to her?

'Hey...' he said, joining her at the window.

'It's gone!' Even her voice had shrunk.

'It hasn't gone,' Galen said.

'It's all disappeared into the sea…'

'No, no…' Galen gently refuted. 'I work over there.' He pointed. 'And you are here so that I can see you more.'

Her room was beautiful, and there were multiple photos on the shelves, but Roula's eyes were drawn to one of Galen in his military uniform. Her gaze darted away, back to where Galen was now guiding his *yaya*.

'Come and sit. I have someone for you to meet.'

She ran a hand over the arm his dark suit. 'Are you here for a funeral?'

'No funeral,' Galen said.

'Your tie should be black,' she said as he led her to a seat.

'Yaya, this is Roula,' he introduced her. 'You might see her a bit over the next few weeks.'

'Kupia Florakis,' Roula smiled. 'It is nice to…' She hesitated, for surely she should say that it was nice to see her again, rather than deny knowing her. 'It's good to see you.'

Galen watched as his *yaya* turned her currant eyes to Roula, and then he watched as she did what he must not. She reached up and took hold of the single strand of hair that she had been twirling.

'Kyrios?' Yaya said.

'Yes.' Roula nodded, but did not glance over to see Galen's reaction to the fact that she had been recognised, albeit by her previous name.

Yaya looked her slowly up and down and then turned to Galen. 'Roula shopped for me.'

'Did she?' Galen took a breath. 'I didn't know that.'

'Well, you were gone,' Kupia Florakis rebuked him. 'No help. Go back to your books Galen.' Now she looked back to Roula and tapped the side of her head. 'He's not right up here. The doctor said. Damaged.'

Roula saw the tension behind his smile as he ignored her cruel words, and, yes, she might be confused now, but Roula rather guessed Galen might have heard much the same growing up.

'Roula brought you this,' Galen said, and opened the glowing cool bag. 'Come on,' he said gently. 'Eat.'

But Kupia Florakis hadn't finished with her observations yet, and she looked over to Roula.

'What happened to you? You were so pretty once.'

Galen tried to distract her with the cheese.

'Why is she hiding?'

'Yaya…' Galen said as Roula stood, her face one burning blush.

'She's so ugly now.'

The nurse came in then. It was pill time for his *yaya*, it would seem.

To her shame, Roula felt somewhat relieved, for she felt more than a little exposed.

'She says things…' Galen said, and he sighed once they were back in the car, leaning back on the headrest, his eyes closed for a moment. 'You know, she spent the first decade of my life telling me to engage my filter before I spoke, and the last decade has been spent…' He opened his eyes and looked over at her then. 'I'm sorry if she was rude. I have to buy flowers for the staff all the time to apologise.'

'No flowers required.' She smiled back.

'She doesn't mean half of it…'

'I know that.' Roula nodded.

But it was the half that was true which burnt…

Kolonaki Square was beautiful.

'Leo's studio is over there,' Galen said. 'You're more than welcome to get a new work wardrobe…'

'I have plenty of clothes, Galen.'

Her response was a little acidic, but with every sentence spoken the division between them grew wider. He flew—she took the ferry. He dressed in designer clothes and turned heads—she…

Oh, it was more than that, though, and the division actually helped. Even walking through the square, she was aware of him in such an unfamiliar way.

'Unless you *prefer* your staff to be dressed by Leo Arati?'

'Kristina asked for it to be in her contract. I was just...' He shrugged and nodded to a doorman, who opened one of the old wooden doors.

And there the square evaporated.

The ancient building was still there, but its imperfections had somehow been enhanced. Stone walls were exposed, and old windows too, yet there were glass cloisters and elevators, and it was so vast it felt as if she was looking up to a spaceship.

'It's stunning,' Roula croaked.

It was so much more than that.

'It's a bit confusing at first,' Galen warned as they walked past a security guard. 'Costa's got the second floor, though he's still on honeymoon. And my development team's main workspace is through there...'

She looked at the handful of people behind glass, all working away and completely oblivious to them.

'There are also private offices on my floor. I'm sure Kristina will explain.'

He showed her the codes to the glass elevators and that felt overwhelming, but then she recalled her terror on her first day of work at the retreat.

She could do this.

'Roula, this is Kristina.'

'Welcome!'

Kristina was indeed dressed by Leo Arati!

For her last day in the office she wore a little black dress, and her make-up was so 'after-five' she would have parted a velvet rope anywhere. Even her baby bump, though large for her petite frame, seemed to want to oblige, and was so neat and round that it fully deserved its own little bow—not that she would ever wear one.

I want to be her, Roula thought. Well, not specifically Kristina, but she wanted to wear red lipstick as if she simply always did, and to own every part of herself as she crossed a room.

For a moment Kristina discussed a dinner booking with

Galen, and then she addressed Roula. 'This will be your office—well, after today...' Kristina smiled a very brittle smile.

'Oh,' Roula said, as she looked at the bare surroundings. There was so much glass she felt as if she stood inside an ice cube. 'You didn't have to clear out your personal effects and things...'

'I didn't,' Kristina said tartly. 'I like a tidy space. I'll give you a tour and a rundown, then take you to the apartment.' She glanced to Galen. 'We'll be fine.'

'Well, very best wishes,' Galen said. 'I hope all goes well.'

'Thank you.' Roula smiled.

'I think he was talking to me,' Kristina said rather pointedly. 'Thanks, Galen. I guess I'll see you in six weeks.'

That was it? Roula tried not to gape at this very matter-of-fact farewell. Gosh, at the retreat if a member of staff was leaving to have a baby—well, it was a wonder that any work got done on that day!

And this was his personal assistant!

Kristina made no attempt at conversation as she packed up her bag.

'So are you all out celebrating tonight...?' Roula attempted brightly, wondering if that was the dinner booking that she had mentioned.

'Sorry?' Kristina glanced up.

'The dinner?'

'Roula, may I be blunt?'

'Go ahead.'

'You worked for Costa, yes?'

'Correct—well, Yolanda was my direct boss...'

'I know he has several hotels, but it's a family business—yes?' Roula nodded.

'Well, this *isn't* a family business,' Kristina warned her. 'If I want a cake and a party, then I'll ask my husband or my friends.'

Roula considered herself told!

The whole place—including the people—were just so cold. It was beautiful, but so clinical Roula was sure a forensics team would struggle to find a fingerprint, let alone signs of life.

'This is the guest lounge,' Kristina said. 'But there is another downstairs. I prefer visitors to wait down there.'

All the staff were so engrossed they barely looked up as she was shown around. There was an open-plan staff lounge, but no one was gathered there. Perhaps because their boss's office was opposite, and most of the doors were glass.

Not that Galen looked up.

He was a man of many screens! Roula counted six as they passed.

'Nico…' Kristina introduced her to a young man. 'This is Roula.'

He barely looked up, just mumbled, 'Hi…'

'Now I'll take you to Dora, the laziest woman on God's earth. She'll be playing games online, but the second she sees us…'

Sure enough, Dora reminded Roula of her nieces when they were pretending to do their homework. Except Dora was in her fifties and her curls were grey. She jolted to attention and pretended to be busy as she quickly closed down her screen in the same way the twins did.

'Dora,' Kristina said, in a very bored voice. 'This is Roula, my temporary replacement. I've told her that if she has any problems she is to come to you.'

'Of course.' Dora smiled. 'It's lovely to meet you, Roula.'

'Thank you,' Roula said as she received her first real smile since her arrival. 'Likewise.'

'Dora?' Kristina soon broke the pleasant exchange. 'Can you please get off whatever game you're wasting time on and sort out Nico's leave, and then chase HR for Roula's contract…?'

'I was actually just doing that.'

Kristina gave a scoffing laugh, but stopped as her phone bleeped. 'Galen wants me.'

'He *texts* you?' Roula checked—because they were literally a few steps away from his office, should he deign to look up.

'Of course,' Kristina said.

Roula's jaw gaped as Kristina, as if she was training a puppy, told her to 'Stay!'

No, she did not want to be Kristina any more.

'She's like that with everyone.'

Roula turned as Dora unwrapped a chocolate ball.

'Don't take it personally...'

Who were these people who texted and offended, but took no offence...?

Oh, she wanted to be back in Anapliró, where at least at work she knew who she was and was the best at her job...

In fairness, most of the time Galen had no idea where Kristina was in the building, and texting her was an efficient method of communication.

The trouble today was that he knew exactly where Kristina was—or rather Roula.

'Galen?' Kristian checked.

'Perhaps take Roula over to the apartment now?'

'I'm just showing her around while I wait for HR to send over her contract.'

'Maybe take her now.'

'Sure.' Kristina turned to go, but then turned back. 'Galen, I just want to say... Well, both Ruben and I want to...'

'Can we please drop it?' Galen said, for he had made it clear more than a year ago, when he'd paid for his loyal PA and her husband to be treated by Athens's top IVF specialist, that he would prefer the fact not to be raised. 'I'm thrilled you finally got there. Well, aside from the fact that I am now destined to six weeks of zig-zags.'

Kristina laughed. 'Do you want me to tell Roula about your issue with patterns?'

'Are we even allowed to do that now?' He rolled his eyes. 'Or will we offend the pattern police?'

'We need you to be working, Galen. I'll have a word.'

'Good. Now get the hell out of here and go and have your baby.'

Roula watched as Kristina gave Galen a half-wave and then marched her efficient way over.

'We should get over to the apartment.'

'Kristina…' Roula was starting to have serious doubts, both about her suitability and her qualifications, and decided it might be better to just state it now. 'I don't think I'm cut out—'

'Let's discuss this at the apartment.'

The apartment was in a very narrow lane, so the driver dropped them a short walk away and they made their way down.

'It's a nice location,' Kristina said as she clipped along.

Nice?

It was on the edge of everything.

The beautiful church of Aghios Dionysios was close. There were cafés, restaurants, boutiques…a whole new world at her door…

'This is yours.'

They climbed a steep staircase with detailed iron rails—a gorgeous slice of old Athens.

'Ground floor,' Kristina said as she let them in and they walked down a long, high-ceilinged corridor. 'This one's yours. Just the one bedroom…' Kristina snapped on the lights and opened all the doors, speaking like a realtor. 'It's serviced weekly…'

It was beautiful. The apartment alone almost tempted her to stay and fake it until she made it—or whatever the saying was.

Roula looked out of the bedroom window.

'No views,' Kristina said.

Oh, but there were. There were people and cafés and life pulsing outside. Except…

'I'm really not sure I'm qualified.'

'You're overwhelmed?'

'Yes,' she admitted. 'I told Galen I was computer literate, and until now I honestly thought I was, but…'

'Roula, when I was interviewed for this role I insisted that I wanted the title of Executive Assistant. But, as Galen pointed out, it would be a lie. I have degrees in both business and computer science, and yet I still don't really understand what the hell he does.'

'Oh…'

'He's a genius,' Kristina said. 'And I don't say that lightly. There are a few of them working there.'

Roula nodded, and there was a quiet sadness as the truth was acknowledged. Galen had been called so many things growing up. Different…odd…damaged… And today she had found out that his *yaya* had clearly thought he was too.

'I run the edges of Galen's life so that he can do more of what he's good at. That role will be yours, while I…' Kristina gestured to her stomach. 'So, shall we go through everything and then you can decide if you're up to it or not?'

Roula found that she rather admired Kristina's directness and, despite appearances to the contrary, there truly was kindness in her, for she had waited until they were well away from the office to address this.

'Yes,' Roula said, ready to hear more about the role.

'Okay…' They both took a seat and Roula got out a new notebook and pen. 'Galen has to do corporate stuff for the gaming Tuesday to Thursday—he hates it. That's when you'll appear to be busy.'

'Appear…?'

'Lots of phone calls, sitting in meetings—just all the usual. There's a big ball coming up…' She waved that fact away. 'But I should be back on board by then. And there's a new release. The directors are pushing Galen for progress reports, so they can announce it. What you need to understand is that everything corporate and/or family falls in that Tuesday to Thursday timeline. Today is an anomaly. Usually on Friday he has a development team meeting at seven a.m.…'

'Do I need to be there for that?'

'I'm always there at six. The café delivers breakfast, but you don't need to stay for the meeting, thank goodness—they eat like horses at the trough.' Kristina pulled a face. 'Usually they all go off, and then Galen locks himself in his office and does all his programming and coding.' She held up her hands. 'Don't disturb him for *any* reason.'

'Got it.'

'I mean it. You don't have to be in the office, but Galen's

phone lines will be diverted to you, so that *nothing* interrupts him—well, apart from one.' She fixed Roula with a look. 'Unless his *yaya* is actually dead, or very soon to be, just deal with it. The care home will call all the time.' Kristina rolled her eyes and moved swiftly along. 'On Mondays Galen is awful—just bring in coffee, put it down, leave. At some point he'll rise from the ashes... What else...?' Kristina thought out loud. 'Sex and food.'

Roula let her pen hover over the paper.

'He gets food and coffee delivered all the time—I mean *all the time*. Just take it from the driver, put it on his desk. He won't look up.'

'Okay...' Roula looked at her list. *Grow up, Roula. You deal with stuff like this at the retreat.* She'd had to find a vibrator for a client once! 'What about...?'

'Sex? Oh, don't worry, he factors that in himself. Thankfully I don't have to run that.'

'So I just order flowers and book restaurants and such?'

'God, no.' Kristina shook her head. 'His lovers are as practical about it as he is. That's the one phone line he keeps open, but if you get a text from one of them by mistake, just text back "PA".'

'How will I know it's one of them?'

'They'll say "Bored?" or "Catch-up?" That sort of thing. Don't worry, there's nothing lewd.' Kristina shrugged. 'Honestly, it's not an issue. Also, if he disappears for a couple of days, that's probably why.'

Gosh.

'Or if there's an afternoon when you can't find him.'

'I see.'

'Or...'

'I get it, thank you.'

There was also his doorman, whom she could call if any dire events occurred while Galen was missing!

Roula's usually neat lists were pages of scribble by the time Kristina was through.

'Look, if you have any doubts,' Kristina said as she stood, 'particularly when he's in lockdown programming, run them by me—don't disturb him.'

'You're sure? But you're…' Roula honestly wasn't sure if she was allowed to mention that Kristina was clearly very close to being due!

'Absolutely.'

'Thanks for being so thorough.'

'Well, it's best to know what you're getting into. Your time will no longer be yours, but if you don't want the position say so now—believe me, there are many who do. I have three people I usually fall back on…'

Roula knew she was being warned that this really was a coveted job.

'I just had a wobble back at the office,' Roula admitted.

'I get it,' Kristina said. 'But you wobble in here—not there.'

'Noted.'

'I'll leave you to settle in,' she said, but as she clipped towards the door she turned around. 'Bring his coffee from the café on Monday, remember?'

'Got it,' Roula said, and read back his complicated order. She frowned when Kristina pressed her thumb and fingers to her forehead. 'Are you…?' Gosh, was she even allowed to ask? 'Is everything…?'

'I have a headache. I've had it since last night…'

Kristina suddenly didn't look quite so photoshoot-ready—she looked as if she might faint.

'Kristina, sit down,' Roula told her.

'Don't say anything to Galen.'

'I shan't.'

Roula didn't quite know what to do with this very private, very bristly woman, but she quickly worked out the complicated curtains and they sat in semi darkness.

Kristina took off her heels and lay on the couch. 'Excuse me,' she said, and then admitted, 'I'm embarrassed. I don't tend to lie down at work. Ruben would freak if I told him that I'm having headaches. My husband,' she added.

'Would you like me to leave you?'

'It's fine…' Kristina said. 'I'll go in a moment…the driver's waiting…' She grimaced as her phone buzzed.

'Let me…' Roula offered, and took the phone. But she blinked as she read the message.

'The care home?' Kristina checked, without opening her eyes.

'No, it's Galen, asking if you've told me about my "awful zig-zag skirt".'

Kristina gave a soft laugh. 'He hates patterns. They cause some kind of overload to his brain. Don't be offended.'

'I'm not.' In fact, it cleared things up a little as she thought back to the bed linen and her opinion that he was picky and precious. That he'd changed.

Maybe he hadn't completely changed, Roula realised. Perhaps she just knew him a little more.

And Roula also knew what her guest services manager self would do…

'Kristina, why don't I tell the driver we'll be a while and that you'll call him when you're ready to be picked up?'

'You don't mind?'

'Of course not.'

Kristina dozed for a full hour, and Roula sat, a little awkward in her new home, looking at the late afternoon sky and the pile of suitcases waiting to be unpacked.

Most of them were full of things she had retrieved from his *yaya*'s home—though it would seem that wasn't allowed in this cold, get-ahead world.

Roula's own phone chimed loudly and, expecting it to be her mother, she swallowed when she saw that it was Galen.

How's Kristina?

She looked over to Kristina, who had stirred and come awake at the sound of Roula's unfamiliar and loud phone.

'It's Galen,' Roula said. 'Asking how we're getting on.'

'Shh…' Kristina put a finger to her lips.

Roula texted back.

Wonderful.

'Thanks for that.' Kristina sat up and drank the water Roula had placed next to her. 'I feel a lot better. I'll call the driver and head back.' She nodded when she saw Roula's worried face. 'I'll call my doctor.'

'Good.'

It was odd but they seemed to be…well, not friends, exactly, but a lot friendlier as Kristina left.

And it was odder still to stand alone in the apartment that was now her temporary home. It was gorgeous, with a beautiful bathroom and a gleaming kitchen, but it was the bedroom she paused in. The bed was high, and dressed in smart white cotton with a shot of silk through it, and the pillows were plump.

It had been a very long time since Roula had slept in a bed. And a whole lot longer than that since she'd enjoyed sleeping in one!

She opened a window and took in the sounds of the city on a Friday evening. Traffic and people—all there on her doorstep. Roula was a little too nervous to venture out, but then her phone buzzed again, and she saw it was Galen.

'Galen?'

'Sorry about this… I have dinner with a client tonight. It's unexpected, but…'

'It's fine.' Roula smiled at his attempt to be polite. 'I didn't expect you to entertain me on my first night.'

'This isn't a social call. Kristina isn't available, so you'll have to come with me.'

She winced at her own presumption. 'What time?'

'Now,' Galen said. 'Well, by the time you get up the lane the car will be there. Also,' Galen added, 'we need to speak.'

CHAPTER SEVEN

'I DID WARN YOU the job was full-on,' Galen said as she climbed into the car.

'You did.'

'And I'm aware that you haven't signed your contract yet.' He held up a folder. 'We can go through that after dinner—hopefully it won't drag on. The guest is Hector,' he explained. 'Chairman of the board. I didn't think he'd actually fly in.'

He pressed the intercom and spoke to his driver, and Roula went a little pale as the driver confirmed that they were on schedule.

'Galen?' She was taken aback when she heard the name of the restaurant they were headed to. It was such an exclusive restaurant that even for the retreat guests reservations were not always able to be secured! 'You should have said where we were going?'

'Why? It's just dinner.'

For him, perhaps.

No wonder Kristina was photoshoot-ready, Roula thought as they drove up the hill. Then again, the only halfway decent dress she had was black—the one she used for funerals. Another hand-me-down from her mother.

Roula sighed, but then snapped to attention as Galen spoke on.

'Hector wants to find out if there's any progress on Game Four.'

'The Anapliró game?'

'It's not Anapliró,' Galen corrected. 'Just loosely based on it. Anyway, he's really pushy.' He told her what Kristina already had. 'They want to announce the release date at the ball.'

'Is it nowhere near ready?'

'I'm not discussing that until your contract's signed.'

That stung a little too much, but Roula took a breath and reminded herself of the warning Galen himself had delivered—he was very different at work. They were not friends going out or catching up.

Roula was so underdressed for such fine dining that she actually did turn heads. A nudge when they saw Galen…a gape for Roula. Her face was actually burning as they were ushered to a table—or rather, one of *the* tables...

As the waiter held out her chair Roula attempted a little joke to Galen as she took her seat. 'Best tuck my skirt away!'

'Sorry?' Galen frowned.

'I saw your message to Kristina about it.'

'Oh!' He grimaced. 'I asked Kristina to broach my issue with patterns.'

'You could have just said.'

'Well, I find those sorts of topics difficult,' Galen admitted. 'I'm not allowed to notice Kristina's girth or she gets annoyed.'

Roula gave a little laugh.

'Don't order a starter,' he warned. 'I don't want this to drag on.'

'Okay.' She looked over. 'What about dessert?'

'Hopefully he won't last that long,'

The glug of wine being poured welcomed Roula on this, her first night in Athens. Yet they sat pretty much in silence as she turned and drank in the view, for it was as if they were seated on the edge of heaven, encased by hills with the sea beyond, the centrepiece the beautiful citadel and its gorgeous ancient buildings.

'Gosh!' Roula sighed. 'It beats the school trip.'

Galen didn't respond. He was checking his phone. 'Someone is ill on Hector's plane and they can't disembark,' he said.

'You seem pleased?'

'I am—it's usually me cancelling him.' He looked over to the approaching waiter. 'Could you give us a moment, please?'

'Are we leaving?' Roula checked, assuming the night was over.

'No, no,' Galen said. 'I told you that we need to speak... Did Kristina explain everything?'

'Yes.' Roula nodded. 'She was very thorough.'

'Any concerns?' he asked. 'Because now is the time to air them.'

'I don't think so.' Roula shook her head. While there was no way she would be able to work for him permanently, she was only here for six weeks. She could survive in the fridge where he worked for that long. 'As I said, she was very thorough. Though it's Friday—shouldn't you be locked in your office now?'

'I'll be headed there soon.' He nodded. 'It's been one of those days. One PA leaving…another one arriving.'

'Yes.'

'I actually have some concerns myself, Roula,' Galen said, and though his voice was calm and even there was no mistaking a certain edge to his tone. 'Kristina is, as we speak, in hospital, strapped to monitors.'

Roula's eyes flashed up as she realised she'd been caught lying on her first day. 'Is she okay?'

'Well, she's certainly not "wonderful", as you made out. I specifically asked you how she was.'

'Galen, I thought you were just messaging to see how it was all going,' Roula admitted. 'If we were getting along…'

'Why would I care if two professionals who will never see each other again are getting along?' he asked, clearly irritated. 'Do you think I suddenly looked up and thought, *Oh, I hope they are having a nice time*…' He shook his head in frustrated annoyance. 'I messaged you to ask how Kristina was. You should have told me.'

'You really want me to tell you when a staff member has a headache?' Roula checked. 'I didn't think it was that kind of place.'

'Excuse me?'

Roula was assertive at work. 'It's clear your staff leave their private lives at the door,' she said.

'Don't we all?' he said. 'Or do you smile like that at home?'

'Like what?'

He flashed her an odd bright smile and then halted. 'Look, I get why you didn't tell me,' he conceded. 'She's nearly due, though.'

'Yes.'

'My driver returned concerned, so I texted you to see how she was.'

'I see that now.'

Subject closed.

'Shall we get menus?'

'Sure.'

Not quite closed.

'Roula, I overreacted. But it was clearly panic stations for Kristina.'

'Can you find out how she is?'

'Ruben said he will call.'

'Will you let me know?'

He nodded. 'Nico would *not* make a good doula.'

Roula found that she was smiling, and not her corporate one. There were unfamiliar muscles stretching her lips as they parted over her teeth, and she could actually feel the edge of the top row on her mouth.

As they looked through the menus his gaze fell on the plaster on her middle finger. She'd worn one last week, but it had been on her thumb, and that was still there too. Galen noticed such things.

He guessed she was biting her nails.

'The calamari is amazing here...' Galen suggested.

'I hate fish.'

'Not brilliant if your husband's a fisherman...' Galen stopped. He really was awful at jokes and that had been a dreadful attempt.

'Risotto,' she said, and then added, 'Please.'

They were awkward. Impossibly so.

She had gone through her contract for the retreat with Costa, in the retreat's restaurant. And Leo always treated her to a lovely lunch whenever they caught up. What was this? Roula asked herself.

But she knew...

She'd never dined with a man she was attracted to.

Had never known this feeling at all.

'How are you, Roula?' he asked when their meals had been served. 'Really?'

She looked up. 'I thought we weren't going to engage in idle conversation.'

'You haven't signed the contract,' Galen pointed out. 'Maybe, just for tonight, we can catch up? How were your family about you leaving?'

'A little upset,' Roula admitted. 'They don't believe it's just for six weeks.'

'Is it?'

Gosh, a real conversation—it had been a long time since she'd had one of those. 'I don't know,' Roula admitted. 'For now, I'm on leave from the retreat. Yolanda was a little cross at first. She said I'd given no indication…' She shrugged. 'You know what it can be like when staff leave.'

'Not really.' He tore some bread. 'I can't get rid of mine.' He gave her a half-smile, a little sad that she clearly felt unable to tell him about her brother. 'We might seem cold at first, but you should give us a chance.'

'Yes,' Roula agreed, for this job really was a serious opportunity. 'I should.' But first… 'How are *you*, Galen?'

'I'm trying to make you feel welcome, Roula.'

'So tell me how you've been.'

'I've been well.'

'How was the military?'

'That was years ago.' He cast his mind back. 'It was good. I liked the training, and I got to fix computers instead of mopping and cleaning. After that I settled in Athens. I went back to Anapliró a couple of times to visit my *yaya*.'

'I heard.' She looked at him then, and Galen found that he was frowning at her expression, for she looked a little cross.

'She often spoke about you.'

He didn't want to visit the past. 'Right, shall we do this?' He opened the file he had brought along and pushed it across the table. He took out his pen and Roula looked at the contract.

It was just a contract.

Generous, but not some major cash dump for an old friend from Anapliró, and her accommodation was a separate contract for an eight-week term.

'A couple of weeks' leeway,' Galen explained. 'So you're not looking for both a new job and a place to live.'

'That's very thoughtful.'

'I can be.'

He smiled, and Roula did not know what to do, for she had never known a smile to have such effect.

She was acutely aware that she was probably the worst-dressed woman in the restaurant, yet when he smiled at her she felt almost a little beautiful…and a little bit teary too.

She did not know what this was.

Did not know how, when he pointed out a line on the contract, his finger seemed still to be before her eyes long after it had left the page.

Perhaps Galen was her version of seeing pattern, because this was sensory overload, and Roula did not know what to do with it all.

She even liked his gentle chiding as he tutted when she told him, 'I don't want a bonus in crypto currency.'

'Philistine!' he teased, and then added, 'Roula, it's a minor detail.'

'Well, I'd rather have cash.'

'We call it fiat currency—however, the "cash" equivalent wouldn't pay for a glass of wine at the moment,' Galen said. 'It's more a morale thing to do with the potential of the project…'

She picked up the pen and it felt cold and heavy in her hands. 'I'm having a wobble,' she admitted. 'According to Kristina, I should only have them at home.'

'Then take it home to read,' Galen said, and she watched as his hand returned. She felt the warm brush of his fingers as he took the weight of the pen, yet she felt no lighter. Instead she felt heavy with indecision, for it was no longer the job that felt challenging, but the six weeks in close proximity to Galen she was struggling with. Or rather, her new companion: awareness.

Such awareness.

And not just for the man who sat before her, but of her own body in the chair. She prickled all over, as if tiny shards of glass were working their way to the surface of her skin, not so much pain, more a rising presence.

And so, instead of signing, she nodded in relief at the waiter's suggestion they move to the balcony to enjoy their coffee.

Only there was no relief there, for they were guided to a plump couch to savour the sunset.

'Still better than the school trip?' Galen said, as pinks blazed in the sky and the temples were lit on the sacred stone, and in the distance the Aegean turned shifting purple.

'So much better.' Roula sighed. 'This is surely the best view on earth.'

'Truth?' he said. 'I prefer the view from my home. A different angle, but...'

'You're so arrogant!' She half laughed.

'Am I?'

'I don't know...' Roula admitted.

She didn't know!

She was remembering him—remembering Galen who said things as they were, and offended at times, but was always kind.

He was the most honest person she'd ever known. At times so direct it was confrontational. And yet there was a rare sense of security to be found in that too. Truth.

'There was snow here this winter...' Galen said as she gazed out.

'I heard.' Roula nodded, though she did not turn her head—for who would turn away as the setting sun seemed to set the Parthenon on fire?

She wanted to turn her head, though. So much so her neck felt taut.

'I woke up,' Galen told her, 'and I had never heard Athens so silent.'

'Truly?'

'I walked around in it for hours.'

She could feel his breath, and his thigh was against hers, and still Roula stared ahead. Because her neck ached to turn, but her mind told her she would ruin things. That he would laugh in her face if she moved in to kiss him, for she was surely misreading things?

It wasn't even the fact that he was soon to be her boss that was the issue right now.

For even if he did not laugh in her face...even if he moved to kiss her back...she wouldn't know what to do.

This new want, this genesis of desire, was too much and too soon. She wanted to want from a distance, not seated by his side.

'I should get back,' Roula said as the sky slipped into night. 'I had a very early start today.'

'Of course.'

He got a call on the way out, and it was good news.

'Kristina is fine,' he told her. 'She has to have her blood pressure checked again, but the babymoon is on.'

'I'm so pleased. You should call Nico.'

'I'll tell him when I get back to the office.'

The drive home was a silent one except for the drum of his fingers on the walnut trim as Galen pondered how it must feel for Roula to be in a new city, in a new workplace, and to know that any day now her life would become headline news.

And, while he chose not to get involved in the dramas of other people's lives, he felt a reluctant yet definite responsibility.

She really was on her own.

'Roula...' As they neared the apartment he turned and saw the lights of the city flash on her pale cheeks. 'We used to talk, yes?'

'Yes.'

'On Monday things change,' Galen said. 'As I said when I offered you the role, things are different at work, but that doesn't mean...' *Merda*, he was bad at this. The car pulled in at the top of the lane. 'I'll walk you down.'

'There's no need.'

'We're not on Anapliró now.'

Tell me, Roula, Galen thought as they walked down the lane in tense silence.

'Thank you for dinner,' Roula said as they came to the steps. 'And for meeting me this morning.'

She was getting out the keys, about to go in and face this alone.

'Yolanda's right,' Galen said. 'You give no indication as to what's going on with you.'

Roula swallowed. 'Perhaps its wiser not to.'

'Tell me, Roula.'

'I think it's better I don't.'

'Surely you know you can tell me anything?'

'Anything?' Roula checked.

Once she had trusted him in a way that was hard to define. Once she'd been able to share what was on her mind with him, and Galen was inviting her to do so again now.

He had been her first real friend.

Her first dance—well, the first that she'd enjoyed…

And now, for the first time in her life, she wanted a kiss. It felt like a butterfly flitting past, and it was so fleeting, so rare, so impossible, that she was scared the feeling might never come again.

Roula had taken notes on his sex life this afternoon—she knew how little one kiss would mean to him.

Yet it would mean the world to her. To know…

'I want to be kissed goodnight,' Roula admitted. '*That* is what is on my mind.'

He looked at her. Hell, he had meant her just to tell him about all the drama going on with your brother.

'You want me to kiss you?' he checked.

'Yes, but if you kiss me here, can we end it there? I mean, I won't ask you in.'

A kiss?

Two weeks ago he would have laughed at the thought of just a kiss—at least on the inside—but he guessed it would be her first since her husband.

'Sure.' He was practical. 'But then we're done.'

'Completely.'

Roula felt his hands on her arms and breathed in, in nervous preparation for his mouth. Except it was the softest brush of lips, and she felt as if there must be snow in May, for Athens had become silent.

There was nothing she could liken it to, for it was soft and slow, and yet it made that deep breath pointless, for she was hungry for air when his kiss did not end with that brush of lips.

The pressure of his mouth was a relief, and as his hands moved from her arms to her head she felt his fingers in her thick hair. Then it was Roula who parted her lips, and the slip of his tongue was the most beautiful thing she had ever known.

It was like dancing, and it was like laughing, and it stroked her and gently coaxed her, until her hands were in his hair.

This was how it felt to be kissed, to kiss, to want the touch of another.

His fingers stroked her back and moved to her bra strap—or rather straps, because she felt them linger to check. And then his hand moved down, his arm circling her waist, and for a second she opened her eyes.

His eyes were closed, so Roula returned to the darkness, and the deep, deep kiss, and the citrussy clean scent of him, and the slow thrill of his tongue and the mouth that made her want more.

And then he ended it.

Their mouths shiny and wet, her skin a little raw, they stood, bodies apart, heads together, both breathless.

'Go in,' Galen told her, and his voice was a touch uneven.

She knew that in his world they should be up against a wall now, with her legs wrapped around him. Yet for Roula everything felt right with the world.

She stood and savoured her first kiss—well, the first kiss she had enjoyed—simply lingering in the ripe deliciousness of it.

'Thank you,' she said.

'My pleasure.' Galen nodded. 'We might do it again on your leaving day, but not a moment before.'

Roula laughed as he walked off.

Then he abruptly turned and walked right up to her, but it did not feel confrontational...it felt necessary. 'Roula.'

'Yes?'

'Wear zig-zags.'

She frowned.

'Spots, stripes...'

They were staring at each other, and it was both tense and a relief to be lost in his eyes and to see that their kiss had affected him.

'Whatever you've got in that luggage...'

'Will do.'

She took for ever though to sort out the unfamiliar keys and get inside the door, and from there she gave him a wave. 'See you on Monday.'

'Yes,' Galen said.

In stripes, spots *and* zig-zags, preferably!

CHAPTER EIGHT

ROULA'S PHONE BLEEPED. And then it gave another bleep, and it took her a moment to work out quite where she was.

In bed.

The cover was heavy, the pillow soft, and she lay on her stomach and flicked off the alarm, then lay there.

She *had* contemplated male beauty before.

Once.

That photo of Galen in uniform she had seen long ago. In fact it had been years old by the time she'd even seen it.

'Is this Galen?' she had asked, and smiled, looking at the picture as she dropped off Kupia Florakis's shopping. Studious, happy, hopeful for her exams and not really interested in boys, she'd been feeling a shy curiosity over her body she had deliberately ignored.

Or she had tried to.

Yet that photo had somehow embedded itself and hooked in her mind...

One morning, weeks, perhaps months after she'd dropped off that shopping, Roula had awoken to a loud knock on her bedroom door, hauling her back from a place she did not know. A place in her dreams of torrid, rough kisses and heated skin and no trace of her usual shyness as Galen boldly explored her.

'Roula!'

Her mother had told her she'd be late for school even as she'd lain there, breathless, aware of a heavy heat between her legs and wishing the morning had not invaded just yet, for she wanted to get back to that place she'd glimpsed.

'I'm up...' Roula had croaked, and although perhaps guilt should have propelled her from the bed she'd lain there a while longer, trying to get back to the place she'd been, with a Galen she did not know, who in his curiosity over her body had not been shy.

Nor had she been. For when she'd dreamed it had been her kissing him, prising open his mouth as his hands roughly squeezed her breasts. And that morning Roula had tentatively done the same. Trying to blot out the sounds of a waking house and slip back to that place she'd almost found. Her curiosity had become less shy as she'd explored her body, thinking of his closed eyes and that mouth that rarely smiled tussling with hers.

'Galen...'

She had said his name as if summoning him, trying to get back to that place they had been, her hand creeping down, and she had felt for a moment that if she dared turn the key she might enter beyond...

'Roula!'

Her mother's second knock had hauled her back to reality. Soon to be a new reality. For it had been that very afternoon she'd returned from school and been informed that her husband had been chosen.

For a fleeting second her heart had soared.

Galen was coming home!

'Your husband will be Dimitrios Drakos.'

Roula had forgotten what she'd glimpsed that morning. Her experience of sex had been so far removed from that distant half-dream that she'd flicked the memory off, like an unwelcome show on the television.

And now here she was, frigid in a warm bed in Athens.

All desire leeched from her.

Yet she'd had that kiss...

And she started working for Galen today.

There was no guilt, no regret, and certainly she was not worried to face him, for she knew their kiss was no doubt nothing but a distant memory to Galen. A brief pleasure to him, like a glass of wine he had drunk—tasted and then forgotten.

She chose a brown dress with yellow squiggles and a matching fabric belt, as well as her brown shoes, but could not be bothered to pin up her hair, so just tied it back.

Then she checked her bag.

Four new pens: two blue, one black, one red.

A pencil.

Another new notebook.

And now she held the phone with so many contacts, and he must have diverted his calls because it lit up as she neared the square.

'*Kalimera...*' Roula said, as she ordered his coffee from the café and took her first call.

'I'm on my way,' said a voice.

'Who is this?' she asked.

'Joe.'

'Thank you, Joe. I'm Roula—'

He'd already rung off.

The doorman wasn't particularly friendly either, as her name hadn't been added to his list. 'I was with Kristina before she was unwell on Friday,' Roula attempted to explain. 'I'll be working for Galen.'

Reluctantly the doorman relented and waved her in.

Then her bag was checked.

Goodness!

By the time she reached Galen's office Roula had few expectations. Apart from the screens it was all in darkness, and she placed his coffee down quietly.

Reluctantly, Galen noticed.

He caught a feminine scent wading through the stale air of his office and despite himself looked up.

'*Kalimera,*' he said.

What a difference a weekend makes in Roula time, Galen thought. For her hair was loosely tied back and its colour displayed, but—and he thanked God for small mercies—her dress was appalling.

'*Kalimera,*' Roula said.

And to be polite—it was her first day after all—Galen did not look back to the screen. 'How are things?'

'Wonderful. I had lunch with Leo on Saturday, and I went

to mass— Oh!' She realised he was talking about work. 'Joe is on his way.'

'Good. I'm going to have a quick shower.'

Galen headed through one of many glass doors and she grabbed a trash bag and, just as she would have done in her old job if she'd found a suite in chaos, started a massive tidy-up.

She was collecting coffee cups, wrappers, when Galen's voice startled her. 'The cleaning team does that.'

'I'm sure,' Roula said. 'I was just…'

'Please don't.'

'It's habit.'

'Perhaps.' Galen nodded. 'But I like things left as they are.'

'Okay.'

His scent cut the air now. Citrussy. And he must have shaved in the shower, Roula thought, because he had been gone just a few scant minutes and returned, clean shaven, wearing fresh dark jeans and a thin grey jumper that was a little damp on the shoulder.

Perhaps from his wet hair, or maybe he really hadn't dried off.

Well, not to Roula's exacting standards.

Actually, she did not have exacting standards about men drying their shoulders except where Galen was concerned, and the blush that had stayed down on her first glimpse since that kiss emerged a little now.

'All okay?' Galen asked.

'Yes.' Roula nodded.

'We're not awkward?' he checked.

'No,' Roula said, and she gave him a smile. 'Not awkward at all. I've had ten kisses since then…'

Galen smiled at her little joke.

He wanted to add, *I haven't.*

Nada.

In fact, since Costa had informed him about a certain wedding on Anapliró there'd been nothing.

Save for one kiss…

And, despite the state of his office, he had not got an awful lot of work done, either. Well, certainly not enough for Galen's obsessive standards.

He'd been cross with himself when he'd come back to the office late on Friday.

Then he'd been distracted by the prospect of her arrival on Monday.

And now he was distracted because she was here.

For there was that sunshine scent and those wavy patterns before his eyes.

Only it was not the patterns playing hell with his mind.

It was a very different type of sensory overload Galen was dealing with this Monday morning.

'I need to get on.'

'Of course.'

Roula happily gave up on his appalling office and found, to her surprise, that there was a gorgeous coffee machine. Yet he preferred his from the café?

There was also a fridge, piled high with flavoured sparkling caffeinated beverages. Her addiction of choice! And a whole jar of chocolate balls on the table—the ones with the liquid centre and others with pieces of praline.

She had to walk past ground control to get there, but Galen was always lost in his screens.

He was trying to be.

He breathed out and watched as she wandered over to the glass table and took another handful of chocolate balls.

Everyone did.

It was just what they did.

Yet now he was considering moving the glass jar because he was looking at her bottom—and, God, that was *not* Galen at work.

The whole lot of his staff could be naked and feeding each other chocolate balls and he'd barely glance up from the screen. Yet he was looking now at a brown and yellow wavy bottom and watching how she reached right down to the bottom of the jar to get the last of the praline balls…

She was everywhere.

Her scent, her voice, those clumpy shoes…

On Thursday she returned from lunch with an armful of flowers, to brighten up the 'glass factory', as she called it, downstairs.

'Roula!' he called. 'Get those flowers out from the ground floor now!'

'It's like a mortuary down there,' she said. 'They brighten it up.'

'The staff will be in the mortuary soon. It'll be like an ER. They're all on puffers and nasal sprays…'

And then, before she left, she dropped a meal delivery on his desk.

'Galen?'

He ignored her.

She was more than used to that in guest services—except he was not a guest and nor was she the bearer of discreet nuts and a cocktail.

'Galen?' she prompted again. 'Your meal.'

'Oh, yes…' He stirred and reached for the silver-wrapped food.

'Thank you!' she said rather sarcastically on her way out. And then, as she closed the glass door perhaps a little noisily behind her, instead of freezing on the spot at her own audacity Roula actually wanted to dance.

She was herself—or rather, Roula was glimpsing herself… whoever she was.

Saturday morning found Roula surfing the net for jobs and updating her CV. Then, of course, the care home called.

Again!

'Kupia Florakis had a very unsettled night. More nightmares. We want to discuss increasing her night sedation.'

'Well, I can't give permission for that,' Roula said. 'I'll come in.'

The old lady was smiling when Roula arrived.

'Kupia…' Roula took a seat. 'How are you?'

'Cold.'

'I bought *lipsopita*,' Roula said holding up a bag, 'I need to stop, but honestly…' She could not resist the Athenian bakeries and cafés, and today was indulging in little buns with orange zest.

'That's good,' said Kupia and, teeth or no teeth, she certainly liked the bun!

'You had bad dreams last night?' asked Roula.

'No.'

She shook her head and asked Roula to hand her a photo, and as she took the frame down Roula felt a lump in her throat. It was a smiling baby Galen with his parents. Gosh, he was the image of his father. Well, a decade younger perhaps.

'Too old for her,' Kupia said. 'I said it would come to no good.'

'They look happy.'

His mother had been black-haired and black-eyed and in the photo she wore a simple white top and a gold cross. Her eyes were shining as she looked at her son.

'Galen's smiling,' she said.

'No.' Kupia denied it. 'He put soap in his eyes once, pretending to cry…he has no feelings.'

'Kupia Florakis…' Roula stopped herself. Oh, it must be so hard for Galen to hear this. 'Your daughter was very beautiful.'

'Yes.' And then she pointed to Galen and smiled. 'Cheeky boy. Talk, talk talk…'

'Did he?'

'*Why? Why? Why?* Every minute…'

They chatted a while, but after that it was mainly nonsensical, although Kupia was smiling when Roula left. And, no, there was no need to disturb Galen with the staff's sedation request.

Roula found herself outside a boutique so exclusive it had only one item in the window. It was a pale blue linen shift dress with a red flower on one hip, and this was the first time Roula's gaze had lingered so.

Her clothes, her hair, her absolute desire to be invisible had worked in Anapliró. It had been expected of her, even. But here

Roula did not blend in. She ventured inside, but before an assistant could even approach Roula turned and walked out.

Then there was a hair salon that caught her eye—though not like the one at home, where her mother went…where everyone went.

Of course she could not afford the one at the retreat. But here she wanted to be brave, and walk in, find how to tame her thick curls and…

Stop hiding.

Be seen.

She felt seen by Galen.

'I was wondering…' She looked at the hairdresser, a woman about the same age as she. 'My hair is so curly…'

'We'll cut it dry and then wash it.'

'Just cut it a little,' Roula warned.

She took loads off, and she sat there in silent horror as her hair fell to the floor. And then she lay head back and closed her eyes at the sink, wishing she'd never set foot in the place.

'Better?' The hairdresser smiled as Roula returned from having her hair washed.

No, it wasn't.

In fact the day got worse. Because her phone buzzed then— or rather *his* phone.

I need a break

Roula frowned as she read it, and then a follow-up message came in.

Do you?

It would seem that someone called Pandora would like to 'catch up' and was wondering if Galen would like to do the same.

God, she wanted to text Galen and tell him that he was supposed to be working! Actually, she wanted to message him about his *yaya*. But she swallowed it down and was a dutiful PA and messaged Pandora back.

PA

Roula even got a reply.

Whoops, sorry!

Pandora had even added a little crying/laughing face!
'That's better,' the hairdresser said.
And, expecting the worst, Roula looked up. To her surprise it *was* better. It was still almost as long, except it was no longer one vast triangle. There were ringlets and curls, and she felt glossy as she stepped back out on to the street, and kept looking in shop windows at her new hair.

Nobody noticed at work.

Well, she was busy taking calls.

Joe was cancelling, the care home was impatient…

There were so many she actually had to warm Galen's coffee up in the staff coffee lounge.

Galen gave her not so much as a glance as she placed his coffee down.

'*Kalimera,*' Roula said, and broke the silent Monday morning rule.

He didn't respond.

Because, yes, he had noticed—not her hair yet, but even her presence in the building was invading his peace, and now her scent was back, and he was so behind he *needed* to get on.

Yet he looked up, red-eyed and unshaven, and there she stood in a calf-length polka dot dress, with a matching belt and those Medusa curls…

'What?'

'Surly' would best describe his tone, she thought.

'The care home called, looking to increase Kupia Florakis's sedation.'

He glanced up. 'You didn't authorise a change to her treatment regime?'

'Of course not.' Roula frowned. 'I told them they'd need to discuss that with you—though she seemed fine when I saw her.'

'You went over?'

'Just to check for myself.' Roula nodded. 'We had coffee.' Really, it had been just a fifteen-minute visit. 'Oh, and Pandora messaged…' She said it as lightly as she could.

'Yes.'

'I let her know that the message had come to me by mistake…'

'Pandora told me.'

Galen turned back to his screen, when he would have liked to pull her around his desk and onto his knee. He wanted to kiss away that scowl he was certain was behind the plastic smile as he told her that he'd declined Pandora.

He reached for antacid rather than the coffee.

This really wasn't working.

'Oh,' she added on her way out, 'you've got Hector at ten.'

'No, no…' Galen said. 'Not on Monday…'

'I know—but he felt terrible that he'd been held up on the plane, and given that Joe has cancelled…'

'Joe is head of my development team,' Galen said through gritted teeth. 'Joe is working his ass off right now…' He held his breath.

'Oh, God!' Roula screwed her eyes closed as she realised her error. 'I got the gaming stuff mixed up; I'll cancel Hector now.'

'Just leave it as is.'

'Hector!' She greeted him warmly and took him up to the visitors' lounge. 'Please, take a seat, Galen shouldn't be too long.'

She was lying.

He'd be ages.

And the trouble with glass offices… Well, Hector kept looking over at her.

Channel Kristina, Roula decided, understanding now why Kristina preferred visitors to wait downstairs.

'Galen…' She stood at the door to his office. 'Hector's getting restless.'

'Roula,' said Galen. '*He* demanded this meeting. I told him I had not got the time…'

'But he's here now,' Roula said. 'You'll feel better when it's done and not hanging over you.'

'*You're* hanging over me, Roula,' Galen said.

And then he stood up and walked into a meeting he didn't want to go to, with his PA who sat there like an umpire at a tennis match.

He was too aware of her, Galen knew.

Too aware of that jack-in-the-box hair that might uncoil at any moment, and too aware of the way she laughed when Hector made a little joke.

'Yes, the third game is the charm, ho-ho-ho…'

'My nieces love those charms.' Roula nodded.

'What we're trying to gauge,' Hector said, 'is the progress on game number four?'

Galen was silent.

'I'm aware we agreed on next year, but we're nearly halfway through this one…'

Silence.

Roula took a drink of water. He could see her out of the corner of his eye.

'Ideally,' Hector pushed, 'we'd like to announce a launch date at the ball…'

More silence.

It was not because he was playing hardball. Just that Galen liked to work in a vacuum—a silent, blacked-out vacuum—and if Hector got so much as a sniff that he was close, that in fact it was for the most part done, the hell of it all would start up.

Galen had done this three times before and he was determinedly putting off number four. Except he could feel, not just Hector's but Roula's eyes upon him, demanding that he elaborate.

'I mean,' Hector persisted, 'just some idea as to where you are…'

Galen spread his hands.

And now it wasn't silence filling the room—it was the sound of

Roula's breathing. And he was too aware when she took another sip of water and pushed that crazy, amazing hair back from her face.

He could *feel* her frustration.

Certainly he was aware of his own—and it had nothing to with work.

'I said the game would be completed this year,' Galen finally responded. 'There are still several months left, I believe.'

'There are.'

'Then I'm still on time.'

It was all handshakes and smiles—well, between Roula and Hector—but she was breathing hard as she packed up.

'What?' Galen demanded.

'Nothing.' She looked up then. 'Just that the game's practically finished.'

'Oh, you know that, do you?'

'Nico said…'

'Your new friend?'

'Yes.'

'You have no idea of the circus that will start the moment I give a completion date.'

'Just get it over with,' Roula said.

'I don't need career advice, Roula, and I don't need you staring me down in a meeting.'

'I wasn't…'

'I was waiting for a kick under the table to prompt me,' Galen said—because that was exactly how it had felt. 'And, while we're discussing things, I don't need you to bring me coffee and pastries and then hover until I say thank you…'

'I just want to be sure you know it's there,' Roula said. 'So that you don't spill it.'

'No!' He would not have that. 'You stand there and…' *Make me notice you!*

They were having a row, Roula realised. Only it wasn't the type of row she was used to. Oh, she'd had rows at work at the retreat, and she'd dealt with them. And, of course, there had been rows with Dimitrios. But this in no way compared.

This was not personal, but it was not work.

It was the first exchange of words with a man that Roula had found exhilarating. Not scary, nor intimidating. It was not at a level she was trying desperately to ignore, and so she fumbled on.

'I apologise for messing up with Hector,' Roula said.

'This isn't about Hector…'

His hazel eyes were like two infernos, yet she still wanted to step into their fire.

'I'm going out,' Galen snapped. 'No calls.'

She stood breathless after he had gone, unsure of the energy that still swirled in the room, and then she tried to locate her phone, that was buzzing in her bag.

Or was it Galen's phone?

'Hello…?' she croaked.

'Roula.'

One word—that was all it took for the balls to clatter down. Roula briefly wondered if detectives went to voice training school, because she knew who it was even before she confirmed her full name…

And as for her own voice—well, she thanked the detective for letting her know in a voice that sounded oddly normal.

'Thank you,' she said again, and then somehow made her way on shaky legs and to take a call from her mother.

'The police are all over Nemo's…' Mamá was frantic, breathless. 'Roula, I don't know what's going on.'

Roula swallowed.

'There's a car outside!' she cried out, and Roula could picture her, peering out of the window. 'The police are coming to the door. What the hell is going on?'

'Mamá…' Roula attempted, but was saved from answering as presumably her mother opened the door and those deep detective voices were there in the background.

'Kupia Kyrios?'

The phone went silent.

CHAPTER NINE

'WHERE'S ROULA?' ASKED GALEN, frowning, when he returned from his walk.

Dora shrugged.

He guessed she was at lunch—though it didn't really matter. Well, it *shouldn't* really matter. His staff were not chained to their desks, and there were a million places she could be, but he wanted to discuss the morning's events.

Calmly.

He wanted to reset the tone.

Have sex?

Seriously, for the first time he was actually willing to sleep with someone he worked with just get it out of the way.

Hate me in the morning, Roula!

Oh, and she would—because he wasn't her husband—but then perhaps they could get on.

He took another swig of antacid.

No…

He met with Joe, and with Nico too, and then just sat there. At least without her there he could work in peace.

It was an empty peace, though.

So he called out for a delivery of *bougatsa*—a sweet custard in pastry. Not because he was hungry, more because…

Only it was a silent delivery—from Dora.

'Where's Roula?' Galen checked, when usually he didn't even look up.

'She took the day…' Dora said, and went to leave him to it.

'Took the day?' He frowned.

'Galen, don't worry about it.'

'What's going on?'

'She has some family issues,' Dora said. 'You just get on.'

Dora closed the door on her way out, and in that moment Galen loathed his carefully structured life, and his absence from the world. He'd so carefully crafted it, but as he scrolled through the news on his phone he felt as if he'd been smacked over the head with a cricket bat.

Roula's life had fallen apart, and no one had thought to tell him.

It was odd to sit in her office and take calls.

Costa: 'How is she?'

Leo: 'Oh, tell darling Roula to call me, please...'

Yolanda, in tears: 'I knew something was wrong.'

Just an endless stream of people, and he was curt, or vague, or polite if it was called for.

Galen still had the news on, watching the updates and gleaning facts from the little they told and combining them with the bits he knew.

And then there was another phone call.

Her mother.

'I need to speak with my daughter...'

'Roula is not in the office today,' Galen said, as if he was the receptionist.

'Then I need her home number.'

'I'm sorry. I don't have it.'

'But she's not taking my calls.'

She wasn't taking Galen's either.

'What?' Roula asked as he buzzed the intercom.

'It's me.'

'If you're here to fire me, just say so.'

'Fire you? Roula, just let me in.'

She buzzed him through and he found her in striped pink pyjamas, with a lot of curls and ringlets. Her hair was down for the first time.

How inappropriate of him to be turned on, Galen thought.

'I just wanted to check in,' he said. 'I heard.'

'Yes...' She gestured to the television that was on. 'So has everyone.'

'I'm so sorry, Roula.'

'Well, don't be. I've been expecting this. I know I should

have told you, but…' She shook her head. 'I thought I might get through the next few weeks before…' She gestured again to the screen.

Christ, Galen thought, they had a helicopter over Anapliró. And there were reporters both there and in Athens, where it would seem her brother was in custody.

'Nemo's house,' Roula said as a picture of it came on the screen. 'I found Dimitrios's gas cylinder in the garage. They haven't said that yet…'

'Okay…' He had to remember he wasn't supposed to know. 'Your mother called a short while ago.'

'I just tried to call her.' Roula nodded. 'I think she's giving her statement.' She shot him a look. 'She doesn't know yet I was the one who went to the police. She'll never forgive me.'

'You don't know that.'

'We *both* know that, Galen.'

'If he killed your husband, you have every right to hate—'

'Shut up!' Roula put her hands over her ears.

He was so bad at this type of thing…

'Turn it off, Roula,' Galen suggested.

But still she stood and, no, she was not feeling as together as she had first thought.

'I want to see my little cottage.' Oh, she really was starting to lose it. 'I want to see what they say.'

'Roula…' Galen took her arms and held them firmly.

It was a move that might honestly have spun her, only she felt secure rather than confined.

'Stop,' he said.

'It's my life.'

'I know it is,' he said, and it felt as if his two hands were the only things holding her in place on this earth right now.

'I thought I was prepared.'

'I know.'

'You don't know…' No one did.

'Listen to me,' Galen told her. 'We're going to my place.'

'No.'

'Yes,' he insisted.

'Hiding won't help.'

'For a little while it might. I can police your phone and we can lie and watch movies.'

'They'll be screaming for me…finding out it was me who informed on my brother…and you want to watch a movie?'

'Yes,' he said. 'That's what I do every year on the anniversary of my parents' death.'

He shared so little, and suddenly he was giving her so much.

'I black out my apartment and watch movies and I wait for the clock to move past…'

'All that day?'

'All the moments of a day I can't even remember.' He was still holding her arms. 'Pause with me,' Galen said. 'Don't do this on your own.'

CHAPTER TEN

ROULA WAS STILL in her pyjamas as Galen drove beneath some vast building and pressed a lot of buttons to get them into an ancient elevator. And then they were going up, to a world that was so blacked out it was like walking in the dark.

'Here…'

He put on some lights and dimmed them, and she saw there were couches, and no doubt beautiful artwork and such things, but her eyes were fixed on a huge globe.

'Come on.' He took her arm. 'I'll show you around.'

'I don't need a tour.'

'Then nor do I.'

It was so dark she had to feel her way to find the sofa. It was vast, and just so nice to half sit, half lie in a silence broken only by their buzzing phones, which Galen checked now and then.

So dark that when she reached for her soda and drank it she pulled a face. 'What the hell…?'

'Antacid,' Galen said. 'Mia poisoned me.'

He'd made her smile, but then her face changed. 'Has she messaged?'

'Not yet,' Galen said. 'But Yolanda called, and Costa, Leo…'

'Can we please not talk about it?'

'Of course.'

He suggested a movie.

'You watch on a computer?' Roula frowned as he set up his laptop. 'I thought you'd be a bit more high-tech than that.'

'The screen's in my bedroom.'

'Galen!' She half laughed as she stood up. 'I'm not exactly dressed to kill…'

It was the biggest bed. They could have lain there like separate stars if they chose. But they sat propped up, and he rang out for food, and they watched the most dreadful movie, and she drank iced soda and Galen drank iced tea.

It was so nice *not* to talk about it—but of course the world was waiting for her, and despite the blacked-out room she knew it was getting late.

'I should have brought a toothbrush and things.'

'I have all that.' He wandered into his bathroom and came back to hand her a lovely little bag. 'I sometimes choose the lady's one when I fly. For guests…'

He must fly first class, because it was a gorgeous bag, crammed with beautiful things. But she was so tense she just grabbed the toothbrush, and as she brushed her teeth she made up her mind.

'I'm going to call my mother,' Roula said when she returned to the bedroom. 'She's surely finished giving her statement now?'

'Why don't I check your messages first?'

Roula nodded.

'I'm going to shower,' Galen said as he retrieved their phones. 'The guest rooms are down the hall, if you want. The second or third door.'

But as he went to the bathroom, rather than heading off, she sat on the bed.

She didn't want to be alone this night.

Yet she didn't want sex.

Or she sort of did—but not in disgusting nightwear, and unshaved, and just…

Oh, it might not be supposed to matter, but Roula had had enough sex where it *really* hadn't mattered. A very different thing. For a while it was perhaps nice to feel wanted, no matter your attire, but for Roula things were a little more complex. She had been taken over and over, no matter what she wore or how she looked.

She wanted to feel nice—not just for him, but herself.

'Still here?' Galen said when he came out of the shower, wrapped in a towel.

'Well, I want to hear what's being said. I assume you've checked my phone?'

'I have.' Galen nodded. 'Do you want to go through to the lounge for a debriefing and then I'll show you to a guest room, or do you want to speak here in bed?'

Why was he *so* direct?

'Here's fine, but…'

'Roula…' He opened and closed several drawers as he spoke 'I have a rule…'

'What?'

He tapped his ring finger. 'They don't turn me on.'

He did not see her burning cheeks, for he was still looking through drawers.

She diverted her eyes as he pulled on some dark grey lounge pants, which were tight at the bottom and had clearly never been worn because they had a price label on the front of the waistband—though she tried not to notice as he got under the sheets.

'Get in,' he said, and she did, and they faced each other, and his shoulders were broad and wet…

'You don't ever dry yourself properly,' she told him.

'I dry the important bits,' he said, and then added, 'I dry them very thoroughly. The rest…'

He liked her pink blush and the temporary receding of pain in her eyes.

It wouldn't last.

Galen had heard her mother's tirade, and it would seem that Nemo's lawyers, along with her family, were rather hoping Roula might want to fabricate a suitable defence and help Nemo.

Galen was not one for affection, but he would have liked to wrap her up right now and hide her for six months. He was incredibly relieved that she lay in his bed, not down a hallway, or streets away, or on Anapliró…

He resisted, though. Even as he saw the trouble swirling in her eyes…

'Your mother did call, but I think you should wait till tomorrow to call her back. Tensions are high.'

'What did she say?'

'I was brushing my teeth,' he said, 'so I didn't get all the details. But anger was the general drift.'

'Did she call me a traitor?'

'Not sure… I was gargling.'

Galen breathed on her, and it was minty and antiseptic, and Roula had never imagined, not even in her wildest panics about what her mother would say, that it would even possible for it to be delivered in such an offhand, calm, minty and, yes, *sexy* way.

And as he went through her messages he took out, not the agony as such—this was too heavy for that—but he dulled the acute sting in a way she could not have envisaged.

'Can I ask how you're doing?' Galen asked her.

'Grateful to pause,' she admitted. 'So, you hide yourself here on the anniversary of your parents' death…?'

He regretted telling her already. 'Yes.'

'You don't remember them?'

'I've always said I don't,' he admitted. 'But now, I'm not sure if it's all the photos I've seen, sometimes… I really don't like talking about it, Roula.'

'I don't enjoy talking about my murderous brother,' she said, 'yet here we are.'

Then she asked what his PA should not. 'You didn't take the flowers that I picked for your grandmother…'

'I'll send you to the guest room,' he joked. Sort of.

'Send me, then,' Roula said. 'Why can't you speak about her home to her?'

'I want to get this last bit right—for her to be peaceful. I've caused enough upset in her life…'

'I think her life gave her a lot of upsets other than just you.'

'Yes, but I was not an easy child. I wandered off…didn't speak till I was four…'

Roula frowned as she recalled some of what Yaya had said. *'Why? Why? Why?'*

She wasn't sure he was right.

'Galen, there weren't exactly a lot of specialists available then—even until recently there wasn't a clinic. We were all fumbling along...'

'I was angry. She wanted me to love my parents, to kiss their photos, to cry, and I said they were strangers to me.' He gave her a grim smile at the admission.

'Well, I did everything I was told and now my family is not speaking to me.' She looked at him. 'Galen, she just wants to talk of home.'

'And I cannot stand it. Because she shouts and then she cries...'

'I know it's hard, but if you just listen to her it might help you both.'

'Thanks, Dr Roula. I'll let the specialist team know your recommendations.'

'Good!'

'I was being sarcastic.'

'I know you were, but I wasn't!' She took a breath. 'Galen—'

'My turn for questions now,' he interrupted.

'I told you—I don't want to talk about it,' Roula flared.

'See?'

But he moved his hand to much nicer distractions, up to her shoulder, and then a little question that had beguiled him when they'd kissed came to his mind again. 'There are a lot of straps...'

'Yes.'

'Two bras?' he questioned as he felt under her arm and then undid the top two buttons of her pyjamas.

Roula felt her throat constrict. It was with a delicious anticipatory pleasure and also a dash of embarrassment at her rather appalling underwear.

But he undid only the two buttons, and perhaps didn't even see the shabby grey. It was like a brief check, an observation, as if he might pop his head in and check all was okay...

Galen looked at the squash of her cleavage and then back to her dark brown eyes. She completely fascinated him.

He did up one of the buttons.

Just that.

'Are we crossing lines here, Galen?' Roula asked.

'A little,' Galen said as he ran a hand down her arm. 'Extenuating circumstances.'

'Yes…'

'But we're being good,' Galen said. 'Because we have to work together.'

'True.'

'As well as that…' his hand slid over her bottom '…you told me yourself—you're not like me.'

'When?'

'You know when. At the wedding…when I propositioned you.'

'I don't think it was quite that.'

'It was exactly that,' Galen said. 'I offered a one-night stand and you declined. Remember?'

Roula met his eyes and nodded.

'I want you,' he said. 'I think you are so hot, and so cold, and there are times I think you want me too, but…'

'But?'

'Okay…' Galen had come up with a couple of theories of his own—a few, in fact—and now he offered her one. 'Given you've waited this long since…' *Argh!* He couldn't even say his name. 'Well, perhaps you're holding on for someone who can give you more than sex. But that's all I give, Roula. I am terrible at relationships. I just don't do them—'

'Galen,' Roula cut in. 'I'm honestly not ready for one,' she admitted. 'I'm just not. But can I say this one thing?'

'Go ahead.'

'You *are* good at relationships. You have amazing friends, and not by chance, and I was wrong about your work—you have staff who are devoted to you. Again not by chance.'

'Perhaps,' Galen said, 'but I don't want an intimate relationship. I don't want to lie here and say the wrong thing, or ask, *Honey, how was your day?* and pretend to listen as I tune out. All that…' He shrugged. 'I tried all that when I was still going by the *Find the One and Settle Down* rule book. It never worked.'

'How?'

'First one?' Galen said. 'She asked where we were going—I said, "Back to bed, hopefully." You get the drift…'

'Second?' Roula smiled.

'That was a very big row. She asked what I was thinking in that moment, when we were lying there—you know…we'd just… And so I told her.'

'What *were* you thinking?'

'Well, Costa was wanting a cheaper office rental. We were really broke then, but the slightly more expensive one came with utilities included. I wanted to mine crypto…'

'Oh?'

'It takes a lot of electricity,' Galen explained. 'I was wondering how long I could get away with it before the landlord noticed.'

'That's what you were thinking?'

'Yes.' He nodded. 'After sex. When you're just supposed to…' She stared back, nonplussed.

'You know,' Galen said. 'Float…'

Roula did not know that feeling.

'I ticked some things off your list while I was playing secretary today,' he went on.

'Like what?'

'I declined dressing like a charm for the gaming convention—so you don't have to run that one by me.'

'I was actually going to make an executive decision there and decline for you.'

Her hair had moved forward as she'd rolled over, and to Roula it just felt good when his hand pushed it out of her eyes.

'You smell nice,' she told him.

'So do you,' he lifted a strand of hair and inhaled it. 'Sunshine. But we're being good, because you're upset tonight and I am not taking advantage.'

He made it easy to breathe even with her racing heart. Always he reassured her—always.

Perhaps more to the point, there was no way she'd let anything happen. No flesh beneath her pyjamas would be touched or seen.

Roula was more than aware that she needed some kind of major intervention, but it was bliss just to lie talking. It was nice to just lie face-on and to really look at his beautiful eyes, to be locked away with Galen for a while.

'What else did my secretary do?' Roula asked.

'I got through quite a bit,' Galen said. 'One thing: "Ask about Pipéri?" What does that mean?'

'Dora's dog.'

'Oh?'

'He's having knee surgery tomorrow.'

'Seriously?'

'He's going to be on wheels…'

'Are you kidding?'

'No. Little wheels on his back legs, so that he can get around.' Roula nodded. 'I'd have done it for my dog…'

'Benji?'

Roula nodded.

'How did you know about Pipéri?' Galen asked.

'I asked. You should try it.'

He saw that tiny raising of her eyebrows. 'I do ask. I ask how she is… I ensure that I speak… And Kristina sorts out gifts…' Galen took a breath. 'Maybe you can send her flowers from me?'

'I'm on stress leave.' Roula smiled. 'Anyway, you don't know how his surgery went yet—perhaps you should call and ask her tomorrow?'

'Get out.'

Galen smiled, but he was staring, and Roula was back in another time in her life with Galen when a conversation was being had without words…when she could see he was thinking about what she'd just said.

But then his attention was back on her. 'I did something not on your list,' Galen said.

'Such as?'

'I spoke to Leo. I am your fairy godmother, Roula—you shall go to the ball.'

'No.' She shook her head.

'I thought a night out in a few weeks' time might be something to...' He rolled over and looked at her. 'Get dressed up... have fun?'

'I can't see it.'

'Of course you can't,' Galen said. 'But we'll dance, though we both hate it, and I'll mingle.' He rolled his eyes.

'I won't be working for you by then.'

'Exactly.' Galen smiled again. His hand was on her hip, and then he moved to her bottom. 'No more watching you pinch all the praline balls.'

She liked his hand there, just the ease of it. 'Galen, you said no sex.'

'We're not having sex,' Galen said. 'Just being a bit inappropriate.'

His palm was warm on her bottom and his fingers pressed a little into her flesh.

'That's all,' he told her.

His hand moved to her waist, beneath her pyjamas, and she liked his slow perusal. But there was vigilance still.

'Is that okay?' Galen checked.

'Yes,' Roula said, because she liked his hand sliding over her waist, and then back to her candy-striped bottom, and she liked it that she wanted to move in closer, and that she could— if she so chose.

And she felt his circle widen a touch, so that her hip was just a little bare now, and it was so nice to cave in and hold his bare arm. No longer damp, but still cool from the shower, and so firm and yet silky.

'You're going to the ball,' he told her. 'When you no longer work for me. If you so choose.'

'Outside of work?' Roula said, unsure what this meant.

'Yes,' he said. 'No crossing lines then.'

'Oh, so we're talking about your "catch-up" list?' Roula asked, and it was actually so freeing to lie in bed and just talk about... well, sex, and a time when this would have all blown over, and they might know mutual desire.

'Nothing wrong with a catch-up list,' he told her.

'There's *so* much wrong with it.'

'No,' he refuted. 'Much like in my professional life, I focus on the things I can do.'

'And outsource the rest?'

'Pretty much.' He nodded. 'Insource, maybe,' Galen said and his hand slid up between her thighs.

It was so bizarre not to tense…just to feel his hand move there and feel him cupping her through the fabric.

'Do you want to come a little to help you sleep?'

Galen spoke as if he were offering her a glass of wine or a couple of headache pills, and she stared back at him, a little stunned, for she'd never climaxed in her life.

'No,' Roula said. She did not want another first in her life.

'Okay.' He removed his hand. 'Get some sleep.'

Roula did.

A real sleep.

In fact she awoke with her head on her new and very favourite firm pillow, and she was not sure for a second which legs belonged to her, for they were knotted with Galen's, one of hers hooked high over his thighs. A little too high… He was holding her hand as if they were dancing, and then they both sleepily realised what had stirred them out of slumber.

His hand dropped and he moved her leg just a little, back down, and rearranged himself beneath those lounge pants. In fact, he must still really be more asleep than awake, for he picked up her hand again and drifted back off with soft snores.

And it was so nice that she did as her body wanted and just went straight back to sleep.

CHAPTER ELEVEN

GALEN WOKE AND turned on his phone as Roula coiled into him, and was stunned to see the time, for it was after eight. He unknotted himself from his bedfellow and then went out to his unused kitchen to check the messages...

Roula woke to see Galen sitting on the bed.

'Your mother remains keen to speak...' He must have read and heard all her messages.

'Who else?'

Her detective, her lawyer, members of the family, friends, her late husband's mother... It really was quite a list.

'I'm going to be busy.'

'We're in hiding, Roula,' Galen said, and climbed back into bed. With a groan, he checked his own messages.

'I might have a shower,' she said.

'Sure, help yourself. The bath is nice, but takes ages to fill. Do you want a shirt? There's underwear in the top drawer.'

'I'm not wearing your partners' leftovers, thank you.'

'I meant mine.' He gave her a smile. 'It'll probably be a bit big for you.'

Roula took the 'lady's' flight bag and padded out to have a shower, but as she closed the bathroom door she blinked. Gosh, his en suite bathroom was stunning! Roula had only brushed her teeth and used the loo last night, and had not really been up to examining her surroundings.

Now, as she stripped off her pyjamas and her most appalling massive knickers, she looked up at the marble and columns. The subtle opulence was daunting. Seriously so.

Aside from the columns and such, two of the walls were mirrors—but certainly not the measure-and-cut kind.

Oh, my...

Roula stepped closer to one vast wall and saw the speckles and grey-green hue, and then she looked at the ornate frame. Of course she could not touch it, for it was saved from further damage by a thick layer of modern glass.

She spun and looked to the other wall.

It was a smaller mirror, though still vast. This one was unframed and had a crack running through it, and was so beyond beautiful it made her reach out.

Again it was set behind glass.

Roula looked at the beauty around her, and as she took off her first bra she felt shabby. For a very long time it hadn't mattered. In fact, the shabbier and more hidden the better she'd felt.

She unhooked the second bra and felt the drop of her heavy breasts. She stared at the pale reflection of the large breasts she tucked and strapped away, and then looked down to her pale stomach, and lower, to the bright red curls that seemed too vibrant for someone who was dead inside.

Yet she did not feel so numb now.

She turned and looked at her bottom—the same bottom that Galen had stroked last night, through fabric—then back to her reflection. Roula lifted her arms and looked at the hair there—only it was not black and beautiful, like Galen's.

Unfortunately the lady's toiletries pack didn't come with a razor, so she looked at his razor, picked up the heavy metal, then stood under a deluge of warm water.

She could have been standing there a thousand or more years ago, Roula thought, being drenched by the rain. Except the rain was hot in Galen's world, and there were glass jars with bubbles and lovely fragrances and oils.

She shaved for the first time in for ever. Well, since her teenage days, and the eve of her wedding. And she borrowed his nail scissors too—though not for any practical reason! And she pinched some lotion and sniffed his deodorant, but replaced it unused. It smelt very male.

She felt not.

Roula pulled on her horrible pyjamas but left off the underwear. And as she bundled it, the she had when she'd wet her knickers all those years ago, something changed in her head.

She wanted pretty things.

And she wanted him.

Galen was not exactly husband material...

Bad comparison.

Well, not even relationship material...

Roula took a breath. If she was being honest, Galen didn't even tick the 'transition guy' or 'dating' box...

Yet Galen had turned something too awful to contemplate into something rather beautiful. And that languid moment when she'd briefly woken in the early hours... Well, Roula had gone back to sleep, but that moment rather fascinated her now.

There was a certain peace and harmony that came over her when she was with Galen.

He was on the bed when she stepped back into the room.

'I borrowed—' she started, but then saw he was on his phone.

Fine, he mouthed, and waved her away, thankfully oblivious to the transformation that had taken place.

Not so.

As Roula sat on the bed, combing her hair, he glanced over and tried—really tried—not to notice that her breasts had honestly doubled in size.

'I'm very pleased to hear that, Dora.'

Roula smiled as she combed her thick hair.

'I can't. I'm sorry. I have to keep it a pet-free space,' he said, and pulled a face at Roula. 'For allergies and such. But if you need a few days more at home...'

He spoke for two minutes more, then scowled at Roula as he turned off his phone. 'See what being nice does?' he accused. 'Now she wants to bring her dog on wheels in to work. I said no.'

'I heard.'

'Roula, I am not having dogs and babies and bring-your-pet-ferret-to-work days...'

'I get it!' She laughed. 'It's nice that you called, though. Send flowers.'

'Later.'

'What does—?' Roula stopped her question. She knew Galen

did not speak about his staff, and certainly she wasn't about to dob Dora in.

'Go on,' he invited.

'Nothing.'

'Are you asking what does Dora with her lazy get-out-of-any-work ass do?'

'Galen!'

'I love her,' Galen said. 'Now, no one knows this—not Kristina, not anyone… Well, Nico does. But you can never tell.'

Good God, what was he about to tell her?

'Dora is my number one beta tester,' Galen said. 'Not that she knows it.'

'So you know she sits playing on games all day…?'

'Not all day.' He smiled. 'She checks her horoscope, does a little shopping, occasionally sends the annual leave sheets over to HR or stocks up the mini bar. But she gets through all the levels and we see the bugs, what bits she loves…'

Roula found she was laughing. On a day when her life was just crumbling she felt a surge of something new and she sat there and laughed.

'It's back…' Galen said as her laughter faded.

'What?'

'"Ha-ha, breath, ha-ha-ha, breath, ha-ha-ha-ha…"' He repeated the actual beats of her laugh. 'That's the laugh I remember. I haven't heard it in a long time.'

'Nor have I,' Roula said.

They looked right at each other then, and it wasn't the look he had given her at the wedding—it was a little more questioning than intense. Yet she knew so much more, and it felt almost as if his hand was cupping her down there, as she felt a stir in her body and an ache to step forward.

'I do want you,' she said.

'I'd be your first, since…?'

'Yes,' she said. 'You'd be my first.'

He must never know just how true her answer actually was, because she'd never really once made love.

But it was too much baggage—Roula knew that. Especially

for a man who very deliberately avoided such a thing. And there would be ground rules.

'Roula, I won't change.'

'I don't want you to.'

'And I don't want to hurt you—I really don't. So I'm just making sure. What happens when I ignore you at work?' Galen checked.

'I shan't notice,' Roula said. 'I'll be too busy working, as well as applying for other jobs—though for the next few weeks you should do a better job of diverting your phone.'

'Fair enough,' Galen said. 'But I get to state my wants too...'

'Of course.'

'Take your ring off here, Roula.'

He would be the first person to see her without her wedding ring.

She stood and removed it, and as she dropped it on his dresser it felt as if she was dropping a lead weight rather than a sliver of gold.

Nervous, Roula went to take a step towards him, but Galen climbed out of the bed and walked over to her, and then he took her face in his hands and gave her a kiss such as she had never had.

It was not like the one he'd given her on the steps. This kiss was more silky than before, slower, and this one was leading to other places. She was lost in the bliss of his mouth, of his hands soft on her breasts, stroking her nipples and then cupping them.

And then he was pausing and stripping off his one garment.

Roula had seen him in a towel—had seen most of him—but she did not look down yet, just felt his beautiful shoulders and pulled at the little hairs on his chest as he undid the little buttons of her pyjama top.

'Thank God for zig-zags,' he whispered as he exposed her breasts, and then it was Roula who shed her shabby pyjamas, desperate to be free.

She closed her eyes as he took a nipple and sucked it to an indecent peak.

His skin was incredible, it was a relief to touch it, to hold on to his torso, but also not a relief, because it was too heady to be pulled into him, to be pressed against him as his fingers stroked her.

And then he stopped, half lifted her, and it was a kiss that dizzied her as he lay her down.

Now she saw him, and she lay there with Galen standing over her, and he looked at her and gave her a smile, and she looked up at him. At his jet-black hair and the thick length of him. And she was so burning for him that she frowned as he knelt and lifted her knees.

'What are you doing?' she asked, a little confused, a little breathless, a little awkward.

But his eyes were not holding hers, for they were trained *down there*.

'Looking at you,' Galen said. 'God, Roula…'

A part of her wanted to close her knees, unused to this, and yet there was something in his voice that made her tremble inside, and the light touch of his fingers had her curious for a little more of the feelings he evoked.

He swore, but gently and nicely. As if his own pleasure was somewhat inconvenient. As if he liked doing this—stroking the little knot she'd never even known was there.

Roula found she was tense with delicious conflict as he slid his fingers inside her. This strange push-pull feeling was consuming her, making her just a little dizzy as he stroked her, and then she was a touch bewildered as he lowered his head, because certainly her thighs had never been kissed before.

Nor licked.

And as his fingers slid inside her he kissed the most tender flesh of her upper thigh, and her bottom started to lift towards his hand.

She was caving in to the pleasure building—and then she sobbed in frustration when he removed that skilled hand.

'Galen…' Confusion reigned for a moment as he slid further down the bed. '*What* are you doing?'

'What do you think I'm doing?' Galen's words were dark with sensual torment, but he frowned slightly, as if he'd registered the note of bewilderment in her voice. 'Don't you like…?'

Roula felt as if her heart was lodged in her throat as she realised he was about to go down on her with his mouth. She'd had no idea such a thing actually existed. Well, perhaps she'd got some idea from a couple of TV shows, but she'd always flicked them off.

'Please…' Roula said, because she *wanted* the full Galen experience—honestly. She trusted him that much and he readily obliged. His fingers and his kisses had been enlightening, but his mouth made her feel as if she were chasing the eye of a storm. 'Galen…'

It was too much, and at the same time not enough. It was as if his mouth was attached to her, not leaving her, and then she was lifting up on her elbows, watching his dark head between her legs, hearing the desirous noises he made.

Or was that her?

He moved her legs over his shoulders and Roula had a sudden urge to laugh—but then he moaned into her.

One hand was under her bottom, the other pressing her stomach. It was Roula trying to lift her hips up, except he kept pushing them down, and she fought it a little, crying and red from the exertion of going nowhere except to bliss as he tasted her deeper.

Roula came against his mouth and it shocked her that she might—that she could.

'You taste amazing,' he said, licking his lips, and then he came up on the bed and sort of crawled up to her, rolling her to her side. They faced each other as they had last night. And there was a question she couldn't read in his eyes.

He took her hand. 'Stop biting them,' he said.

And then he moved her hand down and she closed her eyes, feeling his strength beneath her fingers.

'It's…' She felt the silky skin, and the power of him, and shot bewildered eyes up to his.

She didn't know what to do, Galen realised.

She felt him put his hand over hers and together they stroked him, and she was a mixture of desire and this deep pit of sadness, because she'd just never known anything like it before.

He was slippery in her hand and she let go, but then he moved down so that he was stroking himself, close to her.

'Please…' She was urgent. It was knotted desire and desperation, and there could be no halt in these proceedings.

They were side on, their legs scissored, knotted together as he slid in, and Roula closed her eyes as he filled her, so slowly she thought she might faint from the source of this pleasure.

'Never stop,' she said as she moved her hands up his chest and held his shoulders.

And he moved within her and she just watched him, felt him inside her, felt his heavy thigh over hers. Her hips started to move to meet his, in a motion that just came to her.

Then he moved, angled himself a little differently and drove deeper in.

'There,' she said.

'There?'

He pulled her hips closer till they were so locked together that her breath came out sharp with each measured thrust.

Galen had never been into a woman so much. He was watching her unravel before his eyes and resisting the urge to go faster, which was in such opposition to his own command to go slow. He was trying to hold on, but the intensity was beyond him and he started to thrust harder.

And she clung. And he caved.

His breathless shout as he shot into her was a mix of annoyance with himself and utter release.

To Roula it felt like permission.

She gave in to the place he'd led her, felt the throb of her body and the pulse of him, and so deep was the pleasure that the world lost colour, sound, as if her every sense had been diverted to capture every last beat of this.

They were breathless and still looking at each other as they came down. Still facing each other as she felt him slide onto her thigh. And then Roula found out what floating meant, because her thoughts were up in the air instead of reined in. And although she didn't

want to, she started to cry. Not the squeezed-out tears of her first
orgasm, but a cry for something else—her younger and other self.

Galen, who was more used to a smile, and zipping up, or lying in
sated leisure before the next round, did not know quite what to do.
    'Are you all right?' he asked, and hated his own wooden voice
and his stupid choice of words after they'd just exploded together.
    Even he had been taken aback by the intensity of their union.

    'I'm just…' She wanted to tell him she'd never come before,
never liked sex, hated it… But she was certain her truth would
spoil things. 'It was amazing.'
    'Maybe too good,' he said, as if he was cross with himself. 'I
should have used something.'
    'Something…?'
    'Roula!' His eyes were wide. 'I swear, I always—'
    'I know.'
    She believed him, because she had been drowning in him, and
actually it was she who was the practical one.
    'I can't have babies,' she told him. 'So that takes care of that.'
    'Good,' Galen said, and then winced. 'I mean, I'm sorry…'
    'No, you're not!' Roula laughed, her tears receding, and lay there
wrapped up in his arms feeling better, just feeling this gorgeous
harmony. This was surely what Galen had meant about floating.
    'What are you thinking?' Roula teased.

But Galen's mind was back there, hearing again the slight waver
and question in her voice as to what he was doing before he'd
gone down on her. And Roula's naivety… He did not like the
conclusion he was coming to. Had already been forming the first
time they'd danced.
    'Charts,' Galen said.
    Roula laughed.
    Oh, God, he thought. How did she feel peaceful in this the
worst of times?

CHAPTER TWELVE

THE REAL WORLD was waiting, of course.

There were hundreds of calls to be made, but the people she needed to speak to refused to take her call.

Roula left a message. 'Mamá, please call.'

She walked back into the bedroom, where Galen sat holding his phone.

'Costa called,' he added. 'I've told him you're fine.'

'You didn't tell him I was here?'

'Of course not,' Galen shook his head. 'I said you'd checked into a hotel and were sensibly keeping your phone off. I told you I am always discreet.'

'You did.' Roula took a breath. 'Galen, I don't want to take advantage, but I might need to take a couple of days off.'

'That's my plan.'

'I mean, I'm going to head home.'

Galen sharply looked up. 'You're going back?'

'Yes,' Roula said. 'By the time I've called everybody it would have been easier to just…'

'Roula!'

He was appalled at the thought. Galen had heard her messages and, no, the cauldron of Anapliró was so *not* the place she needed to be right now.

'The whole point of you being here—' He stopped abruptly.

'I get it,' she said. 'It was nice to hide for a night, but…'

She looked at him then, and frowned, because the very suave Galen, who was so upfront about so many things, looked uncomfortable as he got back to his phone.

'Well, I'm not sure it's the best idea.'

'What else did Costa say?' Roula asked.

'Not much.' Galen shrugged. 'He just wanted to check you were okay. He and Mary are heading back.'

'Honeymoon's over, then?' Roula said in a voice that held a question—and it was *not* in regard to Costa and Mary's marriage.

Galen would know that. He rarely slipped up and was clearly rather hoping Roula hadn't noticed, yet she had.

'I'm trying to find a florist for Dora,' he said.

Head down, Galen, Roula thought. As he had done all those years ago—only it was not bruises to his face he was hiding now.

She felt angry tears pricking her eyes and she swallowed them down—for, yes, this brief honeymoon, for want of a better word, was over. And she took a breath and spoke, as she would for any issue at work.

'You said the whole point of me being here…?' Roula checked. 'Did Costa ask you to employ me?'

'Sorry?'

'Galen.' She pulled the phone from his hands. 'Answer me.'

Her cheeks were pink, her eyes angry, and it was truth or lie time. Galen never broke a shared confidence, but he preferred honesty over lies.

'Yes,' he admitted. 'Costa spoke to me after the wedding.'

Her face lost all colour.

'He was concerned about what might happen, as was I.'

'Galen, we hadn't spoken for nearly two decades—don't play the white knight here. You didn't give a damn until Costa asked you to step in. If he hadn't asked you to hire me, then Nemo's arrest would have been something you skimmed through on the news.'

'No.'

'Yes,' she said. 'Absolutely yes. You cut off contact the day you left. This was nothing more than a favour to Costa.'

'I don't agree,' Galen refuted.

'I don't recall you sending flowers when Dimitrios died. I don't recall—'

'He was just some guy from home who died on a boat,' Galen snapped back. 'Boo-hoo.' He stopped himself from voicing his emerging thoughts on her husband. 'You're wrong, Roula, because, had I read this news I'd have been on your to-do list to call.'

'Rubbish!' She was furious. 'Do not move me around like a chess piece! You don't get to decide when I'm in trouble, or...'

Her anger was white-hot, and perhaps out of proportion. Irrational, even. But this hurt at a level he could not know. Where had White Knight Galen been when she'd really needed him? Where had her friend been then?

'My God, Galen!' She was close to shouting—close to telling him that this was nothing, *nothing* compared to what she'd endured. 'Don't you dare control my life. Don't you dare play God with my career.'

'Damn it, Roula...'

She had her phone out now and was calling for a taxi, or trying to. She was shaking with anger.

'Don't go like this.'

'Oh, I'm going.'

She was. Galen could see that.

Seriously, she was going to walk right out onto the street in pyjamas and in a rage.

He said the only thing he could think of. 'I'll drive you.'

Roula told him what he could do with that suggestion, and not politely. But he would not let her leave like this.

'I'm driving you. I will not talk. I will not ask to come in. I will apologise. In fact, I'll do that now. I am sorry. However...' Galen took a breath. 'You are in pyjamas, and I think it best that I see you safely back to your apartment.'

She looked down to her candy-striped pyjamas and bare feet and he saw a tiny flicker of logic occurring in her angry mind.

'Yes,' she said, 'but I don't accept your apology.'

It wasn't the gentlest end to their hideaway.

Galen kept to his word and said nothing as he drove her the

short distance home, and Roula sat there, angry, embarrassed and hurting.

And conflicted.

The raw edges of her anger were receding, but instead of calm invading her there was a new and unfamiliar turbulence rattling her. His car glided through the streets, yet she felt as if there should be oxygen masks dropping down and bells pinging.

She'd never been so angry in front of someone.

Never dared to be.

And certainly she had not expected to be driven home.

She felt more naked than she had in the shower.

Worse, she felt lower than shabby.

A fisherman's wife...

Galen turned at her mirthless laugh but said nothing until he was pulling the car in at the top of the lane.

'We're here.'

And really, thank goodness he'd driven her—because he silently handed her the apartment keys that she'd forgotten to bring.

'You forgot this too.' He handed her her wedding ring.

So she had!

'Obviously I shan't be coming back to work.' Roula's voice was shaky as she said what she had been practising on the drive.

Galen stared out through the windscreen and forced himself to keep his temporary vow of silence, but when he tried to take her angry clawed hand she would not allow it.

'If I could have a bit of time to sort out the apartment, I'll return the keys by the end of the week.'

'Don't do this,' Galen said.

'What? You want me back at my desk doing some cooked-up job, pretending I'm needed?'

'It isn't a cooked-up job, Roula. You know that. You just have friends who want to help. I told Costa that I didn't like the idea from the very start...' He gritted his jaw. 'Look, I don't know how many times I've tried to give you an opportunity to tell me about your brother.'

'When?'

'When I picked you up from the airport.'

'You walked me home.' The angry flush on her face leeched away. 'That night when you asked what was on my mind...'

And she'd asked for his kiss.

She could not feel more humiliated.

'I'm going.'

'Roula, you can have the rest of the week off, but I expect you back at work on Monday.'

'Get lost!' she said.

'As a friend, you can use the apartment... I said that to Costa at the time. But I also warned him that I don't run a charity. I accept that you have some personal issues to deal with, so I will call in one of my regular temps to cover this weekend, but either you're back at work on Monday or you'll be replaced. Oh, and you have a gown fitting too.'

'You seriously expect me to go for a gown fitting?'

'Not if you don't intend to return to work,' Galen said. 'But if you are going to leave that window open, then don't go home till you've been measured. Leo is already cutting it fine to have it ready in four weeks.' He looked right at her. 'Unless, of course, you already have something suitable...'

She slammed the door and ran down the little lane in her pyjamas. Galen drove off, angry at himself, but at the same time glad the truth was out.

And worried.

As a friend would be, of course.

Roula stood in her lounge, breathless, and felt as if she had been running for ever—not just up the stairs to her apartment.

Her hand was holding the one he had reached for, but she let it go and tried to get back to her life, listening to the messages, reading the texts—and then the long-awaited call came from Mia.

'I don't know what to say,' Mia admitted.

'I know,' Roula agreed. 'I'm sorry for the pain your family are going through, Mia, but I couldn't tell you.'

'Of course not,' Mia said. 'But it's just back to square one, isn't it? Grieving for him all over again.'

Roula closed her eyes, for it felt a little as if she were being told how to feel—told that she should arrive back on Anapliró looking suitably widowed and ravaged to appease the Drakos family. Or defensive of her brother to appease her own.

Really, she would like to crawl into bed. Preferably Galen's. And just escape as he had allowed her to.

'Dimitrios's mother is bereft,' Mia said. 'I'm not sure what reception you'll get.' There was a long pause. 'Roula, I want to say it's fine, that we can be friends again, but I don't see how we can be. To be honest, I can't see me staying on at the retreat if you come back.'

Roula had learnt a lot from watching Galen, she realised, for instead of filling the gap she stayed silent.

'Do you know what I wish?' Mia said.

'What?'

'It sounds selfish, and I know you did the right thing, going to the police, but I wish you'd said nothing. I wish you'd just stayed quiet. It's all too big and too sordid, and I don't see how we can get past it.'

Roula felt a little ill.

'I mean it,' Mia insisted, even though Roula wasn't arguing. 'I wish you'd just kept your mouth shut.'

And therein lay the problem.

Not just with Nemo, but with all of it—it was the story of her life.

Stay quiet, Roula. Don't spoil a pretty picture with the truth.

Roula found her voice then. 'Mia, I'm sure you're not alone with your thoughts. In fact, I think most people would quietly agree with you—some things are best left unsaid.'

Roula ended the call.

Perhaps it was time to take a leaf from the *acceptable* rule book that everyone wished she'd abided by? To examine this with a more selfish slant? Roula thought, as Mia's words played over in her head.

She was better—so much better than she had once been. In fact, Roula knew she had moved on in leaps and bounds. Galen had introduced her to her body and shown her the beautiful side of sex. And career wise...well, it was exciting.

No more working on her past.

Healed.

Done.

Over.

On a day Roula knew she should be sorting out the drama of others, she was urgent in her need to deal with herself.

Urgent.

She pulled on a dress…any dress—she had an endless selection thanks to her mother's hand-me-downs—and put on shoes that made her slender legs look heavy. Then she picked up her purse and half walked, half ran through the Athens streets to Kolonaki Square.

Only she was not headed for work. Instead it was Leo Arati's studio she arrived at, and pressed and pressed on the bell, then realised she was too early.

'Roula!' Leo moved to embrace her. 'I've been calling. You poor darling… Come up. I've slotted you in.'

'No.' She stopped him. 'I don't just want a gown fitting, Leo. I want a make-over.'

'Fine,' he said, 'We'll do both. Galen has put you on his account.'

'Leo, I don't want designer clothes, or to be on Galen's account. I have my own money. I just want a friend to come shopping with me.'

'Shopping?' Leo gaped.

'Yes,' Roula said. 'I don't know where to start, Leo, and I don't know what I want…' Oh, yes, she did. 'I want to reinvent myself.'

'A new Roula?'

'Yes.'

A tougher Roula.

A more ruthless Roula.

One who allowed no one in!

There was just one teeny issue with her plans…

Roula loved Galen.

Always had.

CHAPTER THIRTEEN

FINALLY!

Galen woke in his temperature-controlled bedroom to a distinct lack of drama. He took coffee on the terrace and gazed not upon the stunning view but at his laptop, and the results of a couple of days' neglect, work-wise.

Well, a couple of weeks of neglect, really—things had not been running to his meticulous schedule since Costa had hauled him back to Anapliró for his wedding.

He *refused* to allow his mind to wander towards Roula.

So they'd had a row?

Certainly he was more than used to that with women.

Deliberately he didn't check the news—it was none of his business if she chose to go back to the island.

At least with Roula off until Monday, Dion, his regular temp, was due to commence work and order was about to be restored.

He went in and showered and shaved. To say he nicked himself shaving would have been a severe understatement, for his razor was beyond blunt.

Roula!

He looked like a teenager after his first meeting with a razor, Galen thought as he surveyed the dots of tissue over his jaw.

Oh, and it was a corporate day, so instead of his preferred jeans he pulled on a suit and tie.

He bought coffee on the walk to work and decided to get his visit with Yaya done early today.

'*Kalimera*...'

She was sitting up in bed, all rosy-cheeked from her latest blood transfusion and eagle-eyed. 'You cut yourself shaving?'

'Yes,' Galen said, 'thank you for noticing.'

'It looks like nail marks...' Yaya said.

'No, just a blunt razor.'

'As if she dragged her nails down your face.'

'I got you this...' He took out a bun and she chewed on it.

'Where's Roula?'

'I don't know.' He gave an impatient shrug. 'On some days off…'

'Did Roula do that?' Yaya asked dragging her fingers down her own cheek. 'Did you two fight?'

'What the hell do you think I get up to?' Galen said. 'No! Eat.'

Galen didn't stay for long, instead heading to the relative peace of work—except as he stepped in to greet those who were there it was as if a hundred screen flicked away from the news on Anapliró and they all pretended to get back to work.

'Morning, Galen!' Dora called as he walked past and then came dashing out. 'Thank you for calling about my dog. it meant so much…'

'That's fine.'

'It was unexpected.'

Well, it had been Roula's idea, but he enquired after the dog anyway, when really his mind was elsewhere, and found out that Dora's sister was staying for a few days.

'Good.' Galen said, trying to stop his eyes from crossing with boredom.

'Any updates on Roula?'

'Why would I know?' He knew he was a little defensive. 'I haven't even turned on the news this morning.'

Thankfully Dion arrived. He had no questions of personal nature, and didn't even blink at his slashed face as they went through his schedule for the remainder of the week.

'Meeting with Hector?' he said.

Galen frowned. 'Who arranged that?'

Dion pulled up the information. 'Dora.'

Galen rolled his eyes—and then recalled what he'd been in the middle of before he'd let the details about Costa slip. 'Flowers,' he said. 'I meant to send Dora flowers—not today, but over the weekend.'

'Sure. Saying what?'

'Best wishes for…' He shrugged. 'Whatever her dog's name is—find that out. If it dies send sympathy ones.'

'Of course.'

'I'm really behind,' Galen admitted. 'It's been a disaster here of late.'

'Well, I'll let you get on.' Dion stood.

Ah, the efficiency of Dion. Perhaps not quite the absolute control that Kristina kept, and in all honesty Dion was a little bit...well, *pouty*, as he'd expected to be employed for the full six weeks that Kristina was away, but order was certainly being restored. And the programmers were all safe from Roula's endless pops of pollen.

Dion just placed down his food and coffee orders and completely understood that he was grateful for them. That when he was lost in work he didn't even notice they were there until his hand reached for an empty cup, or he found his drink was cold.

His cup was always full when required. Perfect.

Except, without Roula's little hovering, no matter how full and warm his cup, he felt empty.

And it was back to long silences at meetings, which should be running so much more smoothly now.

At the meeting with Hector he took notes on all the research and feedback that Hector relayed, and all his hopes for the next game.

'We really would like to make a formal announcement at the ball,' Hector persisted. 'There'll be a lot of press and industry representatives there.'

Silence. It wasn't as if Galen didn't know that already.

'So are we?'

'What?' Galen asked. 'Are *we* what?'

'Are you close?'

Dion was a consummate professional—so much so that Galen had actually forgotten that he was even in the meeting room—and there was silence...lovely silence. No little prompt from Roula. No feeling his ankle was about to be kicked under the table if he didn't give a timely response.

Yet, despite her absence, he could hear her voice.

'Just get it out of the way,' Roula had said, and had told him about her lists, and how good it felt to add a tick.

The game *was* actually ready—well, for the most part. But a million things had pinged in to distract him, and he really, seriously needed to focus on the work that was vital to him. And he didn't want to deal with the social side.

Yet, look at what Roula was dealing with right now...

Why did all roads lead there?

'Hector,' Galen said, 'you will be able to announce a date by the ball.'

'Really?'

Even Dion looked up.

'Yes,' Galen said. 'There are a few glitches to iron out, but we're on them.'

And on Friday he met with the development team, and thanked the very efficient Dion, who would be taking his diverted calls all over the weekend.

'So *she's* back on Monday?' Dion pouted. 'The one with all the personal issues?'

'Yes,' Galen said, 'to the former. I would never discuss the latter.'

Dion flounced off, and although Galen still sat in his blacked-out world, it didn't feel the same. Yes, Dion would take all the calls from the care home, but... As much as he might have resisted her invasion, blocking out the world had felt a little safer to do, knowing Roula was fielding those calls...

Saturday he was productive. Sunday not so much.

He found himself checking the news instead of his charts and looking for updates on her—in Roula's words—'murderous brother'.

Nothing.

'Hey, Leo...' Galen called his friend, oh, so casual, when he never called anyone casually. 'How are you?'

'Hungover.'

'Oh?'

'Galen, you know I don't rise before midday—especially on a Sunday. What do you want?'

'Did...?' He halted, stopping himself from asking if Roula

had kept her appointment—because Galen didn't snoop, nor delve into other people's lives. 'I just called to see how you are.'

Leo had already rung off.

Mondays were never his sunniest days, but Galen found himself awaiting the arrival of this one and wondering if his ultimatum had worked. If Roula would return.

It wasn't the scent of sunshine that cut the stale office air, though, instead it was Dora. And she seemed to have caught Roula's hovering habit when she brought in his morning coffee and thanked him profusely for the flowers.

Galen held in a tense breath and pushed out a smile. 'How is…?' *What is the dog's name?* 'How is your lovely dog?'

'He's doing very well.' Dora smiled, but still hovered. 'I thought Roula was supposed to be back today?'

He said nothing.

'She's not?' she asked.

'No,' Galen said. 'She's not.'

It was after nine when finally he addressed it—the first ever meeting for *everyone*—and they all gathered rapidly, agog for updates on the news they already knew.

'Roula is taking some more time off,' he said, when he knew he should just take her off the books. 'Also,' he added, 'Dora's dog continues to do well.'

'Should we send Roula some flowers?' Nico suggested. 'And a card?'

'And what do we write?' Galen fired back. '"Sorry to hear your brother killed your husband"?'

'We could just say that we're all thinking of her,' Dora suggested.

'No flowers,' Galen said. Because presumably her absence meant Roula was in Anapliró, and the thought made him feel ill.

Or was it his ulcer?

'How about chocolate?' someone else chimed in.

'Very well,' Galen said. 'Maybe send her a jar of praline balls.'

'No need…'

They all looked round at the sound of Roula's voice. 'But

thank you for the thought.' She glanced over to Galen. 'I apologise for being late. I had a meeting this morning.'

'That's fine,' Galen said—it was all he could manage.

Far from fraught and ravaged, she looked sensational. Seriously so.

Roula wore a wrap-over dress dotted with red poppies with black velvet centres, tied at the hip with a red velvet bow. And shoes that were far better suited to her pretty feet than those brown ones.

Yet she still wore her wedding ring.

He would never know her. Galen was quite sure of that. Reading Braille would be easier—and that was not an idle thought, because he'd actually dabbled in it once.

'Roula!' Dora jumped up. 'We've all been so worried.'

'Honestly, I'm fine…'

She smiled a new smile—one he hadn't yet seen. For it was neither her PA smile, nor her guest services manager smile, just a bright, breezy smile that went absolutely nowhere—certainly not to her eyes.

'I knew this was coming. I'm just embarrassed at all the drama it's caused.'

He caught up with her a short while after, feeding paper into a shredder, and she looked up and gave him that smile.

'How are you?' Galen asked. 'Really?'

'I'm actually relieved.'

'Come off it, Roula. How has it been?'

'Fine,' she said. 'You were right—it was sensible of me not to go back to the island just yet. So I've dealt with most of it over the phone. I had a legal meeting this morning—that's why I was late.'

'That's it?' he checked.

'Pretty much.'

'I'll call Leo, then.' Galen shrugged. 'And get the gossipy version from him. And Costa's due back next week…'

'I thought you didn't chat about your staff?'

'I don't. But I do have a social life, and I'm sure we'll catch up soon, and they'll talk. I don't police the topics.'

'You just listen?'

'Yes.' Galen smiled. 'You learn a lot more that way. Look, do you want to go for dinner later and—?'

'No, thank you. I just want to get through these next few weeks as professionally as I can. I've put you down as a reference, as I've filled in a few job applications. I hope that's okay?'

'Of course.'

And Galen really *was* arrogant and aloof, because he went to walk off.

Despite her best intentions the new Roula couldn't quite leave it there.

'I'm glad I've made it all so convenient for you,' she called to his back, but instantly regretted her words. Because, watching his demeanour change, she knew her embarrassment had made her lash out in a way that wasn't fair.

Still, he quickly rallied.

'Convenient?' Galen checked. 'That's the last word I'd use to describe you.' He looked right at her. 'But do turn me into the bad guy here if it helps, Roula.'

'Meaning…?'

'Roula.' Galen was sharp. 'I have walked many people to their door, the lanes here don't always allow for car access, and…'

'And what?'

'I'm saying that if, say, I walked Dora or Kristina to their door and they asked me to kiss them…' He thought for a moment. 'Well, the answer would be no. And I can't even envisage a time I'd be lying in bed with either of them…' He gave a little shudder at the thought. 'I'm not a tap you can turn on and off. We had great sex and now, for whatever reason, you're regretting it.'

'I regret that you lied in the first place.'

'I've already apologised for that,' Galen said. 'But I'm not apologising for kissing you, nor for our having sex. I gave up self-flagellation a long time ago.'

'Along with your morals?'

'I'm not the one wearing a wedding ring,' Galen pointed out. 'I'm not the one feeling guilty because I happened to enjoy it.'

'Well, it won't be happening again.'

'Probably for the best,' Galen agreed. 'This Monday morning post-mortem kind of takes the shine off it a bit—even if it is a week late. Now, if you'll excuse me, I'd really like to get on with my work.'

Yet *still* he couldn't.

He had never second-guessed himself over sex but there he sat in his office, doing a Dora and pretending to work, but really he was just staring at the screen.

There was something wrong, something missing... It was a problem he could not solve, and for once it had nothing to do with numbers.

Kristina had had her baby—bang on her due date, of course— and it was Galen who told her.

'Hey, Roula.'

He came to her door wearing a really nice smile. He looked all scruffy in black, and up-all-night-looking, and she wanted to run to him.

'Yes, Galen?'

'Kristina just called,' he told her. 'The baby is here...'

'And?'

'Sorry...' He turned away. 'I thought you would like to know.'

God, had she changed so much that he thought she would give such a surly response to the news?

'Galen?' She called him back. 'I meant and is there more information?'

'Oh, mother and baby are well.'

It was like trying to get mustard from an empty jar.

'What did she have?'

'A boy. But we knew that.'

'I didn't.' Roula shook her head. 'Do you want me to get a gift?'

'No, she had a registry.'

God, she got things so wrong, and while the new Roula should not care, she ended up in his office after her lunch break.

'Take this in to Kristina.' She put the wrapped present down.

'Why?'

'Galen…'

'Okay.'

He was sulking—not just because he hated the thought of a visit to Kristina, but because that damn ring on Roula's finger was flashing like a beacon.

'What did I get her?'

'A cream cashmere blanket.'

'Didn't they have blue?'

'She'll love it.'

'Thanks.'

He stopped by her office later, just before she was due to head out.

'You were right,' Galen said. 'The blanket was a hit.'

'How was the baby?'

'All scrunched up,' Galen said. 'I think I offended Ruben. I held the baby and said he was like a whole little person, just condensed, and he said, actually, he was average height.'

Roula smiled.

'And they think he's a genius, and knows his own name already, but I tried calling him and he didn't even open his eyes.'

'What *is* his name?'

'Luka,' Galen said. 'Luka the genius.'

'Maybe he is.'

'I don't think you'd know at one day old. Apparently, my parents thought—' He stopped then, because Roula was back on her computer, and they didn't talk like that any more. 'I'll get on.'

'Sure.'

Galen never chased gossip, but for once he headed up to level two of the building purely in search of it, and dropped in on Costa.

'How was the honeymoon?' he asked.

'I told you—good.'

'What did you get up to?'

'Hill walking,' Costa said. 'How's Roula going?'

'Well, she doesn't really talk about it.'

'I meant work-wise?'

Galen could not do small talk. 'Costa, what's happening on Anapliró with the families?'

'Crazy guns at dawn stuff.'

'Such as?'

'Just toxic. I've only heard gossip around the retreat, but Mary went and got her hair done in the village—she said she'd find out a lot more that way... Anyway, the Drakos family want the cottage back. The Kyrios family say it's theirs. They've decided that Nemo did what he did to save Roula...'

'A bit extreme,' Galen said, tongue in cheek.

'Ah, but, Toto, we're not in Kansas any more. We're in Anapliró now.' Costa looked over. 'That's a *Wizard of Oz* joke...'

'Thank you,' Galen said sarcastically.

'Oh, and I'm going to be without a head chef if Roula comes back... Mia's threatening to resign.'

'Bitch.'

'Whoa!' Costa said, because that was not the Galen he knew. 'I guess you've had it all from this end...'

'No. I told you, Roula doesn't say much about it.'

That gnawing feeling was back in his gut and Galen didn't like it—not because it smacked too much of feeling, more because he was starting to be sure about her husband. It wasn't like an ulcer—just a plain old gut feeling that had been markedly absent in most of his life, but ever-present when it came to Roula...

'Mind you,' Costa continued, 'Mia might not want to push her own agenda too much.'

'Meaning?'

'Yolanda's looking to pull back. I'm going to be looking for a manager.'

'Roula?' Galen frowned, but then put up his hand. 'I don't want to know.'

God, another thing that would get him in trouble if they ever spoke again. Still, even though he was usually less than interested in gossip, Galen was here with a question in mind—and he hadn't asked it yet.

'What was he like?' Galen was rarely nosy, but he knew that Costa read people better than he did.

'Who?'

'The man who died?' Galen said. 'I can't really remember him—just that he was very popular...'

'You know the type.' Costa shrugged.

'No,' Galen said. 'You read people better than me.'

Costa thought back. 'I couldn't stand him,' he admitted.

'Yet he got on with everyone?'

'Yes, but he was a smiling assassin. You know the type. He's a saint now, though.'

CHAPTER FOURTEEN

'ROULA?'

They were sharing the glass elevator and Galen's citrussy scent was too much…too strong. Death by bergamot, Roula thought as she stared ahead.

'Just how many jobs have you applied for?' he asked.

'Quite a few.'

'I feel like a reference machine…'

'Sorry.' She grimaced. 'I honestly didn't think I'd get so many responses.'

'London?' he said as the lift paused between floors.

'It's an amazing job,' Roula said. 'But I seriously doubt I'll get it.'

'Well, I gave you a great reference.'

'Oh!' She flashed her new smile. 'That's nice to know, thanks.'

'I didn't want to,' Galen said. 'But apparently you're not allowed to do otherwise.'

And then there was a moment. An awkward one. Because Roula had called in sick the day before. Actually, she'd taken the red eye flight to London, and guiltily called to say she was sick from the airport.

'Are you okay?'

'I'm fine. Just a migraine.'

'I used to get migraines,' he said.

'Did you?'

'Really terrible ones,' Galen said, and she realised he knew she'd been lying. 'With an aura and everything.'

'Oh?'

'Thankfully, I don't get them now.'

'I'm pleased to hear that,' Roula said.

'Well, I was very concerned for you,' Galen said, 'Dora suggested flowers, but I said they might make you feel a bit nauseous.'

'Probably.'

'Roula, can I ask you a favour?'

'I *am* your PA.'

'Exactly,' Galen said. 'I wouldn't ask Kristina to do this, nor Dion, but Yaya isn't eating.'

'Oh…' Roula swallowed. 'Since when?'

'Well, she's eating a bit, but…' He was rarely uncomfortable, but she saw he was now. 'Could I ask…? I know this is beyond the scope of your contract, but she wants fava soup, and the chefs there don't make it the right way, apparently.'

'It's not a problem.'

'You're sure?'

'Of course,' Roula said. 'I can take some over tomorrow.'

'That would be great,' Galen said, relief evident in his voice. 'She'll eats for you.'

But then the moment was ruined as Roula turned a favour for a boss—or a long-ago friend, or whatever they were—into something far more personal.

'I divert her with conversation while she eats,' Roula said, and then she caved for the second time. 'Whereas you just try to divert her with food.'

'Don't worry about the soup,' Galen snapped. 'I'll make it myself.'

Good luck with that, Roula was tempted to call as he stalked off.

It was a taste of home, Roula thought that night as she unpacked the ingredients—and not just ones from the store.

She'd actually brought a packet of yellow split peas from home especially for Kupia Florakis, and she'd brought the dried mushroom powder from there too. It was a dish famous on Santorini, and also Anapliró, where the rich volcanic soil meant it could never be quite replicated.

Roula sniffed the fragrant garlicky air and found her mouth pooling with saliva. The scent was just too strong.

She walked out into the hallway but the scent followed her there, so she went into the bedroom and opened the window and breathed in the fresh air.

It was like having Covid in reverse. She'd suddenly *gained* a sense of smell.

Galen's scent…the soup…

Stop it, Roula told herself, even as she walked into the bathroom and stared at a box of tampons that had been there, unopened, since her arrival.

New job, Roula told herself. New city… Brother facing prison for murder. Family disowning her.

There were many reasons for her period being late.

Yet as the soup bubbled away so too did her emotions, and there were long-ago memories of Dimitrios's temper at the arrival of her period each month.

Of course it had got worse when Ella, already having two sons, had announced that she was pregnant with twins!

But then she remembered getting her period one particular month, when that little baby who never was had made her brave. Roula stood there recalling it—the moment of decision. How could she bring a baby into a world that even she didn't want to be in?

Oh, please, not now…

Thankfully Roula had the foresight to turn off the fava soup before she curled up on her bed and cried.

Galen wasn't having a great night either.

Of course he hadn't made it, but the chef at V's might well weep to see Galen actually wearing his special recipe fava soup.

'No!' Yaya had shouted as she'd flung it towards him.

'Shh…' Galen said now, trying to soothe her. 'Come on, take your pills.'

She spat them out, and for a woman of ninety she was very strong, because not even Galen and the one-on-one nurse were quick enough to stop her from pulling her IV out—and that was before the transfusion had even started.

'Leave me alone!' she shouted. 'Enough!'

'Yaya,' Galen said. 'You need it.'

'You never listen to me!' she yelled. 'I tried to help you and what did I get? Trouble. Every day you bring home trouble. Get out! Give me peace…'

CHAPTER FIFTEEN

'*KALIMERA*, DORA,' SAID ROULA as she joined her in the lift.

'You look amazing, Roula. Glowing.'

'Thank you.'

Dora followed as Roula put the soup in the fridge. 'I've found a new baker's...do you fancy going—?'

Roula cut off the attempt at friendship. 'I'd better get this to him.' She held up the vast coffee mug and made her way in.

'Hey.' Galen looked up as she placed it on the desk and got an eyeful of cleavage. 'Thanks for that.'

'I made the soup...'

'Thanks,' Galen said. 'And I mean that. I faked it and got some from V's, and I ended up wearing it...'

It was sort of unspoken that his *yaya* was getting worse.

'I have a meeting at the care home at five—maybe we could take it over then? We can find out if there are any treatment changes before I dive into lockdown tomorrow...'

'Sure.'

'Then I'm in Rome next week,' Galen said. 'Back Thursday night...'

It must be very, *very* hard for him to leave, Roula thought. And, really, what a wonderful grandson Kupia Florakis had.

'I can visit,' she said.

'Would you?'

'I go there at the weekends anyway. I'll make sure I go and have my coffee with her next week.'

'Thank you.'

Roula peered at him. 'You look dreadful.'

'Thank you,' he said again. 'You don't.' He gave her a thin smile. 'I should never have told you to wear zig-zags that night.'

'Galen!' She raised her eyebrows. 'Let's not talk about personal stuff at work.'

'Where else, then?' He shrugged. 'I just want you to know that I wasn't trying to keep you down.'

'I know that…' She gave him a smile, because it was nice of him to say that. And then she did a dangerous thing. 'You were hot for me. I got that.'

'Yes—and it wasn't convenient in the least.'

'Well, I'll be out of your hair soon.'

'Yes, London's calling,' Galen said. 'Well, they've called HR for document checks, at least.'

'I didn't think they'd move so fast.'

'Funny, that,' Galen said. 'I was just thinking the same about you.'

And though those moments between them were getting less, they still happened. And if it sounded as if she was counting them—well, in reality she was. Wrapping them up like precious jewels and storing them in the trunk labelled 'Galen' in her heart that had been there for ever.

'You used to practise your English on me…'

'Yes,' Roula said, and then it was Galen who took out one of those precious jewels she had stored away and unwrapped it right in front of her.

'"*Does this bus go to town, Mr Conductor?*"' Galen said, and they shared a little laugh at the thought of her ten-year-old self and that time long ago when they'd sat under a tree. A memory so precious to this very day.

'Roula, I know I lied to you…but was what I did so terrible?'

'No.'

'So why the big freeze?'

'There's no freeze.'

'Come off it.'

'I don't want to be on your catch-up list, Galen. Once was empowering—but no more than that.'

'I don't believe you.'

'Excuse me?'

'There's something you're not telling me.'

'I have no idea what you're talking about.'

'Really?' Galen checked. Because, if there wasn't something then we'd be at it now.'

'Now?'

'Yes,' Galen said, and he clicked off the lights, and the room was blacked out apart from the computer screens. 'Seriously, you'd be on my lap now.'

Yes, she wanted to say, *but if you touch me I'll fall apart in your arms, and I can't.*

'You're so full of it…' the new Roula said, and walked off.

They were both very bristly as they walked into the care home later.

'Can you please not mention to her that you're finishing at the end of next week?' Galen asked.

'Of course.'

'Galen!' a resident called.

'Sir.' He nodded, and then turned and gave Roula a little nod. 'Thanks for this. It's appreciated.'

'Kupia Florakis.' Roula gave her a wide smile and sat down. 'How are you?'

'Cold.'

She was very bright this afternoon—and hungry!

'Where's Galen?' she asked.

'He'll be in soon.'

'He's tired.'

Roula breathed in, because she'd been trying not to notice the dark rings under his eyes or the fact that he'd lost weight.

'Look at him here,' his *yaya* said as she slurped Roula's soup and laughed at a photo. 'He was so cheeky… Some days his *mamá* would say, "Galen is too bold."'

'Did she?'

'Oh, yes. His father was a professor,' Yaya said as she gulped down more soup. 'I was so cross… He was too old for her, but he did love her so.'

'Your daughter?'

'They were so happy.' She nodded and ran a finger over the photo, stopping at the little gold cross round her daughter's neck. 'I had to sell all the gold to buy books for Galen and for him to go to summer school.'

'I'm sure they would have approved.'

'I could never sell this, though.'

God, just talk to her Galen!

She wanted to drag him out of his meeting with the carers and bring him to her bedside. Because these were some beautiful memories his *yaya* had. Funny and kind and filled with so much love.

But, yes, it was tough at times to listen.

Galen would have loved to be dragged out of his meeting.

'So without the blood transfusions…' He stopped, because he knew the answer to that. 'We can try now she's calmer?'

'Yes.' The doctor nodded.

'But she gets distressed at the needle insertion,' Galen said. 'Even with the numbing gel.'

'Yes.'

It wasn't as clear-cut as he would like it to be.

He wanted to call Roula in, but that really would be pushing the limits of friendship, or even an occasional lover, or anything really.

And until now he had always preferred making decisions alone.

Walking back into his *yaya*'s room when he'd just signed off on her life was the oddest moment.

She wasn't frail, or visibly dying. Instead she was perky and sprightly and scoffing her food!

'You're eating!' Galen said as he came in. 'That's good.'

'Galen!' She beamed. 'Roula came to see me.'

'She ate it all.' Roula smiled and stood, then addressed Yaya. 'There's more in the fridge for you. I'll say goodnight, Kupia…'

'Kyrios?' Yaya suddenly said.

'Yes.' Roula nodded.

'Nemo…' she sneered.

'Yaya…' Galen tried quickly to intervene. 'Do you want some more soup?'

'Brute,' Yaya said, and then she turned her little currant eyes to Roula, as if seeing her for the first time. 'Roula Drakos?' she checked, and Galen saw, almost before it manifested itself, the flash of contempt in Yaya's eyes. *'Bástardos!'* Yaya shouted. 'That Dimitrios.'

Yikes, Galen thought. *Not so coherent after all. Or just very accurate…*

'Roula.' He tried to pull her away. 'She says stuff.'

'Pig!' Yaya shouted.

'Galen!' And it was Roula who lost it then as Yaya raged loudly on. 'She's right!'

And then he had it in stereo.

'Bástardos!' Roula said, with so much venom. 'Your *yaya* speaks an awful lot of truth if only you'd let her…' She shook her head as the nurse approached with sedation. 'She's fine,' Roula snapped. 'Just close the door if she's being too noisy for you.'

And then she took Kupia Florakis's hand.

She would do this.

For Galen.

As hard as it would be, she would sit there and let his *yaya* be heard.

'Nemo beat Galen…' Kupia Florakis wept. 'He would hide the bruises.'

'Yes,' Roula said. 'I know.'

'And your husband,' she sneered. 'Horrible boy.' She raised a gnarled finger and jabbed it in the air. 'Little Benji…he kicked him down the street. I shouted at him. Every time I saw him I let him know. They called me *trelós…*' she shouted. 'But I know what I saw. No one believed me.'

'I do,' Roula said, but her voice was husky. And then she felt Galen's hand, warm on her shoulder. 'I believe you, Kupia.'

'Bástardos!'

'Yes,' Roula agreed. 'He really is. But listen. Nemo—he's in prison…' she saw Yaya's eyes widen '…and Dimitrios has a bigger judge to deal with.' She pointed skywards. 'So now they have to pay their dues.'

'I couldn't stop them…'

'No,' Roula agreed. 'But you did the best you could. Look at Galen now,' she said. 'Look at the lovely man you raised.'

And then she moved her shoulder to remove Galen's hand, because she couldn't do this any more, and she gave Kupia a hug and walked out on legs that were shaky, and found the restrooms and threw up…

But that was for Benji.

When she came out Galen was waiting, looking as grey as she felt.

'I'm going to get some air,' she said.

She sat on the steps outside and almost wished she hadn't said anything, or that the nurse had come in with the sedation five minutes earlier. But, no, there was an odd relief that it was out in the open now.

With the one person she trusted to never tell.

'Go to her,' Roula said when he followed her out. 'Galen, it's not Anapliró disappearing that she's worried about—it's the memory of her daughter.'

'I can see that. But right now I'm more worried about you.'

'Please,' Roula said, 'she hasn't said anything I don't know. Well, I didn't know about Benji. But, yes, I'm quite sure he was capable of that. Go back in.'

'No, I want to listen to you now.'

'It's done,' Roula said. 'Galen, I know you keep your word… well, apart from that one time.'

'I don't regret telling you that,' Galen said. 'I just wish it hadn't come out in the way it did.'

'Galen, you can never speak of this to anyone.'

'I would never do that.'

'I'm not talking about respecting my privacy.'

'I get that it might change things for Nemo.'

'That was about money,' Roula said. 'No one knew about my marriage. They were both bad.'

'Yes.' He paused for a moment. 'You're not on your own, Roula.'

'Oh, I am in this,' she said.

'I know now…'

'You don't!' she refuted. 'You don't know anything about me

or what it was like. I was eighteen and I had no idea. That night with you was the first time I'd ever actually made love.'

Galen sat there, and in his eyes she saw she'd confirmed what at some level he'd already known.

And then she shared details she'd never thought she would.

'I looked at that bed,' Roula told him. 'And every day I prayed that I'd never have to lie in it again. What does that make me?'

'Normal.'

'Culpable.' She saw him frown. 'I mean in court. If they questioned me…' She shivered in the warm night air. 'He's pleading guilty, though. I'm dreading it.'

'Of course.'

'I was planning to leave him,' she said. 'I didn't know how, or where I could go—there was no retreat then. I didn't have a job. It took me a long time to realise just how bad my marriage really was,' she went on. 'After he died, I mean. It was a lot easier to be a grieving widow than to deal with it all. I was just coming to the point when I'd decided to speak to someone—a counsellor or something—but then I found the gas cylinder and that window closed. I knew I couldn't reveal it to anyone.'

'Well, I'm glad that you've told me. Well, not *glad*. I wish you'd been able to tell me before we—'

'Please,' Roula sneered. 'You'd have run a mile.'

'I wouldn't have.'

'Or you'd have treated me like glass.' She was adamant. 'It was better for me that you didn't know. I *hate* it that you know!'

Galen sat silent.

'Can we never speak of this again?'

'If that's what you want. But if you ever—'

She shook her head. 'I won't.'

'Roula?'

'I mean it, Galen. I loathe what he did, and I hate it that you know, and I can't stand how you'll look at me now.'

'What?'

'Would that night have happened if you'd known what you do now?'

Galen took a breath, because so many times he said the wrong thing, and he knew that he could not get it wrong now. Not for his sake, or their sake, but for her sake and for the sake of the next sex she had.

Because in bed… Well, he'd paused for a moment and then thought about it later…

But did he tell her?

'Would you tell me to get on your lap now?' Roula demanded.

The old Galen would have said, *Settle down, Roula, we're outside the care home*—but he didn't know what to say now.

'It kind of takes the spontaneity away, doesn't it?' She looked at him, and for once he stayed silent. 'I want a new start,' the new Roula announced. 'I'm taking that job in London. I'm leaving next week.'

And then, as simply as that, she took off her wedding band. She didn't even toss it away with venom—just let it slip to the ground with a little clink and then watched it roll away.

'Dues paid,' Roula said. 'I'm going to go.'

'I'll walk you…'

'Galen.' She stood up and looked at him. 'I don't need you walking me home.'

'Maybe I'd like to,' Galen said. 'To tell you the truth, I wouldn't mind a drink.' He took a breath. 'Just to talk… I don't know.'

She gave a mirthless laugh. 'I don't need your carefully crafted words, Galen.'

'I might need—' He stopped. 'Whatever you want.'

Yaya was as docile as a lamb when he returned.

'What did they do to you today?' she askedm and frowned when she saw his strained face.

'Who?'

'They hurt you?' she said.

'No.' Galen attempted a smile. 'Maybe…' he admitted. And he took the little scrawny hand, all covered in bruises from the drips and the medicine he'd insisted upon. 'They hurt someone I care about.'

'That's worse,' Yaya said. 'I would have taken ten beatings to spare you one.'

CHAPTER SIXTEEN

ROULA LAY ON her stomach and thought she had never wanted to call in sick so much in her life.

She was bitter with regret at telling Galen, and raw with shame. And, yes, she'd read all those self-help books, and, no, it wasn't her fault.

Her very soul felt tainted, though.

She closed her eyes when she thought of some of the more intimate details she'd shared.

Oh, she did not want to face Galen and witness the awkward dart of his eyes.

But then she remembered that, as of now, Galen would be boarding a flight and soon winging his way to Rome.

It was a relief, and yet not… In six short weeks she'd become accustomed to having Galen in her days, and after Friday she would not.

And so she climbed out of the lovely bed—second only to Galen's—and went into the bathroom. Through sheer will power alone she refused to cave in to the nausea.

Roula dressed in one of her new dresses—a linen dress chosen by Leo, in a gorgeous burnt orange—chose flat shoes today, and arrived just before eight.

'Good luck,' Dora said as she walked past. 'It's Monday.'

'He's here?' Roula was startled. 'But I thought he was in Rome.'

'Clearly,' said Galen. 'Given how late you are.'

'No.' Roula shook her head, blushing as she turned to face him. 'Actually, I'm five minutes early.'

'Oh, so we're on contract time now, are we?' he snapped.

God, he didn't even look at her—just turned on his heel and walked off. And for the hundredth time she regretted baring her soul.

'Don't take it personally,' Dora said, just as she had the first day.

However, it *was* personal this time. Roula was sure.

Not that she would let it show.

So she held her palms skywards as he stalked off and turned to Dora. 'What does "on contract time" even mean?'

'Don't worry—he told me off too.' Dora was affronted. 'I was just checking my horoscope before I started, and he saw and said, "Are you ever going to do some actual work?"'

'That was mean of him,' Roula said.

'I told him this place would fall apart without me,' Dora grumbled. 'Well, I didn't actually say that…'

Roula was trying not to smile. Galen actually had the patience of a saint where Dora was concerned. In fact, he'd created an entire job around her lack of commitment!

'It's his *yaya*…' Dora whispered.

'What?' Roula stepped in. 'Was she taken ill?'

'No…' Dora motioned for her to close the door. 'Apparently there was a meeting. I just heard him on the phone to Galilee, asking about a bed.'

Roula swallowed. Galilee was a palliative care home.

'I think he's actually going to keep her where she is, but you know Galen—there'll be a thousand second opinions before he makes up his mind.' Dora looked up then. 'Were you there?'

'Not at the meeting.' Roula shook her head. 'I was just dropping off some soup.'

'Well, that's all I know.' Dora gave a worried sigh. 'Poor Galen. From the sound of things, I don't think it will be very long.'

Oh, no…

Vividly she recalled him standing at the door, smiling, pleased to see that his grandmother had eaten, and then…

And then it had become all about *Roula, Roula, Roula*. Dealing with her stuff when there should surely have been a moment for his.

He'd asked her to go for a drink.

He had actually been asking to speak with her…

Damn!

'Galen?' She knocked on the open glass door. He didn't look up. 'I just heard about Yaya.'

'It's fine.'

'Clearly it's not. Galen, it never entered my head that you'd been through a difficult meeting. It should have…she's so frail. I just wasn't thinking straight.'

'Of course not.' He let out a breath. 'Nor was I.'

'They'd just told you?'

'No,' Galen said.

'I'm not with you…'

He relented a touch. 'I kind of told them.'

'Oh.' She waited for details, but none were forthcoming. 'What did you say?'

'Roula…' he was very direct '…we can't talk about you, correct?'

She nodded.

'Yet you feel we can talk about me?'

'I'm your PA.'

'Till Friday.'

'Galen—' she started.

'Save it for the sympathy card, Roula…' He glanced up. 'Airmail, I presume?'

The bite to his tone had her breath catching.

'When do you fly?' he asked.

'Monday.'

His phone buzzed then. 'If you'll excuse me? I need to take this.'

It wasn't a great week.

There was just a pall of sadness in the gleaming space—and him saying, no, he did not need more fava soup, nor any of her endless offers to bring in food.

Her last day was as flat as Kristina's had been.

Just a matter of tying up all the loose ends.

'Roula!' It was Dora at her door. 'Kristina's here.'

And for all Kristina's coldness there was so much kindness. For there was genius Luka, wearing the blue booties Dora had knitted and with a blue teddy given to him by someone else, everything blue, blue, blue…

'You look amazing,' Kristina said to Roula. 'I hear it's all gone very well.'

'Thank you.'

'No, thank *you* for agreeing to go to the ball. I thought I'd be able to go but, as I was just telling Galen, I can't be way from my breast pump for more than two hours. He said not to worry.'

It was funny to see the guys all blushing, and Kristina actually gave Dora a little wink as a few of them scuttled off.

'Wait!' Dora called them back. 'Kristina's here for another reason. Surprise!' she said to Roula.

'*You* get cake?' Kristina said.

And champagne, and cola, and even Galen made a brief appearance.

'Will you miss us?' Dora asked.

'Yes.' Roula smiled.

'We've still got the ball,' Nico reminded her, and Roula could feel Galen's eyes on her as she flushed.

They all ate cake, and then Galen asked if he could have a word with her before she left.

'Could you close the door?' he asked.

'Why?'

'It's all right. I'm not going to dim the lights…'

Roula blushed.

'I want to talk to you in case I don't see you again. What I have to say has nothing to do with us.'

Roula closed the door.

'Sit down.'

She did.

'I might not be able to say the right thing, but Dora's a good friend to have—so stop shutting her out.'

'Pardon?'

'That's it,' Galen said. 'All I have to say on the matter. Thank you for everything you've done—and I do mean that. You've cheered the place up…well, for the most part. And, on a more personal note, you've been a great help to me and my grand-mother. It's appreciated.'

'Thank you,' Roula said, and stood. 'I've really enjoyed my time.'

'Go.'

Oh, but she didn't want to.

Not just because of the Galen thing, but all of it.

But that was what they did here—a little wave... 'See you...' Only Roula couldn't do that.

'Can I ask you something?' Roula said. 'Your honest, unfiltered opinion...?'

'Are you sure you want it?'

'Yes,' Roula said. 'Am I making the most dreadful mistake?'

'Career-wise?' he checked.

She felt as if they were sitting under that tree sharing lunch, back to where he'd helped her with the bits she didn't understand.

'No.' He sounded honest. 'I think it's a great move. For all Yolanda's talk of semi-retiring, she'll never hand over the reins...'

'What about friendship-wise? Yaya, I mean.'

'Roula, I wouldn't ask Costa or Leo to cancel a lunch over Yaya. I hope they'll come to the funeral, but only if they're in Athens... So, no, you don't owe me anything friendship-wise.'

'Us-wise?'

'Us?' Galen checked. 'We had sex once... Had ouzo been involved it could have been twice...'

'Thanks,' she said. 'For being honest.'

'I haven't finished being honest yet,' Galen said. 'Why now, Roula? Seriously?' he said. 'Why, when we were getting good, would you choose to go now?'

'You said you didn't want a relationship.'

'So did you,' Galen fired back. 'That was the deal we made. But then things changed. You told me some things that I don't believe you would drop into any casual conversation. You brought me right up close to here...' he jabbed at his chest. '...and then you told me you were on the next flight out.'

'It wasn't like that...'

'Pretty close.'

'I told you so that you'd open up too.'

'You're not that magnanimous,' Galen said, and Roula swallowed at his confrontational words. 'Deny it all you like, but we were getting close—and now you've decided to run.'

'Some things are just too big and too sordid to come back from.'

'Says who?' he challenged. 'Are you still reading from the *Book of Drakos*?'

'That's mean.'

'Yes,' Galen said. 'I can be. But so can you. Like it or not, I know you—or I did once. And before you tell me you can't make it to the ball, know this: I don't think *I'm* going to be able to make it. Believe it or not, it's work. I would like some notes made now Kristina cannot be there… And Leo has got quite a bit hanging on this bloody gown getting photographed, so just know that too, before you run off.'

'I'm not running off,' Roula said. 'I'm here, aren't I?'

'You haven't been here since you got out of my bed, Roula,' he accused. 'Now, will you be there tomorrow?'

Caught, she nodded.

'Good,' he said. 'I suggest you bring your Dictaphone. It says "no recording" on the invitation, but if you do it will be easier for you to write up your notes.'

'Anything else?'

'Not that I can think of,' Galen said. 'How about you?'

Roula shook her head, too petrified to share her unconfirmed fears. 'No.'

CHAPTER SEVENTEEN

'OH, MY GOODNESS...' Leo stepped back and admired not so much Roula as his new creation.

The gown was almost white, but not quite, and of the softest velvet with a halter neck. Roula didn't even recognise herself. The gown clung everywhere, and her hair was up so high that even her neck felt exposed, and as Leo and Deacon drove her to the offices in Kolonaki Square her teeth were chattering with nerves.

And she couldn't even have a glass of champagne.

'Roula!' The doorman smiled and in she went. Everyone looked stunning. Nico in a tux, Dora in floor-length silver... This ball was far bigger than she had envisaged.

It would seem Galen really was a no-show. But everyone was beautiful, and there was such a buzz in the air that she didn't even need Galen to feel excited for tonight.

She'd just prefer him to be there, that was all.

To think she'd nearly missed this, Roula thought as she stood with Dora and Nico and all the people who had been strangers to her just six weeks ago.

'Champagne?' Nico handed her a glass.

'No, no.' Roula smiled. 'I'm sticking to water for now. Maybe later.'

She had tampons in her bag, but then she thought of the dress she was wearing and it was odd... In the moment she hoped she *didn't* get her period tonight. She actually wasn't sure she wanted it after all. Or rather, she would be okay if it was nine months late.

Yes, she had a new job, and they wouldn't be thrilled, but look at Kristina...

And she had always lived frugally and had money saved.

It was odd to stand there and return to the absence of fear that she had found in Galen's arms.

To feel strong alone for the very first time.

To feel happy.

She smiled widely at Dora, who was chattering on.

'I said, maybe she's died!'

'Oh, sorry…' Roula wiped off her smile. 'My mind was miles away.'

'Well, the ball won't be the same without him,' Dora said. 'For all he's difficult, he's the best boss.'

'Yes…'

'Galen was the first person I told that I wasn't happy at home.'

Roula swallowed and thought about what Galen had said about Dora, how he'd suggested they pair up.

'He helped me to leave.' Dora sighed. 'Anyway, I'm sure he's where he needs to be tonight.'

Galen wasn't.

He was all dressed up—well, for the most part—but Yaya would not let his hand go, and he did not know how to pull it away when finally they were speaking.

'I saw the *kandylakia*,' he told her. 'Candles still lit.'

She smiled.

'I put flowers there, and there were some other recent ones.'

'Where's Roula?' Yaya asked, as she often did.

'At a work function,' he said. 'And she heads off to London for her new job soon.'

'Hiding.'

'Not any more,' Galen said, and brushed the little strands of grey hair back. 'I tell you, once the shackles came off…' He gave her a smile. 'She's doing what she needs to.'

And he needed to see her before she went. Because yesterday's exchange had left such a bitter taste in his mouth.

Was it selfish to ask her to put her life on hold and be here for the next couple of weeks?

He'd hoped for more.

And offered her so little.

'I bought her a leaving gift,' Galen said.

He'd put more thought into this gift than he ever had before and was rather pleased with himself. It was an olive branch. A very expensive olive branch. He would take it to the office tomorrow.

'A nice one,' he added.

'Why would you do that?' Yaya sneered. 'Stupid boy. Go to your party.'

'It's not a party—it's work.'

'Go.'

He kissed her bony cheek and pulled the blanket up around her shoulders. Finally he felt that with Yaya he'd got things right.

He was late, but they were all meeting for a drink at the office, so he told his driver to take him there first.

Galen was nervous when things like this didn't faze him. He had lozenges from the doctor now, little minty squares of chalk, and he sucked on one as he saw that the cars were all outside. They hadn't left yet.

Would she even be there? he wondered, and then reminded himself, as he had to an awful lot these days, that this was work.

'We should keep in touch,' Roula said to Dora. 'I mean, if you want?'

'I'd like that.' Dora smiled. 'Maybe I'll come to London. Do you think I could get a business trip out of him?'

'Probably!' Roula laughed.

'I think we have to move down to the cars,' Dora said. 'Oh, look—here's Galen.'

There was a lurch to Roula's heart as she turned around and Galen came dashing in. He was so stunning that it was hard to believe she had once been coiled around him, that his beautiful mouth had devoured hers. And elsewhere!

Her face flew to fire just at thinking about that.

'You look beautiful, Dora,' Galen said. 'Can you sort this?' He pulled out an arm and Dora started sorting his cufflinks.

Clearly he was late with sad reason.

'How is she?' she asked.

'Comfortable,' he said as he put on his tie. 'Hate these.'

Then he spoke to Nico and a few of the others as the cars waited to take them for the short drive to beautiful Syntagma Square, where the ball was being held.

And Roula looked on, a spectator now, until he saw her.

'Roula.' He came over and as always was polite. 'You look stunning.'

'Thank you.'

That was it. All those hours spent getting ready and he simply nodded, and complimented her just as he had Dora. Well, perhaps even a little less than he had Dora.

But it was not a night for sulking.

Even Nico seemed enthusiastic. 'I thought Roula might come with us in the second car,' he said.

'Roula will come with me,' Galen said. 'You are with the development team. I need Roula to go through my speech.'

They were already a little late, a little rushed, but they were all present and correct and it was their night of nights in a world she didn't know.

And she thought she would remember this for ever—how he rolled his eyes as they all argued about who was getting in what car.

'You want me to go through your speech?' she asked.

'No, I was just being helpful,' Galen said. 'You have a fan.'

'I know!' She blew out a breath. 'How old *is* Nico?'

'Nineteen.'

'God…'

Galen laughed, but it faded halfway and he closed his eyes for a brief second, as if he couldn't quite believe he'd got here.

'How is she?' she asked again.

'As I said, comfortable.' Galen nodded, and then she realised he was putting his game face on.

The passed the Hellenic Parliament and surely Athens was taunting her for leaving? For it was as if all the stops had been pulled out tonight. Everything was lit up as if to tell her to stay.

'Better than the school trip?' Galen asked.

'So much better,' Roula said, and wanted to add, *But only because you're here*. 'I lied,' she admitted. 'I have been to Athens before.'

'To see the police?'

She nodded. 'I did the right thing, didn't I?' she asked, because it might be the last chance she'd have to ask this man she trusted so very much. 'Going to the police?'

'Completely,' he said. 'I always said you were brave.'

'You did.' And it meant the world that he thought she was right—his opinion mattered very much.

Galen watched her look skywards in the little ritual she did when she was trying not to cry.

'No tears,' Galen said.

'Do you have a tissue?'

'No.' Galen said, but there were little serviettes for the drinks, and he passed her one of those. 'Yaya's in a good place,' he said gently. 'I owe that to you.'

'You don't.'

'Seriously, I've told them she's never been in a peaceful place in the thirty-five years I've known her, so they must stop sedating her.'

Roula laughed.

'She won't stop talking…' He squeezed her hand. 'So thank you for facilitating that.'

'I'm so glad.'

He looked at her then. 'You're allowed to leave, Roula.'

She wasn't sure that she wanted to, though.

'I'm sorry if I sulked about it,' he added. 'You don't deserve that. And now we're going to have a great night. We deserve that, yes?'

'Yes.'

'So let's do it.'

'Arati,' Roula said, whenever she was asked who had made her gown—just as Leo had told her to do.

'From his NYC collection?' they asked.

'I believe so,' Galen said, and named the colour on Leo's behalf. As they walked in, he said, 'Mist over the Aegean… That's what you remind me of tonight.'

It was the most beautiful thing anyone had ever said to her.

'You're famous here,' Roula said, as they stepped off the red carpet.

'In odd ways,' Galen agreed.

There were game charms on the tables, and Roula collected a few for her nephews and nieces. Even if the adults in the family weren't talking to her, she would send them with love.

'Red or white?' the waiter asked.

Galen declined. 'Not for me. I have to give a speech.' He looked at Roula.

'Nor me,' Roula said—and not just because of potential mini-Galens, but because really she was having great difficulty holding on to her emotions.

He hated these things, Roula knew—not that even she could tell, for now they were seated and he was laughing.

'No Kristina?' asked a guest wandering past.

'Not tonight,' Galen said.

'Oh, is she still on maternity leave?'

'Roula is my guest tonight,' Galen said.

No, he was not discussing Kristina and her pumping situation. God, he hated these things...

But then he took a breath and spoke to the man. 'Roula is from Anapliró...'

'Where the new game is based!'

'Loosely based,' Galen corrected, but he smiled. 'Do you know,' he told Roula when the man had drifted on, 'HR has informed me that I have to provide a room for Kristina?'

'For what?'

He glanced at her breasts. 'You know...'

'Oh.'

'And a fridge,' Galen said. Except he had lost his thread a little bit...because had Roula's breasts doubled in size again?

'You could put it next to the dogs-on-wheels room,' Roula said.

They both laughed, and it was the first time Galen had sat at one of these things and really laughed. Even while he was sad.

He remembered rest of the table. 'Dora, what do you think of the new version of the game?'

'I can't wait to try it,' Dora said.

Roula watched as Galen and Nico shared a small smile.

Aside from loving Galen, she adored them all. And, honestly, it was the best last night in Athens, with the most amazing, wonderful man, and if she didn't love him it would be perfect.

'Roula doesn't like fish,' he said as he swapped their dishes, and then he pulled a face. 'Actually, nor do I tonight.'

She had a creamy pasta dish, that was very nice. Dora didn't want the fish either, but it seemed Hector was happy to swap with her.

'You're quiet Galen,' Hector commented as Roula slipped off for some air.

'Hector…' Dora warned, and she must have given him a little kick, or said something, because Hector quickly stopped asking why Galen was quiet.

Only Roula knew it wasn't about Yaya…

'There you are.' Galen found her on a balcony, drinking in the delicious view. 'Speeches soon.'

'Coming.'

'We've got a few moments.'

'Yes.'

'So, London here you come?'

'Yes…a clean slate.'

'Your slate's already clean, Roula.' He looked at her then. 'If you do meet the perfect guy, will you tell him?'

She thought for a moment. 'No.'

And still Galen stood there, and he knew he could stay quiet, and perhaps that would be wise, but he preferred honesty.

'Roula,' he said. 'I already knew.'

She turned.

'I knew before you told Yaya. I knew there was something wrong when we danced—not the specifics, but…'

'You knew?'

'I don't delve into people's sex lives. I don't care if someone here's slept with half the ballroom. But after we danced I knew you'd been hurt, and then when we made love… I hoped I was wrong, but…' He took her hand and he pressed it not on his chest but high on his stomach. 'I feel it here…with you.'

'What?'

'I've cancelled my endoscopy. It's his name that's been making me ill.'

'Oh…'

'So when you asked me to kiss you—yes, I was surprised, but I was also very mindful that you do not give away kisses. It was the most impractical kiss,' Galen said, 'given you were due to start working for me, but…'

'Sympathy?'

He thought for a moment. 'I was trying to do the right thing for you. It seemed right at the time.' He looked at her then. 'I guess I was wrong.'

'No.'

'Then why can't you talk to me?'

He went inside, leaving her staring up at the sky.

It was such a lovely night, and she could never have nipped out and taken notes, for as she listened to the speeches his name was quite a regular occurrence.

Hector announced that the game was near completion and would be available in the New Year, to thunderous applause.

'I can't wait!' Dora clapped the loudest.

Roula honestly was bemused. Did she not even know she'd been playing it all this time?

It would seem that this man did a lot of good in the world.

But a rather more hard-ass PA might be required for a man trying to set up a financial system that would work in an impoverished part of the planet. Or when society collapsed and fiat currency was worth nothing…

That brilliant brain, Roula thought.

They were all applauding as Hector returned to his seat, and she went out to the loo for a little cry and checked her phone.

Catch up later?

He had a nerve. That was her second thought.

Her first was, *Yes, please.*

Except she'd be a terrible catch-up girl. She'd cry over Kupia Florakis, or confess her undying love, or admit that her period was late.

And so she didn't answer.

Galen didn't seem bothered by her lack of response.

'Hey, Dora, come and dance,' he said.

She watched as he danced with Dora. Clearly the ball was her night of nights.

Galen danced with all the women at the table, in fact, and Roula danced with Nico, and then had to make a dash away from him because she had a dreadful feeling that he was about to ask her out.

She gulped water.

'Come on,' Galen said, taking her hand. 'You haven't turned him down?'

'He hasn't asked yet.' She breathed out. 'I managed to get away.'

'We can dance two dances,' Galen said. 'I did three with Dora, two with the lady who smells of roses, so we have a clear run.'

'Good.'

'Can I ask you something?' Galen said, and he felt her stiffen in his arms.

'Of course,' she said.

'Do you think Hector and Dora…?'

'No…' She looked over and saw they were dancing. 'Maybe…'

'Please, no,' Galen said. 'It would be hell having them both pushing me for the next game.' Then he told her a something, that he hoped would show he trusted her more than anyone. 'She does deserve to be happy, though. Talk to Dora sometime.'

'I have.'

'Good.'

'She's going to ask you to send her on a business trip.' She draped her arm around his neck as they danced. 'I thought you were gamer boy?'

'I am.'

'Crypto kid?'

'That too.'

'I'm not coming back to your apartment.'

'So I'll make you come here.'

'Galen!'

'Yes,' he said. 'Can't you feel me?'

Roula said nothing.

'I can feel your breasts flat on my chest,' Galen said. 'Are they taped up?'

'No…' she smiled.

'They must be,' he said. 'Because this dress is backless, and they are very beautiful, but I can't feel…'

'I think the bra is inbuilt,' she said.

He put his hand in the small of her back, and her skin felt so warm she might have been standing in front of a fire before placing it there.

'Maybe dancing isn't so pointless,' he said.

'No…'

He dusted her arm with his fingers, as he had wanted to that night, and pulled her in closer. And he knew that for all the things he didn't get in this life, he *did* get Roula. Of that, he was sure.

'I knew you were about to cry on the beach,' Galen said into her ear. 'That's why I came over.'

She was very still.

'You do this thing with your hands and your eyes. And when you're upset you get angry…'

'Galen…' She felt as if she were being pulled apart even while held in his arms. This was a character assessment when she did not want scrutiny. But he held her in a way that she did not want to leave.

'I don't know what I've done,' he admitted. 'I can't work that out.'

'Good,' Roula said, for she did not want him to know how much she loved him.

'Our dance is over,' Galen said, and she heard the music still a little more gently than it had the night they had met, when Leo had crashed. 'History repeats itself.'

'Does it?'

'You went off into the night last time.'

'If it wasn't for Costa we'd never have seen each other again.'

'Believe what you want, Roula, but I'd have got in touch.'

'I said no to you.'

'Yes,' he agreed. 'And I respected that. But I knew something had been left undone…'

Roula swallowed. 'As I said, history repeats itself.'

They were back at the table.

'Come on Dora,' Galen said. 'One more.'

Roula was left with Hector, who was looking longingly at Dora.

Thankfully Nico had discovered someone from social media, who was now draped around him, and so Roula collected up her purse and knew she could leave.

The sensible part of her mind was reminding her that having this conversation with Galen might be better done from afar, because she really didn't want him to see her breaking down.

Except she felt ridiculously alive tonight.

On fire.

Brave, even.

So it was Roula who took out her phone and sat at the table as if butter wouldn't melt in her mouth and replied to his text.

Yes.

She got a smiley face in return.

CHAPTER EIGHTEEN

'YOU'LL HAVE TO close your eyes,' Galen said as he led her through the apartment. 'Your gift is in the bedroom.'

'What a surprise!' Roula said in a droll voice, but he came up behind her and his hand covered her eyes.

'I'm serious,' he said. 'I didn't have time to wrap them.'

'Them?' she checked.

'Just close your eyes.'

He led her into the bedroom and she stood there waiting—for what? A naked Galen? Gosh he made her thoughts depraved…

But she was not scared. It was odd, but even in the dark she wasn't frightened.

'Open them.'

'Wow!' Roula said, forcing a smile as she surveyed a new luggage set. Gosh, clearly Galen wasn't the King of Romance! 'It's beautiful.'

'Isn't it?' Galen said. 'They all come with a lifetime guarantee.'

She guessed in his own way he was giving her his blessing to leave. 'Thank you,' Roula said. 'I mean that. I'm…'

Underwhelmed.

Except she shouldn't be, Roula knew, for it was the best luggage set ever, and he was the sexiest man in the world, and he was trying to make this right.

'I'm touched.'

Sort of.

Not.

She felt as if she'd got on a bus headed in the wrong direction, or on a ferry that was taking her to a port she didn't want to go to but had insisted upon. Everything was chugging along in the wrong direction, and she didn't know how to turn things around.

'Come here,' Galen said, and he took her hand and led her towards the terrace and the view she had missed the first time around.

She loved Athens, Roula thought as she stepped out onto the terrace. And, yes, Galen had the best view. For the Temple of

Olympian Zeus was lit up in the foreground, so close, and high and proud behind it stood the Acropolis.

'Worth it?' he asked.

'So worth it,' Roula said, and even as she drank in the view her words were for him. 'You can never move,' she smiled. 'I mean, how would you top that?'

'I'm very lucky,' Galen said. 'I know that.'

'So am I,' Roula said, because tonight she felt so too. 'I never thought I'd be...' *Where to start?* 'Dancing, making new friends, firing off texts requesting sex!'

'It's such an effective method of communication.' He smiled. 'I'm teasing.'

She smiled as he took her arms in his hands,

'It's been a brilliant six weeks,' Galen said. 'Well, perhaps not for you.'

'It's been the very best that it could have been. I honestly thought I'd be facing it alone.'

Yes, she was minus a family, but she had a cast of new friends and a new sense of herself now. She was no longer Guest Services Manager Roula, the woman he'd first met, or PA Roula as she'd tried to be, or 'poor Roula', as some of them back home called her.

But neither was she the New Roula she'd tried so hard to create. The one who stood in a sexy ball gown and knew what to do and how to say goodbye.

'I don't want to cry,' she said.

'Tomorrow,' he said, and kissed her...softly at first.

Roula had guessed she was going to get gentle Galen, all tender, now that he knew the truth. Except she didn't know Galen, nor the way he could kiss her in full view of Athens.

He sucked at the tip of her tongue, just a bit, and then he sucked at her bottom lip. And then, when she thought she knew his kiss, he changed it. He kissed her so hard, so deep, that if the sky hadn't been navy then it might have turned pink, for he was devouring her with his mouth and then denying her his kiss.

They were right on the edge, looking at each other, almost challenging each other—to what, neither quite knew.

'Come inside,' he said.

She knew she must, or they would be arrested, or filmed, or who knew what.

He led her not to his bed, but to the most beautiful bathroom in the world.

'Are we having a bath?' she asked.

'Takes too long to fill,' Galen said. 'Maybe later.'

'I love your bathroom.'

'It's the best.'

She looked in the mirror and he stood behind her. 'Why are we in here?'

'So I can look at you,' Galen said. 'At us.'

He looked stunning, end-of-the-night beautiful, and somehow her dress looked even better in the soft antique mirror and she could admit something.

'It feels vain, but I think I look beautiful...' She couldn't stop looking—not so much at herself, more at *them*.

'Tonight, everyone is beautiful. Monday, not so much...' Galen said.

Roula did not want to think about Monday, and she didn't have to right now—because he was undoing the little hooks on her dress between deep kisses to her shoulder, and she watched his lips on her skin and the gentle suck of his mouth. Every now and then the hooks irritated him, so he gave in and pressed his hands into her breasts, kissed her neck as she watched.

'I don't want to leave a mark,' he said, getting back to the little clasps. 'Not a good look for your first day at work.'

She flushed with tense anger as he brought up Monday again, when they would be no more, but then he dealt with the last clasp and exposed her breasts.

Roula stared at them, all white and creamy, and the ridiculous thing was it was as if she had never really seen them before—well, at least not until Galen. She had just stuffed them into a bra. Now they fascinated her. He was stroking them from behind and his head was lowering, so she could only see his hands. He kissed the notches at the top of her spine, and then her scapula as if it was the most vital part of her. She had barely known it existed, let alone that his mouth upon it might make her want to fold over.

'I've wanted to do that all night,' he said, coming up to

stand. 'And this...' Galen said, and he helped her step out of the dress so she stood only in lacy knickers and heels.

'Look,' he told her.

'Galen...'

She was the only one near naked, and she knew it would be a whole lot easier to be buried in his kiss than to confront the sight of herself in the mirror. 'Galen behind glass,' she said, looking at his hands on her stomach. His fingers were creeping into the lace, and she told him one of her secrets. 'I touched myself once, thinking about you.'

'Did you?'

Roula nodded. 'Before...'

'I like knowing that.' He was kissing the skin between her neck and her shoulder.

'I didn't know what I was doing.'

'Show me.' He took her hand and he guided it down, and his hand was over hers.

'It was one morning,' she said. 'I pictured you in uniform.'

'Did you do it like this?' he asked, taking her finger and making it stroke her slowly.

'No...' She was upended with the memory of a kiss that didn't exist, of how it had felt when the only desire she'd known was Galen. 'Like this.'

She turned, and now it was Roula leading, undoing his buttons just to get to his skin, kissing him as she had wanted to then. Hungry, desperate kisses. And even if her mouth didn't know what to do, it worked, because he met her as she climbed up him and gathered her in.

His tongue was duelling with hers as he tore her brand-new knickers. She was at his neck now, feeling the slap of his belt coming undone on her inner thigh, and then he guided her onto him.

'Look,' he told her.

And she rested her head on his shoulder and watched his taut buttocks in the mirror as he thrust in. Her breasts were flat against him and her hair was falling down.

'My turn,' he said.

She felt the cold of marble on her bottom. Galen was looking down on them and very slowly he took her, stroking her curls, playing with her, and Roula could see her own thighs shaking.

'Slowly,' he said, and then he swore, and his hand went for the cabinet behind her.

They were giving in. They were having the sex they should have had way back then, because now they were beyond sensible.

'You're really bad for me, Roula.'

'I know.' She was coming just a little, right on the edge of it, and just so fascinated by him…by them, by the absolute freedom he allowed her. 'I want to see you come,' she told him.

'Shh…' Galen said, because he was doing all he could not to do that.

'I want to.' Her voice was rising, urgent—imperative.

As he swelled he pulled out, and she glimpsed the brief pulse of his come, and then he slid back into her and she folded. Dizzy and frantic, she came so deeply that he gathered her in, his hands warm on her bottom, as she gripped the last of him.

And then, drunk on pleasure, they kissed each other all the way to bed, and she lay there so happy and watched him undress.

'You have to hang your dress up,' he said as he looked at her.

'No…'

'You do,' he told her. 'I don't want Leo telling us off. Go on.'

'No!'

But she was laughing, reluctant, obliging, hanging up her dress. And it was the nicest moment as she realised she could laugh, and that her night with Galen wasn't over.

They weren't done with the other yet.

Floating. That was exactly what it was. Just as Galen had described it.

'What are you thinking?' he asked, and she knew he never usually did.

'That I haven't checked in for my flight,' Roula lied. 'You?'

That you're pregnant, and yet you can't tell me.

Galen was certain now. And not just from the changes in her body…

But what caused the real disquiet was the fact that he was certain she knew, too.

He was certain she was terrified, and perhaps that was why she was running away.

Perhaps she didn't want him to know, Galen considered, and who could blame her?

Maybe she wanted freedom after the hell of her marriage.

'Charts?' she said, and he dragged his mind back to their little in-joke.

'Actually, I was just thinking that you didn't open all your present.'

'I did.'

'There's a handbag,' Galen said.

'Oh, yes?'

'To go with the luggage.'

'Thank you,' Roula said. 'That's really thoughtful.'

Perhaps there were flags and bunting in one of the cases, Roula thought, and a goodbye card signed by all the staff.

As Roula lay there she kept wanting to poke him, because she had loathed his quiet anger at her leaving, and yet she was opposed to his nonchalance.

She drifted off—only it wasn't her usual nightmare that jolted her awake, but the thought of a world without him.

She listened to his soft snores. How could he be asleep when she was leaving?

She waited for dawn before prodding him awake. 'Galen? I don't know if I want the job.'

'Why?'

'It's all happened too fast.'

'Not really.'

'Too much too soon.'

'I get that.' He pulled her in, blinking himself awake. 'Any other reason?'

'I love Athens.' Roula lay back with him. 'I didn't expect to fall in love with a city, but I think I have.'

'I fell in love with it too,' Galen said. 'It just blew me away. But you might feel the same in another city.'

'Yes…'

'So what else is tearing you up?'

'Yaya,' she said. 'I feel I let you down with her.'

'No, I told you—you've helped.'

Oh, she preferred him cross and sulking, or at least putting up a little resistance to her leaving, but it would seem Galen had made his peace with it.

'Any other concerns?' he asked. 'Because now is the time to air them.'

'You said that at our first dinner.'

'Yes,' he agreed. 'I remember—and you asked me to kiss you.'

Roula groaned, and wished she had the energy to cover her face with the sheet that was crumpled around them.

'Say it, Roula.'

'Okay,' she took a breath. 'I do have a concern.' Although she truly did not know how to share her troubles. 'Us,' she admitted.

'Us?' He turned and looked at her.

'I know there's not supposed to be an "us", and I know I really am the worst catch-up girl, but I just thought…'

'What?'

'That I wanted sex—and I did. But…' She blew out a breath. 'You're right…we were just getting good.'

'Yes.'

She screwed her eyes closed. 'And it's just…'

'What?'

'I have feelings for you.'

'I have feelings for you too.'

'I have a *lot* of feelings for you, Galen,' Roula said.

'How many are we talking?'

'I'm not sure,' she said. 'Quite a lot.'

'Roula,' he said, 'I'm going to get coffee and some pastries.'

Not the reaction she'd hoped for!

He was gone for ages and she lay there, the neediest catch-up girl in the world. But if she couldn't tell him she was crazy about him on her last full day in Athens, then when? And not just head over heels in love with him, Roula thought, biting the skin around her thumb, but very possibly pregnant too!

She didn't know what to do. Truly. So she wrapped the sheet around her and went into the kitchen to get a drink of water, grateful for a quiet stomach, and for the fact that she wasn't head-down in the loo this morning.

His kitchen was gleaming, a chef's dream, and entirely wasted on Galen, who probably didn't even know how to turn on the kettle.

She was going to cry, Roula knew, so she clenched her fists and looked up—and then caught her breath when she saw the ceiling...not so perfect after all.

'Shocking, isn't it?'

She turned as Galen came in and looked up at the sooty ceiling and wall and the terrible scorch marks.

'When did this fire happen?' Roula asked.

'Ten...twelve years ago.' Galen shrugged. 'When I first moved in.'

'And you haven't had it repainted?'

'Why would I?' he said. 'It's just another designer kitchen without it.' He grinned and looked up. 'You can almost see Costa's panic, knowing I was on the plane on my way back. It happened. I like it.'

He held up a paper bag that looked full of greasy goodies and a tray with two cups.

'Breakfast in bed.'

Roula wandered back into the bedroom and climbed onto the bed, feeling a bit sick now—but with nerves.

'Coffee?' he said.

'No thanks.' The thought made her stomach curdle.

'Tea, then,' he said. 'Mint tea.'

'Oh!' She perked up a bit. 'Thank you.'

'Roula,' Galen said. 'It was very brave of you to just do what you did. I mean that.'

'Thank you.'

'We *do* have feelings for each other, but...'

It was like one of those job rejection letters, Roula thought. *Dear Ms Drakos, Thank you for your application, but...*

'You still haven't opened all of your present.' He handed her the handbag. 'There's something inside.'

A coin, probably. Or some lucky charm.

'Thanks.'

There was a sliver of velvet inside.

'Open it,' Galen said.

And when she unrolled it Roula found the pure sound of silence in Athens, for there were no words from her. It was a thin gold chain with a cross.

'This was…' he started.

'Your mother's,' she said.

'Yes,' Galen said. 'And I'm giving it to you.'

'As a leaving present?'

'No, because I love you.'

'You don't.'

'Roula, I completely do. And it's very important that you get that. I love you, and I feel sick at the thought of you leaving, but if you want to go to London I'll come too.'

She looked at him and frowned.

'After Yaya's dead.'

God, he was blunt sometimes. 'I don't think London's the issue…' she began.

'No, but are we clear? I love you.'

'I think so,' she said, because she was lifting her hair and he was putting the gold chain on her, his most precious thing.

'Know so,' Galen said. 'I love you because you are everything. You are strong and brave and…'

'Galen, I'm not brave.'

'You are.'

'I'm terrified.'

'Of what?'

He lifted her chin and his amber gaze met hers, held hers… And, yes, she was nervous, and worried, but more noticeable than that was the absence of fear. It was as if the terror that had resided in her heart had simply exited, and now she looked back at the man she trusted, with all her heart.

Even the wobbly bits.

Even the scary bits that might blow up their plans and change their lives.

For the first time in as long as Roula could remember, she believed that she wasn't on her own.

Yes, there might be an issue, but she didn't have to face things alone.

'My period's a bit late,' she said.

'How late are we talking?' Galen asked.

'Late!' Roula said. 'Quite late, actually.'

'Have you done a test?'

'No.'

'Why not?'

'I don't want to know.'

'Well, I do.' He handed her a paper cup. 'Go and pee in that.'

'Pardon?'

'I bought a test this morning. We'll deal with facts.'

'But I can't have babies.'

'Who told you that?' he said. 'A qualified fertility specialist?'

He tried to rein in his contempt, but he did know a little bit about it—not that he'd tell her about Kristina and Ruben's battles. Somehow he could not picture Roula and him sitting nervously, holding hands in a waiting room, awaiting results.

'On a trip to Athens to check if anything was wrong?'

'No...' She shook her head. 'I feel so naive.'

'And I feel I let you down.'

'No.'

'Roula, go and pee.'

She took a breath as she climbed out of bed.

He caught her wrist. 'I love you.'

'Stop...' She shook her head. 'You're just saying that in case I am...'

'Roula, why would I say it?'

'I've trapped you.'

'How?' he demanded. 'I can have only monthly access, send a card now and then, pay you maintenance—we have a lot of choices.'

'Do we?'

'Loads. And if you want London I have a very mobile job...'

He took back the cup from her hand, and although he wanted to know, there were more important things than facts. 'If you are pregnant, will *you* feel trapped?'

'Galen…'

She flashed him a smile. He wasn't sure which one—her guest services manager smile, her fake PA smile, her new Roula smile? Anyway it died on her lips. How did she feel?

'Roula? How do you feel?'

'Better than I did a few days ago,' she said. 'What about you?'

'We're talking about how *you* feel.'

'If I am pregnant, then I want to be—with or without you. Because I want honesty more than I want you, Galen. I mean that. I would rather you kept your catch-up list and we did this apart than be in a relationship the other didn't want.'

'You want my truth?'

'Yes.'

'In my old ideal world,' Galen said, 'we would have had sex for two selfish years and then perhaps talked about babies. But I am surprisingly open to persuasion here. I don't know when I fell in love, but I think it's been the case for quite some time. I know you won't believe this, but even before Costa asked me to employ you I was considering staying on the island. It grew from there. And you can call me arrogant again, but I think you might love me.'

'I do.'

'Since when?' Galen asked, pleased at her honesty.

'Always,' Roula said. 'Not like this, of course, but I cried when you left, and you know I had a crush on you, but…' She looked at him. 'I wondered if you ever thought of me,' she admitted. 'Not all the time, just now and then. I would look back on times when I'd been happy, and most of those times included you.'

And then for Galen it all slotted into place—her anger, her hurt, all aimed towards him.

'I did let you down, then.'

'How could you when you didn't know?'

'No,' Galen said, 'but I'm finding out that love is very illogical.' He meant what he said next. 'I'm so sorry I wasn't there for you.'

'It wasn't even the real you I had a crush on, Galen.' Although it felt as if she had loved him all her life.

'Go and get your bag,' he said. When she didn't move, Galen got it for her. He took out her Dictaphone and fiddled with it for a moment. 'Press "Play".'

'Why?'

'I recorded a message last night. You were meant to hear it today, when you typed up the notes. Press "Play".'

'Roula...'

His voice was low and there was music playing in the background. She knew the very moment, because she'd been standing in the loo, reading his message.

'I don't come with a ring, but there is a present in a handbag which I think should tell you how much you mean to me. Can we talk before you go? Because I think I am falling in love with you.'

'You are romantic after all!'

'See?' He gave her a nice smile. 'I had it all planned. And then I saw your amazing bust and...' He looked down at her stomach and then up to her eyes. 'We can decide now that we'll always be together. Whatever that pregnancy test says.'

It was time to find out.

She walked into the bathroom and did what she must, and then came back to the bedroom, where he'd opened the drapes. And there was the very best view.

'Where's the test?' she asked.

'I'll do it,' Galen said. 'Drink your tea.'

But not even mint tea and the sunrise and the Acropolis could distract her, for she turned around and he was like some naked Greek god in the bathroom, standing with his back to her, as if he was doing a scientific experiment with a pipette, when really he should just dunk it in.

She could see his expression.

His eyes were on the stick.

She'd have three minutes of this—or was it five? He would feel her looking soon and fake a smile.

But then she looked at the mirrors. They were cracked, and

rather than fix them he adored them and didn't hide the cracks. And she thought of the sooty ceiling that he kept, rather than paint over, because it made him smile. Then she caught her own reflection in the damaged mirror, saw herself sitting on the bed, and the chain around her neck, and she thought of that line she had held on to.

And I will restore to you the years that the locust hath eaten.

And she wasn't scared because this really was love, she knew. Real love. Coming now…ready or not.

'Roula!'

She heard his excited shout. It was so absolute she jumped.

'You're pregnant!'

It was as if they had been trying for five years, and yet they had not even been trying. Galen was swearing and panicking and delighted.

She was in love, and pregnant, and as he kissed her all over there was just one more thing—and he'd made her brave enough to say it. To state her needs upfront.

'I want a ring, Galen.'

He stopped mid-kiss.

'And a wedding,' Roula said.

'Roula, I have very strong opinions—'

'Well, I don't want to be Roula Kyrios or Roula Dra—'

'Marry me,' he said hurriedly—because that name would never be said in this bedroom. 'It would seem I do believe in marriage after all.'

And the most illogical thing was that as he got down on one knee he actually did.

CHAPTER NINETEEN

MIST OVER THE AEGEAN, Galen thought as she walked out of the bedroom. And for all the reasons he loved her—and there were many—one of them was because she wore that gorgeous dress all over again.

It really was perfect.

And so were they as he drove them to their wedding.

'Oh, my God!' Leo was dancing on the street as Roula climbed out, holding a cascade of vivid pink bougainvillea. 'She's wearing *me*!'

Galen was in the same wedding suit he had worn for Costa and Mary's wedding. They were there too. But no one knew his and Roula's secret just yet.

'Should we…?' Mary suggested, indicating that they go in.

'Or maybe…' Leo held back.

Costa just stood there, leaving it all to the others.

'I have spoken with the staff…' Kristina started, but Ruben, holding the baby, hushed her.

'Let them…'

'Thanks.' Galen nodded, because this wedding no one had been able to organise. This was a wedding arranged quickly, be-cause—well, some things needed to be done rapidly.

'We'll call you in soon,' Galen said. 'Ready?' he checked with his bride-to-be.

'I am. Are you?'

He took a breath and nodded as they stepped in and walked along the hall.

Roula's breath caught, because one of the residents of the care home was playing the piano, and all of them were dressed in their finery. Diamonds and jewels and a very smart gentleman holding up a stick.

'Galen!'

'Sir,' Galen said, and this time he went over. 'Thank you for your help organising the guests. Everybody looks amazing.'

'Well, it's a wedding.'

'Yes, it is!'

It really was.

'Can I correct something?' Galen said, just before they went in.

'Of course,' Roula said.

'What I said about us having a baby in two years or so... I want to amend that. *Now* is ideal.'

'It is,' Roula agreed, because she was safe in his love now. But there was another love that needed him too.

'Hey, Yaya...' He gently shook her and she opened her eyes.

'Home,' she said, when she saw the bright pink flowers.

'They *are* from home,' Galen said. 'Picked this morning, trailing down from your roof...'

'Galen...' She breathed in the scent and then looked up at Roula. 'Oh, you look like a bride.'

'Roula *is* my bride,' Galen said. 'The celebrant is here, and when you're ready we would like you to see us marry.'

'Galen!' She was tearful. 'Married?'

'Yes.' He nodded. 'I am in love, Yaya, and it would seem she loves me.'

'Good, good...'

'And,' he told her, 'no one else knows this yet, but we're having a baby.'

'Before marriage?'

'We're sorting that out right now. We're having a little girl.'

Sometimes it was better to lie, because it was actually a little too early to be sure.

'We're going to call her Constantina.' Roula told her what Galen could not, for today there was no need for pretence. 'After Galen's mother—and it's your middle name too.'

'Yes...'

'Yes,' Galen said, and then in front of these two women he cried. 'I remember everything you ever told me about her. I love because of you. The best *yaya*, the best parent—you are every-thing I want to be for my child. You loved little robot me.'

'Horrible boys,' she said, just as she had then. 'Clever you are.'

'I have been blessed to have you.'

It was the shortest, the sweetest wedding, in a room full of Anapliró memories and love, toasted in Anapliró water with a very light sponge cake and just a little smear of fig jam.

'Constantina…' Yaya beamed.

'Yes!' Roula smiled.

'Honeymoon?'

'We're saving it for Christmas,' Galen told her. 'We're going home to have the baby.'

'Home?'

'Our Anapliró home.'

It would not be dissolving into the sea.

EPILOGUE

'Wow…' said Roula.

They sat on the steps of the *theatron*, gazing down on the world.

They were on their way back from Athens and had just visited her mother, for a little meet-and-greet. It had been emotional, but had gone surprisingly well. Then, as they'd been driving up to their Anapliró home, Roula had suggested they stop.

Galen had put a few flowers from a pink bouquet into his parents' *kandylakia*. The candle was still lit.

'Yes, wow,' Galen said.

Only Galen was wowed by little blue eyes and a very red face, all of a week old.

Roula would not be snapping back quite as quickly as Kristina, but she'd been able to take a gentle walk with their very precious wrapped bundle, and now they sat on the steps of what was the best place on earth to share their happy news.

Leo and Deacon, and Costa and Mary—with little Costa, of course—had dropped everything to visit them at the hospital. Kristina had been in too. As well as Dora and Hector! But there were plenty more they were ready to reveal the details to.

'I have a phone signal,' Roula declared.

'Tell them,' Galen said, not taking his eyes off his daughter.

It was quite a group message—especially for two people who had no real family.

Yolanda and Stephanie, and then there was Joe and Nico, and the guys on the ground floor… And really, for someone as supposedly socially backward as Galen, there was a very long list of essential people all waiting for their first glimpse of Constantina Pallas.

It took for ever to send the message—for *ever*—and they sat gazing down at their daughter. A little late, a little bit of a worry, a whole lot to love.

'A whole person…' Galen just stared at her. 'Condensed!'

'I know!' Roula agreed. 'I mean, she's everything—an entire person. Yet this tiny little fragile creature at the same time.'

She got him.

'Home?' Galen said.

Up to their Anapliró home, to get to know their little girl. For he got her too, and home, with their little family, was where her heart was right now.

Galen knew Roula.

* * * * *

CONSEQUENCES OF THEIR WEDDING CHARADE

CATHY WILLIAMS

MILLS & BOON

CHAPTER ONE

'FLOWERS? FOR ME? An hour and a half ahead of schedule, Curtis, and you've come bearing flowers...heather...narcissi...pussy willow, no less! I had no idea you were so well acquainted with the English winter garden!'

From his towering height of six foot three, Curtis Hamilton looked down on his much more diminutive godfather and grinned.

'I know absolutely nothing about English winter gardens,' he drawled, shutting the front door on a snowy February landscape and taking a few seconds to breathe in the familiarity of his godfather's cottage, with its unique smells of a house lived in by a bookish bachelor with a flair for home cooking. 'Nor,' he continued with lazy amusement, as he divested himself of his cashmere coat and handmade Italian loafers, both of which were ridiculously unsuitable for heavy snow in Cambridgeshire but there hadn't been a flake when he'd left London, 'do I know a thing about flowers of any description, English or otherwise. Got Julia, my PA, to get them for me. And, just for the record, the flowers aren't for you, William.'

'No, I suspected not. Care to divulge, dear boy?'

'In due course. What can I smell?' He sniffed the air but his eyes were trained on his godfather, looking for anything that might hint that things weren't as they should be. From the very moment he had walked through the doors of the foster care home where Curtis had been miserably languishing—an eight-year-old statistic in an uncaring and impersonal machine—he had bought himself all the love and affection Curtis had within him to give.

After his health scare eighteen months previously, William Farrow had retreated into himself, knocked back by a body that had let him down combined with his scheduled retirement from the University of Cambridge, where he had lectured in Classics for decades.

A double whammy.

But, thankfully, right now he looked himself, bustling ahead of Curtis towards the kitchen with the flowers, giving a detailed account of what was on the menu for dinner, from where he'd bought the ingredients to how they had been put to use and leaving nothing out in the telling.

He was a small, round man who always dressed formally. Curtis often teased him that it was on the off-chance royalty might just pop by unannounced for a cup of tea.

Curtis knew that tonight his godfather would have made a special effort and was not surprised to see that he was wearing a snazzy red bow tie with his crisp blue shirt, and some *slacks*, as he insisted on calling them. Not quite funeral formal but definitely not the sort of casual gear most people might associate with dinner at a kitchen table.

Curtis's heart swelled with affection. In a life where emotions were never allowed to intrude, his godfather was the only person who could lay claim to his unconditional love. Neither ever spoke of it, but Curtis was very much aware of the fact that William had rescued him from his damaged past and saved him from the unknown horrors of a future that would not have been kind to a child raised by a drug addict and then thrown into foster care when his mother had finally overdosed. There were so many statistics in that setting—children who were lost for ever when they were spat out as young adults—and he could easily have become one of them.

'I haven't seen you for over three months. Yes, you managed Christmas Day here, but that was the sum of it.' William busied himself with a vase but there was intent behind that throwaway observation and Curtis, sitting at the pine kitchen table, breathing in the fragrant aromas of beef and oyster pie, felt a prick of intense guilt.

'I know and I can only apologise for that. Would you believe me if I told you that I would have visited if I could have?'

'I would,' William said wryly, 'which is the problem. You work too hard, Curtis.' He stood back to inspect his handiwork with the flowers and then carefully placed the vase on the dresser against the wall before bringing a couple of wine glasses to the table.

'It's a blessing and a curse,' Curtis murmured, mind wandering as the conversation took a familiar turn.

Where was she?

He'd shown up with the flowers which, admittedly, had been a tiny bit bruised because he'd chucked them on the passenger seat of his Range Rover and then inadvertently dumped his computer bag on top, but still perfectly acceptable as a prelude to a favour.

But where had she been? At six o'clock on a Thursday evening in the depths of winter? On the outskirts of Cambridge? With snow falling? Was there anything to actually *do* on the outskirts of Cambridge on a snowy winter's evening? When he thought about that, his mind hit a road block.

At any rate, she hadn't been in and he'd been so surprised that he'd waited an inordinately long time in the freezing weather before giving up on the doorbell and making his way over to his godfather, who lived twenty minutes away.

He surfaced to the tail-end of his godfather warning him about blood pressure, stress and all the various ailments that could afflict someone who worked too much.

And thereafter followed a comfortable journey for both of them. Gentle nagging, curiosity about some of the bigger projects Curtis was working on—state-of-the-art buildings that defied laws of gravity, the vast commercial sites which were additions to his multimillion-pound portfolio—and then, over the beef pie and roast potatoes, the inevitable questioning about the future.

A wife…children…all those things which had eluded William Farrow, making it doubly important for his godson to achieve, apparently.

How could anyone know what might be good for someone if they'd never experienced it themselves? His godfather had never been married, had never had children, had never, to Curtis's knowledge, desired either.

So where was the logic in recommending those very things to him? Certainly, when it came to lessons learned on the journey through life, his were resoundingly clear when it came to love and all the happy-ever-afters it always seemed to preface.

Not for him.

He was no longer a lost child, pouring love into a parent who had no time for him. He knew better than to hand his heart over to anyone. Waiting by a window with no food to eat for a mother who had viewed parenting as something way down the list of priorities had put paid to all his illusions and if that hadn't been enough, then there had been the shambolic disaster with Caitlin...

He shut the door on that particular memory with a decisive clang.

The subject of a rosy future that wasn't on the cards for him was adroitly shelved when William asked without preamble, as they sipped coffee after an exemplary pie, 'So who, dear boy, were the flowers destined for?'

Which focused Curtis instantly on the thorny question he had been asking himself for the past couple of hours.

'Jessica, as it happens. Rang her doorbell for half an hour! No answer. Where the heck is the woman?'

'Flowers...for *Jess*?'

Curtis flushed, glanced at his watch and fidgeted in the chair, which suddenly felt constricting. His godfather's sharp blue eyes were pinned to his face with undisguised curiosity.

'*Why?*'

'It's not a crime to buy a bunch of flowers for someone,' Curtis said with just a hint of defensiveness in his voice.

How was it that in the world of the billionaire he was the leader of the pack and yet in a cottage on the outskirts of Ely he was reduced to perspiring round the collar at the prospect of a couple of awkward questions from his sixty-eight-year-old godfather?

When he had absolutely nothing to hide whatsoever.

'I...er...it's been a while since I saw her. Naturally, I've emailed a couple of times...always good to know what's...er...happening around here...'

'You mean you get in touch when you want to find

out if I'm all right...' William said shrewdly. 'Make sure the old codger hasn't fallen into a state of utter despair because his ticker isn't what it used to be...' He chortled and waved an admonishing finger. 'Appreciate the concern, my son, but I'm doing fine! And now that you ask about Jess,' he continued smugly, 'the girl's finally doing what I've been advising her to do for the past two years. She's getting out there and dating!' He cast a jaundiced eye over the flowers. 'And no suitor worth his salt is going to appreciate some other chap bringing flowers to his intended!'

Curtis had never heard such a string of old-fashioned terms in his life before. *Suitor? Chap? Intended?* Never mind that he was *none* of those things!

'In that case—' he flattened his hands on the table and rose with fluid grace to his feet '—I'll take doughnuts...'

Jess surfaced groggily to the insistent ringing of her doorbell.

When she looked at her phone, it was to discover that it was a little after eight. That made it an hour past her usual waking up time, whether she was working or not.

Thank God it was half-term and she was *not* because she would have had a crazy rush to get to the school in time.

Nevertheless, she felt slothful at having slept in, even though it had been a long and wearisome night.

How could a date with a friend of a friend of a friend, who had sounded so perfect on paper, have turned out to be so...dull?

He was a fellow teacher at a school in York, he had a degree in philosophy from Oxford Uni, which should have guaranteed an active and energetic mind, plus he taught PE, so how bad could it be, and yet…

She shook her head, flung on the dressing gown from behind the bedroom door and flew to the front door.

She lived in a tiny terraced house and whenever the postman decided to do what he did best—relax on the doorbell for minutes on end—she was terrified that one of her lovely but extremely old neighbours would be upset at the resulting din.

She pulled open the front door to yet another grim and wintry sky and was busily tying the cord of her dressing gown tightly round her as her mouth fell open when for a few seconds she had the sort of brain fog that only descended when one of her kids at school got it into their head that paying attention in class meant talking at full volume over what she was trying to say.

Curtis.

Curtis Hamilton…six foot plus of prime alpha male, so insanely sexy that perfectly normal human beings with their heads firmly screwed on started doing stupid things when he decided to turn the full wattage of his attention on them.

Jess had known him for so long, had been his *friend* for such a long time, that she should have been immune to his looks, his charm and his wit but she never had been.

He'd been ten and she was three years younger when he had appeared at their primary school and, of course, all focus had been on the new kid.

She'd seen him around and about but it was when her mum had taken the job as housekeeper to his godfather that she had really become friends with him. She could remember long summer holidays, poling over to the Farrow place, as her mother used to call it, hanging around while her mum cleaned and tidied and sometimes sat and had a cup of tea with Mr Farrow, an adorable little man with fastidious ways and a knack when it came to baking.

Curtis was older but he was patient. He'd never seemed to mind taking her fishing or including her with his group of friends. Looking back, she could see that he had sensed her insecurities, her inherent shyness, the bookish personality that had concealed, as she had entered adolescence, her intense awkwardness at being the 'big girl' in the class.

Later, she thought that maybe he *had* minded, but had been too kind to say anything.

As they'd got older there'd been a brief spell when he seemed to disappear but then, when she turned thirteen, she suddenly seemed to become *visible*. He'd told her about his plans to make it big, laughed when she quizzed him about his girlfriends, rolled his eyes and confided that he just didn't have sticking power when it came to relationships...

She preciously guarded that place in his life. Girlfriends came and went but she was always there and how dependent she had gradually become on the confidence he gave her, patching up her anxious hesitation about her looks, making her feel good about herself at a time in her teenage years when being 'one of the lads' had not been what she'd wanted. Her parents had always been there for her, but they were biased. She'd needed a different kind of affirmation and he'd given it to her in spades just by being there for her.

And what would she had done if he hadn't been there for her when her beloved dad had died five years previously? Curtis had been away but had returned as soon as he'd heard and he'd been the perfect shoulder to cry on.

Childish adoration and teenage infatuation usually never stayed the same, fizzling out as Life took over, but not for her. For her, those feelings had deepened into something else.

How she'd wished that he could have been more than just her buddy, but by then she'd fully read and understood the writing on the wall. The category she occupied was unique but it would never extend where she wanted it.

It frightened her to think just how long she would have stayed there, happy with crumbs, in defiance of all the signposts that had been emblazoned for her to follow from the beginning...if he hadn't got engaged to Caitlin Smyth.

That was a year and a half ago and the engagement had been short-lived because Caitlin had broken it off, but it had been the learning curve Jess had badly needed to turn away from the spell he had always weaved over her.

She had purposely avoided him for the past few months. She'd answered emails and occasionally spoken to him on the phone when he'd called, but she'd made sure to be busy every time she knew he'd be turning up to visit William.

School trip...visiting her mum, who had moved to Devon to be closer to her sister...buried under work so, oops, so sorry but no way could she snatch any time off...

The list had been exhaustive, but she'd succeeded. On the rare occasion when she had been in his presence she'd made sure to time it so that other people were around, a safety buffer against herself and her weakness.

Until now.

Because here he was, at her front door, with a box

in his hand and a smile on his face and looking every bit as wickedly sexy as he had the last time she'd set eyes on him.

Of course the unbuttoned cashmere coat was crazy in this weather, as were the loafers. Underneath, she could see he was in a pair of faded jeans and his old rugby jumper.

So beautiful, so sinfully perfect in every way... Thick brown hair streaked with caramel, green eyes the colour of the sea in a certain light, the hint of a dimple in his chin and thick, dark lashes to die for.

'Are you going to let me in or should I start calling the paramedics to come out because I'm about to get hypothermia?'

'Curtis!'

'Ah, so you do remember who I am... Move aside, Jess, I need to get out of this cold. My coat and my shoes weren't made for snow.' He nudged past her as she fell back and helplessly watched him dump the box on the little table against the wall so that he could get rid of the coat. 'Don't tell me, it was crazy to come up here with nothing but a wool coat, but who knew that it would be snowing? Thought I'd left that old waterproof in the shed but it would seem not.'

He looked at her and she fought down a blush.

She'd woken from her slumber when he'd got engaged, recognised where she stood, acknowledged where she'd *never* stand, and she'd accordingly made a concerted effort to get her house in order.

So she was never going to be the sort of petite, adorable little blonde thing he was attracted to. She was five ten and had always been prone to generous curves. When her dad had died, her curves had unfortunately expanded with her comfort eating, but bit by bit she had cut back on the chocolate and in the past few months had returned to her usual figure.

'Where are your specs?' he asked, frowning and strolling towards her, green eyes intent on her face, scrutinising as though she had somehow contrived to let him down by withholding vital information about her eyesight.

'Laser surgery,' she said, gathering her scattered self-control and preceding him into the kitchen, where she waited until he was seated at her kitchen table before asking him what he was doing here.

'Doughnuts.' He nodded briefly to the box that he had deposited on the kitchen counter. 'Since when were you interested in having laser surgery?'

'You came here to bring me…*doughnuts*?'

'Why not?' He shrugged. 'What else are friends for?'

'Curtis, I was asleep when you rang the doorbell.'

'You do look a bit groggy. Late night?' His eyebrows shot up and he shot her a wolfish grin. 'Don't answer that. At least, not yet.'

'I need to get dressed.'

'You've done something to your hair as well…'

'Curtis, I'll be back in a sec, but honestly…today's a very busy day for me…'

'Doing what? It's half-term. William told me. So you can't possibly be going to the school.'

'Teachers don't just work during term time and there's a lot going on at the moment,' she gritted, and he grinned and patted the chair next to him.

'No need for you to change. I'm accustomed to seeing you *ébouriffé*…'

Jess ignored him. Yes, he had seen her dishevelled a million times in the past, notably one night when she was eighteen and he'd been back from university, having broken up with yet another small blonde called Mickey. He had turned up at her mother's house and they had watched two horror movies in a row, making their way through several bags of crisps and a bottle of wine. By then the childish adoration and the teenage infatuation had coalesced into something altogether more dangerous.

She changed fast. Suddenly self-conscious about her new and improved figure, she donned some old sweats and an extremely baggy jumper. She would have tied her hair back but he was right, she'd changed her hair along with everything else.

Instead of long and utterly unruly, it was now shoulder-length and more or less manageable. Tying it back was no longer an option.

She paused, looked at herself in the mirror. Still way too tall but the shorter hair suited her, framed her face, and it was nice not wearing specs. Her eyes were an unusual shade of deep, navy blue. No specs made the most of them.

She took a deep breath and returned to the kitchen to find him halfway through one of the doughnuts, having pushed back his chair so that he could stretch his long legs out at an angle.

'Aren't you going to have a doughnut?' He nodded to the box and she shook her head.

'Maybe later.'

He'd kicked off the loafers and she tried not to stare at his feet as she moved to make them coffee.

Her nervous system was all over the place and she hated the fact that he could show up here and after all this time, after all her strenuous efforts to move on from limbo land, could *still* manage to have such a dramatic effect on her.

It was as though his larger than life presence had sucked the oxygen out of the air, leaving it difficult for her to breathe and she was so acutely conscious of his eyes on her as she stirred the boiling water into the coffee. Her entire body felt weird and prickly.

Before, she had been aware of him. Before, he had got under her skin, made her blush, sent her thoughts into disarray. But now that she had decided that he was forbidden fruit he was having an even more devastating effect on her senses and she knew that she had to control her reactions. He wasn't going to be around for long. She would urge him out just as soon as he'd finished his cup of coffee and then she would perhaps think about going to see her mum.

Or maybe not. Would that be a little too close to running away?

Certainly she would be letting his godfather down because she had promised to do two days with William working on his memoirs. It was a labour of love he had begun when he'd retired from lecturing and she helped transcribe them once a week, using it as an opportunity to have a chat and some dinner with him, make sure he was okay because she knew he was lonely at times.

'So...have you been avoiding me, Jessica Carr?' Curtis sipped his coffee, looked at her over the rim of the mug, his green eyes amused and questioning.

'Don't be crazy. Why would I avoid you, Curtis?'

'No idea, but I'm open to suggestions...'

'I've been busy. There's been a lot of fundraising at the school to help pay for the new wing and computer equipment. I've had a lot on my plate.'

'I know. Seems there's been a lot on your plate every time I've tried to arrange to see you when I've been here... You know what they say about all work and no play. But no…wait… I hear through the grapevine that life hasn't been a case of all work for you of late…'

'What are you talking about?'

'Dropped by yesterday evening on the way to William but you weren't in. Hot date, I gather?' He grinned, his keen green eyes pinned to her face.

'You're so nosy.' She looked at him impatiently but the weight of history between them… How could she not respond to the teasing in his voice? She smiled and rolled her eyes. 'You *do* know that my private life is none of your business, Curtis.'

'If it's not my business, then whose is it? So? How did it go? Where did you meet him?'

'A friend of a friend and yes, thank you, it went very well. He's a teacher, like me, so we have a lot in common.'

'Sounds dull. Don't they say that opposites attract?'

'How do you find your godfather?' She changed the subject before she could become immersed in a conversation instinct told her to avoid. 'He seemed a little subdued when I saw him a week ago.'

'Subdued? How? He's always upbeat when I talk to him on the phone.'

'He doesn't want to worry you, Curtis.'

'Why would he think that he would worry me by being honest about anything that might be bothering him?' There was impatience and bemusement in his voice.

'Why do you think?'

He frowned and tilted his head to one side. 'Am I sensing an atmosphere between us?'

Jess felt the charm within that utterly sexy drawl feather over her and she had to fight not to shiver with treacherous awareness because this was what he was so good at…this was what made Curtis Hamilton such a health hazard when it came to the opposite sex. It wasn't just about those incredible looks or the money, what was *really* dangerous about him was the fact that he was so gifted at interacting. He knew how to listen, he picked up on things quickly, knew how to steer a conversation to elicit those little confidences you might not have wanted to impart. The very fact that they had been friends for so long, on such familiar terms, made her all the more conscious of the dangers of being lured back to that place from which she knew she had to flee. She had fallen for a guy who only saw her as a one-dimensional girl next door.

She had no intention of admitting to any kind of *atmosphere* between them, but she was certainly going to tell him what she thought on the matter of his godfather, of whom she was deeply fond.

'He's in awe of you, Curtis.' This was the most blunt she could remember being, but then it was also the first time he had been away for such a long period of time—several weeks, only popping back for Christmas. Into that void, Jess had certainly noticed signs of depression, something she was well adept at spotting given her own mother's descent into mild depression following her husband's death.

'Don't be ridiculous.'

'Sometimes you can be so…*blind*. Honestly!' She clicked her tongue as he continued to frown, mulling over what she had said. 'He doesn't want to bother you, Curtis. You're his golden godson who's conquered the world… You're his pride and joy who got a first in Maths at Cambridge and then developed an app to deal with weight load that had every architect and engineering company in the world begging to pay you a king's ransom for it. You're the whiz-kid who was already formulating a property portfolio at twenty-three whilst opening his own company to deal with sexy, high-end constructions and then, as if that weren't enough, began taking over companies and making yet more millions…'

'Stop, please.' He held up his hands in a gesture of mock surrender. 'It's all going to go to my head and you wouldn't want that, would you?' His tone was light. His mind was whirring. William? Depressed? Just thinking about it sent a coil of clammy alarm curling through him. When it came to the rest of the world, and certainly when it came to women, he might have locked his heart away and thrown away the key to protect himself from ever being hurt, but not so when it came to his godfather.

'I think he feels that you might find it boring if he starts dwelling on his own problems. And these past few weeks… You haven't been around that much. I guess, when you have been here, he just wants to enjoy your company without bringing up anything troublesome…'

'Do you realise that you're the only woman who has ever been able to talk to me like this?' His voice was absent-minded, his thoughts dwelling on what she had said, his keen brain already trying to source ways to remedy a problem of which he had been unaware.

Jess looked at him, so familiar, so stupidly dear to her, so oblivious to how she felt about him.

He stretched and she compulsively and guiltily drank in the sinewy length of his body and the sliver of hard skin exposed as the jumper rode up ever so slightly.

She wondered whether he was seeing anyone. Many times, she got wind of girlfriends thanks to the diligent paparazzi, who couldn't seem to get enough of someone clever, stupidly rich and insanely good-looking. It was as though they'd hit jackpot with him and so kept bouncing back to cover whatever he happened to be up to. All had been quiet on the Western Front for some time.

Not your business! She shook her head, clearing it to focus on what he had said.

'You say that but that's because all those poor women you date are so desperate to be with you that they'd do anything to hang on, including agreeing with everything you say. If you ask me, it's not healthy...'

He burst out laughing and looked at her with warm appreciation. 'Thank God I have one nag in my life, making sure my ego doesn't over-inflate.'

'Thanks for the compliment, Curtis.' But something inside her twisted painfully even though she knew that actually, in his eyes, it really *was* a compliment.

'I'll keep an eye on him while I'm here and I've wrapped up a heck of a lot of pressing business abroad, so my time is going to be a little less pressured for the next few months. I'd planned,' he mused, 'on staying for the weekend but maybe I'll stretch it out a bit longer. Hang around for a week instead. What would we do without the World Wide Web? Business on the go wherever you happen to be and thankfully the internet connection at the cottage is first rate.' He sat up abruptly, slapped his hands on his thighs and looked at her with sudden seriousness. 'I haven't come bearing gifts for no apparent reason,' he said gravely.

'I had no idea that the doughnuts were meant to be a gift,' Jess replied politely. 'My birthday isn't for another three months, as it happens, but I appreciate the thought.'

'It's not so much a gift as more of a...how shall I put it...?'

'Please don't be coy, Curtis. That's not like you.'

He grinned and stood up and strolled over to her fridge, which he opened so that he could peer inside. 'Would you like to make me some breakfast?' he asked. 'Somehow doughnuts don't quite do the trick. Or I could make you something. What have you got?' He pulled out a yoghurt pot and inspected the lid. 'Aside from some Greek yoghurt three days past its sell-by date?'

This, Jess thought helplessly, was where being *good friends* got a girl. A guy who felt comfortable rooting through your fridge in search of food as opposed to the guy who showed up with red roses and tickets to the opera.

'Sit down. I guess I could do some eggs.'

'Or, better still, I could take you out for breakfast…'

'I can't,' she said hurriedly. 'I have a busy day ahead.'

'So you've said, even though you're not working this week. Busy doing what?'

'Meeting some of the staff,' she said vaguely, 'to discuss what else we can do to raise money for the school. There's a real risk it might be merged with the really huge secondary five miles away, which would be a disaster.'

'You need a generous donor,' Curtis murmured thoughtfully, but she was already turning away, fetching eggs and bread and concocting a breakfast she hadn't banked on making.

'So…' she said a few moments later as she plated up for both of them—scrambled eggs and toast. 'What do you have to ask me, Curtis?'

There was a reason he was sitting at her table, sprawled in the chair, watching her with those amazing cut glass green eyes. He wanted something and the very fact that he was beating about the bush was not a good sign.

'I need something of a…ah…a favour…'

'What?' She looked at him briefly, then back at her egg as a shiver of awareness threatened to bring way too much tell-tale colour to her cheeks. She'd always been aware of him but never so much as now. The fine balance between friendship and illicit, forbidden attraction had tipped far and fast into the illicit, forbidden attraction side, and the friendship element was struggling to keep pace.

'I'm best man at a wedding in two weeks' time. John Jones, a youthful Lord, as it happens. Have you heard of him?'

'Are you going to get to the point?'

'What would I do without you?' He grinned and reached forward and absently stroked her wrist with his finger.

An unthinking gesture and yet it fired up a response in her that was terrifyingly dramatic. She felt dampness pool between her legs and her breasts were suddenly heavy, her nipples stiff with a tingling sensation. Had he touched her before? Of course he had. A hug on her birthday, a peck on the cheek at Christmas. Once, and she burned when she remembered this, a kiss on the lips when they had been caught out under the mistletoe. She had been nineteen, he twenty-two. Afterwards he had pulled back and laughed and everyone around them had clapped but that kiss had burned for weeks afterwards.

If she'd wised up a little earlier to just how deep she had dived when it came to Curtis Hamilton she might have got her act together a little sooner instead of something like an engagement having to force her to confront her issues.

She subtly removed her hand and knew that he actually hadn't noticed that evasive withdrawal.

'So?' she asked politely, but her heart was still thumping and her skin was still tingling because her body had, just for a minute, gone AWOL.

'The point is that I want you to come with me.'

'You want me to come with you? I'm not following.'

'The invite includes a plus one,' Curtis explained, 'and I want you to be my plus one.' He looked away briefly before returning the full glare of his undivided attention to her.

'Why?'

'I think it would be nice for you,' he replied smoothly, his slow smile so coaxing, so seductive, so…*tempting* that Jess had to count to ten to clear her head.

'Nice for me…' she parroted, for want of anything better to say.

'As you've told me several times in the space of…' he made a show of consulting his luxury watch '…a little over an hour, you've been run ragged, barely able to function.'

'I don't think I actually used those words,' Jess pointed out, a little dazed.

'It's easy to become disillusioned with one's profession when you find yourself in a position of having no leisure time to yourself. There's a thin line between positivity at all hands to the tiller in a moment of crisis to negativity at the suspicion that you're being taken advantage of. And yes, I know you're going to tell me that you've been out and about on dates…' he paused, left a door ajar through which he invited her to step; Jess ignored him and he continued with a concerned sigh '…but you've barely stopped recently. I know that because William mentioned you haven't been coming as often to help out with the memoirs…'

'Yes, I admit I've been busy but…'

'But nothing, Jess. You need a break and I'm here to provide just such a break for you. One weekend and it'll be somewhere you'll love…'

'Curtis, I can't just…'

'Courchevel.' He produced that with a flourish, like a magician producing a rabbit from a hat. 'A much-deserved weekend away at a lavish, all-expenses-paid five-star hotel doing the one thing in the world you love doing most. Skiing. Additionally, you'd be doing me a huge favour, Jess. You know my thoughts on weddings…'

'Yes,' Jess retorted with sarcasm, 'you think you're going to be a number one target for women with dreams of happy-ever-afters brought on by wedding contagion.'

'Exactly. I need you there to make the whole damn experience more bearable. A couple of hours I can deal with, but four days might become a little challenging.'

'You want a chaperone, in other words.'

A chaperone he knew wouldn't be foolish enough to get any wild ideas in her head—a chaperone who was a good pal and therefore immune to all thoughts of happy-ever-afters with a guy like him.

'And, tempting though you make it sound, Curtis Hamilton, the answer is an emphatic *no*!'

CHAPTER TWO

'WHY NOT?'

He looked genuinely startled and Jess could understand why. In his well-organised world, she had her place. She was his friend, probably the only woman on the planet he could count on as being his *friend*, with no annoying, unwelcome agenda. Why on earth, he was probably wondering, would she flatly reject his offer of an all-expenses-paid holiday which would give her a real battery-recharge after months of hard work trying to raise funds for the school?

She hadn't even bothered to offer any kind of explanation! She had rejected his offer out of hand.

He would be even more bewildered at the fact that she had turned down the chance *to ski*. She adored skiing and was so good that she could instruct.

While she struggled to come up with a plausible explanation, his face cleared and he looked at her knowingly.

'I get it,' he murmured.

'You do?' Jess queried, alarmed.

'I do. We've known each other a long time, Jess. I can read you like a book.'

Alarm blossomed into panic. He was shrewd when it came to reading undercurrents. Show him a signal barely visible to the naked eye, and he could ferret out what it meant in a matter of seconds. Had all her dodging and evasion pointed him in the very direction she had been so desperate to conceal? Had he gleaned, somehow, that she was *attracted* to him? That their so-called platonic friendship, which he treasured, was something she longed to take several steps further.

Had he guessed how she truly felt about him?

She blanched. Honestly, she could think of nothing worse. It wasn't just the mortification, it wasn't just the thought of him laughing his head off at the thought of her actually imagining that she might be competition for the glamorous blondes he was fond of dating... *No*, it would be the loss of friendship that went with that because he would run a mile in the opposite direction.

'You can?' she asked weakly and he nodded.

'You've hit the dating scene big time,' he expanded. 'The fact that you're so secretive about it, secretive about your hot date last night, is telling me something.'

'What is it telling you?'

'It's serious.'

He waited. She failed to embellish so he continued, a little jerkily. 'Frankly, I'm a little hurt that you don't feel you can confide in me.' Surprisingly, he *did* feel hurt and...what else? A feeling of edginess that nestled on the periphery of what seemed acceptable to him. He dismissed the uneasy feeling quickly.

'Why should I confide in you about my private life?' Jess asked, sounding genuinely puzzled.

'You know all about mine!'

'Curtis, so does half the country.' She burst out laughing, expecting him to follow suit, but he stared at her with such a disgruntled expression that she carried on laughing, couldn't help herself. 'You're in the tabloids more often than the daily weather reports,' she said wryly. 'You don't actually need to tell me who you're seeing because all I have to do is grab a newspaper from the corner shop.'

Her stomach tightened but she kept smiling. Yes, she saw all those cute, tiny blondes he went out with. None seemed to last longer than ten minutes.

He said that he was an open book. Was he though? When she thought about it, there were huge gaps in her knowledge about him. He'd never spoken about his childhood, aside from to tell her in passing that he could not have hoped for a better father figure than William. He was adept at deflecting questions he didn't want to answer and questions that were too probing were adroitly side-stepped.

He was approaching thirty and, yes, young enough to be wary of being tied down, but when he talked about women and relationships there had always been an edge of cynicism in his voice, a flat determination that marriage was an institution he had no time for.

And yet he had been engaged. He hadn't been the one to break it off. Had a broken heart accounted for his aversion to commitment? Jess could swear that he had never wanted to be tied down, that he had always been wary of commitment...or was that just her imagination playing tricks on her?

'You never really told me what happened between you and Caitlin,' Jess said, treading on ground previously untrodden. She'd tentatively asked at the time but hadn't pursued the matter when he'd failed to explain. Yet weren't they supposed to be great *friends*?

Well, this friendship wasn't exactly on a par when he

felt hurt because she had chosen not to blurt out everything about her private life but *she* was handed precious little real information about *his*.

Suddenly, she felt the stirrings of an anger she had never felt towards him before. Her anger ratcheted up a notch or two when he stilled because clearly he wanted that untrodden ground to remain untrodden.

'That business with Caitlin is ancient history,' he dismissed in a guarded tone.

The question had come at him from left field and Curtis shifted uncomfortably. For a few seconds he seemed to look down into deep, dark water that swirled lazily beneath him, so full of things unspoken and buried sadness.

'I must say, Curtis,' Jess mused sweetly, 'that it's a bit rich for you to feel hurt because I happen to want to keep my private life to myself, when you have no qualms about keeping *your* private life to yourself. The whole world knows what women you date because you don't mind them knowing, but you're very good at keeping yourself to yourself when it comes to making sure no one oversteps the mark…'

'Okay. Spit it out. What's going on, Jess?'

'Nothing. I'm just pointing out the obvious.'

'So you don't want to tell me who you're seeing?' He shrugged with exaggerated indifference. 'So be it. It's not the end of the world.'

That stung. She hated the feeling. It had been bearable keeping her distance, thinking about him but building up her immunity, but now that he was sitting across from her she *missed* their easy familiarity.

His suddenly unreadable green eyes were locked

speculatively on her face and she felt her heart speed up. She wanted to cry, which was ridiculous because it was perfectly healthy for her to keep her distance. In time, they would resume their friendship but when that happened she would no longer be in thrall to him.

'I'm assuming,' he drawled, 'that that's your reason for turning down my generous offer...'

What to say? How to respond? She thought about her 'hot date'. Poor Mike...so nice, so pleasant-looking—so many boxes ticked—and yet not enough.

That was information she didn't want to impart so she shrugged but, instead of backing away from the topic, he shamelessly prodded, 'Well? Am I on the right track here?'

'How is it,' she said, frustrated, 'that I never realised how much like a dog with a bone you are when it comes to getting what you want?'

He visibly relaxed and she was cravenly grateful that the status quo was back.

'I have no idea. You should have. Are you concerned that the new guy in your life might not like the fact that we're spending a long weekend together?'

Jess marvelled that he could make a statement of fact sound so disconcertingly intimate without even realising it.

'I would never let anyone dictate how I spend my time,' she retorted and blushed when he grinned with smug approval.

'Thought not, but if that *had* been the case then you could truthfully have told him that we would be in separate rooms and, quite honestly, you would be free to more or less do your own thing for most of the weekend. Yes, we would be together for the ceremony, but that's about it. You could ski to your heart's content the rest of the time...' He leant towards her and murmured softly, 'Don't tell me that you're not tempted...'

Jess blinked.

Temptation was a finger's touch away if he but knew it and when it came to temptation the prospect of skiing paled in comparison.

'But,' he continued briskly, 'just in case you need further persuasion, I would very much like to dangle a carrot in front of you...'

'What carrot?'

'A very healthy donation to your school.' He smiled. 'I know that if it's not because of a guy, then it must be because you don't think you'll be able to spare the time because you're all engaged on a fundraising drive to get new desks for your school...'

'Computer equipment.'

'I already contribute generously to many charities via my various business holdings, but I would like to personally donate towards whatever equipment you need.'

He named a sum that took her breath away because not only would it cover all the equipment the school needed, but also repair work to two of the buildings caused by water damage the previous winter.

'It's *that* important for you to have a chaperone to a wedding, Curtis?'

'You should have come to me if you needed financial assistance for your school.'

'Of course I'm not going to do that!'

'Why not?'

'Because I... I just *wouldn't*.'

'You're one of a kind, Jess,' he said softly. 'You have no idea how many people would think nothing of coming to me with a begging bowl to support whatever cause they needed money for. You're one of the least opportunistic women I've ever known.'

Pleasure bloomed inside her and she pinkened.

'We go back a long way,' she admitted. 'I knew you before you made it big.'

'So will you come with me, Jess? You really would be doing me a huge favour...'

There were no other reasons she could possibly give for rejecting his offer. They weren't on the same page emotionally, but how was he to know that?

And if she kept avoiding him, surely he would begin to smell a rat? She valued his friendship. She would hate to lose it and she knew that in due course, once she'd broken free of whatever spell he had cast over her down the years, they would once again be pals, but this time on an equal footing.

Would she now want to jeopardise that? Mike the teacher might not have been the one for her, but there *was* someone out there for her and when that someone came into her life all the foolish feelings she had towards Curtis would disappear like dew in the summer sun.

That was the way life worked.

And, additionally, it now struck her, maybe it *would* be a good idea to go on that skiing weekend. Maybe a burst of Curtis would get him out of her system once and for all. Maybe seeing him in fits and starts over the years had fed her infatuation. Maybe a weekend in his company would do the trick when it came to stifling all the inappropriate feelings she still seemed to harbour towards him. She would see first-hand, in the presence of all the beautiful, eligible women who would be there, just how out of reach he was for someone like her. She would be firmly reminded of her status as *friend*.

It was exhausting thinking about all the permutations of the situation. A simple invitation and she'd been thrown into a tailspin that was giving her a headache.

'The school *would* benefit from your kind generosity,' she agreed. 'I'll come but please don't think that you have to stick to your promise about the money. You're right. It would be nice to relax and to ski.'

Curtis smiled, satisfied. 'I'm a man of my word,' he told her. 'By tomorrow evening your school's bank account will be considerably healthier...'

Jess managed to keep her head firmly down over the next week and a half. The money which he had donated to the school was so greatly appreciated that she thought the governors might actually declare a day's holiday in celebration.

When she knew that he had returned to London, three days after having arrived to see his godfather, she cycled over to William, where news of her weekend's escapade had reached his ears.

'I'm thrilled for you,' he confided as they sat at his kitchen table with a plate of homemade scones between them and Earl Grey in cups. 'You're just like Curtis. You work too hard, my dear.' He looked at her shrewdly and then asked whether whatever chap she might be going out with wouldn't object to her accompanying a man for a weekend away.

'So far—' she laughed '—I've been on three dates with three guys and, as the song goes, William, I'm still looking...'

'There's always my godson,' William returned with a sly twinkle in his eye and she coloured like a beetroot.

'Don't be ridiculous,' she huffed in an unnaturally high voice. 'Curtis is my friend and *that's all*.' She cleared her throat, looked at her phone for the time and shifted her eyes away from his piercing blue ones. 'We might be going to this wedding together, but it's only because he's scared that some scheming cute blonde with wedding rings in her sight might make a beeline for him…'

'He does enjoy his cute blondes, not that any of them ever seem to work out…'

'He's a commitment-phobe, William.'

'You think so, my dear? I would say he wants commitment more than he thinks. He's just in the process of making his way to the right recipient.'

'I should get going.' She stood up, began putting on her thick padded coat. She didn't dare glance in William's direction. Had boredom got the better of him? Made his imagination a little too overactive for his own good?

She would put him in touch with a few clubs as soon as she got back to Ely. She knew a lot of people and she could think of some very nice organisations that would welcome a clever retired lecturer who was also a fantastic cook. Was he too confirmed a bachelor to think about letting a suitable lady into his life? It would certainly distract him from a life without the routine of his university lecturing job.

Left to his own devices, the last thing she needed was for him to start second-guessing how she felt about Curtis.

'There's a lot more to my godson than meets the eye.' He patted her arm fondly as he walked her to the door. 'There are a lot of hidden depths there, my dear.'

'I'll bear that in mind,' Jess replied, laughing, 'when I see him forcing himself not to flirt with all the women who will be flinging themselves at him at the wedding.'

Hidden depths? Sure, many times she had wondered

at what stirred under the surface of his easy charm. She knew nothing about him prior to when he had joined her school, and now William's murmured words had unleashed questions in her head she knew had always been there...

The last thing she needed at this juncture was curiosity, which was on an equal level with nervousness when it came to something else she didn't need, but she was still as nervous as a kitten when, bags packed and long weekend in sight, she pushed her way through the crowds at Heathrow to spy him lounging by the First-class check-in, looking at something on his phone.

Every single time Jess saw him, it was as though she were seeing him for the very first time. He was always just so much more dramatic than she remembered.

He looked effortlessly cool in a beaten leather motorbike jacket, faded jeans, black sweater and sturdy tan loafers. On the ground was a luxury case. He looked up at her approach and straightened.

'Thank you for the driver, Curtis.' She launched into speech to still the butterflies in her tummy. In her layers of bulky clothing she felt frumpy and unexciting.

'I wouldn't dream of putting you through the hassle of getting on public transport. You should get yourself a car, Jess.'

'I already have a car.'

He wasn't looking at her. He had relieved her of her passport and had flipped it open to inspect her picture, while she tried not to cringe because it was a stunningly unflattering one taken when she still wore thick specs and was just a little too overweight to be called voluptuous.

'Mmm. I was talking about one that works when you want it to work instead of when it feels like it.' He checked his watch. 'Not much time to kick around here. It's going to be a long trip. No idea why I didn't take the jet.' He eyed her. 'Very good idea that you chose to wear comfy clothes.'

'You should see the stuff I've packed,' Jess said, walking fast to keep pace even though she was only a few inches shorter than him.

'Including to wear to the wedding?'

'Yes, Curtis. Jogging bottoms and a sweatshirt. Is there a problem with that?'

This was the banter she was accustomed to, light-hearted conversation between friends, but she could breathe him in as he walked alongside her and when she glanced across she was achingly aware of the leather jacket, the tight jeans encasing his muscular legs, the stubble on his chin, the thickness of his slightly too long hair.

'You'll have to excuse my lack of chit-chat, Jess. I have a hell of a lot of work to do on the plane. My routine was thrown out because I hung around for a bit longer than I'd planned with William. Kept an eye on him, by the way. He seems in good humour and...' he slanted his green eyes across to her; there was an amused half smile tugging his mouth and Jess felt her breath hitch in her throat because he was just so damned *sexy* '...he seems curiously excited at the prospect of us spending a long weekend together.'

Jess didn't know what to say to that, but she was spared having to make any response because he was obviously in a hurry to get down to work.

He cut a swathe through the crowds, oblivious to the heads swinging in their direction. He oozed sex appeal. Tall, commanding, movie star looks with an apparent lack of vanity that his whole urgent body language implied without him having to work at it.

No wonder he had women flocking to him in droves.

She still didn't know exactly what had happened between him and Caitlin, but if he'd had his heart broken it was no wonder he wanted to deflect any unwanted hopefuls who might want to target him at the wedding. Once bitten would definitely be twice shy.

They hit the First-class lounge at a brisk pace.

'Coffee…tea…food…pastries… Take your pick, Jess.' He wasn't looking at her as he said this. He was making a beeline towards a nest of deep chairs surrounding a low table, already pulling out his laptop, so at ease in her company that there was no attempt to disguise the fact that he intended to spend the time working until their flight was called. She would have to do her own thing and that suited her just fine.

'Want anything?' She dumped her bag on the table and remained standing as he sat down, briefly looking up at her.

'Nothing. I'll be a little less antisocial just as soon as I've answered this string of emails.'

'I don't expect you to socialise with me, Curtis.' She began unzipping the puffer jacket. Thoughts crowded into her head and she fought against them—thoughts she'd never seemed to have had before, or at least acknowledged. Mean, spiky thoughts that he would be making a mammoth effort to socialise with her if she'd been one of his dainty blondes. He didn't see the need to put himself out when it came to her because there was just too much familiarity between them.

'What do you mean?' For the first time since she'd arrived he actually focused on her, his sea-green eyes riveted to her face.

'I mean—' Jess cleared her throat '—I know why I'm here.' She hoped she sounded airy and wryly amused. She feared she might just sound defensive and a little hurt. 'I'm here to protect you from the fan club waiting to get their claws into you.'

'Bit of an exaggeration.' But he grinned, eyebrows shooting up as he relaxed back to focus fully on her with lazy, lingering amusement.

A prickle of heat coursed through her and she abruptly turned away with a shrug. 'I've brought my laptop and some schoolwork I'll have to get through because I'm taking a couple of days off. I have more than enough to occupy myself while you work.'

He looked at her. What was he missing here?

He hadn't seen her in a while, but it wasn't the first time that weeks had elapsed without contact. Wasn't that the nature of good friendships? Time could pass but catching up was always seamless.

Except this time…

This time something was a little off-kilter, although for the life of him he couldn't work out what it was.

Surely she wasn't offended because he'd offered her an all-expenses-paid free trip to Courchevel where, aside from a few hours in a frock drinking champagne and chit-chatting with a few people, she would endure nothing more gruelling than eating great food, drinking fine wine and skiing down some of the most invigorating slopes in the world?

What was there not to like in that scenario?

He uneasily wondered whether she was miffed because there was a limit to how far he would go when it came to confiding.

When he thought about it, she'd been a bit odd ever

since the Caitlin fiasco. He absently watched her. She was taller than most of the women in the vicinity, her body concealed underneath a navy-blue jumper that reached to mid-thigh, where it merged into the navy-blue jeans and navy-blue trainers.

It was a revelation actually seeing her eyes, though. Deep, deep blue. He'd never noticed how unusual they were behind those thick spectacles she used to wear.

In front of him his laptop blinked, demanding his attention, but his mind was stubbornly drifting as he tried to get a grip on what it was that jarred.

No one knew the full story about the disaster he had narrowly avoided. Despite his openness when it came to the women he dated, despite his willingness to allow the paparazzi to peer into his life, he knew that he rigorously controlled what the public knew about him and the truth was that, despite the parade of women and his willingness to be photographed with them, he was intensely private.

He frowned. The past was a place he never visited. It was too dark and there was no point. Information about him was scant on the Internet. It worked being open to all intents and purposes because it meant that no one really had any interest in delving beyond what was on the table and he liked it that way.

It had not occurred to him that he could or should explain the situation with his ex to anyone. Even William knew precious little. The story was that he'd been dumped by a beautiful woman who'd become bored with him. He was very happy to leave it there.

He shifted. He was uncomfortable with this bout of introspection and bemused that the woman now helping herself to coffee had managed to bring it on.

Still brooding over an atmosphere he couldn't quite

put his finger on, he watched as she spun round and began walking carefully towards him, coffee in one hand and a bottle of water in the other. She should have just got waiter service but that wouldn't have occurred to her, which made him smile.

Just like that, she looked across to him and their eyes met and tangled and for a few seconds his breath caught sharply in his throat. But then he smiled more broadly as she neared, easing back into the low chair, ready to tease her about helping herself to coffee when there were eager attendants waiting to do it for their privileged customers, ready to share a wry joke about the quality of the delicacies on offer being as good as in any restaurant, ready to ask her why she hadn't helped herself to any of the sweet morsels. He knew from old that she loved nothing more than a slice of cake or a chocolate bar.

But then she leant forward to deposit the water and the coffee on the table and in one smooth movement, straightened to remove the bulky sweater.

And he stared.

It was rare for him to be disconcerted to the extent that he was rendered speechless, but in this instance he was because the figure on display underneath that shapeless blue sweater was…definitely not what he'd expected.

He had a moment of pure confusion at the dichotomy between the reality of what he was seeing and his memory of her hiding behind her thick specs and untidy hair and shapeless garments. Wasn't she just the tiniest bit overweight? She had been…hadn't she?

The specs had gone and the hair was gloriously shiny, falling in dark waves to her shoulders, and her body…

He was shocked by the dramatic response of his body. Since when was he in the habit of losing control? He made a futile attempt to drag his eyes away but for a few seconds all he could take in, as she leant to shove the jumper into the holdall, was the sway of her full breasts, the rounded curve of her hips and legs that were incredibly long and surprisingly slender. She brushed her hair away from her face, tucking it behind her ear. She wasn't looking at him and he concluded that that was a relief because she would have been startled to see how compulsively he was staring, but he just couldn't seem to help himself.

When had *that* happened? When had she turned into a sex siren? Why hadn't she given him any prior warning as to what to expect? He really hadn't seen much of her at all over the past few months and it dawned on him that this body transformation was in line with her sudden exploration of the dating scene. It was a sobering thought. She wasn't one of these hard-edged women who knew how the world turned when it came to guys! She was…well, she was *Jess*! Sweetly innocent and endearingly straightforward.

He thought about her with some sex-crazed guy on the lookout for a one-night stand and congratulated himself on the surge of protectiveness that smothered him just for a few destabilising seconds.

'Is there something on my face?'

'Come again?'

'You're staring.'

He flushed darkly, shifted, scowled.

'Mind was a million miles away.' His voice was more abrupt than he'd intended and he saw her face tighten with hurt but, caught out as he had been, the last thing on his mind was an apology. 'Work,' he offered, staring at his laptop while his mind tried to compute a shift inside himself that he didn't care for.

'Okay.'

He heard her laugh and was aware of her sitting down again and reaching for the coffee. All he could see in his mind was the abundance of luscious breasts straining against the stretchy black fabric of her skin-tight T-shirt.

It could not have been a more modest garment, with a high, round neck and long enough to ensure not even a sliver of stomach was revealed, however much she twisted, turned and stretched. And the jeans encasing those long, long legs? Blue denim without a designer label in sight, and high-waisted enough to pretty much classify as unfashionable in most of the circles he mixed in, and yet she could not have looked sexier.

'I should go sit at one of those desks.' He nodded to the bank of desks by the wall, with all the accoutrements for hooking up to the Internet. He tried to kill the uncomfortable flush of discomfort and the zinging awareness of her looking at him with those surprisingly beautiful almond-shaped navy eyes. 'Charging banks,' he muttered. 'Useful.'

'Sure.'

The smile was frozen on her face as he stalked off without a backward glance.

Could he have made it any clearer that he couldn't be bothered with her company?

Was this a terrible mistake? Was their friendship only workable when they met in passing? They weren't kids any more, sitting on the sofa and watching movies with a bag of popcorn between them. Life had separated them. Life and experiences. Was she jeopardising what they had by being here? Some things that thrived in a certain environment wilted and died in another.

They were so close, she mused, pointedly not looking

in his direction but fishing into her bag for her laptop, and yet there was a gulf between them that had become glaringly apparent in the wake of his relationship and engagement to Caitlin.

First-hand, she had seen how the important stuff had never been shared. She knew precious little about his past and nothing at all about how he really felt about... love and marriage and parenthood or anything else that really mattered.

He was the least likely guy she should ever have had a crush on, never mind nurturing deeper feelings that would never be returned.

Maybe he was regretting inviting her along for four days of together time.

Maybe she should tell him that he should feel free to ditch her if he wanted. It wasn't as though she would lose sleep if she missed a wedding where she knew no one!

She would wait and see how things played out but already she longed for the safety of her little terraced house and the peace of not having her feelings challenged.

CHAPTER THREE

THE HOTEL—WHICH, Curtis had told her en route, had been hand-picked by his PA—was one of those dreamy locations only within reach of someone with extremely deep pockets.

Unlike most of the hotels, this one was more like someone's private country house. Neither of them had brought skis, in her case because she didn't actually own any, but she had given her shoe size a couple of days ago to his secretary and not only were skis waiting for her but also boots in exactly the right size.

They were ushered into a foyer warm with subdued earth-toned colours. An expanse of cream and caramel marble led to a desk behind which two smiling women, who would not have been out of place on the cover of a fashion magazine, were waiting to check them in.

Despite the fact that it wasn't an adults-only hotel, there was a marked absence of any families. Jess was so accustomed to sharing her space with kids of all ages and sizes that she found herself whispering, the way she would in a library.

'Lovely.' This to Curtis as they stood in front of the blonde magazine cover receptionist who was busily trying not to pay the slightest bit of attention to the hunk standing in front of her.

'You're whispering,' he whispered with a grin. 'You approve then…?'

Checked in, he took the credit-card-style keys handed to him without glancing in the direction of the receptionist, instead gazing at Jess, eyes still amused.

'It's certainly a step up from the last place I went to with the school kids,' she said crisply. Those green eyes on her did crazy things to her breathing and she broke eye contact to look around. It was awe-inspiring. Where he had grown up, if not in the lap of luxury then in the lap of well-to-do comfort, *she* had been brought up with the motto that *Every penny counts.* Her contact with any kind of luxury had been all those many times she had hung out at his godfather's place while her mother had cleaned, bringing in some pin money to bolster the salary her dad got from the glass factory where he worked as a foreman.

She'd never in her entire life ever imagined that somewhere as perfect as this could possibly exist. It was a prime example of what happened when a top interior designer shook hands with limitless budget.

'Have you been here before?'

'Every year,' Curtis said wryly. 'I like the fact that it's small and it's private. One of the advantages to having money. It buys you peace, if that's what you're after.'

'Is that why we're here?' she asked shrewdly.

She dragged her eyes away from the breathtaking surroundings, reminding herself that there would be ample time for her to explore on her own at some point, and looked at him as the concealed lift pinged shut behind them with the hush of bank vault doors softly sealing closed.

Suddenly the space felt suffocatingly intimate and her skin heated up as he continued to look at her.

'We're in separate rooms,' he said. 'Adjoining thanks

to a connecting door, but separate. Bearing in mind you're supposed to be my plus one, it made sense not to advertise the fact that we're not sleeping together. My plus ones would usually share my bed.'

Jess could feel her skin begin to burn and her breathing became jerky and shallow because, just like that, her head was cluttered with images of him in bed, naked…

She gulped and her eyes glazed over and thankfully she was spared a response because the lift doors slid open, disgorging them into a plush hall off which their rooms were located.

'Your key.'

Jess took the card and stared at it for a few seconds while her batteries tried to recharge.

'Good idea,' she muttered, turning away and blindly tapping the door with the card to push it open, at which point she turned to him, finally braving his eyes, with the safety of her bedroom behind her. 'No point…you know…wagging tongues and the like…'

'My thoughts exactly.'

Jess wondered whether it was her imagination or did those veiled eyes remain on her for just a tiny bit longer than necessary? At any rate, there was a furnace raging inside her and she couldn't wait to douse it under a tepid shower.

'So…' It wasn't yet six in the evening.

'So?' He'd been lounging against the doorframe, having edged her back without her even noticing, but now he straightened, one hundred per cent business. 'Tonight I'm meeting John and a handful of the guys for a night of fun and too much alcohol, I imagine. You're free to do your own thing. Order whatever you want, explore the place to your heart's content. Everything is on me, Jess. You can buy the entire boutique downstairs if you want to. Alternatively, you can come with me and hang with the bride-to-be and her bridesmaids, who will be doing their own thing, probably with considerably more restraint. I'm sure Philippa wouldn't object…'

'I'll skip that option,' Jess said hurriedly.

'Thought you might. Right. And tomorrow…what say we take to the slopes? Before the rest of the world has time to wake up?'

'Isn't that going to be difficult if you're nursing a hangover?' But that sounded just about right to her. She knew that he was a good skier. There would be no awkward conversations on the slopes and the truth was that she was dying to get her skis on and get out there. She'd gazed at the conditions from the back seat of the limo that had ferried them to their hotel and the snow was perfect. Mouth-wateringly perfect.

'I have way too much self-control to overindulge in alcohol,' he informed her. And it was true. He'd spent too many years knowing what it felt like to have no control over any single part of his life, however minuscule. It was thus the one thing he valued now. 'I've never been drunk in my life before and it's not a habit I have any intention of picking up any time soon. So are you okay to fend for yourself this evening?'

'You're a saint, Curtis,' she teased, relaxed at the thought of an evening to herself and normality being resumed in the morning on the slopes. 'And yes, I think I can manage. I've been doing it for the past twenty-six years after all.'

She thought that she might have spent the evening with her thoughts on him, brooding on whatever the next couple of days held in store and analysing to the point of a migraine whether she regretted her decision to come or not, but in fact she had never felt so relaxed as she unwound over the next few hours.

How long must it have been since she'd had time off? Ages. When her dad had died quite suddenly, her mother had been plunged into the sort of pervasive depression that had cast a cloud over every aspect of Jess's life. Her social life had been put on hold because making sure her mother was okay had demanded most of her spare time. Holidays of any sort had not just been put on hold—they'd been relegated to the deep freezer, from which they hadn't emerged to see the light of day.

Now, she felt like a kid in a sweet shop. She explored the hotel from top to bottom, marvelling at the subterranean labyrinth of steam grottos and saunas, practically enough for each guest to have his or her own. Then there was the indoor pool, carved out to mimic an underground lagoon, complete with a wall of cascading water and a jacuzzi.

There was a comprehensive gym and a Michelin starred restaurant, as well as two further casual dining areas, two bars and a spa, which she peeked into. It smelled of sandalwood and eucalyptus.

By the time she'd ordered room service, she'd forgotten all about the stresses that had been plaguing her over the past few weeks and months.

Her bedroom suite was the last word in luxury, with a sitting room that managed to be comfortable yet scarily perfect and an en suite bathroom with a bath the size of an Olympic swimming pool, in which she luxuriated for a ridiculous length of time.

There were floor-to-ceiling windows everywhere, a clever bit of design that allowed you to look out at the snowy wonderland, an unimpeded vista of white.

The following morning her phone pinged, and she smiled when she read Curtis's text saying that he would be waiting for her in Reception.

Breakfast in bed and then a day on the slopes before the ceremony the following day at the groom's parents' ski lodge, which was apparently more than big enough for the party of nearly a hundred people, a string quartet, a sprawling buffet and all the other stuff that was part and parcel of an aristocratic wedding.

Since she had only ever attended three weddings—none of which were fancier than the local church and, in one case, a marquee on the village green, which had been brilliant—Jess couldn't wait to see how the other half celebrated.

But for now...

She felt an illicit thrill at the thought of seeing Curtis. Forgotten were the edge-of-seat nerves and the back and forth wondering what she was doing.

She'd only bought one new thing for the trip and that was her ski outfit—a reckless splurge but when next would she be in a position like this?

At a little after nine she headed down to Reception, having fully togged up for the day ahead.

Outside the snow was freshly fallen so she was looking forward to some grippy turns and a smooth ride down the excellent pistes. She knew that sometimes the cushion of snow could be powdery enough to make her feel as though she was floating and nothing was more magical.

He was there.

They matched. All black. Her heart thumped as she strolled towards him.

She felt exposed in the ski outfit, which clung to her like a second skin. Had he seen her in anything that hadn't been baggy? Yes, surely so, but in the past few months she'd slimmed considerably and never had she been more conscious of her figure.

Looking up from his phone, Curtis inhaled sharply, eyes narrowing on her as she sashayed towards him.

Because no other word could describe the sexy motion of her hips. Her legs went on and on *and on* and where the heck had she got that outfit? It contoured a body that men's dreams were made of and his legendary fondness for petite blondes disappeared under a haze of lust that leapt out at him and sent a charge of high voltage electricity racing through his body with mercurial ferocity.

He hardened, his body's immediate response, yet one that he could not remember having ever experienced in his life before with such urgency. When it came to the game of seduction he was *always* the one in charge. This time, however, his body was calling the shots and it was infuriating.

What the hell was going on? This woman was his closest female friend—his *only* female friend! He'd never subscribed to the homily that a man couldn't be friends with a woman without sex rearing its ugly head. He'd always known that he had far too much self-control for that sort of indiscriminate response to ever hold sway.

He knew he was staring but he couldn't seem to help himself and his mouth was dry.

And the rest of his body was making him wonder whether he'd ever had an attack of plain old-fashioned lust.

Black outfit, zip running from waist to neck, outlining the most perfect breasts he'd ever seen. Breasts that were much more than a handful and those shapely legs encased in tight black and tucked into white boots.

Her sunglasses were propped on her forehead, as his were.

'Ready?' he half croaked, spinning round on his heel because, despite the two sets of thermals and the trousers, he was very much afraid that she might catch sight of his rampant erection.

'Can't wait,' Jess carolled. She looped her arm through his. 'Tell me how your evening went,' she encouraged when he failed to say anything further. 'I did wonder whether I should text you to find out whether you were in one piece...'

'As you can see—' he couldn't look at her, couldn't risk prolonging his rampant response '—I don't do overindulgence when it comes to alcohol. The plan today—' he could hardly detach his arm but the weight of hers wound through his was just adding to his mental disarray, so focusing on a businesslike discussion of the day ahead seemed a good idea '—is some skiing and then a quick lunch. I have work to do after lunch, so you are free to do your own thing. At six, we're going to John's chalet for a pre-wedding dinner. It'll be informal. No need to dress up.' He had a pang of nostalgia for her uniform of baggy clothes, which had always been so good at concealing her figure. 'You've lost weight.' He deviated sharply from the conversation he had had in mind, and cast a quick glance across at her.

'A bit.'

'Hope you haven't joined those women who think that eating anything that isn't raw or can't be grown in a vegetable patch is a crime...'

'Far from it,' Jess countered politely, removing her arm and focusing on the business of the skiing ahead, because something in his voice was edgy and just a little bit…offensive. Although she couldn't quite put her finger on it because it was the usual sort of teasing remark she would have expected from him.

Did he think that she should somehow have been happy to remain as the five ten, overweight girl next door hiding behind her spectacles and her untamed hair?

She banked down a sudden attack of self-consciousness because she knew she looked just fine. The outfit suited her and if he didn't like it, which was the implication in his voice, then too bad.

The slopes were already busy, but this part of the world was classy when it came to skiing. There were so many ski lifts that no one ever had to wait, and the ski instructors were sometimes ex-world champions.

She was in her element here. There were no kids around to channel and supervise and cajole and tell off for horsing around. An opportunity like this would never come her way again and she was *not* going to let Curtis Hamilton spoil it because he seemed to think that she had no right to try and change.

There was only one way to deal with that, she decided, and that was to pretend that he just wasn't there at all, and for the next three hours that was exactly what she did.

She let the white, snowy slopes cool her mind and she lost herself in the thrill of feeling cold air rushing against her face and the freedom that came with speed. He tried to outpace her but she kept up, enjoying the challenge, equal against equal, both savouring the same thrill that was blessed respite from the tangle of emotions that had been plaguing her for longer than she cared to think.

Buoyed, she declined to join him for lunch and instead told him that she would meet him in the foyer in time for the pre-wedding party.

'And yes,' she said, harking back to their pre-ski conversation, 'I know it's going to be an informal event this evening and I think I've brought just the right outfit to wear.' Which wasn't strictly true but there were shops out there and she was going to treat herself to something nice. So what if he preferred she stood still and never changed? She would make sure she chose something that would prove to him once and for all that she was no longer the girl next door, stuck in her predictable comfort zone.

'There's no need to go overboard.' He smiled a little stiffly. 'John's parents will be there and they couldn't be more old-fashioned.'

'What are you trying to say?'

'I'm not trying to say anything.' He raked his fingers through his hair and looked away. 'Right. If you're sure you won't join me for lunch, then I'll see you later. Six sharp. I have a driver to take us there and bring us back.'

An uncustomary sense of rebellion propelled Jess into boutiques she would never have dared venture into a handful of months before, when she was so self-conscious about her size that concealment had been the key factor when it came to choosing clothes.

She would never be able to compete with the tiny little Christmas tree baubles Curtis favoured but she was proud of her shape and wasn't going to hide it under layers of drab clothes. If Curtis had been implying that she should try and cover up because she wasn't skinny enough to wear tight clothes then he was in for a shock. She wondered whether seeing her in her skiing outfit had alarmed him and grinned when she thought about that.

What a prude underneath that charming libertine exterior! At least as far as *she* was concerned!

She reflected as she threw herself into an afternoon of shopping and to heck with counting her pennies, that we all ended up being stuck in categories and sometimes, when we wanted to get out, it was a whole lot more difficult than we expected.

She wondered where she would end up if she broke free of the category into which she had always been stuck as far as Curtis was concerned.

No longer the comfortable friend, but then what…?

Maybe still a friend but one who was allowed past all those No Trespass signs she realised he always had up, maybe a friend who could openly chat to him about her love life because she would have gone past her inconvenient infatuation to find herself a guy who really appreciated her. Maybe they would go on double dates together, although her imagination found it hard to stretch to that scenario.

At any rate, anything would be better than the limbo she felt she'd occupied for too long.

The only coat she had was a mid-thigh-length, very unbecoming but highly practical black down padded puffer, perfect for intensely wintry conditions. But she'd treated herself to a pair of low flat boots and a long-sleeved woollen dress in a flattering shade of deep blue, with its elegant cowl neck which managed to expose just the right amount of shoulder. It clung to her much like the ski outfit did but left a lot less to the imagination when it came to the length of her legs and the fullness of her breasts.

She was a big girl and she wasn't going to try and play it down.

She hugged herself as they stepped out to the waiting four-wheel drive limo. For a few seconds she breathed in the purity of the mountain air and enjoyed the tingling crispness of the dry cold on her cheeks.

'Beautiful, isn't it?' He paused alongside her, both staring out at the same stunning view of rolling peaks and valleys of purest white, even though it was dark. 'Glad you came?'

'It's been a lovely day skiing.' She moved away, letting herself into the back seat of the chauffeur-driven car and then shuffling along so that he could slide in next to her.

The stillness of everything outside, a stillness that only seemed to exist in the snow-capped silent mountains, seemed to trap them in an artificial intimacy and she hurried to break it by launching into frenetic small talk.

What was the lodge like where the ceremony was to be held? Had he been before? How many people would he know when they got there? Had he managed to get much work done? Had he spoken to his godfather? What a poppet William was...

She was hyper-aware of him next to her, within touching distance. His padded heavy-duty waterproof coat was as thick as hers but still she was acutely aware of his lean body underneath and as the car drew up to the lodge she breathed a sigh of relief. How much more inane chatting could she rustle up before he asked her whether she was feeling all right? If she veered any more wildly from making a point of showing him that everything was as normal as always between them to babbling nervously as if he'd suddenly turned into a stranger then he would definitely think she'd lost the plot.

The sight of the ski lodge, though, provided ample distraction. It was an immense pile, illuminated in a blaze of light and straddling the side of a snowy hill in various steps, with each layer fronted by an enormous wraparound veranda. Five verandas. There were at least a dozen high-end cars parked in the courtyard, each of them snow-covered. To the side, away from the house and in the blackness, Curtis pointed out a helipad, which probably accounted for how many of the guests would arrive.

'I've always wondered how the other half live,' she murmured, sufficiently distracted not to notice the sexiness of his lazy smile in response or the flare of warmth in his eyes as he looked at her straining forward, mouth half open in awe. 'Now I know...'

'It pays its way,' he said wryly. 'It's impressive but it's rented out for most of the ski season and pretty much all of the summer, when it's really very beautiful here, even minus the snow...'

'I guess not many people can afford the upkeep of a place like this,' she sighed as the car purred to a stop.

'I can and I'm always very happy to acquaint you in other lessons about how the other half live,' he murmured, leaning towards her, his breath warm on her cheek, causing her to pull back in startled response.

Her eyes widened and for a second there were just the two of them in the back seat of the car and then she said urgently, to break the sudden electricity that seemed to have built up, 'I can't remember...we're not supposed to be an item, are we...?'

The driver had rushed out to open the passenger door for her, lest she do it herself, as she had earlier, and she stepped out and away from the radius of Curtis's overpowering personality.

'People will assume that we're going out.' He shrugged. 'I've told the guys that I'm here with a woman...so they've reached their own conclusions. People will see me with you and...'

'And all those pesky women will steer clear?'

'I don't need anyone imagining that I'm up for grabs,' he murmured.

Jessica slanted thoughtful eyes on him. 'Not all single women go to someone's wedding and immediately think that the best man is up for grabs if he happens to be single,' she returned. 'Besides, you must have lots of experience when it comes to deflecting unwanted attention...'

'Over a four-day period it could get a little trying, and at this point in time... Put it this way, I would rather steer clear of anyone in search of involvement.'

'Well, just so long as we don't have to pretend to be romantically involved...'

'Oh, we don't have to pretend anything,' Curtis refuted. 'No one is going to ask me to elaborate on our relationship and no one can doubt that we are intimately involved... That's the joy of a friendship that spans more than a decade—there's no need to work at acting relaxed in each other's company because we already are...'

Jess shivered because the last thing she felt at the moment was *relaxed* in his company, but she could see his logic.

Assumptions would be made and it would just be a case of going along with them. They had always been easy with one another and their casual familiarity would answer unasked questions. He was hardly the sort who would advertise a relationship with physical displays of affection.

There had been method in his decision to ask her to tag along.

She had a twinge of nerves as they entered the vast

lodge. The door was opened by a uniformed member of staff and their names were formally taken and checked against a printed list.

Out of sight, she could hear the sound of voices and laughter, the low steady rumble of people having a good time, but she couldn't see anyone because they were all scattered in the bowels of the sprawling villa.

This was the holding pen where guests were ticked off a list because you could never be too careful. Although who on earth would want to gatecrash a fancy gathering in a ski lodge that sat in its own snowy grounds was anybody's guess. Who would dare?

'Your coats?'

As she absently removed her coat to hand to yet another member of staff who had appeared out of thin air, she was busily dealing with a sudden onset of nerves just at being somewhere where she would know absolutely no one at all and already envisaging being left to her own devices by Curtis, who would want to socialise with old friends. She decided that it would be an opportunity to brush up on her small talk skills with strangers.

Likewise, Curtis was gearing himself up for an evening of mingling. Small talk invariably ended up boring him to death, so the prospect was not an enticing one.

It was good that she had asked him about the charade about to commence, although he really didn't think it was about deceiving anyone into thinking anything, merely establishing boundary lines because John's wife-to-be was a model and there would be a bevy of models in the wings and, whatever anyone said, he would be targeted, the thought of which left him exhausted.

Surrounded by John's family and friends, it would have been an unpleasant task having to evade potential predators. That said, he had established Jess's role and emphasised the solid friendship between them. That had been a good idea, given the way his mind had strayed earlier on.

Coat dispatched, he turned to her and froze.

The sterling qualities of friendship, which he had just been mentally applauding, flew through the window faster than a speeding bullet.

His body was jump-started at supersonic speed and what he had felt only hours before when he had seen her in that ski outfit paled in comparison to what he was feeling right now.

Nothing was left to the imagination. Or rather too much was left to the imagination, and his imagination was having a field-day conjuring up all manner of forbidden images.

His hands itched to slip under the neckline of that dress to find the heavy weight of her breasts. He wondered what her nipples would look like, would taste like...

He clenched his fists and gritted his teeth and managed to step forward to politely usher her in the direction of the noise.

'You...' he said in a stifled undertone, 'you've gone the extra mile with the dress.'

'Do you like it?'

'It...it's unexpected... I don't believe...ah...that I've ever seen you in something like that...'

'A change is as good as a rest,' Jess piped up. She didn't want to look at him because she feared that she might find it hard to tear her eyes off him. Underneath the coat, he was wearing a pair of black trousers and a white shirt, with a charcoal-grey V-necked jumper in the softest cashmere. He succeeded in looking both casual and insanely elegant at the same time.

'Ah…'

When he failed to continue, she looked at him quizzically, braced to defend her choice of clothing and to stand up for statuesque women and their right to wear whatever they chose to.

'Yes?' She arched an eyebrow and he flushed.

'Nothing.' He circled her arm with his hand. 'Don't be nervous,' he added, for want of anything better to say. 'I know you don't like this kind of event.'

'I never used to,' she said airily, 'but that was years ago. I've got a lot more confident since I've been teaching. When you have to control a classful of kids and establish order, you can't afford to be too much of a shrinking violet.'

'Got it,' he muttered.

They paused ahead of the sequence of bustling rooms. It was an open-plan space that managed to retain separate areas with the clever use of partitions and banks of plants and two open fireplaces. Through the vast expanse of glass overlooking the mountains, the view was surreal in its empty whiteness.

Waiters circulated, balancing trays of food and drink.

'I thought it was going to be a little less…crowded.'

'So did I.' He shrugged. 'Don't worry. I don't plan on staying long.'

'I'm not worried,' she said irritably. About to reassure him that he was no longer dealing with the insecure girl who'd shied away from parties, she followed his gaze to where he was staring narrowly at a slight figure reaching for a glass of champagne.

'Jesus,' he swore softly under his breath. 'You're not going to believe this, but Caitlin is here…'

CHAPTER FOUR

IT TOOK A few horrified seconds for that to sink in, even though the evidence was standing straight in front of Jess in the form of five-foot-nothing of drop-dead gorgeous Barbie doll in a tight, short red dress and killer heels.

She jerked Curtis off to the side, behind the wall, and hissed, 'Did you know that your ex was going to be here?'

Jess had met Caitlin twice, when he had brought her to visit his godfather. Towering over the dainty blonde, and still in her comfort-eating phase, Jess had never felt more self-conscious, and being introduced by Curtis as '*My best friend...don't know what I'd do without her...*' had failed to help matters, making her sound halfway between shrink and favourite maiden aunt.

'I had no idea.'

'So you *didn't* invite me here as a buffer against awkwardness from your ex...?'

'Would I be so devious? I admit,' he said grudgingly, while handfuls of people continued to walk past them towards the open area just out of sight, 'I knew a couple of girlfriends from distant times past might be on the scene, but you have my word that I had no idea that Caitlin was going to be here.'

Things fell into place abruptly. Vague stories of wanting to dodge female predators with stars in their eyes, true though that might very well have been, had probably come second to a very real desire on Curtis's part to avoid the attentions of women he had probably dumped. He was always unfailingly fair, he had once told her, telling the women he went out with that he wasn't interested in anything long-term, but did that mean all his exes relished the time when he decided that they had gone past their sell-by date? Did that mean that they all shrugged their shoulders and parted with a rueful shake of their heads and the words *That's only fair, I was warned after all* in their minds?

Doubtful.

'We can't huddle out here for much longer,' he broke the silence to say. 'Pretty soon they'll send out a search party to find out where we are. Philippa knows we've arrived. She caught my eye over the waiter with the tray of champagne cocktails.'

'I never signed up to this,' Jess all but wailed and he looked at her with sympathy.

'Nor did I,' he said grimly. 'But here we are and there's not a damn thing either of us can do about it.'

Navy eyes met green and Jess breathed in deeply because he was right, of course, here they were. And it wasn't as though she could skulk out and find the nearest taxi to deliver her back to the sanctuary of the hotel.

She reminded herself that she was twenty-six years old, a woman with a responsible job and why on earth should it matter that Caitlin was going to be around for a weekend that now seemed to stretch into infinity?

She wasn't the insecure girl who preferred to blend into the background and leave the limelight to others. She had moved on since those times.

Unfortunately, she was still paralysed with nerves as

he gently eased her from where she appeared to have taken root by the side of the wall. Fear and the yearning to flee were emotions that could be recalled without warning. It was easy to be driven back to a place in the distant past and Jess made a concerted effort not to find herself returning there now because she was confronted with just the sort of petite beauty who had once made her feel so ungainly and clumsy as a self-conscious teenager. She took a deep breath and steeled herself.

This was no polite gathering. Largely a young crowd, the noise levels reflected scores of slightly tipsy people talking loudly to make themselves heard. Everyone was beautiful. In truth, Jess had never seen a collection of so many glittering peacocks gathered in one room in her life before.

She slanted a sideways glance and was momentarily startled to see something very much looking like jaded cynicism on Curtis's face, although when he turned to meet her eyes she had to wonder whether she had imagined it.

'Deep breaths.' He smiled reassuringly. 'It'll all be over in a couple of hours… Caitlin or no Caitlin…'

'I'm very happy to leave before you—' she hoped he would take her up on the offer '—if you want to stay longer and enjoy the company. Or not as the case may be.' How would he feel about seeing his ex-fiancée? Was he as emotionally detached as he appeared to be or was that just an act? Surely he would feel *something* in the presence of the one and only woman ever to have dumped him? And a woman he had cared enough about to want to marry. Jess didn't think she could bear to see him chatting to Caitlin, reminding her of her own foolish, misplaced feelings.

Curtis killed that wild hope stone-dead. 'Perish the thought.'

And then he was leading her through the throng and she was conscious of eyes on both of them, of heads turning as they walked towards John and Philippa, their hosts. She had to resist the temptation to tug her dress down or fiddle with the neckline and at the first opportunity she managed to swipe a champagne cocktail from a passing waiter. Dutch courage.

She was introduced to the groom and his bride-to-be and to his parents and she chatted and sipped her champagne and, at one point, became quite vivacious on the subject of skiing and the slopes she longed to try. That said, her ears and eyes were vigilant for Caitlin, ever conscious of the frailty of the confidence she had meticulously built up for herself over the years.

She had expected Curtis to leave her to her own devices so that he could mingle with friends he probably didn't get a chance to see much of during the course of the year and she was surprised when instead he chose to stick to her side. Like glue.

There was no formal meal, no buffet with a rowdy queue snaking through the elegant living areas, but a constant supply of exquisite finger foods ferried through the party crowd by an army of uniformed waiters and waitresses. No glass was left unfilled for longer than five seconds.

She had almost forgotten about Caitlin, having made sure to stay put in a very small circle of people, when she heard a voice from behind and both she and Curtis turned as one to find the diminutive blonde right behind them.

Slightly the worse for wear, she tottered on her very high heels with a drink in one hand and her white blonde hair in some disarray. Even so, the woman, Jess thought grudgingly, was beautiful. She had naturally full, pouting lips and huge pale blue eyes and very straight hair that hung in a curtain to her waist. Despite the fact that it was the very depths of winter, she had a light golden tan that spoke of expensive holidays in the tropics.

'Curtis—' she dimpled '—I wondered whether I'd see you here!' She looked up at Jess. 'How lovely of you to bring your friend from the village.'

Jess wondered how it was that she had somehow found herself reduced to village idiot status.

'Caitlin.' Jess smiled politely. 'How are you?'

'You look different.'

'Do I?'

'I'm very well. Would you mind awfully if Curtis and I had a private word together?'

'She really would.' Curtis smiled, not unkindly, and, to Jess's shock, he slipped his arm around her waist, a gesture that did not go unnoticed by the other woman, who narrowed her eyes to slits.

'I had no idea you two were an item,' she mused. 'You kept that one under your hat, didn't you?' She laughed but there was a hard, hurt edge to her laughter.

'There are aspects of my private life,' Curtis said, 'that are not for public consumption. Caitlin, it's been nice seeing you. You look well. Now, if you'll excuse us...'

'Please, Curtis, I just want to chat to you for a moment...'

Next to her, Jess could sense him stiffening. Something about the scene playing out was at odds with the reality of a woman who had been the one to do the breaking of an engagement, but Jess decided that that was none of her business. What *did* fluster her was that hand still securely circling her waist and sending her nervous system into freefall, and what *did* upset her was knowing that the only reason that hand was there was to say something to his ex.

'I should say goodbye to John's parents.' She smiled and inched away from the red-hot branding iron of his arm. They had only just been talking to them but everyone had melted away with Caitlin's arrival. Perhaps they'd all sensed a possible awkward scene in the making, although there was nothing embarrassing about their stiff exchange. No raised voices or muttered oaths or shouty recriminations. If anything, Curtis looked a little frustrated but strangely tolerant where she might have expected a little more anger and certainly a lot more reluctance to be cloistered with his ex, who had given him the boot in a very public manner over a year ago.

Before either could respond, Jess walked away, seeking out the older, amiable hosts who were chatting to a little group and instantly included her in the conversation.

If anyone thought it strange that she had left Curtis and Caitlin together whispering who knew what, no one showed the slightest curiosity.

This, she decided, was *exactly* what she needed to cure herself of her foolish infatuation with him. Seeing him in his natural habitat, pursued by his ex and surrounded by just the sort of blonde bombshells he was so accustomed to dating.

She had no idea who the past girlfriends were but, from the high number of extraordinarily good-looking women present, they could have been any of them.

This was a world where Curtis moved with ease, sophistication and self-assurance. He was one of them—at home in billion-dollar properties where helipads were *de rigueur* and jewellery was kept in bank vaults only to be worn on special occasions. He might be a self-made billionaire, unlike many there who had been born into money, but he was so self-assured, so respected and feared in that complex world where big money was made, that no one would ever have questioned his right to be there.

They were good friends because they went back a long way, but the bottom line was…she was a teacher and very far removed from this glitzy crowd.

She couldn't help glancing over to him as she made small talk with the people around her. What did he and Caitlin have to discuss? He might have been shocked and alarmed to find that she would be part of the guest entourage, but he didn't look particularly uncomfortable in her presence, so what was that all about?

Had he been so in love with the other woman that he was willing to put the past behind him and give her a second chance?

He'd certainly said absolutely nothing about what had been behind the end of the relationship and now all sorts of questions were jumping out from hiding places Jess hadn't even known existed in her head.

Coming here might allow her to put things in perspective insofar as she was being afforded a glimpse of what kind of life he led and how inappropriate he was and always would be as a candidate for her heart because their worlds could not have been more different but, conversely, it was also opening up a Pandora's box of curiosity.

'Huh?' She blinked and realised that someone had asked her a question about the National Curriculum and, by rote, she launched into a conversation about Independent versus State education.

She half turned so that Curtis and Caitlin were no longer in her line of vision and when, after twenty minutes, she felt hands on her shoulders she practically leapt with surprise.

'Time to wend our weary way back,' he murmured and, to her consternation, he did more than slide a hand across her waist as he had earlier done. This time he bent and brushed her neck with his mouth, a feathery kiss that temporarily turned her to stone. The smile froze on her lips, her eyes glazed over. He then rested his hand on the nape of her neck, under her hair, and left it there. The sounds around them suddenly became background white noise, over which she swore she could hear the crashing of her heart against her ribcage.

What the heck was going on?

This wasn't part of any scenario she had imagined! Was he playing games with her? Somehow trying to make his ex jealous? Was that it?

Her body was as heavy as lead and yet, curiously, wobbly and shaky. Every nerve in her body was alive to the thrill of his hand against her neck, absently caressing underneath her hairline. She should be angry but she was too wildly aware of his touch for any other emotion to find a way through.

She breathed slowly, steadying her nerves.

This was what came of an inappropriate crush, she agonised, while her nerves continued to fray and her body sizzled with dark, forbidden excitement.

If she could track back, she could work out just when she'd become aware that what she felt for Curtis had morphed into a crush.

If she traced through time, and she frequently had over the past few months, she could work out that there was a point when adolescence, with all its complexities, had replaced the innocence of childhood.

Everyone in her class and at the afterschool club, all the girls, had started to change, physically and mentally. Boys had gone from annoying and stupid to riveting and worth getting dressed up for. And how her friends, who were all so much smaller and skinnier than her, had enjoyed the transition!

Yet she, Jess, had been the one to develop the fastest, shooting up in height, taller and bustier than all her friends.

And boys had stared. She could remember shying away from the attention, well aware that they hadn't been staring at *her* but at her breasts, which no school uniform could successfully conceal.

She'd become adept at covering up and maybe, she often thought, that had become a habit, a display of insecurity about her body that had lasted for years, dictating what she wore and how she interacted with the opposite sex.

When her father had died she'd turned to comfort eating and the heavier she had become, the more she had hidden herself under shapeless, baggy outfits. As a teacher, it was a manner of dressing she could get away with because comfort always trumped style.

And yet, through it all, Curtis had been there for her, from the very moment she had met him as a kid in his godfather's house, right through adolescence, with all its challenges, none of which she'd ever talked to him about because she'd been just so happy to be in his company.

Was it any wonder that she had developed an almighty crush on him over the years? Was it any wonder that, between her own insecurities and that idiotic crush, there had been no room to actually contemplate the business of getting out there and dating?

Until now...

Until she had woken up in the wake of his engagement, despite the fact that it had not led down the aisle. Until she had seen just how much of her life was being wasted in a hopeless infatuation with someone who would never look at her in *that* way. Until she had got her act together and changed her lifestyle and now, recently, started dating. Her confidence levels had risen so much in the past few months.

Unfortunately, lack of experience when it came to men was not standing her in good stead now, and she couldn't help but feel knocked back when she had looked down at the tiny blonde girl who had stolen Curtis's heart.

So how did she deal with that hand caressing the back of her neck? How did she get past her lack of experience to handle a body that had gone into meltdown? The truth was that Curtis liked the fact that she spoke back to him, that she didn't bow and scrape in an attempt to please. He liked her outspoken irreverence. What would he do were he to realise that that was only a thin veneer concealing an inherent shyness and the hangover of self-consciousness from way back when?

She surfaced to find that goodbyes had been said and she smiled and said all the right things, though her mind whirled with the confusion of knowing, at least for her, that the status quo that had existed between them was being called to account, that foundations were shaking and the comfort of knowing where things stood could no longer be relied upon.

When she looked around, it was to find, to her surprise, that the room had emptied. They weren't the first to leave. They were among the last and there was no sign of Caitlin.

They went to gather their coats, Jess having shaken

his hand off, making sure to keep a healthy distance between them, but when they were in the back of the chauffeur-driven four-wheel drive she turned to him and said, with driven urgency, 'Are you going to tell me what all that was about?'

'Did you find it disconcerting?'

Had she found it disconcerting? Jess nearly guffawed with manic laughter at that question. She couldn't think when she had last been so disconcerted by anything.

'I didn't find it *disconcerting*, Curtis! I found it *bewildering*!' she denied vigorously. 'I thought there wasn't going to be any pretending that we were anything other than friends...'

'Not quite the conversation as I remember it.'

'Meaning?' For once, the spectacular panorama of white snow, dazzling despite the darkness, was lost on her as she feverishly looked at him in the semi-darkness of the car.

'Meaning we agreed that we would let our friendship do the talking. We wouldn't have to pretend anything because we would rely on assumptions being made and, since it would be perfectly clear that we're involved with one another, there would be no need for us to define the nature of the involvement.'

'Well, be that as it may—' Jess sidestepped that interjection because he was right '—you still haven't answered my question. What's going on with the bewildering gestures of affection?' Without thinking, she rubbed the back of her neck in an unconscious gesture to scrub away the feel of his touch there.

Watching her closely, expression veiled, Curtis took in that small gesture and shifted. For the first time in their long history, he had touched her in a manner that wasn't completely platonic.

Scratch that—there had been one time, the only one, single time, when he had touched her and felt his body respond in a way that had shocked him. That kiss under the mistletoe. It was a million years ago but he must have kept the memory lodged in his head somewhere because it rushed to the forefront now, now that he was recognising that something had shifted between them. At least as far as he was concerned.

From her perspective…not so. That was the gesture of someone who had been irritated by the feel of his hand on her neck.

He could barely admit it to himself, but he had enjoyed being by her side at the party, hadn't particularly wanted to branch out because her conversation was so much more invigorating and because she demanded more conversationally from the people she was with, and they duly obliged.

When he *did* veer off to catch up with some of the guys he hadn't seen for months, he'd still found himself seeking her out, his gaze resting on her just a little too long. She'd seemed oblivious to the attention she'd been getting but he hadn't been. He'd seen the way some of the men there had glanced at her, appreciating her curves. They would never have said anything because they'd all been under the impression that she was with him but they still hadn't been able to stop what had been an automatic gesture of appreciation of her considerably sexy assets.

And when he'd touched her…

That same knee-jerk reaction he'd had at the airport when she'd whipped off the shapeless jumper to reveal a body that had stunned him into utter confusion.

'Caitlin seemed to think that for our relationship to go from good friends to lovers was open to question, and...'

He raked his fingers through his hair and fell into momentary silence until she prodded, 'And...?'

'Possibly a conversation best left until tomorrow morning.'

'Why?' Jess asked with genuine puzzlement.

'It's complicated.'

'Does it still matter what your ex thinks about you and your love life?' she demanded sharply.

After some hesitation, Curtis murmured in a low voice, 'Yes.'

One word but it was like a physical blow and Jess recoiled from it because if ever there was confirmation that he was still in love with Caitlin, then this surely was it.

As a rule, Curtis Hamilton had never cared two hoots about what people thought of him. They were entitled to their opinions was his take, but he wasn't interested in letting what they thought influence his behaviour.

He'd once told her that but, even if he hadn't, she would have guessed simply from watching how he dealt with so many situations. He had always had an inner strength that was completely undeterred by what other people thought of him or said to him.

So the fact that he was willing to alter his behaviour because of his ex said something.

'Well, maybe, Curtis, *I* may not want to play games with you and pretend that we have a relationship if that means you touching me.' She rubbed the back of her neck again, more vigorously this time, and looked at him with thinly veiled hostility. She was reminded of just how devastating that casual touch had been, throwing her senses into complete disarray and putting her on the back foot when it came to the whole business of getting him out of her system by putting him into perspective.

He stiffened. 'My apologies if you felt…uncomfortable, Jess.'

'I didn't feel uncomfortable.' She shook her head unhappily. 'I just… I know she still means a lot to you but that's no reason… What were you trying to do? Make her jealous? Was that it? By touching me?' Joining the dots, that seemed the most likely explanation and she did her best not to sound hurt and stung.

'Far from it.'

'I refuse to be involved in whatever situation there is between the two of you.' Jess was loath to let it go. Jealousy was an ugly emotion, in her eyes, yet she could feel it sinking its teeth into her, hard as she fought against it.

She'd barely noticed the scenery moving slowly past them as the car carefully wound its way to their hotel, so she was surprised when it drew to a smooth stop.

The air outside was cold and crisp and they both hurried into the warmth of the hotel. She paused, relishing the change of temperature, before turning to Curtis.

'Let's talk tomorrow,' he said before she could pick up where she had left off. 'It's late.'

Jess looked at him narrowly and he shot her just the ghost of a weary smile.

'You have a very expressive face, Jess, and right now I'm seeing doubt written all over it. You think I'm going to try and avoid the subject come morning…'

'Can you blame me?' She hoped her face wasn't quite as expressive as he seemed to think because the last thing she needed was for him to guess the effect he had on her. 'You're not exactly a guy who likes to have heart-to-heart conversations, and I guess you're sensitive on the topic of your ex, and I don't care. But I'm here now, *at your behest*, and it's only fair that you tell me what's going on.'

'At my *behest*…? Little wonder you and my godfather get along so well…' But as the lift doors closed on them he turned to her and said, utterly serious now, 'No need to fear. We'll talk tomorrow.' Then he smiled. 'Even though you're right when you say that I'm not the kind of guy who believes in tearfully pouring his emotions out.'

They were on their corridor and she reached into her clutch for the door key. She could feel his presence next to her as he leant against the wall and watched her.

'Meet me for an early breakfast,' he murmured just as she pushed open her door to stand framed by the light from behind.

'Okay.'

'We can talk and then we can ski.'

'I think there's some stuff planned…activities for bored other halves.'

'You're never bored when you're with me so that automatically excludes you.'

Jess shivered and dragged in a silent, ragged breath. Did he have any idea how intimate he could make a simple observation seem? How easy it was for him to ignite her imagination until it became a conflagration?

'What sort of activities have they lined up?'

'Trips…tours… I believe there's a wine-tasting experience…'

'Scrap them. We'll have breakfast and then we'll spend the morning on the slopes.' He glanced at his watch and straightened. 'Okay. I'll meet you in the restaurant at…eight tomorrow morning. Or I could order room service, which might be a better idea if we want some privacy.'

'No!' Jess cleared her throat and frowned thoughtfully. 'No, the restaurant will be just fine.' She thought about sitting opposite him at the little circular table in her room, with a bed announcing itself in the background, and could think of nothing worse. 'And yes, okay, eight.' She smiled with genuine anticipation at the thought of a morning skiing. 'And then we can hit the slopes. I believe you have some catching-up to do.' It was a stilted attempt to reclaim some of that shaky ground that had suddenly opened up between them, to regain their easygoing familiarity and to forget, just for a second, that if she stared into those green eyes for too long she would feel as if she were drowning.

'Is that so?' He smiled. 'I believe I gave you quite a substantial head start but...' He shrugged and raised his eyebrows. 'If you really think you're up to proving superior skiing skills then...who am I to argue? At your behest, I'm more than willing to drop the head start...'

In treacherous waters, the absolute bliss of normality between them kept the smile on her face as she shut the door and went straight to the bathroom to have a quick shower.

She let the water run off her and for the first time, after she had towel-dried, she stood in front of the standing mirror and looked at herself.

It was not something she ever did. Ingrained in her from her much bigger days was a certain amount of ambivalence when it came to looking at herself without any clothes on.

She did now. She was tall and she was bountifully built, and she wondered whether Curtis had had to grit his teeth when he'd touched her.

She swung around, pulled on her pyjamas—which consisted of a loose, brightly patterned T-shirt and a pair of stretchy shorts that barely skimmed her thighs.

Despite the cold and snow outside, it was warm in the bedroom. And, despite the buzzing questions in her head, she fell asleep as soon as her head hit the pillow.

Her last thought was, *I wish I'd never come... I think...* And her first thought the following morning was, *Who the heck is knocking on my door? Have I somehow forgotten to flip the Do Not Disturb sign over?*

Before the cleaners could decide to service the room while she was only just out of bed, Jess flew to the door and pulled it open sufficiently to realise that it wasn't any member of staff who had been knocking.

'What are you doing here?' She shuffled as far back behind the door as she could possibly manage and peered at a bright-eyed and bushy-tailed Curtis, dressed in black trousers for skiing and a tight black thermal, which she just about glimpsed underneath his black V-necked sweater. He hadn't bothered to shave and the stubble on his chin struck her as ferociously sexy.

She gulped, conscious of her legs on display because there was only so much concealing she could do without rudely closing the door in his face.

'Have you forgotten our breakfast date?' He looked pointedly at his watch. 'It's eight-thirty. I thought I'd knock on your door to make sure you weren't the worse for wear.'

He kept his eyes pinned to her face. She was pink and flushed and still in her nightwear. Some kind of patterned top and a pair of bottoms that left absolutely nothing to the imagination. Her legs were smooth and long and he could see the sway of her unconstrained breasts, soft and bouncy against her arms, which were across them.

She looked tousled in the sexiest way imaginable.

Hence his focus on her face. He didn't want to risk his eyes straying to more dangerous zones.

Before he could open up a dialogue on the issue of time-keeping, he decided to head back down to the restaurant because the less he saw of her in all her drowsy, ruffled glory, the better. He wasn't sure whether it was a new phenomenon, but it seemed that his prized self-control was under threat when she was around and the worst of it was that he didn't seem to mind anywhere near as much as he should...

'Doesn't matter,' he said tautly, backing away and shuffling ever so slightly before glancing in her direction again. 'How long should I be expected to hang around waiting for you to join me?'

That came out not at all as he had intended, and he noted the way she stiffened but, hell, he wasn't going to apologise because he just wanted to clear off before his imagination had a chance to take over completely.

Looking at him and hearing the curtness in his voice, Jess's voice was cool when she replied. 'Give me half an hour. Will that do, or is that too late for someone as busy as you, Curtis?'

'I'll see you there.'

CHAPTER FIVE

DESPITE BEING BUSY with the early to ski crowd, the restaurant managed to feel calm, quiet and relaxed. No crowds forming an unruly conga line by the breakfast buffet bar. Instead, there was an attractive cornucopia of fresh fruit and a selection of every cheese imaginable, with baskets of freshly baked breads and a comprehensive menu for anyone who wanted anything of the cooked variety.

Jess spotted him before he saw her and she stopped dead in her tracks, an automatic reaction to his physical beauty as he lounged in his chair, staring at whatever held him spellbound on his cell phone.

Unremitting black suited him, she thought stupidly. She took a deep breath and headed directly towards his table and smiled as their eyes briefly met.

'I must say, this is very different to my experience of breakfast in a hotel on a skiing trip with Year Eight,' she told him, sliding into her chair and watching as he straightened and looked at her.

'I imagine it is.'

Jess laughed nervously because of his thoughtful expression, so rare in someone who was essentially the very essence of light-hearted charm and teasing banter. Wasn't this what she had secretly longed for, though?

A Curtis who moved from superficial charm to offer her a glimpse of the depths that swirled underneath?

The conversation she had demanded felt inappropriate over breakfast before taking to the slopes and there was a part of her that almost wished she hadn't. She enjoyed their familiar routine, even if she was restricted by it, and this felt like a seismic shift in something that had been an anchor point in her life over the years.

'You wouldn't believe the chaos,' she gamely carried on as coffee was poured for them and the menu inspected and discarded in favour of the cold continental options, 'when you have twenty-odd kids scuffling to see who can make it to the bacon first...'

'You asked about my relationship with Caitlin...'

'It doesn't matter,' Jess said quickly.

'Doesn't it? What changed overnight?'

'As long as I don't have to pretend to be anything we're not, then I don't care what sort of relationship you have with her, or whether it's over or not.'

'It's firmly over, Jess,' he told her, pausing only to give his order to one of the serving staff. 'Why don't you go and get whatever you want from the buffet and we can talk about this when you're back. Get it out of the way.'

'Honestly, Curtis...' She leaned towards him, elbows on the table, and looked at him earnestly. 'It really doesn't matter. I don't see what the problem is if you're no longer...an item.'

'Why did you imagine that we were?'

Instead of answering that she headed for her breakfast, giving herself time to think about his question and half hoping he might forget that he had asked it at all, but as soon as she sat back down with her plate of cheese and bread in front of her he repeated it.

'I suppose that huddled conversation in the corner of

the room last night.' She shrugged and felt the bite of jealousy again but this time it was muted because she believed him when he told her that whatever relationship they had enjoyed was over. 'You looked... You didn't look like a guy who's over a woman.'

'How does a guy who's over a woman look?' he asked with genuine curiosity. He attacked his food with relish, but she could feel the focus of his laser-sharp attention firmly pinned on her, making her restless and fidgety.

'You looked as though you still cared about her,' she muttered, staring down at her plate. She cleared her throat and toyed with the bread and cheese, eyes flicking up to him every so often. 'And, to be honest,' she confessed, 'you always struck me as the sort of person who ends a relationship without any messy, unfinished strands of it left to resurface at a later date.'

Curtis's green eyes were thoughtful. 'You know me well.'

'So, if that's the case, then how is it that you're obviously still attached to Caitlin? How is it that you still care what she thinks?' Jess hoped that the jealousy she was banking down hadn't found its way into her voice, but she wasn't convinced and when she looked at him his expression was serious and unreadable.

'You wanted to know why we broke up.'

'I *know* why you broke up. It was in the gossip columns. She dumped you because she didn't think you were a long-term match. I think the implication was that you weren't enough fun for her.'

'I admit there might be some who find me a bore.' He half smiled but his eyes were serious when he spoke again. 'I have never talked to anyone about this,' he began, pushing his plate to one side and leaning towards her, his expression as grave as she had ever seen. 'Not even to William, although he wasn't as curious as I might have expected. Probably didn't want to jinx the situation by asking too many questions. Not sure he ever saw Caitlin as a match made in heaven for me.'

'Who knows?' Jess murmured vaguely.

'You, I expect.'

She blushed and inclined her head to one side but could hardly deny that wry observation.

'Caitlin and I got engaged because she told me that she was pregnant.'

His words dropped between them like a rock thrown into still water, spreading ripples outwards until the ripples absorbed everything. For a minute Jess's brain seemed to stop completely. She had never been so shocked in her life before because it was the last thing she'd expected him to say.

She knew she was staring with her mouth open, but she couldn't help herself.

'You're surprised.'

'That's putting it mildly!'

'I say she *told* me that she was pregnant. It was an elaborate lie designed to get exactly what she wanted. A marriage proposal. She showed me the evidence, the positive pregnancy test. What I didn't realise was how she got hold of it. She managed to convince someone she knew who *was* pregnant to hand over one because she wanted to play a joke on a friend.'

'I don't understand… Why on earth would she do that, Curtis? It's not as though she could carry on faking a pregnancy for nine months.'

'No, but she could fake one until we were married, only to tragically have a miscarriage. I found out because the girl she duped, someone who was far removed from her social circle, a satellite she befriended on a shoot somewhere abroad, joined the dots and came to me.'

'This is crazy.'

'I confronted Caitlin and she confessed.' He sighed, raked his fingers through his hair and looked at her. 'Caitlin has…many issues. As soon as I found out the whole shocking truth, I naturally called off the engagement but…'

'But…?

'Caitlin, as I discovered, was obsessed with me. It was something I only recognised in stages and by the time I wanted to bow out…well, it seemed to be too late. She came to me with the pregnancy story.'

'And you would have actually *married* her because she was pregnant?'

'I believe in the sanctity of family life,' he said gruffly. 'Believe it or not.'

Don't we all want the things we are denied? Especially when those things denied are rooted in our childhood?

'So… I still don't quite understand, Curtis.'

'Caitlin has…an unfortunate background. She was pretty upset when I told her I wanted out. Felt humiliated. She mistakenly imagined that I might spread the story of the fake pregnancy. Of course, she could not have been further from the truth, but the fact is that I felt sorry for her, despite what had happened.'

'Because…she had an unfortunate background?'

'Correct.' He looked at her for one long moment, his eyes shuttered. 'I told her that she could tell the world whatever she wanted on the condition that she had therapy, which I was more than happy to pay for, for however long it took.'

So many gaps in the telling, Curtis thought, but even

so he was curiously glad to be talking to Jess. It occurred to him that, whatever she thought, there would be a level of empathy at the very heart of her that would stop her from prying because there were things he had no intention of sharing.

The past, for Curtis, was a place where sadness was buried, where memories were too painful to bring out for inspection. It was a place he preferred to keep locked away because to go there would always feel too steep a mountain to climb. He might occasionally confront the darkness inside him, but he would never share it with anyone else.

He had told her that Caitlin had an unfortunate past. He would never tell her that that unfortunate past was what had kept him tethered to her even when he'd recognised that he should get out. She had been in and out of foster care most of her life and had emerged, at the age of eighteen, tough and determined to leave a miserable past behind her.

He had not been in foster care for the length of time that she had, but he had been there and could remember what fear and loneliness and abandonment had tasted like. The two years he had spent there after his mother died had made him understand what it meant to look at a future where love would be in very short supply because when he'd been put there, at the age of six, he'd been just a little too old to be desirable for adoption. Too old to adopt but not too young to care.

Those dark places he kept to himself and always would, but they had shaped him. Trust and an ability to give his heart away were commodities in short supply. He had the capacity for neither. He had formed a protective shell around himself that allowed no one in, no one but his godfather, the man who had rescued him.

Caitlin had dealt with her ordeal in another way. Her insecurities, so well hidden under that beautiful exterior, manifested themselves in a desperate need to be loved. Had she sensed something in him, some shared background, and that was why she had become so obsessive about him in such a short space of time? Obsessive enough to want him, whatever the cost? He had no idea because she certainly knew nothing about his past.

At any rate, they had broken up, but he couldn't just let her go and damn the consequences. For starters, he feared she might do something rash because she fundamentally held herself in low esteem, however deceptive appearances might have been, and a sense of responsibility also meant that he was concerned for her welfare, whatever lies she had told.

He had continued to check in on her, irregularly but enough to know that she had kept up the therapy. But he had gently held her at arm's length when she'd begged for a reconciliation. He couldn't bring himself to reject her completely and he'd been thankful that she had pulled back to let him get on with his life because he would have had to reject her eventually had she not.

Seeing her the night before had been a stark reminder that sometimes the best laid plans did not necessarily go the predicted way.

He hadn't had contact with her for at least three months. Despite his initial alarm when he'd spotted her last night, he had been reasonably hopeful that there would have been no unfortunate scene.

But she had clocked the situation with Jess, had shrewdly deduced that old friends didn't suddenly turn into new lovers.

Had this reignited a need to have him back? Where she had been happy enough to adhere to his No Trespassing signs when he had dated other women after their split, she had not been happy when he had informed her that he and Jess were serious about one another. Maybe she had been simply biding her time while he went out with other women, but Jess, someone she knew to be an old friend, had suddenly felt more of a threat.

'I'll bet your godfather's thrilled,' she had chirped, watching him carefully. 'He didn't like me—didn't think I was good enough for you. The second time we went there, he couldn't stop talking about the girl next door. So I guess he's over the moon that you two are a serious item…'

He had set that snide observation to one side because the need to demonstrate that he wasn't up for grabs had been more important. She hadn't got over him as he'd hoped, and he was astute enough to realise that she had the potential to become obsessive, which he knew would damage her far more than it could ever damage him.

He would normally never reveal any of this, but Curtis realised that he had to share enough to explain to Jess why he had touched her that way, a first for them both. He had the weirdest sensation of having done something outrageously taboo. Worse, he had *enjoyed* it… That in itself was even more shocking to him, and it was something else he had no intention of revealing.

Jess tried to glean what he wasn't telling her but she had no idea. What he had said was so revealing and yet it raised more questions than it answered.

He was a closed book and she knew that that was probably what gave him some of the incredible authority he wielded in the world of business. He gave nothing away, and right now he was only offering her a selected sliver of a bigger picture. She didn't know why she was so sure of that, but she was.

'So, to recap,' she said slowly, dragging each and every syllable out and, for once, not at all discomfited by those green, green eyes pinned to her face, 'Caitlin is here. She's been a thorn in your side and it's a nuisance, I'm sure, that she's going to be around for the next couple of days, but I don't understand why that would pose such a problem. And I *really* don't understand why all of a sudden you had to give the impression that we really *are* an item when that was never part of the deal.'

Which neatly brought them back to square one. Curtis signalled for a refill for both of them. The beautiful room had also emptied out and she realised that time had flown past since they had begun talking.

A morning aggressively attacking the ski slopes looked to be going down the tubes.

'She doesn't buy that we have a relationship.'

'Do you really care? Does it matter if she thinks you're fair game now?' Jess was still so confused but she managed a weak grin. 'And here I was thinking that you were a big boy who wasn't scared of anything.'

Curtis burst out laughing, his eyes warm with amused appreciation. He sobered up to say, 'I mentioned Caitlin has had an unfortunate background...'

'You did.' Jess frowned. 'Why are you finding it so hard to have this conversation, Curtis?' Then, voice a shade cooler, she added, 'I realise it must be agony being a tiny bit open with me...'

'I'm more open with you than any other woman I've ever known,' he pointed out.

Jess wondered whether she was expected to take that as a compliment because on no front did it feel like one. Did he mean that he was so utterly unaware of her sexually that he found it easier to confide in her? Was she the equivalent of the hairdresser, who was confidante of many whilst being significant to none? At any rate, if he thought that he was truly open with her then he had no idea what it meant to confide, to share.

She wondered when she had started thinking this way, which made her think of Caitlin and she fixed him with a cool, silent stare.

Curtis hesitated. 'Caitlin is mentally…fragile,' he said quietly. 'I'm telling you this because I don't feel I have a choice, not at this particular moment in time. She wants to rekindle something that isn't there. I thought she was over me but, meeting her yesterday, it would seem not. She doesn't think that we could possibly be going out…'

'Why? Because we've known one another for a hundred years, or is it because of the way I look?'

'What does that mean?'

Jess shook her head and backed away from a contentious conversation at speed. 'Nothing.'

'No, talk to me. Tell me what you're trying to say.'

'I'm not tiny and blonde, Curtis. *That's* what I'm trying to say! Of course she doesn't think we're actually going out, because she doesn't believe that you could *actually* ever take an interest in me!' Raw hurt surged through her and she wanted to stand up and walk away but that would have been giving away too much, would have shown him just how much of an effect he had on her.

'Maybe,' he mused, 'she doesn't *want* to believe it.' He sounded a little surprised, as though this was a thought that was only now occurring to him. 'Maybe,' he continued, thinking aloud, going with the flow, 'she was never threatened by the women who came after her but with you…' He looked at Jess narrowly and she flushed.

'Yes, we're old friends...but you're smart, you're witty and you're sexy. Maybe she sees *you* as the threat she doesn't want to face. At any rate, whatever the reason, this weekend should be all about John and Philippa. The last thing I need is for Caitlin to dominate proceedings by trying to commandeer me, and she's unpredictable enough to not care how much of a disruption she causes.' He paused. 'I'm not sure what I would have done had John forewarned me of her presence on the scene but I'm guessing it never occurred to him that it might be a problem. He knows that I don't harbour grudges, and am pretty comfortable meeting women I've dated in the past. Either that or he wanted my presence and so diplomatically decided not to raise the subject.' He grinned. 'I'm inclined to believe the latter. A hedge fund analyst knows how to gamble for the desired outcome...'

Jess's brain had stopped whirring at that word, *sexy.* Had he actually described her as *sexy*?

Suddenly the atmosphere felt close and claustrophobic and the recollection of his hand on the nape of her neck was imbued with all sorts of different, more dangerous connotations.

Had he found her sexy when he'd been stroking the nape of her neck...? Touching her in a way he had never done before?

'I'm glad you explained.' She shot him a one-hundred-watt smile and began rising to her feet. 'I guess, all in all, we'll only be in public when we're at the wedding...and you're right, it would be awful if John and Philippa's big day was clouded by...er...antics from your ex-fiancée...'

She was keen to get skiing, disconcerted by the way the familiar had veered off into the unknown, by the inroads being made into safe territory. 'I guess a few fond shows of affection aren't going to hurt anyone!' she trilled with nervous enthusiasm. 'And now we've gone through all that, shall we head for the slopes?'

Curtis watched as Jess tugged off the black and red striped woolly hat, releasing her hair before running her fingers through it.

Where before her body language had been that of someone trying to disappear into the background, now she was looser, more confident in her sexiness. Was it any wonder Caitlin was now so unnerved by what she must consider a real threat to any chance of them getting back together?

He had had over a dozen texts since they had chatted the evening before. He had answered one and that was to tell her that he didn't want her texting him.

It was true that he had once worried, and still did, about the fragile state of her mental health, which had encouraged her unhealthy obsession with him. He was now concerned about her unpredictability. Her texts had been intrusive and out of order. She had reverted to pleading that he give them another chance because she had changed, because the therapy had done her a world of good.

She couldn't believe he could possibly be interested in someone like Jess. Didn't he remember the fun they used to have in bed?

Curtis was seriously considering telling John that the situation was too flammable for him to stay for the wedding, although there was no part of him that didn't curse the fact that this was a situation that should never have come about in the first place.

Who was it who said that a good deed never went unpunished? He would have been better off walking away from the woman instead of trying to lend a helping hand.

The scars he carried from his own childhood had coloured his responses to Caitlin, had, for the first time in his life, blinded him to the hard-line path he had forged for himself, one from which he never wavered.

Just went to show what happened the minute you opened that door a crack and allowed emotions to start calling the shots, even in the smallest possible way.

Only William would ever lay claim to his emotions...

For once, he fully allowed the past to intrude, without the mental censoring he usually employed. He played in his head, like a movie set to warp speed, the events that had led to him being rescued from the loneliness of life in foster care. William had shown up, just like that—'a visitor' to see him. Curtis could remember sitting in that chair, feet barely touching the ground, and looking across at a kindly man he had never seen in his life before. He remembered being asked to stay where he was while Mrs Evans, the middle-aged lady in charge, who ruled the place with a rod of steel, disappeared for what had felt like ages with the kindly faced stranger.

Then she'd returned and his life had changed course for ever.

Later, in drips, he had discovered what had led his godfather to the doors of that foster care home.

William had been his mother's tutor at university, a caring guy who had done his best to keep her on the straight and narrow, and for a while, after his mother had graduated with a first-class degree, they had kept in touch. But Sophie Hamilton, herself the product of a broken home, without any support network in terms of family, had always hovered on the fringes of a bad crowd. Beautiful, clever and utterly irresponsible, she had dumped her job and vanished with Curtis and her boyfriend of the day to the world of alcohol and drugs.

She and William had parted with angry words exchanged and, soon after, his godfather had, himself, been offered a job abroad. He'd tried his best to keep in touch, he'd later told Curtis, but to no avail. From the other side of the world, he had been able only to pray and hope for the best.

Time had passed and it was only when he'd been returning to the UK, and with a newfound knowledge of all those search engines that enabled people to reconnect with old friends and acquaintances, that he'd laboriously and piece by piece found out what had happened to Sophie and his godson.

Appalled, he had descended on the foster home with rescue in mind and the rest…history.

Yes, his godfather would have the love and trust he denied the rest of the world. Caitlin? A mistake and that lapse in his strict code of behaviour? Also a mistake. Look where it had got him.

'Hello? Where are you?'

Curtis blinked to find that his torrent of thoughts had swept him away and now here was Jess, standing in front of him, smiling, her deep blue eyes curious.

And, just for a split second, he wanted to pull her inside and sit her down and fill in all those bits he had earlier left out, fill her in on the dark motivations that drove him forward and the past that had propelled him into taking his eye off the ball, so that Caitlin, instead of being relegated to the past, was still, unfortunately and despite his best efforts, very much in the present.

Where had that weak compulsion come from? he wondered, confused. Jess was his friend and sure, he was open with her, but confiding his innermost thoughts? He did that with no one. So how was it that suddenly he'd been tempted…? How was it that he looked at her and his self-control felt precarious?

'Thinking that you ski like a pro.'

He grinned and shook himself free from his thoughts. Life was something over which he needed to exert control and it paid to know the parameters of his friendship with Jess. 'But I still managed to beat you, despite the extremely generous head start…'

Had he really been thinking that…?

Jess could swear that he'd been a million miles away. Where? Work? With his wretched ex?

She hadn't had such fun on the slopes since for ever. She had set their conversation to one side and out there, racing with the cold air against her face and the wide-open white wonderland all around her, she had felt completely free.

'I don't think anyone could call two metres a "head start."' But she was laughing as they headed inside the hotel, where various employees rushed to assist them in shedding coats and ski boots. 'And who's to say I didn't *let* you win? Hmm?' She had half turned to look at him. She almost felt that she'd imagined that pensive expression on his face moments before because he was back to normal now, grinning, eyebrows raised.

'I mean,' she teased huskily, one hundred per cent of her straining towards him, caught in the moment, '*everyone* knows that men enjoy thinking that they can win at everything, including skiing down black runs…'

'Is that a fact…?'

He glanced to one side, moving those green eyes away from hers just for a moment.

She felt breathless, wired. He'd never looked sexier than when he'd been hurtling down that steep gradient slope just ahead of her, every muscle in his body ultra-confident in his own abilities. She could come close to catching him because she was such a proficient skier, but he would always outpace her.

This was what having fun felt like. She could go on dates with guys who all sounded perfectly suitable and were perfectly nice, but Curtis Hamilton was top of the leader board when it came to fun and excitement and making her heart beat so fast it felt as if it could burst out of her ribcage.

And now, as he turned to look at her, eyes boring into her until she felt heady and even more breathless, she felt his intense focus and purpose like the feathery brush of a finger against her skin.

He was going to kiss her. She knew it. She saw the way his breathing changed and the way his eyes darkened and when he lowered his head she was, oh, so ready for him.

She inched closer and arched up and the cool of his lips against hers was like nectar. Without having to think about it, she reached up and clasped her fingers together behind his neck, pulling him towards her. His tongue slid against hers and he shifted, bringing their bodies closer, deepening his kiss.

There was no one else around them. The entire world had disappeared, leaving just the two of them, immersed in a never-ending kiss.

It was rudely interrupted by a woman's voice. Even so, it took a few seconds for Jess to register Caitlin's presence next to them and it was with reluctance that she flattened her hands against his chest and took a shaky step back.

Several things came together in her head in the space

of time it took to break away from that devastating kiss and turn to a manifestly upset Caitlin.

The first was that he had obviously seen the other woman to the side and had engineered a kiss because that was what they had agreed... Keep up a show so that no ugly scenes with a volatile ex spoiled what should be the happiest day of John and Philippa's life.

And so he had kissed her.

But the second thing to enter her head was that she had kissed him back with every ounce of pent-up passion and desire inside her. She had thrown herself into that kiss as though her life depended on it and what, exactly, had been the message she had sent to him?

Definitely not the message that she was reluctantly resigned to having to display some kind of physical show of affection for the sake of appearances, lest his ex ruin the fun with her antics.

In a daze, she took a back seat while Curtis, polite to a fault, had a hushed and rapid conversation with Caitlin and then managed to steer her towards the grand front door, where a barely visible nod to one of the uniformed men on duty had the desirable effect and she was politely but firmly escorted out of the hotel and into whatever taxi happened to be waiting outside.

Jess had barely taken in a word of what had been said between them.

'I can't deal with this, Curtis.'

His eyes were still dark, still slumberous, still burning with what felt very much like real desire as they rested on her, but Jess wasn't going to fall prey to any illusions on that score. She'd made enough of a fool of herself already.

'You won't have to,' he told her huskily. 'She won't be around for the wedding.'

CHAPTER SIX

THIRTY-SIX HOURS OF unremitting battle against temptation, Curtis thought.

He'd managed to ensure Caitlin disappeared back to the UK, suitable excuses made to the host and hostess. No fuss, nothing to see here, a discreet exit, leaving the bride and groom-to-be free to enjoy their nuptials without asking any awkward questions or thinking, in any way, that her departure had anything to do with them at all.

Having sleepwalked into an engagement with her on the back of an outrageous and unforgivable lie, he had gone against all better judgement to keep open some lines of communication because he'd felt sorry for her, because, in a strange way, he'd understood.

But enough was enough.

He'd been chilled to the bone by the very real prospect of being stalked and, worse, for Jess to suffer the fallout because of him, because he'd been loose in his dealings with his ex.

'You need more intensive therapy,' he had told her coldly, *'and that will mean a residential facility. I will foot the bill, however long it takes, but you need to get your life back on track and eliminate me from it. Sadly, should you not do so...'*

Had there been any need to go into details? Not really. He wielded great power and that power stretched into all sorts of circles, ones that could impact her in a great many ways, and he had tabulated a few of them for her. He had seen comprehension dawning in her eyes.

She had a job for starters, thanks to him. A nine-to-five job, he had reckoned in the wake of their breakup, would confer a certain amount of stability and open her eyes to the process of co-operation and working with different people. She'd been in fashion, and fashion editing had been right up her street.

Would that job still be hers if she continued to plague him, to delude herself that they could ever get back together? Possibly not. Or possibly she could be transferred. The magazine was global. Life on the other side of the world would be quite different, she would find, and maybe not to her liking.

Who knew?

He had suggested an emergency of an unknown nature, too private to share, might be an excellent excuse for her hasty and premature departure from Courchevel. He was quite certain John and Philippa would understand.

In the end, he had thought, life was all about survival. He had learnt that from a young age. An irresponsible and drug-dependent parent and a couple of years in foster care, at the mercy of strangers, was a terrific lesson in instilling toughness and if he had wavered for a brief window in time, he was determined not to do so any longer.

Caitlin had read his message loud and clear. Her time was up. She'd left on the first flight back and there had been no further need for any public displays of affection.

'So you can relax,' he had informed Jess, and he'd

raised both hands in a gesture of amused mock surrender as she had breathed an audible sigh of relief and smiled.

Since then…? The battle against temptation.

He wanted to touch her. He wanted to touch her when they were away from public scrutiny and he wanted to touch her when they were in the presence of other people and he didn't really care who those other people were.

It all went against the grain. He had never been the kind of guy who liked public displays of affection. His friends were well aware of that, which was why Jess, as his plus one, had been such a good idea. Their 'relationship' would require no physical proof.

But he hadn't banked on her getting under his skin in all sorts of ways he would never have dreamt possible.

The more he itched to touch her, the greater his realisation that it would be a sign of weakness to do so. Worse was the fact that Jess wasn't one of his hot blondes with a sell-by date. He cared about her sufficiently to know that if he ever hurt her, he would never forgive himself. He was incapable of love and would never be willing to try and Jess was a woman who would never want anything less than a proper relationship.

So he fought the urge.

And he was aided by the fact that the attraction did not seem to be mutual. Zero. Zilch.

Aside from that one kiss when he had spotted Caitlin. Then he had kissed her and she had given herself utterly to that kiss, had moved her body against his until he had lost sight of the fact that they should have been kissing for effect only.

But since then she had returned to that comfortable place where they were great friends. Unfortunately, that place was one he no longer had much interest in occupying, even if it made sense.

Waiting for her now so that they could get to the venue for the wedding, his mind was a million miles away, playing with imagery he wanted to banish but couldn't.

Had he learnt *nothing* from his bruising experience with Caitlin? Hadn't it hit home that letting any form of emotion take precedence over common sense was something to be avoided at all costs?

Evidently not because his body was calling the shots and it infuriated him.

In the midst of his mental meanderings, he was only alerted to the fact that Jess had appeared because the noise levels of the people around him seemed to fade for a few seconds and then he raised his head, focused and saw her...

He'd thought that seeing her in that dress the other night, sexy as hell, couldn't be topped when it came to being knocked for six. He'd been wrong.

She was wearing a long red velvet figure-hugging dress that had a sufficiently dipped neckline to reveal the shadow of a bountiful cleavage. The dress was sleeveless, and a cream faux fur wrap was casually draped over her shoulders.

And the shoes... High enough for her to be on eye level with him and certainly to tower over every other woman in the vicinity.

Curtis took deep breaths and forced a smile on his face as he moved towards her.

'You look...'

'Incredible?' Jess laughed and looked up at him. Did she sound normal? She hoped so. She'd spent the past day and a half trying to appear very normal. Everything back on solid ground! Friends as they always had been!

No more nonsense, having to pretend to be in a phoney relationship!

Caitlin had disappeared. She had no idea what Curtis had said to her but, whatever he'd said, it had worked.

She should have been sagging with relief that she would no longer have to put her weakness for him to the test, would no longer have to endure the dangerous racing of her pulse whenever he casually touched her to keep up appearances.

That kiss she had decided to conveniently shove to the back of her mind. He hadn't said anything since and there was no way she had any intention of raising the subject.

But it had been a heroic feat of willpower, trying to reveal nothing for the past day and a half and to be jolly and affectionate, the way she always had been, whilst being acutely conscious of the fact that lines had been breached whether she wanted to face it or not.

Lines had been breached...and words had been uttered that couldn't be taken back.

He'd said that he found her sexy...

Just recalling the words wreaked havoc with her attempt at self-control.

The laughter tapered off at the smouldering heat in his eyes as he looked at her. Her body tingled all over and she was conscious of her nipples pushing against the velvet dress, because she wasn't wearing a bra, conscious of a spreading wetness between her legs. She stumbled back a couple of inches, breathing jerkily but unable to tear her eyes away from his face.

'We should go,' she said roughly, and he nodded but he didn't move for a few seconds and then, when he did, it was without his usual easy grace.

He looked so beautiful, so breathtaking, in formal attire, white shirt, black jacket, black trousers, a uniform that should have made him look average but somehow did the opposite.

His face was darkly flushed, and she could almost breathe in the heady scent of desire.

He'd been so much his usual self ever since he had kissed her that she had convinced herself that what he felt was very distant from what she did.

Now she knew that they were on the same page when it came to *wanting*.

What did she do with that information…? Someone more experienced would not have hesitated to take advantage of it. She was crazy about the guy, for better or for worse. It was only natural that she might want to… have her first experience with him.

The mere thought of that, however, was enough to bring her out in a cold sweat because alongside that resided sheer panic and the horror of knowing that he would probably be either alarmed or amused or both by the fact that she was still a virgin.

But the dangerous thought tingled inside her as they made their way to the wedding venue.

The ceremony was moving, with only a handful of people to witness the exchange of vows in the small church. Then a battalion of white cars delivered everyone back to the chalet, which was a winter wonderland inside. Huge trailing garlands of white flowers formed lacy patterns from the ceilings, as delicate as spun silk, and urns of white orchids worked as partitions ensuring that the huge spaces were broken into smaller components.

There were lots more people attending the actual reception than had been there for the more intimate gathering where Jess had first laid eyes on Caitlin.

She should have been nervous because this was just the sort of event nothing in her entire life could have prepared her for, but she wasn't.

Champagne flowed and the food was delicious. She drifted from group to group, keenly aware of Curtis, who never seemed to stray too far from her side.

In truth, she barely noticed the noise and the laughter and the stunning scenery outside, matched only by the stunning décor inside. At one point she drifted across to the vast bank of windows that gave out over a scene of limitless snowy mountains and behind her was Curtis's reflection. He raised a glass to her and she smiled without turning around.

Her heart was pounding when, several hours later, they found themselves saying their goodbyes to the couple. She was so conscious of Curtis slightly behind her, his body so close that she could feel the heat radiating from him, that she could barely focus on what Philippa was saying. Something about being the only bride to have her honeymoon exactly where she happened to have married because they would be skiing for the next week. She was rolling her eyes and laughing and constantly looking at her new husband with love and tenderness while he reminded her that the Maldives awaited them in four weeks' time.

Jess slipped off her shoes once in the back of the car. She wasn't looking at him, instead choosing to stare at her fingers interlinked on her lap.

'You were pretty amazing tonight.' Curtis broke the silence, his lazy eyes clocking the way she was making a big effort not to look at him when he knew she badly wanted to.

God, he had never before spent an evening in a state of such heightened anticipation.

When he hadn't been right there next to her, he'd been following her with his eyes, noting her every movement, the sexy swing of her hips as she moved through the room, her natural warmth as she chatted to various people and her endearing lack of awareness of the looks she was attracting from every guy at the reception.

He'd felt the sizzle of red-hot chemistry between them even when she wasn't looking at him and now, sitting in the back of this car, he was wired.

'Thank you,' Jess murmured.

He shifted, then reached out and placed his finger on her chin, gently turning her to face him. Then he let that finger trail a devastating path to outline her lips. She sucked in a sharp, jagged breath but she couldn't tear her eyes away from his face and, tellingly, she didn't slap his hand away.

'I couldn't take my eyes off you.'

'You...shouldn't be saying these things,' Jess whispered. 'How much have you had to drink?'

'Next to nothing, and why shouldn't I be saying these things...?' He knew. Of course he did. And she was right. But the devil was in the detail and he couldn't help himself.

'Because...' Her voice trailed off.

'Because we've always been friends?'

Jess nodded and breathed a silent sigh of relief as their hotel came into illuminated view because there was so much going on in her head that she couldn't think straight.

It was cold outside but she was on fire, itching to get out of the car, suffocating from the force of his personality and the intimacy of him so close to her. He was no longer touching her, but he might as well have been.

Amid the flurry of being escorted into the hotel by one of the ever-present uniformed staff who seemed to operate a round-the-clock service specifically to welcome guests, whatever the time of day or night, there was a brief respite.

But her thoughts continued to swirl and her pulse was still racing as, minutes later, the lift doors closed on them. Surrounded by mirrored walls, there was no escaping him. Their eyes met and there was a challenge in his that made her burn from her toes up to her hairline.

Flustered, she practically leapt out of the lift, pulling her wrap tightly around her in an unconscious effort to ward off the heated responses of her disobedient body.

She hit the door to her suite at a rapid pace and fumbled with her key card—then froze when his hand covered hers.

'Want to talk about what's going on here?' he asked softly, and Jess reluctantly gave up her frantic efforts to flee and turned to him.

'Nothing is going on.'

'We both know that's a lie.'

'So we're...' she looked at him a little despairingly and made a sweeping gesture '...out of our regular comfort zone. I guess if it feels as though... I mean...'

'Want to have this conversation somewhere that's not in the middle of a corridor?' He nodded to her room behind her.

'No, not at all.'

'Are you scared to?'

'No!'

'Okay.' He shrugged and began to turn away. 'I'm happy to pretend that none of this is going on and that this conversation never happened. We're heading back the day after tomorrow and we can return to the safety of our comfort zones.'

'No, wait…' She reached forward, one hand on his arm. In an instant, she recognised that she was at a turning point. She'd been infatuated with him for so long…

If he walked away now then yes, they would return to their comfort zones, except would it be quite as comfortable?

And would it cure her of her foolish infatuation?

If he walked away he would never look back, and their friendship would slowly dwindle away under the weight of something that hadn't been dealt with.

Was this business that had to be finished?

Sleep with him, she thought, and she would slay the beast. She would get him out of her system once and for all. She had never gone through this process of giving herself to someone, had never wrestled with the doubts and hesitations and excitement and dread that other girls dealt with when they took those tentative steps with the first guy they slept with. Untouched, she had locked herself away in an ivory tower from which she could watch and fantasise without having to risk anything. She had hidden behind her insecurities, vaguely assuming that she would never have to put them to the test because there was no way a guy like Curtis would ever look at her.

She had presumed that she would get over him and lower her sights when it came to having an actual relationship with someone suitable. Someone suitable would not have been such a nerve-racking experience. Someone suitable would not have been six foot something of hard, honed alpha male who could make her laugh out loud and give her pause for thought, all in the space of five seconds. But here they were and the time for risk was with them. Still, her heart was thudding and her mouth was dry as she searched for a way of saying what she wanted to say, what she felt *driven* to say…

'I'm listening,' he prompted softly.

'I admit that I might be attracted to you.' She stumbled over her words and he inclined his head to one side and gazed at her. It was fallacy that tall men felt protective with women who were shorter, smaller. Watching the hectic colour in her cheeks, he felt a sudden surge of protectiveness towards this woman who had been his friend for so many years.

He was so used to women who were adept at playing the courting game. His heart twisted as she nervously tucked a strand of hair behind her ear and looked away.

His heart was not a commodity he could ever give away, but she knew that. Not just because he'd told her, but because she knew him so well, knew his history with women. They were simply two adults acting on a physical attraction neither had factored into their comfortable relationship. If they slept together, they would be doing so with their eyes wide open.

He reached out and linked his fingers through hers and ushered her the few steps to his own suite and, once inside, he dimmed the lights and led her towards the bedroom.

'I've spent all weekend wanting this,' he said roughly, turning to place his hands on her shoulders and stroking the nape of her neck. 'Relax.' He smiled. 'I know we're friends and, believe me, this is not what I was expecting, but sometimes surprises can lurk round the least expected corners...' He kissed the side of her mouth and flicked his tongue over her lips.

Jess froze. Her body wanted to respond, and her head was telling her to just go with the flow, but deep-rooted panic was trumping everything and she gulped.

'What's the matter?' he murmured as he began to unbutton his shirt. His coat and jacket had been disposed of earlier. She hadn't even noticed but, in fairness, the earth could have moved under her feet and she probably wouldn't have noticed.

'I don't know... I'm not sure...'

He stilled, banking down the surging ache between his legs. 'It's an unusual situation—I get that, Jess. I want you but you know you have every right to change your mind and walk away...'

'No, it's not that,' she said in a stricken voice.

'Then what?' Just talking felt like a feat of endurance when he wanted to do so much more.

'I'm not that experienced,' she muttered.

Curtis smiled reassuringly, oddly pleased at her honesty. He carried on unbuttoning the shirt until she could see his chest, broad and muscled. He shrugged off the shirt and she felt faint. 'I am experienced enough for both of us,' he murmured softly.

He rested his hand on his trouser zip and reached with the other hand to tug her towards him.

This time his kiss was one hundred per cent no-holds-barred *hungry*. He slid his tongue between her lips, tilting her back, plundering her mouth until she was whimpering and clinging to him, restricted in the dress and desperate to get rid of it.

He edged her towards the bed and she felt the edge of the mattress hit her knees. She almost teetered onto it.

Her arms were looped over his shoulders, her breasts pushing against his bare chest, and she moaned when he reached to unzip her dress until it was sagging open.

'No bra.' He nipped the side of her neck and she shivered and sighed, eyelids fluttering. 'I like that. Very much.'

'I'm not as slight… I'm a big girl…'

'Something else I like. Also very much.' He swept down the straps almost before she could protest or take evasive action or even shield herself from his gaze because he took her hands in his and stepped back and looked at her.

Jess closed her eyes tightly. So desperately did she want to cover herself that it took a superhuman effort not to yank her hands free of his loose hold and put them strategically in front of her.

'You're beautiful,' he murmured huskily.

At that, she sneaked a glance at him and their eyes met, his blazing with desire, hers tentative. With hesitation, she touched his chest and then stroked it, marvelling at how hard it was and loving the way he sucked his breath in as she caressed him.

He caught her hand and growled that she would have to watch out because too much excitement would make an experience he wanted to last, finish in way too short a time.

'Let me see the rest of you,' he commanded gruffly.

He slid his hands down her sides, along her waist, and pushed the dress so that it slipped further down. Jess inhaled deeply and shimmied out of it. Should she tell him that by *'not that experienced'* she actually meant *completely green behind the ears*?

No. She couldn't face his reaction. There was no reason for him to know, was there?

She stepped out of the heels, instantly losing five inches in height. Her underwear was practical cotton, nothing skimpy, and definitely no thong.

'You have a body fashioned to drive a man wild,' Curtis told her with searing honesty. 'Feel for yourself...'

He stepped towards her and in one easy motion took her hand and placed it on his prominent bulge. This was what he wanted. This was what they *both* wanted. They were two adults and if their situation was more complex than those he was accustomed to then all that was needed for clarity was for him to strip it back to the bare bones.

Mutual physical attraction.

Irresistible and overwhelming.

He killed the questions tugging at his conscience. He had spent a lifetime controlling his own destiny and if now there was a moment of vague unease that destiny might be controlling *him*, then he was quite certain that it would be a momentary blip, easily remedied in the cold light of day.

His deep affection for the woman who just happened to be turning him on to a degree that was unimaginable would not pose a problem. *She knew him better than anyone. Knew of his aversion to the sort of commitment that led to a walk down the aisle. He had explained about Caitlin...so there were no illusions waiting to be shattered.*

There was no risk to him. His heart was protected, as icy cold when it came to the murky waters of emotional involvement as the frozen tundra wastelands. It was the way he was built—the way life had moulded him. He had no illusions that could be shattered.

They were *both* going into this with their eyes wide open. Had that not been the case, then he was sure they wouldn't be here now, however hot the fire was that burned between them.

He would never—*never* risk hurting this woman and on that thought he promptly closed his mind and allowed physicality to consume his head space.

Jess's mouth went dry. She looked down and inserted her finger under the waistband of his trousers but honestly lacked the courage to actually yank down the zip. It felt surreal. Being here, being with him, having her fantasies roar into life without much warning. She wished she had the experience to handle the situation, to deal with what was happening without feeling utterly out of her depth.

'It's a little weird,' he whispered into her ear. 'I know. I get it. I understand.' He unzipped himself, stepped back and out of the trousers, eyes firmly glued to her face, and then out of the boxers.

Utterly at ease with his nakedness, he stood there in front of her and Jess gaped.

She forgot that she was clad only in her knickers. She forgot her nerves and the bloom of panic rising inside her. She forgot everything as she stared at him, so stunning in his nudity, his body a work of art. Broad shoulders and a broad chest tapered to lean hips and long muscular legs. He was a tall man and beautifully built, with the honed perfection of an athlete.

She stared at his manhood, impressively big, and almost passed out when he absently took it in his hand for a few seconds.

'A little weird' didn't come close to the heightened anticipation and burning confusion sweeping over her but nothing could deter her now. She was so turned on her mind was cloudy.

'Think you can handle a little bit of weird, Jess?' he murmured with a smile in his voice and he didn't give her time to answer. He kissed her and his hands were not innocently exploring now but cupping her breasts and he groaned and moved against her so that she could feel the hardness of his erection pushing against her belly. 'I love the fact that you're so tall.' His voice was thick and uneven as he rolled his thumbs over her nipples.

Jess grunted a reply, but she had no idea what she might have said because, for the first time in her life, she was *feeling*. Her body was alive with sensations, her nipples sending messages straight to that place between her legs which throbbed and ached to be touched.

She squirmed and rubbed her legs together, felt the wetness soaking her underwear.

As if reading her mind, and definitely reading whatever signals her body was giving off, he eased the underwear down too fast for modesty to provide a stumbling block.

He cupped her between her thighs with one hand and Jess froze in shock, but he was still kissing her, her mouth, her face, her neck, while that hand…

That hand moved rhythmically between her legs, slipped into the wet crease to stroke, finding her core and rubbing until she could barely breathe because her rising excitement was so intense.

She wanted to come so badly.

He edged them towards the bed and she gratefully sank onto the mattress and had a few seconds of breathing space, during which she watched as he checked his wallet for something. Protection. Of course.

Through the haze of pure lust filtered the recognition that the last thing he would want, after the fiasco with Caitlin, was an accidental pregnancy.

She was too overwhelmed to follow that thought anywhere useful. Instead, she half closed her eyes and gasped as he sank onto the bed to begin a slow, leisurely and methodical exploration of her breasts, nuzzling and sucking and caressing and driving her crazy. She arched back and groaned as he suckled, massaging them between his big hands. The abrasive rubbing of his thumbs on her sensitised nipples and the lash of his tongue against the tightened buds was beyond erotic.

She laced her fingers through his hair and arched back and writhed under the explosion of sensation. Her legs dropped open and she watched in fascinated trepidation as he trailed a path along her stomach, circling her belly button on the way, eventually finding what he was looking for, the damp mound between her thighs.

He buried his head there and Jess squirmed, embarrassed at such intimacy but then enjoying it way too much to wriggle free of that questing tongue.

She scarcely recognised her guttural moans and only felt a stab of real apprehension when he levered himself up to don protection, taking a lot longer than expected because his hands were so unsteady.

She noted all that and knew that that was the biggest compliment he could have paid her. He was as out of control as she was and that said a lot for a guy who was always in control.

He sank into her and she stiffened instantly. She'd thought she would be able to hide her lack of experience, but she'd been an idiot. That first deep thrust had

been a shock, had *hurt*, and she had reacted accordingly.
Just for a split second but long enough for him to immediately pull out and when she looked at him there was
raw shock on his face.

'Jess…'

'Don't talk,' she pleaded huskily.

'You're a virgin!'

Mortification seared her and she felt the prick of tears
stinging the back of her eyes. She looked away quickly,
but he gently turned her face so that she had no option
but to look at him.

'Don't cry,' he whispered.

'I'm not,' she answered quickly and fiercely. 'So what
if I'm a virgin? I want this. So stop talking and just…
do…'

'I don't want to hurt you…' Curtis sounded as if he
was talking about more than just whatever physical discomfort she might feel at having him inside her.

'You won't—' the fierceness was still in her voice but
she stroked his face '—you won't hurt me, Curtis. So…
please… I want this so much…want you to make love
to me… No more questions…please…'

He did, a little clumsily at first and then gently, easing his way in, taking his time, sending her into orbit
until she was the one calling the shots, at which point he
moved faster, thrusting deeper, filling her and taking her
with him, all the way to a place she'd never dreamt possible, where she shattered into a million glorious pieces.

She clung shamelessly, hooking her legs around his
back and feeling him as he came inside her and then
another clumsy fumble, cursing softly as he disposed
of the condom.

'I'm never like this,' he said gruffly, turning her so
that they were lying on their sides, facing one another,

with her leg between his thighs and his over hers. Their bodies fitted so perfectly together.

'Like what?' She snuggled into him. She felt whole, complete and, yes, she knew that this was just going to be a moment in time, but she wanted to appreciate the absolute pleasure of lying in a bed with Curtis.

'I could barely control myself. That damn condom… think it slipped a bit… Damn…' But already the passing concern was wiped out by a wave of dizzying passion.

'What?' She nuzzled his neck and he reacted by clasping his hands on her buttocks so that he could pull her closer to him.

'No matter. You could have told me, Jess.'

'Why would I have done that?' She looked at him, her expression serious. She wasn't going to be coy and pretend that she didn't know what he was talking about.

'I would have been gentler…the whole way through. I'm sorry if… I didn't know, didn't suspect.'

'You were…perfect,' she said roughly, and he smiled and pushed some of her hair off her forehead.

'So were you.'

'Mutual admiration society.' She blushed and smiled and looked away. 'Who'd have thought?' When she thought about actually lying in bed with him, both of them naked, she felt the thrill of the forbidden. Never had anything tasted sweeter.

'Who indeed.' He hesitated. 'We're here for another day and a half…'

'We are.'

'Jess, I never thought…this didn't cross my radar. No,' he mused, 'maybe it did but us…here…lovers…it wasn't a scenario I predicted.'

'Do you regret what just happened, Curtis?' she asked quietly.

She only realised how tense she had been awaiting his response when he said with a smile, 'Far from it.' He curled one finger through her hair. 'Still feel weird about this?'

She shrugged. *Yes and no*, she wanted to say. 'I might in the morning,' she admitted honestly. 'But things will return to normal.'

'I still want you,' he said bluntly. 'I don't want this to be the first and last time we sleep together.'

'What do you mean?' She felt a burst of pleasure and dared to let her thoughts travel down roads she knew were out of bounds, roads that might lead to a proper relationship. Hope bloomed against better judgement.

'Think about it,' he mused, still playing with that strand of hair, his eyes pensive. 'We've opened a door. If we walk away now, there's a risk that the door will remain open and, if it does, nothing between us will be the same again. We have to see this through to the finish line. That's my opinion. We do that and we will have history between us, but we won't be living with the notion that there's unfinished business festering somewhere, waiting to be dealt with.'

Jess thought that part of the reason she had come here had been to kill the infatuation that had had her in its grip for as long as she could remember. See him in his natural habitat and the chasm between them would snuff out inappropriate feelings. She hadn't banked on this! But was he right? Was this something that needed to be put to bed, literally and figuratively? Lest it fester and remain the unfinished business that would lay waste all her hopes for moving on with someone else?

And who knew...? a treacherous little voice suggested. *Who knew what lay down the road...? From friends to lovers... A road unexplored...possibilities born...*

'You know me better than anyone,' he continued as she chewed over what he had just said. 'You know that I'm not looking for anything long-term. We can be lovers without the worry that you might want more than what's on the table...don't you agree?'

His words hit her like a bucket of cold water, killing dead those treacherous shoots of hope.

The tableau in front of her was now somewhat different. In it, she saw herself continuing with what they had, handing her heart over to him and then, when her sell-by date came, he would politely discard her as he had discarded so many women in the past, as he would have discarded Caitlin had events played out differently.

And she would have no one but herself to blame because he would have given her ample warning that he wasn't in it for the long haul.

Was she willing to do that? Hadn't she spent months striving to move on? What would be the point of throwing the towel in just because he wanted her as his lover for a week or two longer?

'I think,' she said gently, 'that it would be better... healthier...for us to leave things where they are, Curtis. Let's remember this as a wonderful one-off.' She kissed him lightly on the lips and began edging away from him. 'We're friends and, okay, it might be a little odd tomorrow, but after that...? Well, we'll still be great friends. I'll go on dates and stop burying myself in work and you... There's an ocean of gorgeous women waiting out there for you.' She smiled but her heart was clenched with pain. 'So I'm going to go back to my room now.'

The thought of having more of him was so tempting that she had to escape as fast as she possibly could or else risk being talked into something she knew she would end up regretting.

She slid her legs over the side of the bed and tried not to make a frantic, embarrassed dash to the pile of clothes on the ground.

The red dress no longer felt sexy. She was going to walk the plank of shame and thank goodness her room was next to his.

With a final glance at him, she said, amiably and calmly, 'Skiing tomorrow?' She paused. 'It's been really great, Curtis. I'll remember it for ever. I'll see you in the morning.'

CHAPTER SEVEN

AN UNEASY TRUCE. A sticking plaster over something that threatened to ooze out.

That was what it felt like to Jess.

Yes, she had left his bed, had got right back into that red dress and had scuttled back to her bedroom. And, yes, they had skied in the morning and chatted, but she was conscious of whole conversations lying unspoken beneath the surface of their banter and chat and laughter.

Was it just her who had felt the strain of trying to pretend that everything was as it had been *before*?

She'd laughed but made sure to keep her distance physically. She'd teased him while steering clear of all references to anything that could be a reminder of the fact that they'd slept together. She'd watched him and now her eyes were no longer innocent, no longer speculating. She knew what his body looked like and felt like and tasted like, and it had been hell keeping things natural while that imagery was playing in her head.

It had been a relief to hit British soil once again. As if mentally back behind his desk even before they arrived back at the airport, he had disconnected on the flight over, burying himself in whatever work he had missed during his time out in Courchevel.

She assumed that once his proposition had failed he

had shrugged off her rejection with good humour and relegated the whole episode to the back of his mind. Easy come, easy go.

While *for her* that had been impossible.

A breather, she had decided. Once back, she would no longer have to be in his presence and so that spine-tingling, toe-curling, dark, forbidden excitement that had suffocated her would be gone.

They had parted company at the airport and she had firmly refused his offer of a driver to return her to Ely.

'Jess,' he had said, turning his fabulous green eyes on her for the first time since they had left the hotel, 'it's ridiculous for you to trudge all the way back to your house on public transport in this weather. If you don't want a driver, then I will get a taxi to take you back and if you don't want that, then I will have to insist on driving you back myself.'

She had taken the taxi. She had returned to her house and had spent the past two and a half weeks nursing all sorts of memories that had no place in her life. She had half-heartedly checked out a couple of guys on her dating app and rejected both. She had told herself that she just had a very bad case of break-up blues, which was something everyone went through but usually years earlier. She was a late bloomer but that didn't mean that she wouldn't recover, that she would remain trapped in a half-life of yearning for what she couldn't have while desperately trying to embrace what she didn't want.

She had immersed herself in work and repeatedly told herself that in six months' time she would chuckle at the torment she was currently feeling.

Except in six months' time...

Jess stared at the small stick with the pair of blue

lines on it and felt a wave of nausea rise up inside her all over again.

Books to be marked sat untouched on her kitchen table. Although she had recognised two days ago that her normally perfectly reliable menstrual cycle had had a glitch, it had not seriously occurred to her that she might be pregnant. Not even when, two hours previously, she had gone to the local chemist to buy some toiletries and bought herself a pregnancy testing kit on the spur of the moment...*just in case*.

Now she was numb as she stared at the evidence of the price that could be paid for a few hours of stolen pleasure.

How? *How?* He had used protection, but then she thought back to his shock when he had found out that she was a virgin, the way he had fumbled, totally thrown by something that hadn't come close to registering as a possibility on his radar. Had he known that there had been a chance the contraception had failed? She vaguely remembered him muttering something before the moment was lost in the heady passion that had consumed both of them.

Experienced as he was with the opposite sex, he had clearly never been in the novel situation of ending up in bed with a virgin and, in that once-in-a-lifetime moment of utter awkwardness, fate had seen fit to intervene.

And what happened now? she wondered miserably. Outside, steady freezing rain seemed to mirror her panic-fuelled confusion and mind-numbing fear.

Of course she would have to tell Curtis. What choice did she have? On moral grounds it would have been indefensible to keep that sort of information to herself, and on practical grounds it would have been impossible anyway because she saw a great deal of his godfather.

Hiding a pregnancy and a baby didn't begin to be an option unless she turned her back on her strongly held principles and fled the area under cover of darkness. Like a thief in the night.

Facing a very long evening with nothing to do but think, Jess picked up her cell phone, stared at it for a few minutes, her heart pounding like a jackhammer inside her, and dialled his number. *Don't put off until tomorrow what you can do today...*

It was a little after five in the evening which, for Curtis, still left at least two, if not three, hours ahead of him. Two or three work-fuelled hours before his driver returned him to his bigger-than-strictly-necessary house in one of the most expensive postcodes in London.

Life could have been better as far as he was concerned.

Work-wise? Great. More money being added to the coffers. Two enormous deals that would guarantee him as a major player in the cut-throat world of web development and complex data analysis.

But on a personal level...?

Two dates with two small hot blondes had failed to ignite his interest or, for that matter, put to rest way too many fantasies about a certain five-ten woman he had slept with *once* but who still managed to occupy his every waking moment.

For a 'moving on' type of guy, as he was, that did not sit well. Understatement. That sat very, very badly, especially when the blunt truth was that she had been the one to turf him out. Metaphorically.

Of course, as he had told himself over the past couple of weeks, she had been absolutely right. Parting company, when he thought about it, was key to making sure their friendship remained intact and that was the main thing. A bit of a dalliance, however much he had craved it at the time, would never be worth the risk of her getting hurt. Not that there had been the slightest chance of that because she had been very casual and very upbeat when she had turned him down. The last few hours they had spent together before heading back to London had been proof positive that theirs had been no more for her than an enjoyable and brief fling. Which worked for him too. Didn't it?

Every scrap of common sense he had deployed when he'd thought about the situation should have been enough for him to sally forth to pastures new without a backward glance, but unfortunately the opposite seemed to be the case. Was it because he connected with her on a level that went way beyond the physical? Was the bedrock of their friendship the thing that was making it so difficult for him to shut the door on that very brief interlude? However many bracing internal debates he had.

To further complicate everything, William had read something somewhere and that was proving a thorny and unforeseen problem.

'Where did you hear that?' Curtis had asked two days ago when his godfather had casually mentioned that it was nice that the skiing holiday had resulted in the unexpected—in him and Jess 'becoming an item.'

It had taken half an hour of painstaking interrogation to discover that he had featured with Jess in the gossip pages of a weekly women's magazine of the type usually found lying on glass tables in hairdressing salons.

The picture was innocent enough, Curtis had discovered when he sprinted to the nearest newsagent to see what the fuss was all about. The text accompanying the picture, on the other hand, suggested all sorts of things that had given him an almighty headache. In a few short sentences, it implied that the most eligible bachelor in London had finally met his match and found the woman of his dreams. Would marriage follow…? it asked. It appeared that a 'little birdie' and 'good friend' had spilled the beans.

Curtis had no doubt as to the identity of the good friend and little birdie.

Caitlin had finally exited his life in a blaze of glory by making as much trouble for him as she could. Under normal circumstances, this would have amounted to no more than some awkward conversations with his friends but, against all odds, his godfather had read that article and now…

A headache.

'What were you doing with a women's glossy?' Curtis had been unable to stop himself from asking.

'Everybody needs some light relief, my boy!' William had answered testily. 'Happened to see it in a prominent place at the newsagents so got hold of it. Good to know what's happening out there with you young people! And good job I did! Don't suppose I would have heard a sausage about anything otherwise. Jess certainly didn't say a peep when she came round yesterday! Course, far be it from me to start interfering…asking questions…not my style at all.' And then he had added darkly, 'Nice you two have finally seen sense and decided to make a go of it, Curtis, but I'm warning you… Jess isn't one of those floozies you like to go out with, so I don't want you doing your usual.'

If not a catastrophe, then certainly a nuisance because, whilst he didn't care what other people thought of him, he *did* care what his godfather thought of him and so he had spent the past day toying with the realisation that he would have to talk to Jess and explain the situation before William decided to start asking her awkward questions about the relationship that never was.

So, sitting here now, unable to focus, Jess's name popping up on his cell phone felt propitious. For the first time since he'd got back to London his senses were on full alert and he felt *alive*.

He'd tried to contact her, left a couple of voicemails because she'd failed to pick up her phone and in return had received a brief text from her, claiming that she'd been frantically busy at work—telling him to have a good week.

So now…

Yes, he felt alive, senses zinging as he heard her voice. He pushed himself back and relaxed into his massive bespoke leather chair and stuck his feet on his desk, crossing them at the ankles.

'Jess!' For a few seconds, Curtis contemplated the satisfying notion that she might have been calling to tell him that she'd had second thoughts about continuing what they had started two and a half weeks ago.

Hard on the heels of that came the more realistic scenario, which was that William had had a chat with her, maybe shared his pleasure that she was now dating his godson, told her what a relief it was after all those *floozies*.

He abruptly swung his feet off the desk and sat up.

'How are you? Haven't heard from you in a while.'

'I've been busy.' At the other end of the line, Jess felt her breathing slow. Just hearing his voice, so deep and lazy and utterly sexy, caused a racing of her pulse and the faintness of pure excitement, and then she glanced at the stick in front of her and sobered up fast.

Her mind went blank for a few seconds and she surfaced to hear him saying something about his godfather.

'He's fine,' she interrupted. 'Curtis, I need to have a chat with you.'

'Isn't that what we're doing now?'

'I mean a *face-to-face* chat.'

Curtis smiled. William was fine. There had been no difficult conversation where she had had to try and figure out how, having firmly shut the door on their brief one-night stand, they were suddenly newsworthy and involved in a love-fest with wedding bells just round the corner.

But then why was she calling? Not just calling, but he knew her well and she was...*tense*.

Since when had Jess ever been tense with him? If she wasn't herself, then it was because she didn't know how to say what she wanted to say, and what else could that be other than the pleasing thought that she regretted her hasty rejection of his proposition that they continue what they'd started?

He'd spent the past couple of weeks with her inconveniently lodged in his head, and if it had been the same for her then it stood to reason that she had reached the very same conclusion he had.

'I could be with you in a couple of hours,' he said, promptly discarding the prospect of three more hours of work as he moved to rescue the grey cashmere jumper which he had tossed on the leather sofa by the window, along with his coat.

'There's no need to put yourself out, Curtis!'

'I'm already on my way.' He was. 'Where do you want to go for dinner?' He felt energised.

'Nowhere!'

'All the better,' he murmured smoothly. 'I get sick of eating out. Home cooking is so much better. Maybe I'll get William to give me a few lessons on the basics some time—he threatens to do it often enough. Would make an old man happy…' He was out of his office, barely glancing in the direction of all the worker bees still hard at it at their desks, including his extremely efficient middle-aged PA. He winked at her, mouthed that he would see her in the morning maybe…and then he was sprinting for the lift.

Jess realised that he'd hung up on her before she'd had time to fix another more timely date for them to meet. A date that would give her sufficient breathing space to get her thoughts in order and brace herself for a conversation she'd never dreamt she would ever have with him.

Instead, at a little after five-fifteen, she flew into action. Shower, change into jeans and a long-sleeve T-shirt…and then a mad dash to gather up all the ingredients she would need for an unwelcome dinner *à deux*. It wouldn't be the first time Curtis had had a meal at her house. That said, it was the first time she'd felt sick with nerves whilst preparing a meal. Pasta. Tomatoes and some mushrooms. Exactly what she had planned to have for herself, so she just had to double the quantity.

It felt as though ten minutes had passed when she heard the sharp buzz of her doorbell. She flew to the door and pulled it open and there he was. Six foot three of unfairly gorgeous masculine beauty. She breathed in sharply and stood aside to allow him to sweep past her.

He brought the cold in with him, along with a bottle of wine, which he handed to her before divesting himself of his coat and making his way into her kitchen, as comfortable in his surroundings as though he lived there.

Her heart was thumping so hard she felt faint. He'd always had that peculiar ability to somehow consume all the oxygen, until she felt she couldn't breathe, but never was she more conscious of that than now.

'There was no need for you to rush over here, Curtis.'

'Why are you looking so tense? Glass of wine?'

'Er...no, thank you.'

'Let's go relax in the sitting room.' He moved towards the door, having helped himself to some wine from the bottle he brought and glanced over his shoulder at her, grinning. 'Where have you been, Jess? Tried calling you a couple of times. Sure you won't join me in a glass? No one likes to drink alone.'

'I've been busy,' she muttered, already feeling helplessly in thrall to him and incapable of thinking straight. 'And no, thanks.'

He frowned. 'What's the point of an injection of cash if they're still slave-driving you into more fundraising?'

'I haven't been fundraising. I've been catching up on work and preparing the kids for their next batch of exams.' He'd perched on the deep, comfortable sofa and now looked at her with a veiled expression, his head tilted to one side. Expecting what? she wondered. Expecting her to have relented on his proposal, she guessed, because he was just too tempting to resist. Why else would he have rushed all the way up here?

To forestall a conversation that would lead nowhere, she cleared her throat and perched on the chair facing him.

She rested her hands on her knees and thought about that tiny beating heart inside her. It had not crossed her mind even for a second that she might not keep this baby and now she felt a flutter of excitement, against all odds.

He didn't say anything. He was quite still, his green eyes penetrating.

'Curtis…about what happened when we were away together a few weeks ago…'

He relaxed and smiled. 'Yes?' he prompted softly.

'You remember when we…when…?'

'When we made love?' His smile broadened and there was dark, lazy appreciation in his eyes that sent a wave of longing rushing through her with toxic potency. 'Unforgettable,' he added huskily.

'I had never…done it before…'

'I haven't forgotten.' His voice was unsteady in recollection. 'Believe me, it's imprinted in my memory banks with the force of a red-hot branding iron. Come sit by me, Jess…'

'You fumbled.'

'Come again?'

'It was a shock. You were caught on the back foot for a few seconds. You…fumbled…'

'Maybe I did. We all have our moments.'

'Curtis, the protection you used wasn't as foolproof as maybe you thought it was.'

Jess watched as comprehension filtered through the self-assurance that was so much part and parcel of his personality. The easy, sexy smile faded, he frowned, then the frown cleared and the colour drained from his face.

'What are you saying?'

Jess thought that he knew very well what she was saying but he just didn't want to believe it.

He'd had that situation with Caitlin. He'd found himself cornered into a marriage proposal he hadn't wanted because, at the end of the day, he wasn't into commitment. What must he be thinking now? Was he terrified that he was about to find himself in another corner?

'Curtis, I'm pregnant. I took the test this morning.' She shifted her eyes from his shocked, ashen face. 'I know you didn't come here expecting this, but you had to know. I don't… I'm not expecting anything from you,' she rushed on clumsily. 'I realise that this must be your worst nightmare come true, but I'm not Caitlin.' She laughed nervously and slid her eyes back to his face. No change there. He still looked as though he'd spotted that the sky was falling down and there was no shelter in sight.

'You're not Caitlin…'

'I don't want anything from you.' She slapped her hands on her thighs and began standing. 'So, now that I've told you…er…if you still want to stay for some pasta…or you might just want to go away and think about…er…things… No rush—you can call me when you're ready.'

She began walking away, but she didn't make it to the door. He was there in front of her, barring the exit, and the colour had returned to his face.

'*Go away?'* he grated in outraged disbelief. '*No rush?* Call you when I'm ready? Maybe next week…? Next month…? Next year…? Oh, I'm going to be staying for some pasta, Jess. I'm not going anywhere any time soon, until we've dealt with this situation!'

After the most stressful few hours she had ever had, Jess suddenly saw red. She leaned aggressively towards him, eyes narrowed.

'*Dealt with this situation?* How do you propose to do that, Curtis? There's nothing to deal with. It's happening and we just have to accept that!'

'I need another drink. Something less polite than a glass of wine.' He raked his fingers through his hair and stared at her.

How could this be happening? How had this *happened*? He knew she was right. He *had* fumbled. At the time he'd registered that protection had not gone according to plan but then the thought had been lost and had not resurfaced. And now here they were and, although the bomb had been dropped, he still couldn't believe that life as he knew it was about to implode.

But she must be as shocked as he was. Her colour was hectic and her deep blue eyes, always so soft and laughing, were filled with apprehension, anger at him and uncertainty.

Pain twisted, and shame that he had allowed himself to lose control, to hurt her with badly constructed phrases, poured through him.

'Let's go into the kitchen, Jess,' he said rather more quietly, 'and talk. Let's not forget the most important thing. We're friends. Not enemies.'

For the first time Jess felt some of her nerves dissipate because he was right. They weren't enemies. Far from it.

He spent a few minutes helping her prepare the food, which was a first, and they did that in silence.

When they were sitting in front of their bowls of pasta he looked at her seriously.

'First of all,' he said heavily, 'you're not Caitlin and, whether or not you expect anything from me, I intend to be fully involved.' He dug into his pasta, twirled the spaghetti round his fork and ate a mouthful, watching her in silence.

'Yes, and I wouldn't dream of getting in the way of you doing that.' She had no appetite, but she was aware that this was not the time to start toying with her food. For the next nine months she would be thinking about the wellbeing and health of the child she was carrying and again, despite the circumstances, she felt that punch of pure excitement at the thought of becoming a mum. 'I'm happy for us to informally arrange…visiting rights, even though it's early days yet.'

'*Visiting rights…?*'

He made it sound as though those two words were ones he'd never heard in his life before. Jess figured he was probably right on that score. He might have known what they meant but certainly not insofar as they pertained to him.

'I don't think we need to involve lawyers. I will never fight you when it comes to something like that.' She paused. 'And I guess,' she continued awkwardly, 'you'll probably want to financially contribute…?'

'Does that question really demand an answer?' But there was still that dazed look on his face, which made her hesitate for some reason.

'I guess not,' she conceded. 'But, whatever you decide to contribute,' she told him firmly, 'I want you to know that it will never be for *me*. It'll be for the baby.'

'So I buy the clothes and the…the baby food and the nappies and leave you to carry on teaching and trying to make ends meet?'

Jess looked around her and grimaced. Through the eyes of a billionaire, even one who happened to be her friend, was this little house ever going to make the grade? His pockets were deep enough for him to treat her to one of the most expensive ski resorts on the planet. How was he going to feel about their child coming home to a house where there was hardly enough room to swing a cat?

But the follow-on from that line of thinking was one she knew she would find impossible to accept.

A kept woman, given whatever she wanted financially because she was his child's mother. She enjoyed her independence—*loved* it—but how much joy would she have bringing in her own modest salary when she knew that it was irrelevant?

And if she refused, what would he do next?

Yes, they were friends, but the ground would shift irrevocably underneath their friendship with a child in the equation.

Where she lived, the lack of space, the cramped neighbourhood—all of that would now enter the realms of his concern. Would he think about claiming custody of their child? If he genuinely felt that he could provide a better life for a child because of his vast financial base, then wouldn't he just go for it? Whilst still telling her what good friends they were?

Jess knew that the racing of her mind wasn't going to get her anywhere, but the first drips of cold fear trickled through her as scenario upon scenario formed in her head.

'Money isn't everything, Curtis,' she said weakly. 'Think of all the rich people you know who aren't happy.'

'William knows about us.' Curtis abruptly changed the subject and she gaped at him for a few seconds, her mind still occupied with raging worst case scenarios.

'What are you talking about?'

'We were papped at the wedding. The picture was innocuous enough. The accompanying text less so. I had to wrench the hows and wherefores out of him, but the bottom line is that all the innuendo in the very brief few sentences under that picture imply a serious relationship between the two of us.'

'But did you set him straight?' Jess gasped.

'No.'

'Why not? When did you have this conversation with him? He never mentioned a word to me about anything!'

'He didn't want to appear nosy. The reason I didn't put him straight was because, as you pointed out, William's mental health has not been great since he said goodbye to active life at the university. Also…'

'Also?'

Curtis flushed and pushed his bowl to the side so that he could relax into the chair whilst continuing to look at her with brooding intensity. 'Also, he seems to think that I'm the sort of guy to take advantage of you for my own nefarious purposes, only to dispose of you when I get bored.'

'Ahh…'

'Define *ahh*…'

'I suppose…' for the first time during their fraught conversation she was diverted enough to smile as years of friendship kicked in '…you *do* come with some form in that department, Curtis.'

He grimaced and returned her smile. 'My track record doesn't do me justice.' He raised both hands in mock surrender as her eyebrows shot up. 'Okay, I can see why he assumed what he did, but Jess, it *does* leave us in a bit of a quandary in light of this new development.'

'Why?' She stuck her chin out at a mutinous angle. 'William wasn't born yesterday, Curtis. He knows that not all relationships end in marriage, that sometimes that's not possible.'

'Sometimes,' Curtis told her quietly, 'the head doesn't always win the argument.'

'What are you trying to say?' Jess demanded helplessly.

'Marry me, Jess. I suppose that's what I'm trying to say.'

She gaped at him in open incredulity. '*Marry* you?'

She wondered whether she'd missed a vital link or a sentence somewhere, but then she remembered that he had proposed once before to a woman he hadn't wanted to be with for the sake of the child she had purported to be carrying for him. He was a decent guy. It was why she…had always liked and admired him. More than that. But decency didn't win when it came to a lifetime together. Love held all the trump cards in that respect and, as much as Curtis liked her and respected her and had fun with her, and had even made love with her, he didn't *love* her.

He was prepared to do the right thing but, face it, she thought with painful honesty, he was a guy with a very healthy libido and a penchant for 'moving on' when it came to relationships. Once the enthusiasm for doing the decent thing had worn off and once William had been satisfied in assuming that his godson had sticking power when it came to her, Jess, then what would happen next?

Discreet affairs?

He would break her heart. She loved him. She'd loved him for ever and she expected she always would. It was an admission she had managed to bury in her subconscious but now she took it out, aired it, faced up to it and accepted it with a certain amount of dull resignation.

Marry him and she would be left picking up the pieces and she would never be able to glue them back together again. Wasn't that why she had walked away from the temptation to carry on what they'd had in Courchevel? Hadn't she known, even then, that she had to protect herself?

'Of course I'm not going to *marry* you, Curtis! I wouldn't hurt your godfather for all the tea in China, but I also won't sacrifice my entire life to a loveless marriage. I deserve better than that. We *both* do.'

He looked at her in silence for so long that she began to fidget.

'I'm not prepared to be a part-time parent,' he told her.

'What do you mean?'

'I mean I'll do whatever it takes to ensure a child of mine gets the very best that life has to offer, and that includes a full-time father.'

This was the steel hand in the velvet glove, Jess thought numbly. A guy didn't climb the greasy pole to get to the very top by being Mr Nice Guy. He might be fair and generous and witty, and often surprisingly thoughtful, but he could also be tough when he needed to be. Now, it seemed, was one of those times.

'Are you *threatening* me, Curtis?'

'I'm asking you to think long and hard about my proposition and to put yourself at the back of the queue, as I am prepared to do. A child needs two parents whenever possible, Jess. That's something I would fight tooth and nail to achieve. It's more important than any other consideration.'

CHAPTER EIGHT

'TOMORROW...' HE SAID, vaulting upright. 'We can talk tomorrow. You tell me that I need to go away and think about what you've lobbed into my life? Well, *you* need to have some time to think about the only solution I would find acceptable in this situation. I'm going to head to William's, and I intend to stay there until we've come to an agreement on this.'

'No!' Jess sprang to her feet and, rather as he had earlier, she swerved round him to bar his exit. Hands on her hips and feet squarely planted on the ground, she glared at him.

'Come again?'

'No way, Curtis Hamilton, do you get to tell me that you're prepared to fight me over this because you happen to believe in "the sanctity of family life"! One minute you're waxing lyrical that relationships are a waste of time, and then in the next breath you're telling me that we need to get married for the sake of a baby!'

He flushed and raked his fingers through his hair. '*Relationships* aren't a waste of time,' he muttered. '*Love* is the pointless component.'

'So you're prepared to walk down the aisle with a woman even though you don't love her.'

'If there is a child involved, then yes. I am.'

'Why, Curtis?' There was genuine curiosity in her voice. This guy was the epitome of a forward-thinking male, one who was tuned in to women in the workplace, who made sure that there was no discrimination between the sexes when it came to pay and promotions. Three years previously, Jess could remember reading an article about his massive company being a leading light in the war against all forms of discrimination.

So how was it that he could be so stubbornly *traditional* when it came to something like this?

It wasn't even as though she wanted to bar access to his child. She was prepared to bend over backwards to accommodate him!

'I...' He stared at her, at her puzzled expression. 'I wouldn't mind a coffee,' he muttered, shifting uncomfortably under her direct gaze.

'Okay.' She stepped aside.

The atmosphere had shifted, and she couldn't really even work out *how*, but it had. Her heart began to race. There was a peculiar vulnerability she couldn't *see* but could somehow *sense*.

She walked ahead of him to the kitchen and felt his eyes on her as she bustled about making them both a mug of coffee. She didn't have to ask how he took his because she knew. No milk and a heaped teaspoon of sugar. She'd teased him often enough that sugar in coffee was unnecessary.

'You have to see it from my point of view, Curtis,' she told him quietly, positioning herself opposite him at the small table and cradling the warm mug between her hands before taking a sip. 'I just don't get it. I don't want to fight you on this. Not at all. And from where I'm sitting, any child we have will have us both. We just won't be living together. We won't be sacrificing our chance to find true love and happiness with someone else because the unexpected has happened. You should be *relieved* that I'm not trying to force your hand!'

'I... Before William rescued me...' Curtis stared into the depths of the abyss and took the plunge. Confession. He'd never considered it good for the soul. His past was his and his alone but now he felt an unexpected rush of relief that he was going to do what he had never been tempted to do in his life before. Share. 'Before William rescued me... I was in care.' His eyes met hers. He was already resenting any show of pity but there was none in her clear gaze. She simply tilted her head to one side, her expression urging him to continue. He found that that was something he wanted to do.

'I have no idea who my father is. He'd fled the scene, presumably, before I was born. Maybe he took flight at the prospect of an unwanted kid. At any rate, my mother...my mother was clever and beautiful. She was also a drug addict, something she got into when she left university. William knew her when she was a student. He was her tutor and he took a paternal interest in her because she was, I expect, something of a lost cause despite her brains. From the little I know about my mother's background, she had been left to her own devices from day one and by the time she hit fourteen she was pretty much doing her own thing. It's surprising that she ever made it to university at all but, like I said, she was bright. I suppose, in the end, background ended up winning the war over brains. To cut a long story short, William was transferred to Australia shortly after I was born, shortly after my mother decided to get me christened. Maybe she had a premonition that her lousy parenting would require someone to one day step up to the plate. Who knows? At any rate, she overdosed when I was still young and I was put into foster care. And there I remained for over two years until, through sheer good fortune, William found out about me and rescued me.'

'I'm sorry, Curtis.' Jess hesitated, so tempted to delve deeper yet knowing he would shut down if she did. 'You want your own child to have what you feel you never had yourself.'

'It trumps everything.'

'He or she can have that without us getting married. As you've said, we're friends. Not enemies.'

'Which is what makes marriage all the more appealing. No delusions. Solid grounding in a mutual desire to do what's best for the child.'

Jess realised with consternation that that was the very reason why she couldn't marry him. Where, for Curtis, friendship would be the glue between them, creating harmony in the joint desire to do what might be best for a child that hadn't asked to be conceived, for her friendship where she craved love would be a daily torment. It would be a constant reminder that she wanted more from him and, more dangerously, because she knew herself, a constant battle against hope.

'I can't marry you, Curtis. We have to find another way forward and I hope that way won't involve you trying to fight me for custody of our child.'

'I wouldn't do that.' He stood up. His expression was blank. 'William will have to be told.'

'Yes.' She had drawn her line in the sand and her heart was breaking in two. What he had told her had made her want to weep but she knew that she had to stand firm or else end up hopelessly lost.

William, though, was going to be an almighty problem. He didn't want to hurt his godfather, for powerful reasons she was only now fully understanding, and nor did she.

She knew that William would assume his godson had somehow taken advantage of her and had ended up with a mess on his hands, and even if she denied anything of the sort he would still secretly judge Curtis, who would be found wanting for ever.

It would be heartbreaking.

Curtis had inadvertently told her that William had *rescued* him and that was a very telling word. Could she live with herself if that relationship was somehow changed for ever for the worse?

She could live with herself if *their* friendship changed. It almost certainly would now that she had turned down his proposal. But for William to blame Curtis for what had happened…? That would be a great deal harder to stomach.

He began heading towards the door and she reached out and stayed him with her hand on his arm and felt him stiffen under her touch.

Already their friendship was changing.

'I get it.'

'What do you get, Jess?' His mouth twisted. 'That my semi-tragic background is responsible for me making unreasonable decisions when it comes to the fate of a baby?'

'No!' But she reddened.

'You want your freedom to find true love and I can't stop you. The conversation has been had and, as you've said, it's time to move onto another solution to handling this situation. I said I would do anything within my power to give any child of mine what they deserve. That doesn't mean trying to fight you for custody.'

His voice was cool, accepting and practical, and it cut a jagged path through her heart.

'William...' She maintained eye contact but removed her hand from his arm.

'It is what it is.'

'I can understand,' she said softly, 'why it means so much that his opinion of you isn't...doesn't...'

'Like I said,' Curtis grated, 'it is what it is.'

'Believe it or not, it would break my heart if I thought I'd done anything at all to change his opinion of you,' Jess said. 'So here's *my* proposal.'

'I'm listening.'

'Tomorrow we'll tell him...um...about the situation, but I'm prepared to paper over the fact that we're not cementing a relationship by rushing down the aisle.'

'Explain, Jess.'

'We can pretend just for a while that this isn't what it actually is...a one-night stand with unexpected consequences.' She paused but his expression was unreadable. 'I know if it tapers off in due course, he will more easily accept that we had fun but that as lifelong partners it wasn't meant to be. He won't...think that you're the bad guy in this...he won't think that you used me. Which, of course, you didn't.'

She watched as he lowered his eyes, shielding his expression.

As sacrifices went, this was a big deal for her because she would much rather have dealt with things in a businesslike fashion, which might have protected her battered heart, but his story...his heart-wrenching account of a childhood she had never suspected...

We all had our Achilles heel. If he was hers, then William was his.

To pretend a relationship for a short while would

be worth it if it saved William's opinion of his god-son. He adored Curtis and she wouldn't want to see that jeopardised.

'Appreciated,' Curtis said curtly. For a couple of seconds he seemed to be on the verge of adding to that, but instead he inclined his head in a mocking salute. 'Tomorrow,' he told her brusquely. 'Do you want to come to the house or would you rather I swing by to fetch you?'

'I'll make my own way there.'

She felt a shiver of apprehension at a future stretching out in front of her, weaving its obscure way to a place she didn't know and hadn't banked on.

It was nearly midnight by the time she finally curled up in bed and it was a long time before she actually managed to fall asleep.

William was chatting in the background. The kitchen was aromatic. Smells wafting of a full English lunch with all the trimmings. Lounging on the kitchen chair, one eye on the time because Jess would be arriving at midday, Curtis sipped his wine and half listened to what his godfather was saying. There was no need to give undivided attention because he knew the gist of the conversation and the reason he knew was because William had been stuck in the same groove ever since breakfast.

He swerved between utter joy at the prospect of his godson and Jess finally getting where he had hoped they'd get for a long time and dark warning words about him not taking advantage of one of the nicest girls on the planet.

Curtis had more or less been obliged to respond in a series of non-committal murmurs that neither encouraged nor discouraged but he was immeasurably glad that Jess had come up with the idea of maintaining a pretence of sorts for a short while.

She'd read the situation perfectly and he knew that she'd been swayed by what he'd told her, the confession he'd never thought would ever leave his lips.

A confession he did not regret having made, astonishingly.

Had all that hurt he'd carried around like a dead weight for all his life been somehow diffused the minute he'd confided in her? He certainly felt weightless now. In the telling, he had shed the demons that had plagued him, although, and he knew this with gut certainty, she was absolutely the only one he would ever have told.

Trust.

He trusted her.

He trusted her—he enjoyed her company—and, in more ways than one, they were *good* for one another. He couldn't understand why those things weren't enough to sway her, to make her see what he wanted her to see!

He'd told her about his past. He could never love. His heart was cold but that didn't mean that all of him was buried under ice. Affection, surely, ranked as high as love. Strip away the high-minded, exalted, overrated emotional insecurity of love and what you found was that the relationships that lasted could fall back on good old affection.

So far was she from Caitlin, with her manipulative drive to get him, whatever the means, that he knew he should be overjoyed, but he wished there was some way he could get to Jess, get her to see his point of view, get her to marry him for the sake of their unborn child.

He was lost in introspection when the doorbell rang, and he leapt to go to the door even as William was putting lids on pans and wiping his hands on his apron.

'Stay here,' Curtis told him. He smiled but tension was snaking a path through him. 'That lamb isn't going to roast itself without some TLC...'

'Son, are you okay? You've been very quiet this morning.'

Caught on the back foot, Curtis shuffled and raked his fingers through his hair and glanced at his godfather. 'There's something...'

'Something *what*?' William's shrewd blue eyes were suddenly sharp and very focused.

'Something Jess and I need to talk to you about...'

'Don't tell me anything you think I might not want to hear,' William countered sharply.

Another piercing ring of the doorbell saved him from any further elaboration and on his way to open the door Curtis decided that coming clean about the pregnancy was the best way forward. What would be the point of a great elephant in the room, sitting between them at the dining table for the duration of lunch?

'Jess.' He swung open the door and drew in a sharp breath. In the shock of the unexpected the day before, his libido had taken a back seat. Now it came back in a hot rush as he stared at her, dressed in her usual thick padded coat with a yellow and black woollen hat pulled over her head and some faded jeans and sensible wellies visible under the coat. The least sexy outfit on the planet and yet the heat that surged in him could have melted steel. Involuntarily, his eyes zoomed to her belly before he quickly averted them.

'You look amazed,' she returned, but her smile was tentative. 'Did you think I might have bailed?'

'I've told William that we have something to say to him.'

'Already?' Her eyes widened in sudden alarm and she chewed her lip anxiously.

'It's going to have to be done, so why not immediately?'

'I guess...'

'You're scared?'

'I don't like lying.'

'This was your idea,' he pointed out, then added with grudging honesty, 'not that I'm not grateful.' He stood aside so that she could brush past him but they remained in the hallway, facing one another. 'He's...on a high with this news of our sudden romance.' He grimaced. 'Admitting the truth at this juncture would have been a little...'

'Terrifying?'

'Dramatic word.' But he smiled, amused, and raised his eyebrows. 'Hence I am very grateful you decided to...indulge in a very gentle white lie that will smooth the path for all of us.'

She followed him towards the kitchen. The cottage was cosy and comfortable. No sharp edges or stark colours or empty spaces. Nothing jarringly modern. She loved it. This was the first time she'd felt nervous being here but she sidestepped the feeling. Curtis was right. It was better to say what had to be said and get it out of the way. It was also a good thing that they would be indulging in this harmless white lie because William would have been devastated to think that she was going to have a baby with his godson without any attempt at a relationship to cement them. Who could blame him? He was an old-fashioned man who had grown more and more jaded and impatient with Curtis's choices when it came to the opposite sex.

'So,' he greeted them both from the doorway of the

kitchen, arms folded, his eyes sharp, 'what's this big thing the pair of you want to talk to me about?'

Jess smiled and kissed him fondly on the cheek. 'That's a very gruff way to greet me, William. A girl could be offended. What's on the menu today, chef?' She sniffed the air and noted how he relaxed, which then made her realise just how keyed-up he was about Curtis, braced, no doubt, for another speech about his godson not wanting to relinquish his casual approach to relationships, but this time with *her* in the starring role of discarded victim.

'Lamb. Your favourite. And don't think I'm going to fall for you trying to distract me, young lady. Now, tell me what it is you have to say.'

But he was moving off, nodding at the table, because dining was always casual, in the kitchen, at the eight-seater wooden table by the French windows that led into the neatly manicured back garden.

'Would I do that?' Jess teased, exchanging a quick glance with Curtis. Her face betrayed none of her nerves as they all sat, as Curtis looked at her, as they said, speaking briefly over one another—

'We're having a baby...'

Remove all the signposts and how was anyone supposed to know where the next misplaced step might put them?

We're having a baby.

Those four words had removed the signposts. That was what kept running through Jess's head as, two days later, she and Curtis sat in one of the old-fashioned tea rooms in Ely, looking at one another over a pot of tea and a plate of scones at three-thirty in the afternoon.

Outside, wintry skies were leaden with the promise of snow. In here, though, it was warm enough for them both to have shed outer layers and she had to try very hard to ignore his intense masculine appeal, as she had been for the past day and a half, during which time, at William's insistence, she and Curtis had been spending a crazy amount of their free time together.

'You kids might go back a ways,' he had announced with satisfaction over the perfect lamb lunch, 'but that doesn't mean a courtship isn't a good thing and, correct me if I'm wrong, but have you two ever courted one another? You are having a baby together and I may be an old-fashioned fool but I feel it's important you make the most of the free time you have together before a demanding little one starts calling the shots! Not that this old fool won't be more than happy to babysit!'

So here they were, having tea and scones in the middle of a freezing cold Friday afternoon. She should have been at home, prepping her syllabus for the following week, taking advantage of the fact that it was a class-free afternoon, thanks to an induction day for new students. He should have been in London, working. She vaguely thought that they should have been communicating by email or WhatsApp, whereby she would not be forced to try and sublimate responses that ambushed all her efforts at self-control the minute she was in his company.

The evening before, William had cooked them both a fabulous dinner and then promptly abandoned them so that he could go to the pub, where he'd planned on meeting a couple of old friends. *'What friends?'* His answer had been vague. *'Why the urgency?'* Answer also vague.

'When do you have your first scan? Have you been to the doctor? Booked anything?'

'Huh?' Startled out of her brief reverie and surprised because the weather and the possibility of snow had been the last topic on the agenda, Jess looked at Curtis with wide-eyed surprise.

Their eyes tangled and she blushed.

'Not for ages and no, I haven't been to the doctor.'

'Shouldn't you register?' He looked at her narrowly and she reddened even more.

'I've been busy.'

'When you go, I want to be there.'

'Do you?'

'What did you expect?'

'Well… I know we're pretending to be involved for William's benefit, but he's not earwigging here, Curtis, so there's no need to…er…show an interest at this… um…early stage.'

'I'm not,' he told her abruptly. 'I want to be there every step of the way.'

A vision of intimacy swamped her as she imagined him standing next to her while they looked at a scan in a darkened room with her swollen belly exposed.

She changed the subject quickly, to clear the image from her head. 'How long do you think we're going to have to pretend that we're…serious about one another for William's benefit?'

Curtis tensed. Could she make it any clearer just how little she enjoyed the situation?

Of course, neither of them had thought that William would have stuck his oar in to the extent of insisting they spend quality time together instead of just talking to one another on the phone.

Curtis thought that her hair would curl if she knew the full extent of his godfather's belief that they were madly in love, that it was just a question of time before they tied the knot—because why on earth would they want their baby to be born out of wedlock?—and that plans should be made about where they intended to live.

He had done his best to avoid being pinned down but the prospect of disentangling themselves from the fabrication they had concocted was beginning to look a lot less simple than either of them had originally thought.

That should have worried him. This enforced mini break should have worried him. Since when did he spend time lazing around when there were deals to be done? The fact that it didn't worry him was even more disturbing.

Clearly, though, he was on his own when it came to guiltily enjoying this predicament. He'd seen a different side to her in Courchevel. In bite-sized pieces over the years, he hadn't really appreciated just how smart and funny and empathetic she was. It had been a journey of discovery and so what if he was enjoying the fact that the journey hadn't ended? It made sense because they were going to co-parent, whether he wanted more or not, and so he needed to spend this time with her, to further see the woman who was bearing his child.

'He's very much invested in this,' he said, taking his third scone. 'Time, of course, will allow us to demonstrate that we won't be spending the rest of our lives in blissful perpetuity. How much time? How long is a piece of string?'

Jess frowned. 'I don't know how long the piece of string is, Curtis, but maybe we should try and measure it.'

She was aghast at the prospect of having to deal with her wayward emotions for an indefinite period of time. She saw him and she wanted more, and she hated herself for wanting more. He'd dropped all mention of marriage and she could only think that he was relieved not to have been pushed into anything. Maybe he'd had time to think what a nightmare it would have turned out to be—married to a woman he didn't love, a woman who should have stayed firmly put in the *friend* category.

'At any rate, surely he can't expect you to wash your hands of your work commitments in London?' She tilted her head to one side. 'You must be distraught at having to hang around here when you hadn't planned to.'

'Could your language be any more colourful? Distraught?'

Jess ignored the interruption. She hated the way that sexy drawl could make her whole body tighten with sexual excitement. There was a slight smile tugging the corners of his mouth and she ignored that as well but she could still feel a slow burn inside her.

'But I have an idea that I think might work,' she slowly suggested, frowning when he raised his eyebrows in a vaguely sceptical question.

'Can't wait to hear.'

'You head back to London tomorrow, first thing. Maybe even later this evening. You then stay away for a while due to pressure of work—time issues…meetings abroad…money to be made, deals to be done et cetera. While you're away, I'll lay the foundations for a relationship that couldn't possibly survive because of your long absences. Of course, I'll make sure he knows that we will always remain the best of friends, but that we're just not suited for anything more than that.'

'Due to the fact that I'm never around.'

'Well,' she pointed out defensively, 'you *do* devote most of your time to work'

'Hmm. So…to recap,' Curtis mused pensively, cool green eyes boring into her until she had to struggle not to squirm, 'you generously engineer the demise of our short-lived relationship on the grounds that I'm a complete bastard who can't be bothered to stick around for his own flesh and blood because making more and more money is vastly more important.'

'I didn't say that there weren't elements that couldn't be fine-tuned,' she snapped. 'It's just an idea, Curtis, because we both know that, sooner rather than later, we're going to have to come clean and the later we leave it, I'm now beginning to see, the harder it's going to be.'

'I'm not being the fall guy in this little scheme, Jess. I'm the one who was willing to get married and do the right thing. *You* were the one who was so invested in the business of finding Mr Right that you're willing to walk away from marriage. So when it comes to wriggling out of this arrangement you can forget it if you imagine I'm going to be nailed to the wall as the man who won't step up to the plate and do the honourable thing.'

Hot and bothered, Jess glared at him.

Why was he being so difficult? She knew. His background demanded he provided for his child what his own feckless mother had failed to provide for him and she was stricken by a sudden attack of guilt, but then many children who didn't have irresponsible parents managed to do very well in a situation where their parents no longer lived together. Essentially, she argued with herself, their own child would have a very different experience of growing up than he had had.

Of course, she could see that he might have been a bit taken aback by the rough outline of her idea, but surely he was as keen as she was to keep this charade as short as possible.

Did he still imagine that she would rush into marrying him after she'd said her piece?

Maybe he did. It wasn't as though he knew just how

deep her feelings for him ran, just how catastrophic it would be for her to sign up to being his wife, to being with him every minute of every day, knowing that what she felt for him would never be returned.

She was hit by a sudden wave of pure despair as all-engulfing as a tidal wave and she felt tears prick the back of her eyes.

And, just like that, he reached out and held her hand, his eyes filled with concern.

'Don't stress,' he said roughly.

'But I *do* stress,' she whispered.

'You're scared.' He paused and squeezed her hand, a gesture of such tender support that her heart clenched. 'You don't want the uncertainty of our situation hanging over your head indefinitely, like the Sword of Damocles…'

She shook her head, not trusting herself to speak.

Curtis sighed and rubbed his eyes before looking at her gravely. 'I'll make sure…the way is suitably paved.' His mouth twisted into a smile tinged with sadness. 'As it seems I can't persuade him down any other route. He's arranged a small dinner tonight, asking one of his friends over. After that? Don't worry. It'll be…sorted.'

CHAPTER NINE

THE DINNER WAS at six-thirty or, as William would have said, 'six-thirty for seven', being a stickler to the traditional rules of etiquette. With family, there would be casual drinks before dinner at the kitchen table, but he always took great pride in the formalities of 'proper dining' when he had guests, so drinks would be taken in his front room and dinner would be in the dining room, even though there would be just the one guest.

She hoped the evening wouldn't be too awkward and was already feeling a twinge of sorrow for his disappointment when it had to be broken to him that, whilst he would still be a grandparent, he would not have a daughter-in-law in *her*.

How did Curtis plan to take care of this situation? He had told her that it would be sorted. How?

Would he have said something to William already? Or would he do as she had suggested, which seemed a sensible route towards demonstrating through action rather than words that they were a couple who were not temperamentally suited for any kind of long-term relationship, whether there was a child in the mix or not.

The promised snow had turned into a flurry of flakes falling steadily by the time she hopped on her bike for the twenty-minute cycle-ride to William's cottage.

In jeans and her trainers and two layers of jumpers and with her woolly hat pulled low over her head, she was still freezing by the time she finally arrived at the sprawling cottage in its acre of beautifully manicured grounds.

Cold and fifteen minutes late.

She was tugging off her fingerless gloves when Curtis pulled open the door before she had time to press the bell for a second time.

'You're late,' were his first words as he fell back to let her past him, closing the heavy front door on the swirl of snowflakes.

Jess blinked and stared at him. Would he *always* take her breath away like this?

A plain black long-sleeved, semi-fitted T-shirt emphasised the width of his shoulders. He had shoved up the sleeves and her eyes were drawn to the curl of golden-brown hair around the metallic watch strap. His jeans were faded black and he wore a pair of loafers. He looked exactly what he was—a sophisticated, uber sexy billionaire who could snap his fingers and have any woman he wanted.

It seemed just a tiny bit disingenuous that William could actually find it credible that his godson might fall for her.

'I cycled.' She pulled off the woolly hat, which was wet from falling snow, and shook out her hair. 'Took longer than I'd anticipated. The roads are treacherous.'

'Why the heck didn't you drive, Jess?'

'My battery's low.'

He raked his fingers through his hair with evident frustration. 'This isn't going to do.'

'What are you talking about?'

Still divesting herself of layers of clothing because

the cottage was beautifully warm, she was barely looking at him as she spoke.

'Taking chances, Jess! Look at the weather! It's snowing. Of course it's not only going to take longer to get
here, but the roads are going to be worse than treacherous! You could have gone flying over the handlebars
of that bike! Have you forgotten that you're pregnant?'

'Of course I haven't forgotten, Curtis!' She damped
down the pleasurable warmth from his protective, pos-
sessive outburst and reminded herself that this was all
about the precious cargo she was now carrying.

'You should have called me. I would have driven over
to fetch you.'

'I'm perfectly fine to look after myself,' Jess told
him. 'I'm pregnant, not ill. I made sure to be very careful on the bike.'

'It's time you had a new car. I'll sort that out.'

'You'll do nothing of the sort!'

'Since when does anyone fight over the gift of a new
car? I'm rich. You're having my baby. Stop being so sensitive over small things.'

Jess sighed but accepted the offer. Because he had
a very valid point and it was something she would just
have to get used to. She wanted her freedom? Then with
that would come his inevitable desire to make sure she
wanted for nothing, because for her to need anything
implied that his child would, likewise, be in need.

Her independence was about to be eroded and she
didn't think that the erosion was going to be a subtle
advance.

'Okay, Curtis, but please, if you insist, then I will
choose what I think is appropriate.'

'Appropriate for whom?' But he had relaxed and was

looking at her with amusement. 'You're unique, do you know that?'

Jess blushed, at a loss for what to say, but before she could say anything at all he continued, far more seriously, 'I was distracted.' He placed his hand on her arm and turned her to look at him.

The harried expression she had glimpsed when he had opened the door for her was back and she looked at him with alarm.

'Distracted?'

'You arriving on a bike…the snow…the fact that you could have had an accident, cycling like a maniac in weather like this.'

'I wasn't cycling like a maniac!'

'William's mystery guest…'

'What about her? Him? Who is it?'

'I don't think you're going to like who will be joining us for dinner.'

'You're scaring me. Why won't—?'

At which point a beaming William emerged into the hall, and behind him was a short, rotund man with a goatee beard. One of William's friends. Probably a professor from the university. He kept in touch with a handful and was wont to display his culinary expertise for them every so often.

Why is this a cause for concern? That was the thought that sprang to mind as she moved forward, smiling.

'Jess!' William's beam got brighter as he approached her with his hands outstretched, dapper in a pair of navy trousers, a formal long-sleeved shirt and a snazzy royal blue bow tie. 'You look delightful. That colour suits you, my dear.'

'Grey?' She laughed out loud. 'Thank you, William. I'll bear that in mind when I next go clothes-shopping.'

Behind her, Curtis's presence made the hairs on her neck stand on end. She was uber conscious of his presence and uber conscious of her own weakness whenever he was around.

'Don't believe you've met my friend, have you?'

Jess peered past him to the chap behind, who was of similar age to William and also looking rather delighted. She sensed that news of her pregnancy might have been imparted. Was that what Curtis had been worried about? It was certainly a worry he would have to get used to because there was no way her pregnancy was going to remain a secret for very long and definitely not in William's circle of friends.

'No...'

'Allow me to introduce Raymond! Raymond Dale. He's the local vicar and—exciting news—he's agreed to marry you!'

'What...? Sorry...?'

'Don't stand around there in the hall, you two. It's cold out here! Come through to the sitting room. I've prepared some delightful morsels.'

For Jess, where the past few weeks had whipped by with the speed of sound, time now seemed to stand completely still.

The evening progressed in a haze of appalled confusion as they were ushered by a benevolent William into the sitting room, where drinks were being served.

Raymond was as charming as they came and after fifteen minutes he settled into a jovial but thoughtful line of questioning about what they expected from marriage.

Jess suspected that this had been well planned in advance by William who, at this point, removed himself from proceedings to 'see about supper'—which was going to be a surprise, he told her, but she must rest assured some of her favourite things would be served, including homemade tiramisu for pudding.

'Sit, sit…' William encouraged, before his opportune departure from the room. He then proceeded to usher her and Curtis into the small two-seater sofa by the fireplace, allowing his friend to angle his chair so that he was facing them both.

She felt the press of Curtis's thigh against hers, a distraction she could do without.

Even more distracting was when he took her hand in his, without looking at her, so that he could link fingers with her.

With no room to shuffle out of reach, she pinned a glazed smile to her face and let her hand go limp, even though the racing of her pulse was quite enough to remind her of the devastating effect that small gesture was having on her nervous system.

What on earth was he playing at? she wondered.

Of course, he might not want to alert the local vicar and his godfather's friend that their relationship was not what it appeared to be, but surely he shouldn't be actively *encouraging* the illusion by holding hands. Wouldn't it have been more appropriate for him to have taken up a position on another chair? One of the ones in the furthest reaches of the sitting room.

Her jaw ached from the artificial smile she kept plastered on her face as she listened to Raymond's kind words of advice to the couple due to be married.

'Money,' he intoned, carefully sipping from his modest glass of sherry, 'really is the root of many an evil. It's a cliché, my children, but one I would urge you to both consider as you contemplate your way forward together.'

Jess nodded. Next to her Curtis was more forthcoming, holding forth on how much he agreed with the sentiment, having seen many a person come a cropper in their haste to make it to the top, often taking down their loved ones with them.

He squeezed her hand and she smiled faintly. She could feel beads of perspiration breaking out. She didn't want to be discussing a marriage that was never going to happen, and not just because it was unfair to propagate the illusion to someone who was sincerely trying to give them good advice.

She didn't want to discuss this because in her head it raised so many tantalising visions of what could have been if only...

In this situation there was no room for *if only*, so she did her utmost to let the litany of wise advice sweep past her, keeping a low profile, barely aware of how Curtis was responding. Just aware that he *was* responding.

Dinner couldn't have come soon enough.

The food was spectacular and, thankfully, the conversation moved on to less disconcerting waters.

She allowed herself to relax. A bit.

She tried several times to catch Curtis's eye, but his attention was focused on his godfather and Raymond and, sitting as she was, right next to him, there was a limit to what she could do to engage a surreptitious response from him.

And in the meantime...

How her mind travelled down all those forbidden paths that talk of marriage had opened up in her head.

She had so many memories of her parents, of how deeply in love they had been, enjoying the time they'd spent together as a family.

Had such happiness on the home front made her ill equipped for the realities of life and all its complexities?

Shy as a teenager because of her height and the fact

that she had developed earlier than most of her classmates, she had been too reserved to throw herself into the ups and downs of teenage dating games. Instead, she had enjoyed her books, her sport, her skiing whenever she could.

Maybe if she had had her heart broken a few times she would have been more protected against the business of daydreams and unrealistic expectations.

Except what was so wrong in having expectations in life? It was just unfortunate that her expectations had sent her racing towards a brick wall.

As the evening wound down to its conclusion, Jess could only reflect on the irony that she and Curtis were two people so conditioned by their backgrounds that never in a million years would they have found a fit together.

Where her own sheltered and cosy life had prepared her to follow a predictable course of love and marriage and children, his fractured one had sent him hurtling down a different route.

It was her misfortune that she had tumbled into love with him and now faced the prospect of trying to piece her life together without him, even though she would never be able to fully walk away because of the glue that now held them together.

'You've been very quiet this evening, my dear.'

She surfaced and blinked at William, who was looking at her with paternal concern, and her heart wrenched at the disappointment he would be facing when she and Curtis broke the news to him that they wouldn't be getting married after all.

Raymond was beginning to stand, patting his stomach with satisfaction and complimenting William on the quality of the food.

Jess glanced through the window to see that the snow was falling ever harder, teetering towards blizzard rather than angry flurries.

They all began heading towards the door. Raymond had driven and waved aside William's suggestion that he stay the night and give the snow time to blow itself out. He had a sturdy four-wheel drive, he asserted, and he had every confidence that the Big Guy up there would make sure he was in full functioning order so that he could marry his close friend's godson to his partner.

Jess smiled weakly, very much aware of Curtis's hand resting lightly on the small of her back as they clustered in the hallway, reaching for coats and winding down the conversation.

'So...' Raymond paused, winked at William and then smiled at them all. 'I'm ready to marry you two just as soon as you want. Of course, there'll be a few bits and pieces to sort out—i's dotted and t's crossed and all the rest—but I have slots in my upcoming diary and I don't have to tell you that I will do my utmost to accommodate the ceremony whenever suits you both!'

'I think these children would want sooner rather than later.' William beamed at them both. 'With a baby on the way, why waste time?'

'Why indeed?' Curtis murmured, and Jess gaped sideways at him, but no one was looking in her direction because all eyes were on Raymond, who was doing all but fetching his personal calendar from his coat pocket.

'There's no rush,' she interjected weakly.

'Two weeks, Raymond? A fortnight? Give you young things plenty of time to start sorting out the details about where you're going to live. Of course, far be it from me to say anything about the folly of bringing up a baby in central London, however big the mansion might be, but then that's just the opinion of an old fool...'

Those words were ringing in her ears when, less than five minutes after Raymond had gone, William offered his godson's services to return her to her house.

'Although, my dear, you're more than welcome to stay here.' He shot them both a crafty look from under bushy brows and grinned. 'Curtis, your room's made and I dare say a double bed would do for the both of you...?'

She promptly opted for the ride home and waited in dithering low-level panic as William bustled off upstairs, waving down her offer to help tidy the kitchen, whilst Curtis disappeared to store her bike in the garage.

No sooner was the car door shut on them and the engine started than she spun to him and said, restraining herself from shouting, '*What* is going on, Curtis?'

Fists clenched on her lap, she peered at his averted profile as he calmly manoeuvred the four-wheel drive down towards the lane at the bottom of the front garden.

She realised that whilst she had been panicking for most of the evening as she'd felt herself sucked deeper and deeper into a trap not of her making, *he* had remained firmly in control, giving nothing away, as charming as he always was. Charming and doing absolutely nothing to avert the impending storm on the horizon.

Underneath the charm, if only she could read what he was thinking, but she couldn't. He was a marvel when it came to concealing just exactly what he didn't want to reveal and right at this moment she was at a loss to decipher his thoughts. She assumed that surely he must be thinking as she was, alarmed at the fact that they had somehow found themselves manoeuvred into a situation they hadn't anticipated.

'It seems,' he drawled, concentrating on the road,

taking it slowly as the snow gathered in swirls around the car, spraying against the windscreen wipers, 'that William is in something of a rush to get the formalities out of the way.'

'Is that *all* you have to say on the subject?' Jess all but cried in utter frustration.

'I can't focus on driving if you talk.'

She snorted, glowering, but fell into impatient silence as he carefully wended his way to her house, easing the car to a stop directly in front and killing the engine.

'Before you launch into a full-scale post-mortem of this evening,' he began, unbuckling his seat belt, 'let's go into the house. I need warming up with some coffee.'

There was no need to look at her to know that the unfolding of the evening had horrified her.

Her silence had been telling. He had almost *felt* the stiffness behind her responses and had done his best to paper over it.

In truth, he had been as startled as she had been by the presence of the local vicar. The revelation that his godfather and his friend had concocted a hastened schedule towards a wedding had shocked him, but he had kept his reaction firmly under wraps.

Anything else would have been inappropriate.

And really, how surprised should he have been by both developments? Not very. It had become clear over the past few days that his godfather's disapproval of his private life ran deeper than Curtis had ever imagined.

That hurt. Of course he knew that William was fashioned along more traditional lines. Of course he knew that his godfather didn't care for the revolving door approach to relationships that Curtis favoured, but in the past there had been no overt discussions on the topic.

However, things had changed dramatically on that front.

In short order, Curtis had been made aware of just how much William despaired of his history of brief liaisons. There had been relief when he had broken off his engagement with Caitlin because, as William had finally told him in no uncertain terms, wherever that match had been made, it had definitely *not* been in heaven. But since then…? Curtis's return to his bad old ways had been a source of deep concern and disappointment.

That had been the very word William had used and never in his life had Curtis felt so wretchedly *lacking*.

So now that he and Jess were together, with a baby on the way, William couldn't have been happier. Threaded into that happiness, though, he had managed to bluntly inform his godson that any return to his 'love 'em and leave 'em' ways would be unacceptable.

It shouldn't have come as a shock that William wasn't going to tolerate a loose timetable when it came to tying the knot and he had therefore taken matters into his own hands and hurried things along at a pace that had left Curtis spinning.

The fact that he *wanted* to marry the mother of his unborn child was also a source of intense frustration.

Throughout the course of the evening, he had slanted surreptitious looks at Jess and he knew her well enough to establish that she was no closer to accepting his marriage proposal now, in the face of the rushed schedule William had chosen to spring on them, than she had been when he had first suggested it.

She didn't want to marry him. She liked him, she had fun with him, and they were sexually more than compatible, but she *still* didn't want to end up with him permanently by her side. Underneath the liking and the fun and the good sex, it was clear that he just didn't quite cut it.

Now, as they stepped into her small house and he began removing his coat, he realised that that *hurt*.

Why? Why did that hurt? When he had always taken such care to protect himself from anyone having the power to inflict any sort of emotional pain on him. He suddenly felt a wave of nausea wash over him, temporarily dulling his ability to think straight, then his head cleared and he wondered whether it was just a case of his ego having taken a blow.

Made sense, didn't it?

But he still felt rattled as they headed straight for her tiny kitchen.

'Well?' she demanded, hands on hips, as he took his time settling into one of the kitchen chairs that always felt way too tiny for him.

Her deep navy-blue eyes were narrowed accusingly on him and Curtis shifted uneasily, for once in his life on the defensive.

'Are we going to get into an argument about this?'

'Yes, that's a definite possibility, Curtis!'

'Why don't you sit down instead of towering over me like an avenging angel?'

'How on earth could you let William believe that we're going to be married *within a fortnight*?'

'If memory serves me, we were both present when that announcement was made.' But for once his agile mind was refusing to do what it usually did so well, manoeuvre through the problems and cut straight to the chase.

She had managed to break through his defences.

That was the sobering thought at the back of his mind. It wasn't about his ego being a little bruised. He was hurting because…because…because she had managed to break through his defences and leave him open and vulnerable.

When had that happened? Before they'd slept together. Before he had become blatantly aware of her physical attraction. With blinding clarity, he recognised that she had made stealthy strides deep into the very core of him and, bit by bit, she had stolen his heart.

She might not want him as a long-term proposition because she was looking for someone more suitable, and he knew that there was no way he could force her hand and neither would he want to.

Wasn't the depth of love measured by the painful ability to walk away if that was what the person you loved wanted?

Because he loved this woman. He loved her in all her moods. He was addicted to her laughter and her generous spirit and her sense of humour, which was so like his. He loved this woman because she got him in ways no one else in the world did, and that included his godfather.

If he had to take the hit with his godfather, if he had to sink in his estimation in order to be the person who let go the object of his love for her own good, because that was what she wanted, then so be it.

He felt he could no longer look at her and he scowled at the effort of averting his hungry gaze.

'What are we going to do?'

Jess could feel the walls closing in around her. It was one thing to promote a small white lie with an indefinite timeline. It was quite another when the small white lie grew sharp teeth and the timeline shrank from indefinite to just round the corner.

When she thought about being propelled into living

with Curtis, a ring on her finger, trapped with someone who didn't love her and who, inevitably, would grow to resent her oppressive presence in his life, she broke out in a cold sweat.

'How can you be so…so *calm*?' she demanded shrilly. 'Did you have any idea of what was going to happen this evening? Did William say anything to you? Why would he want us to get married *in two weeks*?'

'You're horrified,' Curtis said flatly.

'Of course I'm horrified! Aren't you?'

'It was my idea for us to get married so I'm hardly going to be quite as horrified as you seem to be.'

'I can't marry someone just for the sake of a child, Curtis. We've been through all this already! That sort of union would destroy both of us in the end.' She had a vivid image of him sneaking out in the dead of night for an illicit rendezvous with a small, adoring blonde so that he could have hot sex with someone more to his liking and complain about the shrew he had been obliged to wed because of his godfather.

It jarred that she knew he wasn't that sort of person, the sort to have clandestine affairs, but who knew how anyone might react given certain circumstances?

Married and with a broken heart that got a little more broken day by day was not a future she wanted for herself.

If she could never have a clean break because of the fact that they shared a child, then surely as clean a break as possible would be the best option?

She missed his dark flush and the tightening of his lips as she continued to visualise a future that had been brought to within touching distance by William.

She blinked to find him rising to his feet, turning

away from her, and there was such finality in that movement that she yearned to reach out and stop him.

'You understand where I'm coming from, don't you?' she questioned anxiously, following him out of the kitchen and then hovering indecisively as he began putting on his coat.

'Of course I do,' Curtis said coolly. 'You've made that crystal-clear.'

'It's important we remain friends,' she pointed out with a hint of panic in her voice. She could feel his cold withdrawal like a physical blow. 'We've always been friends. We need to continue being friends because of... well, now that there's a baby on the way. Aside from the business of...of *love*, we both know that it would be hopeless being married.' She laughed but the laugh emerged as a cross between a croak and a sob. He was looking at her in silence now, head tilted to one side, his expression remote.

'Whereas...whereas we can both step back from the brink and deal with this in a civilised and *amicable* manner! Whatever you'd like, I'm happy to go along with.' Her previous mental block when it came to accepting his largesse now seemed petty and childish. 'I totally get it that you might think my house is a bit on the small side...' She waited for him to lighten up, to pick up the bait she had thrown and tease her about the dimensions of her one up, one down, but he remained coolly, disconcertingly silent, which propelled her further into heated, rambling speech. 'So I'll understand if you want to house us both somewhere a little bigger...' Still that shuttered expression and glacial silence. 'I won't fight you over that. I know you think that the best thing for us to do is to get married, but if you really thought about it you'd agree that in the end we would hate one another!'

'And on that note,' Curtis told her, turning away, his voice husky, 'I think I'll leave.' He slung on his coat, turned back to look at her. 'If it would make things easier for you, I am happy to arrange the details through a lawyer.'

'No! Why would you want to do that, Curtis? We're not enemies, we're friends. Isn't that what you told me?'

'Sometimes clarity is needed in certain situations, Jess. I don't want you to feel uncomfortable having to deal with me when you'd rather I took…a step backwards.'

'No!' She wanted to reach out and clutch his sleeve but instead she folded her arms and stared at him, not too certain how it was that the ground had shifted so dramatically under her feet when all she'd been trying to do was find out what the heck was going on and how they could rescue the situation. 'I don't want lawyers involved!'

'Because that's not what friends do? Especially friends who have ended up in bed with one another?'

She went bright red and was momentarily lost for words and into that silence he said, in a flat, calm voice, 'Your bike? I will ensure that it's returned to you first thing in the morning. And as to my godfather—you needn't worry that you're going to find yourself in any awkward situations, having to carry on with a pretence you no longer wish to be a part of. Tomorrow morning I'll sit William down and explain the situation to him.'

'You will?' She blanched at the thought of how disappointed his godfather was going to be, swept from the euphoria of hastening their marriage vows to having to accept that there would be no exchange of vows after all, and all in the space of twenty-four hours, without any time to adjust, as she had hoped might be the case when she'd suggested this charade.

'If you choose to contact him to explain the situation, then fine. If not, also fine.' He spun round on his heel and headed for the door while she disconsolately padded in his wake, shaken to the core by the grim finality of every word that had crossed his lips.

'Of course,' he continued, hand on the door knob, ready to leave, 'I will be in touch often and we will naturally have to meet up to discuss details of how we move forward if there is to be no involvement with lawyers, but rest assured I will not invade your space in any way, shape or form.' He rested an almost gentle gaze on her as he opened the door, letting in a rush of freezing cold and the spray of snow. 'Your personal happiness, Jess? There is no way I would ever think to get in the way of you achieving it…when all is said and done, it's what you deserve.'

CHAPTER TEN

JESS CAME TO a stop outside William's house and dismounted her bike.

The snow of the week before had given way to ice, blue skies and penetrating cold.

Not great conditions in which to hop on a bike and cycle, but her car had finally given up and she was waiting for a replacement, courtesy of Curtis, who had been in touch with her at least once a day since they had parted company nearly ten days previously.

She had mentioned that she was cycling to school because of her lack of alternative transport and, sure enough, he had immediately insisted on remedying the situation by replacing her dud car with something that actually, in his own words, had 'an engine built this side of the Boer War'.

She hadn't quibbled. Ever since their last conversation he had been the perfect gentleman.

Of course, it was impossible to gauge how he felt exactly, because it was very different being face to face with someone as opposed to hearing a disembodied voice or reading a text message but, true to his word, he had explained the situation to his godfather.

'How...how did he take it?' she had asked anxiously and he had set her mind at rest with his answer.

'He accepted it. Don't we all. Accept the things we can't change.'

Like a coward, Jess had left a few days for the dust to settle with William and she had refrained from probing when she'd spoken to Curtis.

Something about their relationship had shifted and she couldn't quite put her finger on it.

He had retreated.

It felt as though their relationship had moved through stages, from the comfort of friendship to the angst of infatuation, from the desperate urge to break free to the magnetic pull of something too strong, from the passion of being lovers to the sadness of accepting a love that would never be reciprocated.

But where she was now felt the worst.

She was in the most intimate place two people could reach, with his baby inside her, and yet she had never felt more separated from him.

For better or worse, he had been a constant in her life for as long as she could remember but now, despite his support, she could feel that constant slipping away.

He was doing all the right things because he was a decent guy.

He was concerned about her, keen to make life as easy as possible for her, asked her whether she was eating okay and feeling okay and doing okay.

They had begun to tentatively discuss housing arrangements which, he had told her, would take time and so should be sorted as soon as possible, because he would rather their baby be born in the place where they intended to put down firm roots so that there was no inconvenient upheaval with an infant.

'Where will you be based?' she had asked and had been fobbed off with a something-and-nothing answer.

'*Perhaps I might think of investing in something closer to William,*' he had hinted. '*Within easy commuting distance of where you are so that visiting can be maintained on as regular a basis as possible...*'

The implication was that he was keen to ensure her happiness and, to that end, would be amenable to whatever she wanted.

It was all going so much better than she could ever have hoped, she told herself with bracing optimism as she slanted her bike against the side wall and buzzed the doorbell.

She'd laid down her rules and regulations, had point blank refused to marry for reasons she knew he privately accepted when you dug beneath his adherence to do the right thing, and he had backed off just as she had hoped.

In the end, they had both found a meeting place where they could now communicate like two perfectly civilised adults with a passionately shared interest in the child they had conceived together.

She felt William would be pleased with that outcome, although the second he opened the door her heart dived and her nerves kicked in and she gave him a watery smile as he ushered her inside.

'No need to be nervous.' He bustled her into the kitchen and cut to the chase before she had time to start on the pleasantries. 'I was an old fool to think the pair of you might actually get married!'

Thrown in at the deep end, Jess let him make her a cup of tea and fuss over her health, all the while bemoaning his short-sightedness in expecting more than would be forthcoming.

There were no accusations directed at *her*, which she interpreted as indicating that all accusations were mentally directed at Curtis, and her heart went out to Curtis, ached at the thought of him losing standing in the eyes of the one person in the world he loved and respected.

Which was why, when there was a breather in the conversation, she said tentatively, 'You shouldn't blame Curtis for anything.'

'Blame that godson of mine?' William huffed, settling into the chair facing her and fussing with his teacup. 'Wouldn't dream of it! My fault. Expected too much. Forgot that the world we live in now isn't quite the same as the world I lived in back in the day!'

'He did suggest that we get married,' Jess countered quietly. 'It was important to him because of what he went through as a child.'

William stilled and looked at her with a suddenly guarded expression. 'Explain, dear child.'

'You know—' Jess looked down to gaze at her fingertips '—being in foster care for those two years, living life as a young child who never got the security and stability kids need because his mother…failed in that respect. Those things made him propose marriage as a way of making sure his own child had the security he lacked, and it's only because I objected that those wedding bells won't be ringing.' She raised her eyes to look at him and, for once, she could read absolutely nothing on a face that was normally so expressive. She hesitated but, having taken the plunge, her only way now was to carry on until she felt her feet on solid ground again.

'I wanted more than duty. I wanted love because, without love, duty would become a very empty vessel. I couldn't bear the thought of the two of us ending up squabbling and unhappy in a loveless marriage, which would have been a disaster for the child.'

'Curtis told you about his past?'

'He did.'

'And you didn't think that was reason enough to wed? There is also the fact that you are in love with him—'

'He would never love me back!' Jess cried, then flushed as the significance of her outburst hit home. 'I mean... What I mean...'

'My dear, there's no need for either of us to dwell further on this.' He waved down her anguished attempt to explain what she meant, and it was fair to say that he seemed remarkably more upbeat now, insisting she stay for some dinner. 'You wouldn't want an old man to eat by himself, would you? Besides, you need feeding up!'

Relieved at the change in atmosphere, Jess would have accepted any invitation in pursuit of further pouring oil over troubled waters. It wasn't yet five and marking schoolwork would have to wait. It wasn't as though she had anything else lined up expect a scintillating evening nursing her thoughts.

'I just have a quick phone call to make.'

She nodded and helped herself to another cup of tea as he bustled out of the kitchen to his telephone in the sitting room. It had been silly to have been so nervous about this meeting. Of course he would understand! He might be the only person left in the county who still insisted on using a landline, but that didn't mean he was a dinosaur when it came to all things modern.

Curtis was on his way back to London from a meeting not a million miles away from Ely when he got the call on his phone and picked up on Bluetooth.

William.

His heart sank. He had spoken to his godfather several times since he had broken the news about the wedding that wasn't to be. Each time he had ended the conversation with the depressing realisation that nothing was going to be the same again between them, or if they *were* to return to what they'd been then it would take a long time.

He shuddered when he recalled the horror of telling William that he and Jess, much as they were going to remain the closest of friends and united as they were in wanting the best for the child they had created, would not be getting married.

A joint decision, he had said, and one they had both agreed on. They would never stop being the best of buddies, he had insisted, and through gritted teeth had muttered something about wishing her every happiness with someone she loved.

He had contemplated heading to Ely after his meeting but, with the ground still so rocky and uncertain with his godfather, he had chosen to postpone a physical meeting until the following week, which would have allowed some of the dust to settle.

It would also have allowed him time to psych himself up to seeing Jess. He had spoken to her on the phone and messaged her, but seeing her in the flesh?

Bittersweet.

He picked up the call and went into something of a panic when the first words William uttered were, 'Son, you need to head up here as soon as you can.'

Jess was chopping some tomatoes when the doorbell buzzed. William, who seemed distracted, had spent the past forty-five minutes flapping around the kitchen, alternately explaining the roux he was making whilst finding fault with her chopping skills.

One of his favourite daily radio shows was playing in the background.

He dropped everything at the sound of the doorbell.

Wrapped up in her thoughts, Jess was vaguely aware of the sound of voices in the hallway but only when the kitchen door was pushed open did she turn around to see what the fuss was all about.

The last person she expected to see was Curtis and how her heart leapt at the sight of him, gloriously handsome in a charcoal-grey suit and a crisp white shirt. He had dispensed with the jacket and if he'd been wearing a tie it was no longer in evidence.

He looked *fatigued*.

He stopped abruptly in the doorway and now they stared at one another, oblivious to William's presence to the side. Indeed, Jess only remembered that he was there at all when he scuttled into position between them and announced with ringing confidence, 'You two need your heads banged together and I've decided that I am the one to do it. I'm going out for a couple of hours, and when I come back I want to find that the pair of you have come to your senses. You love one another and it's time to stop making a dog's dinner of the situation!' With which, he bustled back to the door, only pausing to toss over his shoulder, 'And the carrots, dear girl, still need to be julienned!'

'Jess...'

Curtis was the first to break the silence, giving her time to try and gather her scattered thoughts, but she couldn't, not when he was standing there in front of her, reminding her just how potent his impact was and making a mockery of her pretence that being away from him might have dented the force of her love. It hadn't.

'What are you doing here?'

'William called an hour ago. Said I had to get here. I was on my way back to London... I thought something was wrong, thought he might have had some kind of turn.'

'Curtis…'

'I'm glad I'm here, Jess. We need to talk. We should talk. I need to talk.'

'Haven't we already done that?' But her ears were ringing with William's incendiary remarks. How could he expose her love like that? And to have misinterpreted what his godson felt about her!

'About what your godfather said…' Her laugh was falsetto high and tapered off into conspicuous throat-clearing.

'He's right.'

'Sorry?'

'Let's go into the sitting room, Jess.'

'I have no idea why William thought that I…that…' Her cheeks were stinging and she knew that she was bright red. Pillarbox-red was not the colour of someone innocent of accusations.

She trailed behind him, mind frantically working to find a way out of William's parting shot that would enable her to emerge with some semblance of dignity.

Once sitting, she leaned forward, hands planted on her knees, every ounce of her attention pinned to his beautiful face.

He looked more than fatigued. He looked exhausted.

'You work too hard,' she said shortly and then realised that what should have sounded like concern had instead morphed into accusation. She decided that that wasn't a bad thing because he needed to realise that having a child on the scene would require an end to the twenty-four-seven work regime, and also attack seemed the best form of defence, at least right at this moment in time, when her heart was flip-flopping dangerously inside her.

He looked at her with such searing intensity and uncharacteristic confusion that she went even further into defensive mode.

'You're going to have to do something about that,' she said crisply. 'If you want to have a good, solid relationship with your child. Also,' she added, 'it's just bad for you, working all the hours God made.'

'I haven't been working,' Curtis responded quietly.

'What have you been doing? You look shattered. No, don't tell me...' she said, painfully aware that there was one other thing guaranteed to tire a man out and it involved handling statistics of a completely different kind.

'I've been thinking about you.'

Now it was Jess's turn to look confused. She opened her mouth but nothing emerged.

He was leaning towards her, their postures mirroring one another's, and she sat on her hands to stop herself from reaching out to touch what was forbidden.

'Jess, I asked you to marry me...' He inhaled sharply, waiting for her to interject, but her vocal cords were still in a state of disarray. 'I put it to you as something of a business deal, something that would guarantee the sort of stability that I never had. Of course you're right. A marriage is no guarantee of stability and two people sharing the same goal can provide as stable an environment for a child even though they might not live with one another.'

'That's right!' She found her voice but there was not the ring of confidence in her assertion as she had hoped.

'I made a mistake.' He paused and took a deep breath. Jess had never seen him this hesitant before and it was disconcerting because he was a man who lived life in charge of the world around him. 'I should have been honest with you but, in fairness, that would have meant me being honest with myself and that was something I had no idea how to do.'

'I don't understand what you're trying to tell me, Curtis.'

'I have never bought into the whole love thing, Jess. You know that. I've always been upfront with you...with every single woman I've ever had a relationship with. No love meant no pain and, as far as I was concerned, that was a blessing. I'd had enough pain as a child to last a lifetime. Why would I court any more by letting my emotions take control? But you...you crept under my defences and I can't even exactly tell you when that happened. I just know that we slept together and something inside me was liberated, even though I wasn't aware of it at the time. And far less aware of the consequences.' He looked at her, his green eyes solemn, and tentatively reached out, encouraged when she, equally tentatively, touched his fingers with hers.

'I would never want to hurt you, Jess. I was fully prepared to walk away and give you the freedom you tell me you want, freedom to find the right guy for you, but I would never be able to live with myself if I hadn't first told you how I feel about you.'

'How you feel about me...' Jess's brain was not quite keeping pace with what she was hearing.

'You mean everything to me, Jess. I think back and realise that, in many ways, you always have. You've been my foundation and I never realised just how strong the building blocks of what I felt for you were until, perhaps, we slept together. It was...' he smiled '...would magical be over the top?'

'No.' For the first time she smiled with pure happiness and joy. 'It would be just...the perfect word.' She finally allowed herself to touch his face and it felt good to stroke his cheek and to have him capture her hand between his so that he could place a tender kiss in her palm.

'I've been in love with you for such a long time, Curtis. It was only when you got engaged to Caitlin that I realised I was in danger of becoming one of those sad old spinsters who spend their lives pining for a guy who doesn't want them and eventually filling the void with... I don't know...cats or stuffed toys or stupid online dating...'

'Now she tells me.'

'I never dreamt that we would ever end up in bed together and when we did...it blew my mind. But I knew just where it would lead, which was why I knew that I had to walk away. And then I found out that I was pregnant...'

'And you turned me down even though you were crazy about me.'

'Who could *not* be crazy about a guy as modest as you, Curtis?' She laughed but then sobered to look at him seriously. 'I ached when you told me about your past. I finally understood why you were the person you were, such a giant when it comes to being thoughtful and fair and generous-minded, yet so fiercely guarded with your emotions. I could understand why you would want to marry for the sake of your child, but it would have destroyed me being married to someone I adored, knowing that they could never return my love. And we were friends, as you kept reminding me.' She grimaced. 'The word *friend* had never been one I didn't want to hear from you! But of course we *were* friends, and I knew that if we didn't marry we would always do what was best for the child we had conceived together, and at least then I might have been able to construct some sort of life for myself. Eventually.'

'But now,' he drawled, smiling, 'as things stand…will you, Jess Carr, my friend, lover and the woman I can't live without, be my wife?'

'I don't think you could stop me.'

EPILOGUE

ALICE ELIZABETH HAMILTON was born two days after her due date and entered the world without fuss, to be placed in the arms of her blissful parents who, in time-honoured tradition, had been married for five months.

The ceremony had been a quiet affair in the local church and, with only the smallest of bumps heralding the arrival of their daughter several months into the future, they had had their honeymoon in Courchevel, although this time the weather was somewhat different and there was no skiing on the agenda.

They had stayed a handful of days and then had completed the honeymoon at Lake Como, staying at one of the most beautiful hotels overlooking the flat blue of the lake.

And then they had begun the hunt for somewhere suitably large enough for a family.

Jess had dismissed anything too grand. 'Who needs eight bedrooms?' she had asked wryly when they had looked around the first house, which had been sourced by the relocation company Curtis had decided to use, so that excess traipsing around unsuitable properties could be filtered out.

After a month they had found the perfect cottage just half an hour away from William and from which Curtis would commute to London as and when he needed to. He'd refused to consider any situation that might involve him splitting his time between London and the suburbs.

For Jess, the fairy tale she'd never thought could happen had happened, and only after Alice was born did she finally manage to wean herself away from having to pinch herself every so often just to make sure that the life she was living wasn't just a dream from which she would wake up.

Dreams, she had discovered, really could come true.

* * * * *

COMING SOON!

We really hope you enjoyed reading this book.
If you're looking for more romance, be sure to
head to the shops when new books are
available on

Thursday 3rd
March

To see which titles are coming soon, please visit

millsandboon.co.uk/nextmonth

MILLS & BOON

MILLS & BOON®

Coming next month

REVEALING HER NINE-MONTH SECRET
Natalie Anderson

She needed him to turn. Would she see those disturbingly green eyes? Would she see a sensual mouth? If he stepped closer would she hear a voice that whispered wicked invitation and wilful temptation? All those months ago she'd been so seduced by him she'd abandoned all caution, all reticence for a single night of silken ecstasy only to then—

A sharp pain lanced, shocking her back to the present. Winded, she pressed her hand to her stomach. How the mind could wreak havoc on the body. The stabbing sensation was a visceral reminder of the desolate emptiness she'd been trying to ignore for so long.

She'd recovered from that heartbreak. She was living her best life here—free and adventurous, bathing in the warm, brilliant waters of the Pacific. Her confusion was because she was tired. But she couldn't resist stepping closer—even as another sharp pain stole her breath.

'That's interesting.' He addressed the man beside him. 'Why are—'

Shock deadened her senses, muting both him and the pain still squeezing her to the point where she couldn't breathe. That *voice*? That low tone that invited such confidence and tempted the listener to share their deepest secrets?

Massimo hadn't just spoken to her. He'd offered the sort of attention that simply stupefied her mind and left her able only to say *yes*. And she had. Like all the women who'd come before her. And doubtless all those after.

Now his brief laugh was deep and infectious. Despite her distance, it was as if he had his head intimately close to hers, his arm around her waist, his lips brushing her highly sensitised skin—

Pain tore through her muscles forcing her to the present again. She gasped as it seared from her insides and radiated out with increasingly harsh intensity. She stared, helpless to the power of it as that dark head turned in her direction. His green-eyed gaze arrowed on her.

Massimo.

'Carrie?' Sereana materialised, blocking him from her view. 'Are you okay?' Her boss looked as alarmed as she sounded.

Carrie crumpled as the cramp intensified. It was as if she'd been grabbed by a ginormous shark and he was trying to tear her in two. 'Maybe I ate something...'

Her vision tunnelled as she tumbled to the ground.

'Carrie?'

Not Sereana.

She opened her eyes and stared straight into his. 'Massimo?'

It couldn't really be him. She was hallucinating, surely? But she felt strong arms close about her. She felt herself lifted and pressed to his broad, hard chest. He was hot and she could hear the thud of his racing heart. Or maybe it was only her own.

If this were just a dream? Fine. She closed her eyes and kept them closed. She would sleep and this awful agony would stop. She really needed it to stop.

'*Carrie!*'

Continue reading
Revealing Her Nine-Month Secret
Natalie Anderson

Available next month
www.millsandboon.co.uk

MILLS & BOON

THE HEART OF ROMANCE

A ROMANCE FOR EVERY READER

MODERN

Prepare to be swept off your feet by sophisticated, sexy and seductive heroes, in some of the world's most glamourous and romantic locations, where power and passion collide.

HISTORICAL

Escape with historical heroes from time gone by. Whether your passion is for wicked Regency Rakes, muscled Vikings or rugged Highlanders, await the romance of the past.

MEDICAL

Set your pulse racing with dedicated, delectable doctors in the high-pressure world of medicine, where emotions run high and passion, comfort love are the best medicine.

True Love

Celebrate true love with tender stories of heartfelt romance, from the rush of falling in love to the joy a new baby can bring, and a focus on the emotional heart of a relationship.

Desire

Indulge in secrets and scandal, intense drama and plenty of sizzling hot action with powerful and passionate heroes who have it all: wealth, status good looks…everything but the right woman.

HEROES

Experience all the excitement of a gripping thriller, with an intense romance at its heart. Resourceful, true-to-life women and strong, fearless men face danger and desire - a killer combination!

To see which titles are coming soon, please visit

millsandboon.co.uk/nextmonth

LET'S TALK
Romance

For exclusive extracts, competitions
and special offers, find us online:

facebook.com/millsandboon

@MillsandBoon

@MillsandBoonUK

Get in touch on 01413 063232

For all the latest titles coming soon, visit
millsandboon.co.uk/nextmonth

MILLS & BOON
Desire

Indulge in secrets and scandal, intense drama and plenty of sizzling hot action with powerful and passionate heroes who have it all: wealth, status, good looks…everything but the right woman.

MILLS & BOON
MEDICAL
Pulse-Racing Passion

Set your pulse racing with dedicated, delectable doctors in the high-pressure world of medicine, where emotions run high and passion, comfort and love are the best medicine.